THE COVER WIFE

THE COVER WIFE

Dan Fesperman

Alfred A. Knopf   New York   2021

THIS IS A BORZOI BOOK
PUBLISHED BY ALFRED A. KNOPF

Copyright © 2021 by Dan Fesperman

All rights reserved. Published in the United States by Alfred A. Knopf,
a division of Penguin Random House LLC, New York, and distributed
in Canada by Penguin Random House Canada Limited, Toronto.

www.aaknopf.com

Knopf, Borzoi Books, and the colophon are registered trademarks of
Penguin Random House LLC.

Library of Congress Cataloging-in-Publication Data
Names: Fesperman, Dan, [date].
Title: The cover wife / Dan Fesperman.
Description: First Edition. | New York : Alfred A. Knopf,
a division of Penguin Random House, LLC, 2021.
Identifiers: LCCN 2020050269 (print) | LCCN 2020050270 (ebook) |
ISBN 9780525657835 (hardcover) | ISBN 9780525657842 (ebook)
Subjects: GSAFD: Suspense fiction. | Mystery fiction.
Classification: LCC PS3556.E778 C68 2021 (print) |
LCC PS3556.E778 (ebook) | DDC 813/.54—dc23
LC record available at https://lccn.loc.gov/2020050269
LC ebook record available at https://lccn.loc.gov/2020050270

Jacket design by Kelly Blair

Manufactured in the United States of America
First Edition

MAY 1999

1

The rain clouds parted an hour before sunset, and the hiker's shadow finally rejoined him on the mountain trail, his only companion all day. Or so he hoped.

Ascending to a granite outcrop with a sweeping view, he paused to look back at the way he'd come: lacy spring foliage and a meadow in bloom, with the trail stitched through it like a dirty suture. Not a soul on it.

The air was golden with pollen, and he considered digging into his pack for an allergy pill before remembering he'd already taken one. He cleared his throat, spit, and immediately regretted it. He rubbed the spot with the toe of his boot, only to make a bigger mess. Sighing, he checked his watch and set off.

Still lurking to his rear was the unseen presence that had haunted him since dawn. All in his head, perhaps, but the reports from the briefing had been sobering enough: two men, well trained and unaccounted for, meaning they might be anywhere. He imagined them back there now, moving briskly just beyond the nearest ridge. He picked up the pace.

A mile later, reaching the level grade of a narrow ridge, he eased into a long and limber stride. Better. His scuffed old boots were a comfort, a reminder of past hikes among friends. Their voices returned to him in the murmur of the leaves, the creak of swaying limbs—distant echoes of dewy mornings and twilight encampments, those long-ago weekends when they would cook up a hearty fireside meal and scrub their mess kits in the gravel of a stream. A tin cup of whiskey to pass around the campfire, everyone carried off to slumber on a tide of laughter and familiar old tales.

Caught up in his memories, he imagined himself later that night, rubbing his hands for warmth as he brewed coffee on a tidy blaze. Or, no, because that would be like lighting a beacon in the night. So instead he would boil water on his tiny stove, eat one of those dehydrated meals from a pouch. He would turn in early, listening carefully from his tent to the noises of the night. Sleep as well as he could, and then rise before dawn.

An old song came to mind, so he whistled a bar just to hear the sound of something human, his footsteps keeping rhythm as the trail steepened. The last notes drifted up into the trees and he fell silent, conserving his breath for the climb. He recalled a boyhood tale of a cavalry scout trying to outrun the Comanches, in which days had turned to weeks. He had packed enough food for five nights, but what if he needed to resupply?

From above came the grumble of a single-engine plane, which stopped him in his tracks. He remained still for a full minute, watching as it passed low enough for him to read the tail number. No one had mentioned this possibility, although he supposed it was within their capabilities. Various weapons had been discussed, of course. But this? Yet here he was, cowering beneath the leaves. Sunlight glinted off the fuselage as the plane moved toward the horizon. He exhaled and reached for his water bottle. Yet again he gazed back at the way he'd come.

The trail was still empty, so he allowed himself a moment to enjoy the view. There was much to admire—low sunlight sparkled in the wet branches like diamonds, or the twinkle of a vast city in a valley, stirring to life at dusk. The forest smelled as fresh as a mown pasture, and birdsong was everywhere, the final chorus before nightfall. Such beauty. And for the first time all week, he took hope.

Smiling, he drew a deep breath of the clean mountain air and resumed walking. He had covered fourteen miles today, a tiring distance at his age, but "a good tired," as his wife liked to say, the kind that settled your mind for a deep and healing sleep. So, after another mile, he decided to leave the trail to scout for a campsite.

The good omens multiplied. He quickly found a level patch of downy grass beneath a spreading beech, where a pale band of fallen leaves pointed like an arrow to the optimum spot. It was like an illustration for a fairy tale, a place of enchantment.

He heaved off his pack, set it down by a big log, and unzipped the top. Fresh, cooling air rushed up the back of his shirt, and the crinkly tent released old, familiar smells as he flattened it on the grass. The rituals of making camp were a comfort, and it felt as if the forest had enveloped him in its arms. Nature, so often harsh, was for the moment his cloak of invisibility. This was his home ground, not theirs, and that counted for plenty.

Yet as he slid the tent poles into their sleeves he noticed that the birds were no longer singing. Were they done for the day, or had something put them on notice? The wind shifted, and for a fleeting moment he thought he detected a whiff of something human—sweat, soap, the smell of exertion. Or maybe it was his own scent, coming back to him on the turning breeze. The hairs on his arms stood on end.

A twig snapped to his rear, and he nearly lost balance as he wheeled awkwardly and rose from his crouch. Looking left, then right, then over his shoulder toward the trail, he saw only the brown expanse of the forest floor, leaves and limbs, the white flash of a squirrel's belly as it leaped from tree to tree. But the odd smell lingered, unmistakable now, and he remained still.

To his rear, the thump of a footfall. He spun as a metallic click sounded from the edge of the clearing, and he saw a man dressed in black just as the bolt from a crossbow struck him below the breastbone and plunged into his heart. Crying out in agony, he slumped to his knees and collapsed sideways. Blood pooled brightly on the deflating tent, and his eyes rolled back in his head. He gasped for breath, but no air would come.

The birds held their silence. The only sound now was of footsteps approaching steadily across the leaves. They halted, a moment of peace interrupted by the click of a camera—twice, as if to make sure. Then, two more steps, followed by a grunt of effort, and the slurping, ripping sound of the bolt being pulled from muscle and flesh.

Unable to move or speak, he groaned a final time. His last thought was of disappointment in himself for having mistaken beauty for hope. The woods had failed him, and he had failed himself.

The footsteps receded. The birds again took up their song, sounding the all-clear from the trees.

FRIDAY, OCTOBER 1, 1999

2

The man with binoculars turned from his perch by the window and told Claire Saylor yet again to clear off.

"We've got this, you know. And if Marston calls one more time, I'm not covering for you anymore."

"He's losing it because I'm late for a meeting, for God's sake. This is operational. I'm seeing it through."

A second man, seated at a folding table arrayed with five video screens, joined in.

"Claire, what we're really saying is we don't need you. Your part was over an hour ago. So, seriously, go ahead and . . . *Fuck! Do you see this?* Screen four."

The three of them watched the black-and-white image of a prosperous-looking Frenchman, mid-fifties, suit and tie, briefcase in hand, making his way from the stairway exit of a Metro station. Claire was about to offer an observation when her colleague at the window shouted to the man by the video screens.

"You said he'd be gone till noon!"

"He usually is. Call Clay, get him out of there!"

"Can't. He just turned off his phone for the sound check."

"Well, then, Clay's fucked. We all are. You know the target's history."

Indeed they did. *Dresses like Pierre Cardin, slashes like Jack the Ripper.* All of them had read the dossier.

"I told you we should've given him some backup coms."

"Sure, to make him completely obvious when the gendarmes show."

"Well, Jesus, it would have beaten the hell out of . . . *Hey, where are you going?*"

Claire was headed for the exit at double time. She turned the deadbolt and stepped onto the porch as they called out after her.

"*Now* you bail on us!"

"Thanks, Claire!"

She shut the door on their voices, in too much of a hurry to answer. Glancing up the street, she saw the man from the video screen, thirty yards to the right and closing fast. She smoothed her skirt, took a deep breath, and descended the steps. Mustering the most inviting possible smile, she waved toward the man and called out in French worthy of a lifelong Parisian.

"Excuse me, sir. I was wondering if you might have a phone I could borrow?" She gestured toward the "For Sale" sign on the porch behind her, while hoping her colleagues were staying clear of the windows. "I was supposed to meet a real estate agent half an hour ago, but she hasn't shown. And, well, my battery's dead. So, if you don't mind . . . ?"

She reached the walkway and stepped behind him, so that he had to pivot to face her. His back was now turned to the house three doors down, where Clay was still inside. The man appraised her from head to toe, as Frenchmen tended to do. The contents of his file had made her expect nothing less, and by now he had probably observed that there were no rings on her fingers.

She appraised him in return. Age fifty, five years her senior, but stylistically they were a decent match—fit, poised, polished. The suit looked tailored—Pierre Cardin, indeed. The rub was that his dossier also said there was a better-than-average chance that the inside pocket of his jacket concealed a long, slender blade. If she were to give herself away, she had little doubt that he would use it, right here on the street. She held his gaze and smiled again.

He smiled back, as if in approval, although when he reached into his jacket it was all she could do to keep from flinching. If the blade appeared, she would try to block it with her left forearm while sweeping her right foot across his ankles to knock him to the ground. Instead he pulled out one of those tiny Nokia models that half of Paris now seemed to possess, everyone using them wherever you went. She didn't move an inch.

"A single call for a single girl? I believe I could manage that."

"Thank you. It should only take a second."

Claire took the phone and turned away, partly to conceal her actions, partly to hide her flush of relief. She punched in the number for the landline in the man's house, which she'd memorized from the file. Clay would never dare answer it, but perhaps if she disconnected after a single ring he would realize that someone was sounding the alarm. So that's what she did, while pretending to wait through several more rings.

"Oh, c'mon!" she hissed for show, tapping her foot impatiently.

She turned around to face the Frenchman, again doing everything she could to hold his attention. Eye contact. A sigh of helpless exasperation.

"First she stands me up. Now she refuses to answer."

"These estate agents," he said, shaking his head in sympathy. "You know, if you really want some leads on houses in this neighborhood, I could probably be of greater assistance to you than her, Miss . . . ?"

He arched his eyebrows inquisitively.

"Laveau. Marie Laveau. And I'd be grateful for your help."

Over his shoulder she saw Clay rushing down the front steps as he stuffed coiled wiring into a satchel. He headed up the sidewalk in the opposite direction, toward the nearest intersection, where a van was waiting just out of sight around the corner. She handed back the phone.

"I am Claude," he said. "Claude Durand. Perhaps we will be neighbors soon?"

"That would be something to look forward to."

"In the meantime, how could I reach you to let you know if a more suitable property becomes available? Or perhaps simply for moral support."

Yes, he was an old pro, so she rewarded him with a phone number. He again reached into his jacket, and she again fought off the urge to back away, or make a move. Maybe he was onto her.

He produced a small datebook—literally a little black book—and wrote down her number. If he ever dialed it, he would be greeted by a rushed "Hallo? Take your order?" from Phong, owner of a Vietnamese takeout eleven blocks from her flat.

Durand then wrote his own name and number on a separate page, which he tore out and handed to her as gallantly as if it were a lace hankie she had dropped at his feet.

"In case you should require further consultation."

"Why, thank you. You're most generous. And now, I should move on to the next place on my list."

"Here's hoping you will not be successful, or not without first soliciting my advice."

Claire looked away shyly—maybe he would think she was blushing—and then she was on her way. She felt his eyes on her back, where sweat beaded beneath her blouse, and she stepped briskly and in rhythm, hoping that he would hear the *click-click* of her heels as a Morse code of seduction rather than a drumbeat of retreat. She didn't lower her guard until she rounded the next corner, where she finally allowed herself a smile while imagining her colleagues breaking into applause behind the drawn curtains of the vacant townhouse. They could be infuriatingly dismissive, those two, but they never stinted at giving credit when it was due, and both of them would be buying her drinks for weeks in gratitude for this performance. Clay's debt was greater still. By now Durand would have probably been standing over his body, wiping a blade clean and phoning someone to clean up the mess.

Marston, her chief of station, was another matter. This morning's events would go into her file as a fortunate turn of happenstance, or even luck. Sure, she'd been quick on her feet, but didn't she always go off-script? And maybe that wasn't the sort of behavior the Agency should encourage. Initiative? Well, of course. Reckless independence? Preferably not. Especially when Marston had been hounding her all morning about a purportedly urgent appointment with an important visitor, name unknown, a meeting that had materialized out of the mists of the overnight encrypted communications between Paris and Langley.

The summons had come on short notice, probably to keep everything under wraps for as long as possible. The off-site location was another giveaway of its clandestine nature. But Claire was supposed to have arrived an hour ago, and by now someone more important than she had already been kept waiting long enough to make Marston hyperventilate.

It would take at least another forty minutes to get there by Metro, and she considered hailing a cab. But at this hour—nearly 10 a.m.—that might take even longer, and she couldn't be certain of reimbursement. She also needed a moment to collect herself after her performance on the sidewalk.

Besides, Marston had made the mistake of telling her a trifle too much about the nature of the meeting.

"They're putting together a team," he'd said. "Apparently you're on it."

They're putting together a team.

The words had landed in her stomach like a lump of cold oatmeal. Teams represented the Agency's worst tendencies toward excess and inefficiency, and more often than not she drew the short straw on assignments. The short leash as well. Odds were that by this time next week she'd be making coffee and filling out paperwork just to stay busy. One in every six hours she might actually do something useful.

A team, then. Claire was good at what she did, but she was not always a good employee. So let them wait. She stopped to buy a newspaper and a croissant, and then sat on a bench to eat while her heartbeat returned to normal. She decided on a taxi. She would bill it to "the team."

By the time she reached the site—an office park of beige one-story buildings, most of them unoccupied—she was feeling the hangover from her earlier rush of adrenaline, and she hoped there would at least be coffee.

She strolled past a tile showroom and an electronics wholesaler on a sidewalk with weeds growing from the cracks before reaching suite 11-B. The door was unlocked, with no security in sight, although she had little doubt she was being watched by a camera or a lookout—perhaps both. As directed, she proceeded down a hallway to a room where someone had written "Training Session" in block letters in French on a sheet taped to the door. She knocked twice, already feeling a twinge of guilt. Despite her distaste for these sorts of gatherings, she knew she'd be embarrassed if the door were to open onto a roomful of waiting participants. She had already spent far too much of her professional life seated before men who habitually checked their watches.

A male voice, vaguely familiar, called out from inside.

"Yes?"

"Claire Saylor."

"Enter."

She opened the door. The only occupant was seated with his back to her at a small table, next to a single empty chair. He wore chinos and a wrinkled black blazer. Like his voice, something about the shape of his head was familiar. The walls were bare except for a thermostat, a fire safety notice, and a closed door on the far side of the room. As if oblivious to her entry, the man scribbled on a legal pad, his pen making a sound like a mouse gnawing at the baseboard. She waited as he stood and turned to face her.

It had been ten years since she'd last seen Paul Bridger, but she recognized him right away. She immediately felt younger, and a little flushed.

"Paul! What a . . . pleasant surprise."

He flicked his eyes toward the opposite wall, as if to signal that they were not alone, or maybe he was just nervous. Just as well either way, because she wasn't yet sure what sort of greeting to offer. Their last time together had ended in a mix of complicated events and emotions, some of which they had never shared with their superiors. Or she hadn't, anyway. As for the personal repercussions, even Bridger still had no idea, mostly because he had never asked. Since then, he'd moved up the ranks, and he now managed selected ops across most of Europe. And now here they were, face-to-face in a silent room, alone but probably not alone.

For a moment, neither of them spoke. His eyes shone with eagerness even as he seemed to hold himself in reserve. She wondered who or what might be hiding behind the thermostat, the fire notice, or the closed door. But her earlier annoyance with the idea of becoming part of a team was gone, because now she felt certain her talents would not be wasted. Bridger wasn't flawless—who was?—but he was known throughout the Agency as a man who knew how to run an op, and who always got the most out of everyone. He could be stingy with information, but that was the nature of their trade. Need to know. Compartmentalize. *Tell me, but no one else.*

He was also a master of the calculated risk, comfortable out on the crumbling ledge where only the nimble kept their footing and you were never sure when you might have to jump. Not unlike where Claire had been only an hour earlier, although in Bridger's case it always seemed to count as a plus.

"Shall we get down to business?" he said crisply, gesturing to the nearest chair.

Ten years, and those were the first words out of his mouth. What a careful performer. It was a little disconcerting. Then he smiled warmly and she felt better.

Claire took a seat, certain that life was about to get interesting.

3

In a profession built on duplicity, Paul Bridger was known as trust-worthy. Years of operational success were one reason. His eyes were another—cool and inviting, the blue-green of tropical waters. Take the plunge and maybe you could swim straight through to his soul, although Claire would've added a caveat: Dive too deeply and you'll run out of air. She had long ago concluded that he was essentially unknowable.

She was pleased to see that he looked virtually unchanged from when she'd last seen him—trim and tanned, one of those rare fel-lows who acquired style by ignoring it. The chinos and blazer had always been his uniform, and he still favored an unfashionable buzz cut. Although now there was some gray in the mix.

"Wonderful to see you, Claire. I hear only good things about your work."

"Then you must be a poor listener. Good to see you, too. Even bet-ter to know we might be working together again. Although no longer as equals, I suppose. Not like in Berlin."

"Ah, yes. Well . . ."

He reddened at the reference, although that may have had more to do with whoever was listening or observing, a possibility that was already bothersome. So, with characteristic directness, Claire tried to clear the air.

"Are we alone, Paul? And, if not, should I assume I haven't yet passed muster?"

Bridger suppressed a smile and looked down at his notes.

"Glad to know you're still incorrigible when necessary. How 'bout if we get underway."

"So just the two of us, then. If that's your story, fine. I've always been amenable to that arrangement, as you know."

He again blushed. Then he put on his game face and looked her in the eye, pen poised above the notepad.

"Let's begin, Miss Saylor, with an explanation of why you were late." How bureaucratic of him.

"I was on an op, setting up a surveillance."

"Target?"

"A nasty bit of local freelance who's up to his elbows in corporate espionage."

"From everything I've heard, we've been doing a lot of bungling in that department."

"We nearly did today as well."

"Not exactly a vote in your favor."

"I wasn't the problem; I was the solution. You can ask."

"I will."

"And if I pass that test, will you be bringing me on board?"

"Oh, you're already on board, Miss Saylor." What was up with this "Miss Saylor" business? Was he trying to make up for their shaky start, or covering for himself because of something in the official record? "In fact, you could even say you're due for congratulations."

"For what?"

"You're to be married. Effective immediately. Care to see the lucky husband?"

Bridger slid forward an eight-by-ten glossy. It might have been a publicity still for a character actor specializing in wallflowers and milquetoasts, a meek fellow who kept his head down, his voice low, and stayed out of harm's way. Weak chin, pale complexion, thinning hair in a sad comb-over. Wire rims shielded watery, squinting eyes that made you want to tell him to either get stronger lenses or cut back on his reading. She guessed he was around fifty, but, unlike the dapper Frenchman from this morning, she had this fellow beat by miles for style and fitness. Fleshy jowls suggested a sagging belly somewhere below the frame. This was not a man who often saw the light of day.

Never mind the gym; even a walk around the block would have at least put some color in his cheeks.

The one hopeful note was in the upper-right corner, where a stamped logo for Wightman University signified that he was probably an academic. So maybe he at least had the saving grace of brains and, with any luck, wit. On Claire's balance sheet, laughter could cancel out all sorts of liabilities.

"Name?"

"Winston Armitage, tenured professor."

"Nationality?" She asked because the name sounded British.

"As American as apple pie."

"À la mode, by the look of it. What's his field?"

"A scholar of languages. Aramaic and Arabic, particularly with regard to translations of the Holy Quran. He's married, but we wouldn't want to risk his real wife in this sort of thing, so you're to be her stand-in while we lock her away in some high tower. Figuratively speaking, of course."

"And what 'sort of thing' is this, exactly?"

"Do you know that war cry the jihadis use, about how every martyr to the cause will be welcomed into heaven by the sweet ministrations of seventy-two virgins?"

"Of course. Blow yourself to kingdom come for everlasting sexual bliss."

"Well, our professor has apparently established, through some old Aramaic texts, that everyone has been reading it all wrong. He maintains that the reward is not virgins at all. Instead it's seventy-two white raisins."

"*Raisins?* So, a quick snack in lieu of sex forever?" She laughed. "That has to be the world's cruelest bait and switch."

"I laughed, too, first time I heard it." A flick of his eyes, as if he'd misspoken. "But as word of his findings has leaked out, some Islamic scholars are taking this very seriously."

"And some aren't, one supposes."

"Well, of course. Plenty are certain they've already debunked him. Isn't that the way of all scholarly debate? But in making his case, he has compiled enough evidence to fill a book."

"Good for the professor. But how do we figure into it?"

"We're going to make him a star, and turn his book into a bestseller. A bit of information warfare, if you will."

"As long as no one kills him first."

"Precisely. His publication date coincides with an Islamic studies conference next week in Hamburg, and you're going to accompany him to the grand unveiling. You'll be our point person for security, so you'll be sticking your neck out as much as he is."

"Understood. Will he know who I'm working for?"

"No. Both he and Wightman are quite unaware of our involvement, and we'd like to keep it that way."

"Then who am I supposed to be? To his mind."

"An employee of a private security firm, hired by the think tank that's sponsoring the trip. A private foundation, actually,"

"Is this 'foundation' real, or something we've dreamed up?"

"Oh, quite real. And well respected by scholars. Let's just say it's always been a friend. But you could turn it inside out and not find our fingerprints."

"Same thing we used to say about those Polish émigré groups riddled with Soviet plants."

"We're more careful about those things now."

"Bravo for us, but isn't Hamburg the new favorite gathering place for European jihadis?"

"That's the beauty of it. Yes, we'll be wading into a shark tank, but as soon as the fins begin to circle, we'll lower our nets into the troubled waters."

"Ah. The inevitable Paul Bridger ulterior motive. Does the poor professor know he's about to become an Agency chum bucket?"

"He'll never need to know, because he'll be protected by some of our very best people, including his 'wife.'"

"What about the Germans? What will they do when we start scooping unsuspecting jihadis into our nets?"

"The usual, I suppose. Nothing."

"Which can only mean we're not telling them."

Bridger shrugged, as if that was the least of his worries.

"Violating national sovereignty is no small matter," Claire said. "Maybe even a little unworthy of us."

"You could say that. You could also say the Germans are the whole reason this is even a problem. They're so damn determined to not act like Nazis that every law in their books is geared toward letting foreign radicals do whatever they please, as long as nobody bothers the locals. Hatch a plot against America? Fine. The jihadis and their lawyers know it, and act accordingly. Surveil them? Well, sometimes, if the spirit moves them. Indict, or prosecute? They wouldn't dream of it."

The words came out so rapidly that she wondered how much of the answer had been scripted by someone else, but when she searched his eyes for an answer, all she saw was that impenetrable blue, calm and placid, as revealing as a blank page.

"When do I start?"

"Tomorrow."

A rush job. Not usually his style, but she nodded resolutely for the presumed camera.

"We'll send a car for you in the morning and put you on a military flight to the States. Upon arrival you'll be taken to meet the professor at his home, whereupon man and wife will begin their journey to Hamburg. Wightman is in Western PA, so you'll be flying out of Pittsburgh."

"That's not much time to prepare."

"You'll have plenty of briefing materials for the flight over. Oh, and I left out the best part. To look as convincing as possible for the role, you'll be receiving a substantial makeover."

"Oh, dear."

"Yes, the dowdying down of Claire Saylor. I'll admit to a certain fascination with that prospect."

"Who else will be a part of this?"

"All in good time. Any further questions?"

"None you'd be able to answer, apparently."

He grinned tightly and stood. Such a brisk little appointment. It felt like the operational equivalent of speed dating, and she wondered what sort of impression she'd made.

"I'll escort you out, to let the watchers know everything's sweetness and light."

"So are you ever going to tell me who else was watching that performance?" she asked once they were outside.

Bridger warned her off with a tilt of his head. Apparently, even here their conversation wasn't secure, so she nodded in reply.

"Be ready bright and early. Someone will phone later with the departure time. I probably won't be seeing you much as this moves forward, so best of luck."

The news was a surprise, but she tried not to show her disappointment. Bridger held out his hand for a farewell shake, an uncharacteristic gesture for someone who had always disdained glad-handers and office politicians. But perhaps he was still performing, so she obliged him and was rewarded with a surprise—a small, folded scrap of paper. Claire closed her fingers on the item as she withdrew her hand. She again searched his eyes, and again came up empty.

"Best of luck to you as well, Paul. I'm beginning to think you're going to need it."

He didn't reply.

Erring on the side of caution, she waited twenty minutes to unfold the paper, not doing so until she was seated on a nearly empty Metro car as it rocked and roared back toward the center of the city. The message was handwritten and brief:

7—gimlets on the terrace

Bridger was summoning her to an evening rendezvous at his apartment, and if gimlets were in the offing, then she was probably the only guest. She surveyed her surroundings. Having reassured herself no one was watching, she tore the note into pieces, which she enclosed in her fist. Upon reaching her stop, she climbed the stairs to the exit and opened her hand as she emerged onto the crowded street.

The scraps of paper scattered in the wind like snowflakes.

4

The first time Mahmoud Yassin overheard them, five weeks earlier, the five men at the mosque were speaking of death and martyrdom as casually as if they were discussing what to order for takeout—*What'll it be tonight, guys? Holy war or a suicide vest? Pizza or kebabs?*

He liked what he was hearing. His kind of people. So he introduced himself and told them his story, that of a recent arrival from Morocco, hoping for asylum. He was a castaway of mixed parentage—Moroccan dad, American mom—seeking the fellowship of like-minded believers and, if possible, some sort of task to give his life a greater sense of purpose.

His mother's nationality had raised questions, as it inevitably did in these circles, but he was used to them by now. He told them what he always did: that his mother had been dead for years, that her influence had faded long ago. Would that be enough to overcome their understandable skepticism? Only if he could prove his commitment to a higher cause. His willingness to follow orders.

They had heard similar accounts, no doubt, from other arrivals down on their luck and hoping to fit in. But Mahmoud's delivery—halting, fragmentary, an almost reluctant telling in which the shimmer of his deep brown eyes lent an air of humble sincerity—seemed to have won their attentiveness and sympathetic nods. Although it had yet to win their full acceptance and trust. Weeks later, they had not yet invited him into their homes, or out for a meal. Clearly, they still regarded him as an outsider.

He tried not to take it personally. They were smart to be wary, especially in a country like Germany, where so many people didn't understand their deeper feelings about war, or justice, or the ways of God. Being a patient man, Mahmoud had decided at the outset to let them make the first move toward establishing deeper and more lasting ties. He was ready, and knew he would make a good fit.

But now, with the five men still keeping their distance, Mahmoud was feeling a little snubbed, a little morose, and was beginning to doubt the soundness of his approach. There were other mosques in Hamburg, and other such fellows with high-minded ideals and best-laid plans. Maybe he should try elsewhere.

It was early afternoon on a beautiful and unseasonably warm October day. Mahmoud stood alone on the sidewalk by the door of an office building that housed the Al Quds mosque, up on the second floor. He had put on his shoes and come outdoors after completing his midday prayers.

He craved a cigarette, but that was out of the question. *No more room for weakness and temptation*, he told himself. *Be strong, and remain faithful*. The five were still upstairs with the other worshippers, chattering among themselves.

Mahmoud sighed and gazed down Steindamm toward the city's main train station, six blocks away. This was probably the least German part of Hamburg. Three-quarters of the people you passed on the sidewalks here were men, mostly Turks. Of the few women, some were covered head to toe and others were at the opposite extreme, flaunting thighs and cleavage because they worked at the sex shops and dim cabarets sandwiched into the usual assortment of banks, pharmacies, and hardware stores. There were also kebab stands, Middle Eastern grocers, hijab shops, and travel agencies with peeling Arabic lettering on cloudy windows, where, for a modest fee, the proprietor would arrange your pilgrimage to Mecca on a crackly phone connection to Saudi Arabia.

It was lunchtime. At a small café next door, the diners at sidewalk tables were arrayed as if they'd been specifically positioned to test his resolve—young women with bare legs crossed beneath the table, smokers inhaling luxuriously as they unfolded their newspapers, drinkers sipping beer from foaming glasses, plates of artfully prepared food that was well beyond his budget.

Mahmoud turned away as his stomach growled. He should eat soon. Pizza or kebabs? Anything to take his mind off cigarettes, which he'd sworn off on the day of his arrival. Because how could you truly be one of the faithful while making a habit of a sin? Smoking was a transgression against the body that God had given you, and if you let a small temptation like that trip you up, then surely the larger ones would flatten you when you were needed most.

He stepped forward and glanced over his shoulder, up toward the tinted plate glass windows of the mosque on the floor above, where he could make out the shadowy movements of robed men. He thought he detected a bark of muffled laughter. Maybe they were watching him, dismissing him as a wannabe, an inconstant dabbler. The thought made him weary and a little sad.

At first glance, Al Quds was a dreary place—scuffed linoleum floors, dingy walls, and long rooms that seemed more suited to bowling lanes than prayer and sermons. The imam addressed his flock from behind a chipped brown laminate table that looked like it had once done duty in a government office.

Yet it was also a place of seductive warmth and brotherhood. To enter was to be welcomed instantly into its atmosphere of devotion—as long as you were male and a Muslim. The imam, a stout, bearded Moroccan with a fleshy face and a ready smile, was generous with his physicality, brushing his cheek to yours as you hugged, clasping your shoulder in greeting. When he shook your hand, you felt acceptance and commitment in his pulse.

For any lonely Muslim speaker of Arabic, marooned far from home in this chilly and aloof city, Al Quds offered shelter, refuge, a remedy for homesickness. From the first moments, Mahmoud had sensed a level of zeal among the regulars that was far more intense than anything he'd ever encountered in the churches that his Catholic mother had once dragged him to as a boy.

Those doddering priests in rustling vestments had never exhibited any passion or anger like that of the imam, who invariably began his

Friday lesson in a calm and didactic manner before working himself into a frenzy. By the end he was always eliciting affirmative shouts from the faithful. *Join us in our cause! God is great! Death to the unbelievers!* And the five men Mahmoud had first noticed always answered obediently, and they regularly met afterward for further discussion.

Why, then, hadn't they yet reached out to Mahmoud? Perhaps they sensed his reserve, inherited from his mother, a bearing that possibly made him seem too aloof for their tastes, no matter how earnestly he displayed his passions. His paternal side wasn't much help, either, truth be told. Mahmoud's father—a Moroccan, like the imam—wouldn't have lasted ten minutes at Al Quds. They would have instantly pegged him as one of those Fridays-only Muslims who was fine with an occasional tipple or cigarette, or an appreciative leer at a plunging neckline. For Munir Yassin, those so-called taboos had been part and parcel of a full life, because surely a benevolent God would take our weaknesses into account when it came time to enter paradise.

At Al Quds, that was the stuff of blasphemy, and Mahmoud was fine with that. Sacrifice would lead to brotherhood, and brotherhood to a deeper sense of purpose.

He reached into an empty pocket for his phantom pack of cigarettes, then cursed his craving. His stomach growled again, demanding an answer, so he decided on pizza. Probably all he could afford anyway. He would grab a meatless slice just down the block, and then pedal his bicycle through St. Georg to the eastern shoreline of the Alster, Hamburg's big urban lake. On a day as fine as this one, the gravel footpaths would be filled with lithe young women jogging in tights or walking with hand weights in Teutonic precision. He would settle onto a bench and gaze at the small boats out on the water, sails billowing in the sun, or the rowers, gasping in rhythm as they pulled at their oars. He needed to decompress, to clear his head. Maybe he would come up with a new course of action.

He was about to get moving when the door opened behind him with a gust of noise and laughter, which again made him think of his father. Mahmoud turned, half expecting to see him. Instead, it was Omar, one of the five, who smiled when he saw Mahmoud.

"There you are, Brother Mahmoud! We were just wondering where you'd gone."

"Brother Omar, right?"

"Yes, my friend. As-salamu alaikum."

"Wa alaikum as-salaam."

Omar was the eager beaver of the bunch. Late twenties, thin, a live wire from Yemen, a charmer with a soft voice and a ready laugh, although he was also the loudest and most emphatic whenever they sang some jihadi anthem.

"Are you hungry? We would like you to join us for lunch."

Omar was also one of the group's leaders, so this was a good sign.

Mahmoud nervously shuffled his feet and looked down at the ground.

"I would like to. But . . ." He put his hands in his pockets. His poverty was an embarrassment.

"If money is the problem, do not worry."

"No, no. I can pay, just not at the moment. Perhaps I can join you later in the week, when I have saved up a bit more."

"Please, Brother Mahmoud. We can always make Shehhi pay for your lunch, yes?" Omar broke into a grin. "He is from the Emirates, so maybe he will also pay for mine!"

Marwan al-Shehhi, one of the youngest members of the group, was often hit up by the others for small loans, and Omar was one of his most prolific moochers.

"Well, if it is not too much of an imposition."

"And then, after we have eaten, we will take you to the bookstore."

"The bookstore?"

"Al Wahidi. Do you not know it?" Mahmoud had watched them going into the place but hadn't yet presumed to enter while they were inside.

"I am new to this city. I know so little of it."

"Then we will show you. It is just around the corner. There will be others there who you should meet. Important people for our cause. It is Brother Amir's idea. But only if you are interested in our struggle."

Amir, the short and somber one from Cairo, with the chiseled features of a pharaoh, and the group's other leader.

"I *am* interested. I agree with so much of what the imam has to say, and it helps that he is Moroccan like me. Al Quds is the only thing that I like about Hamburg."

"What, have you not seen any of the women as well?"

Omar grinned and winked, as if to add that the remark would stay just between them. Mahmoud, uncertain whether to play along, shrugged and looked at his feet, prompting a laugh.

"You can admit to your weakness with me, Brother Mahmoud. I'll not go running to Brother Amir, or I'd have to report myself as well. And, God willing, you will join us now. First for lunch, then for tea and talking at Al Wahidi, yes?"

"It would be an honor."

"The honor is ours. Wait here. I'll bring the others."

Omar disappeared back through the door. Mahmoud, heart lifting, recalibrated his schedule. Cancel the pizza and the bike ride. He had even stopped thinking about cigarettes, because now he faced the prospect of a busy afternoon among new friends. Having earned this invitation, he was eager to profess his loyalty, his willingness to trust their judgment and do their bidding.

If all went well, maybe the time would eventually come when they would ask him for more. Give him a job, a task, even a mission. No matter where it took him, or what it called for. He would accept it as the will of God. That was his plan. And now he finally felt hopeful that someday they would oblige him.

For the moment, at least, he was one of them. He glanced toward the diners at the café, indulging themselves on rich food, alcohol, and cigarettes. They were nothing to him now.

5

Paul Bridger's apartment was a roomy, stylish flat atop a six-story building in the prosperous district of Neuilly-sur-Seine, with an eagle's view across the treetops of the Bois de Boulogne. It had been paid for long ago by his grandfather, an American tire baron who made his fortune in the 1930s by helping the auto industry drive urban trolley systems out of business.

Subsequent male Bridgers had tried to live down that legacy by serving their country as spies. Paul's father had ditched a promising academic career at Yale to become an operative for the OSS in wartime Greece. He'd then stayed on in Europe for the postwar birth of the CIA, and risen through the ranks.

Paul, born in Bonn and educated in Britain, had joined the Agency in 1975, not long after his father was summoned by Congress to testify about various embarrassments he'd authorized on behalf of U.S. corporations in Latin America. But through all their turns of fortune, the Bridgers had held on to their pied-à-terre in the City of Light. Recently he had hired a housekeeper, Giselle, whose security vetting had taken weeks. Bridger reputedly paid her enough to be her only client, although visitors had continued to report observations of smudged windows and dusty tabletops. Perhaps there were trade-offs for reliable security. Or maybe, as some suspected, Giselle was employed for more than her cleaning.

He was attached to Paris station, but no one had ever seen him set foot there. No one was quite sure who he reported to, although it certainly wasn't Marston. On the occasions he'd been spotted out and about, the reports were always that he'd been alone—off in some corner with an aperitif, his nose buried in a book even as his eyes kept a lookout above the binding.

Claire took a circuitous route to get to his apartment, using anti-surveillance tactics that involved the Metro, a bus, and a taxi and ended with a mile-long stroll through the parkland of the Bois de Boulogne. Silly, perhaps, especially if anyone was watching the apartment building, but she knew Bridger expected nothing less.

Arriving five minutes early, she emerged onto the sidewalk of Boulevard Maillot, knowing without a glance that he would be up on the terrace monitoring her approach, and that next to him on a small table would be a sweating pitcher of gimlets and two crystal glasses. It was his ritual for all invited guests. Claire knew this even though she hadn't been there since shortly after their shared adventure in Berlin.

She crossed the street to the iron security gate, pressed the button for entry to the grounds, and boarded an empty elevator for the ride to the top floor. Bridger was smiling when he opened the door. In a glance she took in the buzz cut, the tanned face with its crinkly laugh lines, the rumpled chinos and white oxford. The old jacket hung from a hook near the door. He greeted her as if their earlier meeting had never taken place, kissing her on the cheek and saying, "How wonderful to see you, Claire!"

"Likewise, Paul. And, you know, it's the strangest thing, but earlier today I met someone who looked just like you."

"Yes, well . . ."

"I'll take my drink now, if you don't mind. That last mile works up a thirst."

"The pitcher is on the terrace. Although we'll hold most of our conversation indoors, if you don't mind."

"Sounds like you're still in a hurry to get down to business."

"Not at all. Never with you." He paused, as if making a conscious effort to slow down. "You look lovely, by the way. Come on out for the view."

The treetops were in their autumn glory, and there was a nip in the air, with a hint of woodsmoke. His grandfather had chosen well. Nowadays this place would easily fetch a million—dollars, not francs, although soon France would be switching to the euro, and how unromantic was that?

Wet leaves were scattered across the terrace, and there was a film of grime on the table.

"Is Giselle off?"

"As of this morning, for the duration of the op. How do you know about her?"

"Everyone knows about her, Paul. How long do you expect it to last?"

"At least a week. Maybe longer, depending on . . . well, we'll get to all that in a moment. Shall we take our drinks indoors?"

Claire meandered back through the living room, detouring past mementos from Bridger's travels—a photo of an Idaho canyon, a matchbook from a roadhouse near Butte, a framed wooden canoe paddle with a cracked handle and scraped varnish. It was known throughout Paris station that every spring or summer Bridger liked to clear his head by making a solitary pilgrimage to the open spaces of the American West, disappearing down some trail with little more than a rucksack and a water bottle.

Slumped on an end table was a crumpled brown rucksack, which Claire paused to inspect. Even before raising it to her face, she detected the scent of woodsmoke, and it was blackened along the top.

"There's a story making the rounds about your most recent trek."

"Yes?"

"The early version was that you'd supposedly outrun a wildfire up the side of a mountain."

"Sounds pretty outlandish."

"Yarborough, our resident skeptic, certainly thought so. He convinced everyone that the whole thing was a charade, an exercise in image building."

"Plausible."

"I thought so, too."

"Sorry to hear that."

"Then I did a little digging. Found coverage of a fire from that very week in the same neck of the woods. Five people were caught in it. Only two got out alive."

"Interesting."

"I kept it to myself."

"Probably best that way."

"My only question was about that second survivor. A companion of yours? And if so, male or female? Friend or lover?"

"Guess you've still got some research to do." He smiled and gestured toward the couch. "Freshen your drink? There's more in the pitcher."

"Will I need it?"

"You might."

She held out her glass. He poured. She settled back into the cushions, while he remained standing.

"Tell me how you've been, Claire."

A loaded request, and, judging from his eyes, it had come from somewhere deeper.

"We'd need another pitcher for that." She tried for breezy but wasn't wholly successful. "My file probably contains most of the relevant events, yes?"

"Well, of course, but . . ."

"I looked up our Professor Armitage online when I got back to the station earlier today."

Now she was the one talking fast, but he tactfully followed her lead.

"I see. Your conclusions?"

"I've heard of keeping a low profile, but he seems to have no profile at all. The university website didn't even have his picture."

"By design, given the nature of his work. This isn't the first time he's had death threats. And he's been on sabbatical the past few years, nailing down his findings. Hasn't actually taught a class in quite a while."

"Wightman looks like a good place to lie low."

"Yes. Only two thousand students, and the town is even smaller. An ivory tower buried in the woods."

"What does a small-town faculty wife do, exactly? Will I need to know how to make bean salad and Bundt cakes? Or is it mostly making nice to old farts with advanced degrees, who'll talk down to me because I don't have a PhD?"

"Oh, but that will be an advantage, Claire: your seeming irrelevance among the worthies. And feel free to laugh behind their backs. From my experience, that's what faculty wives do best."

"That's right, your father was a professor."

"And from the stories he told about my mom, she had the role down to a science. Apparently one summer she single-handedly dethroned a department head who'd become a thorn in Dad's side. He said it was the deftest covert op he's ever seen."

"So *that's* who taught you the game."

"No doubt. She used to say you've never seen real intrigue until you've been to a faculty cocktail party."

"How did we manage to coax Armitage out of his tower?"

"How do you think?"

"Money?"

Bridger nodded.

"This is his one big chance to cash in. After living on a professor's salary all these years, he's finally caught the eye of a major publishing house."

"Also the doing of this foundation you spoke of?"

"Partly. But everyone at the publisher seems genuinely excited. They say that with enough buzz—book people seem obsessed by that word—they'll sell up to half a million copies. They think it's one of those books everyone will suddenly have to have, even if nobody reads it. The next Stephen Hawking."

"What about our target audience of jihadis? Won't this just piss them off more?"

"Some of them. The rest? At best we might make a hairline crack in their resolve, somewhere at the bottom of the foundation. But over time even a small crack can split a boulder. Sometimes an entire mountain."

"So instead of moving the mountain to Muhammad, we propose to make it disintegrate before his eyes."

"As the wife of a Quranic scholar, you're going to have to stop talking like that."

"I thought you *wanted* to stir them up, so we can start scooping them into our nets."

"That's the plan."

"As long as German intelligence doesn't get in the way."

"Yes, well . . ."

"Tell me, have you considered the possibility that our friends in the BND will recognize me from our previous adventure?"

He winced.

"That was a long time ago. I doubt they even got a photo of you."

"Meaning you're not sure."

"Claire, it's been almost ten years."

"Your way of saying I've aged beyond recognition?"

"My way of saying our makeup people will work their usual magic."

"Fair enough. As long as you're willing to tell me who was listening in on us earlier today."

He frowned.

"With any luck, you'll never have to meet him."

"Will he be in Hamburg?"

Bridger waggled his hand, noncommittal.

"You don't know, or can't say?"

"It means it doesn't matter unless you decide to make it matter, which wouldn't be wise."

"I thought the whole reason you summoned me here was to feed me some forbidden fruit. Why else put that note in my hand?"

"Patience. Forbidden fruit is the next course."

Bridger polished off his drink and settled onto the couch, where he turned to face her. He rested his hands on his thighs and assumed that expression she remembered from years earlier, the one he employed whenever he was about to impart something important—a slight wince, with his eyes narrowed and his head tilted forward.

"In addition to your security role, I'm going to need your help in managing . . . another aspect of this operation."

"The part about netting jihadis?"

"Something like that."

"Is this . . . *aspect* official?"

"Let's not play twenty questions, Claire."

"Especially when so far there have been zero answers."

"A lot more will be apparent once you're in place. For now, let's just say you'll be doing some observing. Taking a few readings, reporting what you see and hear."

"And how will I find time for these extracurriculars?"

"The professor's schedule has a window of a few hours every evening. I've arranged for others to stand in for you during those periods, although they won't know where you're going, or why."

"Where *will* I be going?"

Bridger stood, strolled over to a console table, and reached inside a drawer. He returned with a sealed envelope, which he handed to her as he sat back down. She knew better than to open it on the spot.

"Everything you'll need to know is in there."

"But not everything I'll want to know, I bet."

He smiled.

"You and I will have a separate channel of communications. A secure phone for emergencies, but otherwise face-to-face. The logistics for that are also in there. Memorize everything, then destroy it. Not to be melodramatic, Claire, but lives are at stake."

"Ours included?"

"Isn't that always the case?"

Not really, even though everyone always said so. But his tone, his manner, and this whole setup led her to believe that this time the risk was genuine.

"What's the bigger worry here, Paul? The jihadi sharks in Hamburg, or the ones swimming in our own pool?"

He smiled again but kept his own counsel, just as she'd expected. Then he stood and took a step toward the door. Claire took it as a signal to do the same. It was dark now, and she would head straight for the Metro instead of hiking back through the trees. She probably had a full night of studying ahead at her apartment before burning Bridger's notes and flushing the ashes.

He escorted her to the door and offered a parting kiss, cheek to cheek, but this one felt more awkward than the earlier one, and she couldn't say why.

"That envelope I gave you." He paused.

"Yes?"

"Take it straight home. If anyone approaches, protect it at all costs."

"If you're that worried, why don't I just read it here?"

"That was the plan. I'd also hoped we'd have some time to be more *sociable*, for lack of a better word. It's been so long and, well . . ."

"I understand. But?"

He checked his watch.

"I'm expecting another visitor."

He didn't look pleased, so she doubted it was Giselle.

"Will you be mixing more gimlets?"

He shook his head. That told her something, too.

"Then I'd better be going. I'm guessing my presence would be seen as unauthorized."

"Probably."

He reached for the doorknob, then stopped. Fidgeting, he put his hands in his pockets, and then took them out.

"What is it, Paul?"

"A stray bit of curiosity. And I promise this is the only time I'll ask, but, well, after our work the last time around, did anyone in authority ever question you about my, you know . . ."

"Your what?"

"Failure of nerve."

"Is that what it was?"

"Didn't you think so?"

"Oh, Paul." She touched his hand. "It was your humanity. Something we all have."

"That's a kind way of putting it."

"Whatever the case, no one ever asked, at any level of authority. And it certainly didn't go into my report."

He nodded and seemed to relax. She wondered how long he'd been holding that inside. Not that she didn't harbor her own secrets from that time.

"Besides," she said, "it's what we did afterward that would have really gotten their tongues wagging."

"Well, yes. But I hope you never—"

"I'm insulted you'd ask."

"Of course. Mea culpa."

"For now, or for ten years ago?"

"Touché. And I promise you this, Claire. I won't fail you again."

"Nor I you."

"Safe travels, then. See you in Hamburg."

She raised the sealed envelope.

"One way or another, it seems."

Then she slipped it into her purse and was on her way.

6

Claire did not go straight home.

She descended the stairs of the Metro station, walked the length of the platform, past the waiting passengers, and exited at the opposite end, back onto the street. She was no longer within sight of Bridger's terrace.

Walking a few blocks, she reentered the Bois de Boulogne and doubled back along a darkened gravel path until she was directly across from his building, where she took up an observation post in the night shadows of a mulberry tree. It was chilly, but not unbearable.

She glanced into her purse at the sealed envelope. Bridger's warning had made it feel like she was carrying stolen goods. How could a few vaguely worded operational instructions possibly be so sensitive? It was then that she noticed the shiny digital camera buried among the rest of the items in her purse. They had given it to her that morning while setting up the surveillance post, in case they needed any still images from outdoors before the video equipment was up and running. It was a new model, compact and slim. She got it out and aimed the viewfinder at the gated entrance, which was nicely illuminated by a streetlamp. Perfect.

About ten minutes later, a black Chevy Suburban pulled up. She couldn't see if there were green diplomatic tags, but, given the model, the car had almost certainly been provided by the American embassy. A fairly tall man got out from the back and walked toward the security gate while the engine idled. She zoomed the lens and snapped a few photos, but he hadn't turned his face, even in profile. He leaned forward to press the button for entry.

Claire was too far away to hear the answering buzz, but a few seconds later the man pushed open the gate, and as he did so he turned briefly to signal his driver. For a fleeting moment his face was perfectly illuminated. She snapped two more shots.

He disappeared into the building as the car pulled away. Claire studied the images on the small screen. Pale skin, silver hair, a mole on his left cheek. She couldn't tell whether his eyes were blue or brown, and his face wasn't even remotely familiar, but anyone important enough to merit a car and driver was probably either a ranking officer from another posting or a higher-up out of Langley.

Had she just seen the operation's real boss? If so, why was Bridger covering for him? Every op had its subterranean currents, but these already seemed deeper than usual. Claire backed away from the tree until she had a view of the terrace.

Dark and empty up there. By now the men were probably talking. No gimlets and, probably, no laughs. The Suburban had moved out of sight.

She had work to do, enough to keep her awake for hours. Study the notes, destroy the notes. Then she would put her affairs in order for a prolonged absence, just in case. Not much of that to do, actually—a thought that left her feeling a little empty. Funny how she wouldn't have felt that way a mere twenty-four hours ago. Seeing Bridger had stirred up old feelings, not all of them welcome. She was a little excited, and a little desolate, too. Another drink might be in order after she got home, but it would have to wait until she completed the memorization chores.

Then, and only then, she would allow herself a moment to think through all that had happened ten years earlier. Afterward she doubted there would be much time or inclination for sleep.

Claire popped out the memory chip, dropped it into her purse with the camera, and headed for home.

SUNDAY, OCTOBER 3

7

The limo, a black Lincoln Town Car with smoked windows, bounced through a pothole on the Pennsylvania Turnpike just as Claire flipped down the sun visor, checking the mirror for yet another damage assessment.

"How much farther, Robert?"

"Forty minutes tops, if the traffic keeps moving. The last ten klicks are a one-laner through the woods."

"Thanks."

She was antsy, jet-lagged, and the view from the mirror was still pretty horrifying. A makeup and disguise specialist had completed her disfigurement on the plane, and her face looked pale and drawn, eyes shrunken, lashes practically invisible. Her lips were dry and severe, a moue of disapproval, and her hair was limp and flattened. The wardrobe was no better—a brown polyester pantsuit that hung from her frame like a shower curtain, clunky black orthopedic pumps, an orange blouse with a wing collar. She was the colors of a fall rummage sale held in a church basement with linoleum flooring.

Was this supposed to show the debilitating effect of twenty-eight years of marriage?

Maybe Robert would know. He was an old hand from the Langley motor pool, beefy and capable, with both hands on the wheel and a shoulder holster beneath his jacket. He had driven her around years earlier, during a home visit for a lengthy debriefing following an eventful op abroad. He was pleasant company on a long drive, so she'd gone against the usual protocol by sitting up front.

Robert wasn't likely to be privy to much about this op. But he wore a wedding band, and for the moment that was the kind of intelligence she needed most.

The briefing materials that she'd read on the flight across the Atlantic had offered few clues about the professor's marriage, beyond listing some of his personal likes and dislikes, and a few of his wife's as well. Her name was Brenda, which would be Claire's name from here on out. The rest of his dossier was about his professional side—a list of his published works, previous conferences he'd attended, an assessment of his expertise, some notes on his reclusive nature.

The limo bounced through another pothole.

"How long have you been married, Robert?"

"Twenty years on this one. Nine the time before."

"Ah, doubly experienced. Just the man to advise me on how to best put him at ease."

"You've never been undercover as a wife before?"

"Oh, plenty of times, but always with an Agency partner. You ham it up, have some fun. But this guy won't be used to acting, and he hasn't had the training."

"Hmm." Robert tilted his head, giving it some thought. "Hard to say. Marriages are kind of like foreign countries. They've got different languages and everything."

"Got any phrase books?"

He laughed.

"I do, actually. After about the first ten years, you're either at each other's throats or you've settled into a stalemate where a little silence isn't so bad now and then. So, when in doubt, say nothing. It won't fool him, but it'll fool everybody else."

"Well, that's depressing. But it is a handy fallback."

"What about you?"

"Me?"

"I'm surprised you've never been hitched."

"Oh, that. Well . . ."

"Is it all the travel?"

"That's part of it. I came close a few times."

"What stopped you?"

"Just not the right fit, I guess."

"Better to find out before than after, that's for sure."

But it was more than the fit. She knew that, even if she'd never settled on a fully satisfactory answer. It was partly a question of all the secrecy that her work required. How could you square that with the trust required for a lifelong relationship? A colleague in Rome had fathered children on two continents and kept two separate households, each unaware of the other. He had played it like an assignment, a double agent within his own life.

For the moment, Claire was unattached, a handy status when you were about to be shielding a professor from a bunch of dangerous hot-heads. She smiled as she recalled the stylish but lethal Frenchman she had duped a few days earlier. What would he make of her now, looking like this? She wondered if he had phoned the Vietnamese takeout yet.

The limo was slowing down.

"Here's our exit," Robert said. "Ten more miles. We're a little ahead of schedule if you need a break."

"No, thanks." Then a thought occurred to her, something she'd been wondering earlier but hadn't yet felt comfortable enough to bring up. "Actually, yes. Could you pull over for a second?"

"Perfect spot coming up, just off the ramp."

He rolled the limo onto the wide gravel shoulder. Claire reached for her laptop, opened it, and clicked on the image file, where she called up the photo she'd taken in Paris the other night, outside Bridger's apartment.

"There's a picture I want to show you. A man. One of ours, I think, and I was wondering if maybe you'd ever driven him around before."

He gave her a crooked smile, as if to say he knew this was off-limits but didn't mind. Not yet, anyway.

"I mean, as long as you're comfortable with that."

"Long as I don't have to tell anybody else about it."

"That's my preference as well."

"Then let's have a look."

She turned the screen so he could see it.

He squinted and leaned closer, then he slowly shook his head.

"I've never driven him, but he looks familiar." He looked again, then his eyebrows went up. "Yeah, the guy with the mole on his cheek, I remember now. He wasn't my ride, but I saw him getting into Hal's car a few years back. The director was with him, saying goodbye, which is probably why he made an impression."

"At Langley?"

He nodded.

"Right out front. I was waiting for some other guy to come out. So he's probably one of ours, like you said. But he wouldn't have been based there, not if Hal was driving him. No idea of a name, though."

She considered asking for Hal's full name, and maybe his contact information. But the deeper she waded into this pool, the more ripples she would make, and it was way too early for that.

"Thanks, that's a help."

Robert, to his credit, didn't ask why she wanted to know, or where the photo had come from. She supposed there was still a chance he might report all of this, but she doubted it. Doing so would only draw him in deeper, making his own ripples, which would in turn mean further questions, or even paperwork.

He pulled the limo back onto the road, and soon they were driving through deep forest. Yellow leaves fluttered down beneath an overcast sky.

"Beautiful country out here," he said.

"I was feeling kind of hemmed in."

"That's because you've been married twenty-eight years."

"They don't even have real heat at this house of his, you know. Just a woodstove that uses pellets."

"He's not a vegetarian, I hope."

"No. And he drinks. That always helps."

A deer vaulted from the trees on the left. Robert deftly swerved the limo as Claire held her breath. The car shimmied on its big chassis and then righted itself, hurtling onward. A big buck with a magnificent rack of antlers disappeared into the trees.

"I see what you mean," Robert said. Then, after a pause: "I could never live out here."

Ten minutes later they pulled up in front of a brown brick ranch with white shutters and six mullioned windows across the front. In the middle was a black door with a brass knocker. The yard was unraked, with maples and a towering red oak. In the back, nothing but woods as far as the eye could see. The nearest neighbor was a few hundred yards farther down the highway. Robert wheeled up the gravel driveway, parked by the sidewalk, and got out to open Claire's door.

"Good luck in there. I'll open the trunk."

Claire strolled up the sidewalk with a flutter in her stomach, and tried to place when she'd last felt this way. Probably the night of her junior prom, listening from the bedroom as her parents greeted her arriving date, a football player who had been her second choice. A curtain twitched on a window to the left of the door as she reached the porch. She raised the brass knocker and banged it three times.

Footsteps, then a rattle of the knob as the door opened. Professor Winston Armitage squinted into the daylight, looking exactly like his photo. He was even wearing the same gray cardigan, with the top and bottom buttons undone.

"Winston?"

"Hi. You must be the foundation's security person. And your name is . . . ?"

"Brenda, of course. From here on out."

"Oh, right." He laughed nervously. "Come in." He glanced toward the limo. "Should I, uh, or *we*, invite the driver in?"

"He'll wait. We can get acquainted first."

He nodded and stood aside.

"I guess I don't need to carry you across the threshold," he said, followed by a strangled bark of laughter. Claire answered with what she hoped was a pleasant smile, but she held her purse in front of her in case he needed warding off. Then she thought better of it and lowered the purse to one side as she stepped into the foyer.

Armitage crossed the carpeted hallway toward the kitchen, in the back. To the left was a sunken living room, a darkened universe of knickknacks and framed photos. The house was still, with a faint smell of mothballs and past pot roasts, the hum of a refrigerator.

"I made coffee, if you'd like some."

"Oh, thank you. I take it black."

"Black. I suppose I'll need to remember that."

He rattled out the pot from the coffeemaker and poured a cup. Claire smiled uncertainly as she tried to imagine him delivering an important speech that would reshape worldwide thought on martyrdom and the Quran. And at that moment she pitied him, this shy academic accustomed to hushed archives and leafy campuses, being thrust into such a precarious public role.

"The first thing I'd like to tell you, Winston, is that you are going to be safe and secure throughout this trip. We're going to make sure of that. I'll also ask you to address me as Brenda from now on, just as if I were the genuine article. No offense to the real Brenda, of course."

"None taken."

"The more natural we appear to be, the better for all concerned. The university has hired an additional bodyguard who will meet us there. My employer, Bendix Security, has, at the request of the foundation, deployed a support staff that will also be working undercover, as hotel guests and so on. You'll never be out of our sight. And the foundation has arranged a tight schedule that should keep you too busy to worry. So from here on out you'll be in good hands."

"They didn't tell me you'd be pretty."

"Yes, well." There was no way she was going to thank him for that.

"Did that cost extra?"

He smiled to show it was a joke. Claire wondered vaguely what the real Brenda would've made of the remark, and she pictured the woman in a motel room, miles from here, dressed in an identical brown pantsuit and not missing Winston at all as she watched television with her shoes off and her feet up.

"I've been fully briefed on your work, and also on your wife's background. You don't need to know anything about me except what you already know about her. Well, except maybe for how I like my coffee. Just think of me in those terms—a known quantity—and we'll take it from there. Sound good?"

"Yes."

He smiled and seemed to relax. His shoulders lowered as some of the tension went out of his frame.

"Good. And from what I've already learned about you, I'm betting you've been keeping an eye on the clock and would like to get underway for the airport."

"Yes! You're absolutely right! I'm a stickler for being on time. And, well, thank you for doing this."

He held out his hand for a welcoming shake. Claire responded in kind.

"I guess that wasn't very husbandlike, was it?" he said.

"Not to worry. We'll get used to each other's company."

Then, with a sudden light in his eyes, Armitage leaned forward and surprised her with a wet kiss on the lips.

"Maybe more like that, you think? We could always practice later."

He beamed as if he had said something extremely clever.

"After twenty-eight years of marriage, I'm thinking we're quite bored with all of that, yes? Or should I consult with the other Brenda, to make sure?"

"That won't be necessary."

Armitage sounded crestfallen, but for Claire the moment had jolted her back to equilibrium. This wasn't a marriage at all. It was a role, an op, much like all her other roles and ops. And from here on out, she would be in charge of it.

"How 'bout if we get going?"

He nodded as wearily as if he really were her husband, and picked up his bags. He carried them out onto the porch, where he locked up the house before shambling toward the limo, where Robert waited by the open trunk. Claire followed step for step, already watching his back.

MONDAY,
OCTOBER 4

8

Mahmoud's afternoon was off to a poor start. He'd barely had time to roll up his prayer rug and set it in the corner when Omar, usually the friendliest fellow at Al Quds, began hounding him with questions.

"Where were you last evening, my brother? We were looking for you, but no one could find you." He was scowling, hands on his hips. Mahmoud shrugged and looked down at his feet.

"I went home."

"To Munzstrasse? Shehhi says you weren't there. Not at the hour when we were expecting you."

So they were already checking up on him. Hardly surprising. He knew from his own experience that outliers in a strange land had to be careful about choosing their friends and enemies, especially when the locals were inclined to mistrust you. He didn't blame them, and earlier he had gladly offered the address of his apartment when they'd asked, although now he felt a little awkward.

"I took a long walk. To think about things."

Omar shook his head, still not satisfied.

"Well, you missed an important discussion. We made further plans for the action against the professor we were discussing at lunch. But if you are already falling away from us, then there is no point of including you any further. Did all of our talk at the bookstore scare you away?"

Ah, yes, the bookstore. He'd gone there each of the past few days with his new friends, and the gatherings had been quite an eye-opener: a dozen or so young men singing of jihad, followed by a viewing of herky-jerky combat videos smuggled out of Chechnya or some other battlefront. They watched every explosion with fire in their eyes, shouting like football fans. Mahmoud found it easy to get into the spirit of things, and he joined in at top volume. The exhilaration of the moment put a jump in his pulse and made him feel powerful, like he was part of something important. As a group, they could do anything.

At yesterday afternoon's session, talk had then turned to the latest news of the infidel professor from America. He was due to arrive soon in Hamburg. There had been a story about him in a local Arabic-language newspaper saying that in the coming week he would unveil a book that would profane the Holy Quran. And for the first time, instead of the abstractions of jihad in some faraway place, the group had spoken of taking action on their own, right here, and soon, at a hotel only a few miles away. They vowed to meet that evening to discuss it further.

Exciting, but sobering, and Mahmoud had felt a little overwhelmed. Was he truly ready for this level of commitment? Did he have what it would take to stay with this to the end? So, at nightfall, he had gone off by himself, skipping out on their meeting, and apparently his absence had bothered them enough to send Shehhi after him. Now Omar was getting up in his face, seeking answers while Mahmoud was still searching for them.

"Are you with us, Brother Mahmoud, or are you not?"

He shuffled his feet, groping for the words. Then Marwan al-Shehhi burst through the door, an interruption that felt like a reprieve until Shehhi upped the ante.

"Brother Mahmoud! I was hoping you would return." Then, to Omar: "Have you asked him about the train?"

So they'd followed him, then. Someone must have seen him boarding the S-Bahn, and for all he knew they'd stuck with him the entire evening, an unsettling thought. He supposed it was understandable, but even a committed life shouldn't be without its moments of privacy. Maybe this wasn't going to work after all.

"Yes, the train," Omar said, his eyes lighting up in an unexpectedly friendly way. "A few of us will be riding the S-Bahn tonight to the House of the Followers, and we would like you to join us. It's in Harburg, half an hour south of here."

"The House of the Followers?"

"It's where Brother Amir and some of the others live, because it's near their university. We like to meet there for dinner. It's even better than the bookstore, because we can stay as late as we like."

"Until the neighbors complain!" Shehhi said, laughing. "Germans are too much in love with their peace and quiet. But come. Join us. We will make the joyful noise of the devout."

Mahmoud's fingers unclenched. His smile returned.

"Yes. Of course I'll come."

Shehhi nodded eagerly.

"I will go and tell the others."

Omar was not so easily pacified. There was still a trace of doubt in his eyes, so Mahmoud decided to tell him a bit more.

"You're right, Omar. I did have doubts. On Friday, when you invited me to lunch, I was so happy. It was what I had been seeking. Then, after the weekend I think I became a little overwhelmed by it all. I needed time to think, so I took a train out into the country. It was a long night for me. It's a big step."

Omar nodded calmly and put a hand on Mahmoud's shoulder.

"I understand. I do. We laugh, we shout and sing, and we talk of these things almost like they are a game. And, between you and me, to some of them it *is* a game, and maybe it's my fault for letting them think so. But if you needed time to think, then you know that we are serious. Which is a good thing, yes?"

"Yes. That's the reason I decided to come back."

Omar's eyes shone with empathy, and he squeezed Mahmoud's shoulder.

"Then what I would like to know next, my friend, is if you think you are back for good? And it is all right if you cannot yet say yes. Because you're correct: It's a big step. One that might save you for all time in the kingdom of the afterlife. But, still, a big step in this world of ours below."

"I already know my answer. I've done enough thinking. The rest I will leave to God. I am back for good."

"Well done, Brother Mahmoud. That's a great comfort to me, because last night, after all the others had left, Brother Amir and I discussed you for quite some time."

"I see."

Omar must have noted the uncertain look in his eyes, because he again put a hand on his shoulder, as if to steady him.

"He is not yet sure you are prepared to serve us. So I told him I would give you a task. A job to do, as a sort of test. It is a small job, one that you would do for us this afternoon. Small, as I said, but very important, maybe even critical, so it must be done correctly or not at all. Would you be willing to do this for us?"

Mahmoud's inclination was to ask for more details, but he sensed that unconditional acceptance was part of the test. After a pause, he nodded.

"Yes, I am willing. Large or small."

Omar squeezed his shoulder.

"I told him you would say yes. He doubted it, but I was sure, so this pleases me. But first I must know whether you can drive a car?"

"I can. But I do not have any sort of license."

Omar waved away that worry.

"I don't think any of our brothers is licensed to drive here. As long as you drive with care and correctness, that will be of no concern. Here, then."

He reached into his pocket and handed Mahmoud a set of keys. Then he pointed out a car parked just down the block, a silver four-door Toyota Corolla sedan with Hamburg plates.

"You must listen to me closely, because there must be no variation from what we are asking of you. Yes?"

"Of course."

"Precisely at four o'clock, you will take these keys and unlock the car. Inside the glove box are instructions for what you must do next, and also a map. You must not contact anyone else while you are carrying out these orders, and you must follow them to the letter. Once you complete the job, you will destroy the instructions and return to us directly at the mosque, so that we will know you have been successful. But you will not telephone us at any moment along the way. Do you understand?"

"Yes."

"And if, for any reason, you are stopped by the police or any authorities, you will say nothing. No cover story, no explanation for how you acquired the car. Nothing. Would you be able to maintain your silence if that happens?"

Mahmoud knew better than to hesitate.

"I would."

"Very good. You will be strong, I am certain of it. And for now, that is all you need to know. The rest, as I said, will be explained in the instructions."

Mahmoud had questions, of course. Chiefly, whether this had anything to do with the group's plans to disrupt the visit by the infidel American professor. The assignment's timing certainly made him suspect that it did. But Omar's words and manner told him that questions were not only unwelcome, but off-limits. Unquestioning faith was required, faith in his brothers to neither lead him astray nor abandon him to something foolhardy or unwise. By correctly following their orders he would presumably be welcomed deeper into the fold, and the next job would have even greater meaning. Spiritually, it was the only path forward. And that, after all, was why he was here.

"Thank you for your trust, Brother Omar."

"Thank *you*, Brother Mahmoud. You will do well, I am sure of it. Come with me, then, because now we must confront the great stone face of Brother Amir!"

Omar burst into laughter, and Mahmoud knew why. Facing the dour and demanding Amir was intimidating under any circumstances. Doing so after everything they'd just discussed would be even more daunting.

They found him holding court in the main room of the mosque, seated on a folding chair before six men squatting on the floor, faces upturned in rapt attention. One of them asked a question and Amir stroked his beard, deliberating. Spotting Shehhi across the room, he called out, "Brother Shehhi! You are our expert on beards. Mine is yet too short, so how should we determine what is the proper length?"

The six men turned as one. Shehhi smiled and gripped his beard with his right fist.

"It must be long enough so that when you grab it this way, at least a few inches still show below. Do you see?"

The men nodded and turned back toward Amir.

"He's nearly done," Omar whispered. "Amir only allows questions when the lesson is over. He's very strict about that. Interrupt him sooner and he starts chewing on his lower lip to keep from losing it. Watch."

Omar shouted from the back just as Amir resumed speaking.

"What was today's topic, Brother Amir?"

Right on cue, Amir bit his lower lip. But it was his sharp, steady gaze that got Mahmoud's attention—seemingly capable of drilling a hole in your forehead. The men on the floor stirred uneasily, recognizing the warning signs. Omar laughed.

"I am testing your self-control, Brother Amir. It is a reckless joy of mine."

Amir announced stiffly that the session was over and rose from the chair. Omar closed in, with Mahmoud in his wake.

"And now," Omar said, "I suppose you will tell me that too much joy kills the heart, and makes us grow soft."

This finally drew a grudging smile.

"You know me too well," Amir said. Then, to Mahmoud: "I am pleased to see you have returned, my brother."

"I am pleased to be here. I am pleased to serve you, and to serve all my brothers."

Amir glanced at Omar.

"So you have asked him?"

"And he accepted."

"Without questions or conditions?"

"Completely. Just as I expected."

"Very well," Amir said. He looked back at Mahmoud and nodded, although he did not smile again.

"I also invited Brother Mahmoud to the House of the Followers for dinner," Omar said. This drew another sharp glance from Amir. Was that a flicker of disapproval? His eyes were alive one moment, dead the next. Where did his thoughts go when the light went out?

"Our plans for dinner have changed."

Shehhi, who had just rejoined them, looked disappointed by the news.

"There will be no dinner?"

"We have received a better invitation from Brother Haydar. His family has one of those garden houses on a plot near the Stadtpark.

He will be grilling lamb kebabs, and he has invited us all. You, too, Brother Mahmoud. He wishes to meet you. He wants to talk further about our planned action against the infidel American who has profaned the Quran."

Mahmoud again wondered how his own assignment might fit into those plans, but he knew better than to ask.

"I'm glad he wants to meet me."

"Haydar's garden house is a fine place," Omar said. "A wonderful garden, a cabin with a table out back. This is one thing the Germans do well, putting a little bit of the country into their cities. You'll enjoy it. If we're not careful, it may be too much pleasure for Brother Amir to endure."

Amir again bit his lower lip. Of all the members of the group, only Omar was bold enough to talk to him like this. Mahmoud supposed the dynamic was part of the reason for their joint leadership.

Amir's eyes then went from glassy to sparkling in an instant as he looked over their shoulders. Mahmoud turned to see an unfamiliar face as Amir called out in greeting.

"Brother Jarrah, you are back among us!"

Ziad Jarrah, the new arrival, was a revelation, mostly because he wasn't dressed at all like the rest of them. Trim and fit, he wore jeans and a crewneck sweater. Even with his beard, he could have passed for a young European professional, and his wide smile lit up the room. Spotting Mahmoud, he nodded and stepped closer.

"Who's this fresh face, Omar?" he asked. Omar made the introductions.

"It's always good to welcome a new brother," Jarrah said.

"My feelings as well," Mahmoud answered, taking Jarrah's hands in his own.

Jarrah nodded amicably and excused himself, strolling across the room toward Amir.

"Brother Jarrah cannot always be with us as much as we like," Omar said, "but he is wholly committed to our cause."

"Where's he from?" Mahmoud asked.

"Beirut." Then, with a gleam in his eye, "Another one with money, so stay close whenever a bill arrives."

When Jarrah reached Amir, the two men hugged, a warmer greeting than Mahmoud had received, which told Mahmoud he still had work to do. Omar must have sensed his reaction.

"Do not feel slighted," Omar said. "Brother Amir has great plans for Jarrah."

"Plans?"

"Maybe he will speak of them this evening, at Brother Haydar's. If not tonight, then later. Rest easy—you'll know more about all of these things soon enough."

When he glanced again toward Amir and Jarrah, they were conferring head-to-head in lowered voices, their eyes gleaming with intensity.

9

A mere hour on the ground in Hamburg and Claire was already on high alert. A knock at the door of their hotel room set everything in motion just after she had finished unpacking.

She motioned Armitage away from the door.

"Step back until we know who it is."

Checking through the peephole, she saw a familiar face, but feigned ignorance to protect her cover. The visitor's as well.

"It's some guy. Seems friendly enough, but you better have a look."

Armitage strolled over, and brightened at the sight.

"It's my publicist, Tony Fleischman! Let him in."

Claire knew him as Tony Goldman, a Bridger regular based in London. Mid-thirties, with a gift for acting and regional dialects. She'd last seen him in Marseilles, posing as a John Deere international sales rep out of Arkansas.

Armitage handled the introductions while Tony and Claire pretended they'd never met. She'd already spotted two other colleagues from Madrid station checking into the room to the left as a Spanish couple on holiday. Tony was staying in the room to the right. Another Agency operative had arrived earlier and was posted in a room down the hall. Bridger had also arranged for help from the Hamburg police. Two uniformed officers and a plainclothesman were on duty around the clock in the downstairs lobby, keeping an eye on every coming and going.

Claire's only complaint with the arrangements was that the hotel had put her and the professor in a room with one king-size bed, when she would have preferred a pair of doubles. Armitage, predictably, had seemed to think the setup was just fine. The things she endured for cover.

"I'm ready to roll on those interviews this afternoon," Armitage said to Tony.

For such a reclusive fellow, he seemed pretty excited about all the media attention.

"Great," Tony said. "Because we're starting off with a bang—*The New York Times* and BBC World Service. And that's just for starters. Once we get going tomorrow morning, your schedule's pretty full from here on out."

"We'll, uh, have some time to get out and about, too, won't we?"

"Out and about?"

"To kick back a little, maybe see a few sights?"

Tony and Claire looked at each other.

"We're not here as tourists, Winston," Claire said.

"Of course not. Still, this might be my only chance to raise a big mug in a German beer hall. And, well, it *is* Oktoberfest, so—"

"Oktoberfest was in September."

"It was?"

"Sorry."

"Think book sales," Tony said. "By the time we're done, you'll be making enough in royalties to travel to Oktoberfest as many times as you like."

"It's really in September? I had no idea."

"Not to worry. You and I will have plenty to keep us busy. But for the moment, could I have a private word with your bodyguard?"

"Oh. So they told you she's not the real Brenda?" He sounded disappointed.

"The foundation told me. It's in your own best interests if everyone coordinates."

"Sure." He nodded and headed for the bathroom. "I need to use the facilities anyway. Then it's nap time. This jet lag's a real bear."

They moved to the far side of the room and waited for the bathroom door to shut. Tony lowered his voice.

"We've got a problem."

"Already?"

"Bridger got a tip that a hotel insider is planning to make a move against the professor, maybe as soon as today."

"That was fast."

Tony grimaced and looked down at his feet.

"I'm afraid I may be partly to blame. I placed a story about the professor in an Arabic daily that circulates here. Two days ago they ran an editorial calling him the Raisin Infidel, and they printed the whole damn schedule for the convention."

"Jesus, Tony. I know Paul wanted to stir them up, but—"

"Not my idea. Or Bridger's, either."

"Then whose was it?"

"Don't ask."

There it was again, another sign of a second spoon stirring the pot. The man she had seen in Paris, or maybe someone based here, with better local knowledge.

"Does 'insider' mean hotel employee?"

"It might. For now, 'insider' is all we've got. If it's an employee, that leaves you with two hundred possibilities, with around fifty foreign nationals. Judging by the names and countries of origin, maybe thirty are Muslim. But then you've also got contractors—groundskeepers, restaurant and bar suppliers, exterminators."

"For killing bugs, I hope."

"If we're lucky."

"What about the other academics here for the conference? You gotta figure at least a few might be out on the fringe."

"Two guys in particular are pretty radicalized, and they've posted passionate rebuttals of his findings. But one of them is boycotting the event in protest. The other guy's an Algerian who couldn't get an entry visa in time. Everyone else vetted out okay, not that we aren't keeping an eye on them. Frankly, the best thing we've got going for us is that only a few of them even know what Armitage looks like."

"And I handled check-in, so no one at the front desk has seen him. But at some point he'll have to come out of his cocoon."

"Only to a point. We're using a privacy screen and a voice modifier for the press interviews. It's mostly a matter of moving him from point A to point B without incident, and sealing off access to the room. But

I suppose 'insider' could even mean it's another guest, and you've seen how big this place is."

Indeed. At thirty-two stories, the Hamburg Plaza Hotel was the city's second-tallest building, looming over the surrounding parks and rail lines like a slab dropped from the heavens. It was the centerpiece of the city's convention complex.

"Where'd the tip come from?"

"Bridger didn't say. The cops freed up the hotel personnel records, although they turned down our request to post extra officers at either end of the hallway. We've also got the private bodyguard the university hired, Lute Sherrill, so that's an extra body for the good guys."

"You met him yet?"

"Briefly. Next room down from mine. Ex-cop, nice enough, and seems eager to do what he can. A bit of a fish out of water, but he's big and strong, so that should count for something. You'll see. He should be dropping by. Oh, and one other thing. A warning."

"Another one?"

"This one's minor."

Tony got out a photo of a smiling, bearded fellow in his fifties, tweedy, a little impish. He looked American.

"Keep an eye out for this guy. Tom Warden, an old friend of the professor's. From Georgetown, and he's staying up on six, so he'll probably be looking to make contact."

"Wouldn't that be a good thing? Maybe have him down for a drink, keep Armitage from getting so antsy."

"Bridger's orders. The fewer distractions, the better. You know his rules: The moment you throw somebody unexpected into the mix, you start to lose control of the situation."

"What if he sees me? Won't he know I'm not the real thing?"

Tony shook his head.

"The only time he and Armitage ever get together is at these conventions. For drinks, comparing notes, that kind of shit. No wives. So keep an eye out, and make sure he doesn't get close enough to become a problem. As tight a schedule as we're keeping, it probably won't be an issue."

"Got it. What's your thinking on the plan for today?"

"Everything's clear until those two interviews, beginning at three.

We're doing those on the next floor down, and we can take the back stairwell and be back here by four thirty. Bridger said you might want some time later for a few duties of your own?"

"Yes. I'll probably need a couple hours."

"Care to say what for?"

"You know his rules."

Tony smiled.

"Lute and I will hold the fort while you're gone. Tomorrow the professor's got four more interviews, bright and early, plus the big symposium in the midafternoon. We've thoroughly vetted everyone with an invitation, but we'll still be using the screen and voice modifier.

"It's the next day when things could get hairy. A full press conference. Same setup as the interviews, with the privacy screen and voice modifier, but you'll have all those cameras and sound equipment, plus a roomful of unruly hacks. And there's bound to be a mad scramble at the end when we give away the book. Two hundred galleys, boxed and ready to go."

The bathroom door opened. They put on their most cheerful smiles for Armitage, and he smiled back.

"Isn't Tony great?" he said. "He's going to have this thing selling like hotcakes."

"He's made it a hot item, all right."

Claire lowered her voice for a final aside to Tony. "What about vehicles? How protected is the building?"

"The only access is via a single driveway. The police are screening everything that comes into the parking deck below the building, so we shouldn't have to sweat a car bomb, and the clearance is too low for a truck to make it in. A delivery truck or vehicle could try something from the rear loading dock, but the hotel security people say they've got a handle on that, and, let's face it, the local jihadis haven't exactly had much time to prepare. They've only known about this a few days."

"Any good spots for snipers?"

"Well, you're on the third floor, facing the park, and there's no building with a clear line of sight to the window. All the same . . ."

Claire nodded. Armitage piped up.

"Did you guys just say something about snipers?" His smile was gone.

"Only to observe that they're not a threat," Claire said.

He nodded but didn't look convinced. He walked over to the mini-bar fridge and began poking around for a drink.

"Okay, then," she said. "Let's start getting you ready to face the lions, Winston."

"The lions?" He looked ashen.

"From the press. A figure of speech."

"Right. Sure."

But the fun seemed to have already gone out of the day for him, and Claire couldn't help but feel a little sorry for him.

There was another knock at the door. Armitage flinched, and Tony checked the peephole.

"It's the bodyguard."

Lute Sherrill was big, all right. Probably lifted weights, judging from his thick neck and broad shoulders. His face was as flushed as if he'd just run a wind sprint. Nerves, maybe. He was young, late twenties, and probably hoping to make a good first impression.

"Hi, guys. I'm Lute. The U told me to stick as close as I could to the professor, but I was figuring you'd know the best way to use me, so I'm at your disposal."

"Thanks, Lute. I'm Brenda, glad to have you aboard. Tony said you used to be a cop?"

"Iowa City. College town." He shrugged. "My employer seemed to think that made me the perfect choice for guarding a professor. I don't speak any German, though."

"That shouldn't be a problem. Just keep your eyes and ears open."

He nodded. His enthusiasm was infectious. Even if his inexperience wasn't a plus, his willingness to follow their lead would help make up for any shortcomings.

"Where would you like me to get started?"

"You can come with us to the interviews," Tony said. "Cover the hallway while we're inside."

"Sounds good."

"Then later you can double up with me on room protection while Brenda heads out on some errands."

"Sure."

"Afterward, maybe you could pick up the professor's registration kit from the people running the conference," Claire said. "He'll need his credentials to move around, and they said they'd prefer for someone representing the university to take care of that."

"They're the ones at that big table down in the lobby?"

"Yes."

"Consider it done."

Tony called out to Armitage.

"So how 'bout it, champ? Ready to start prepping for those interviews?"

The professor poured a whiskey. The glass in his right hand quivered ever so slightly. Then he smiled queasily as he did his best to show resolve.

"Absolutely, Tony. You the man. Teach me to, uh, tame those lions."

10

Mahmoud nervously kept his distance from the silver Toyota until a few minutes before four o'clock. He walked there from the main train station, hands in his pockets, as if that might help him hold it together.

Was anyone watching, if only to ensure that someone carried out this task? If he failed to show, he assumed they had a backup. Or hoped they did. Although, considering the group's threadbare resources, maybe he was the only option, a thought that made him feel more important, more trusted. Carry this off without a hitch and he would rise to a new level of acceptance.

That thought comforted him only until another worry shoved it aside: What if the trunk of the car was filled with explosives, and he was about to wheel it into place? Scarier still, what if, as soon as he reached a designated destination, someone else remotely activated the bomb?

Being trusted was one thing. Being expendable, quite another, and he could easily imagine Amir deciding he belonged in the latter category. Those eyes of his were at least ten degrees below normal body temperature. But would Omar go along with that? Maybe. For all his warmth and outreach, there was also an air of opportunism about him. Whatever it took—that was Omar's vibe. A great fellow to have on your side, as long as he felt the same about you.

Mahmoud swallowed hard and approached the car. It was four o'clock. He took the keys from his pocket and opened the door.

The interior smelled like warm vinyl from the sunlight on the seats. Whoever owned it was a smoker. He shut the door, put the keys in the ignition, and opened the glove box. A map of central Hamburg and a folded sheet of paper were the only contents. Not even a registration document in case he was stopped, which made him wonder if the car was stolen. He opened the sheet in his lap.

The instructions were typed. They were brief and straightforward, and consisted mostly of directions. From Steindamm he was to head northeast, on a route that would take him to the eastern side of the Alster, where he would turn south and make his way around the bottom of the lakefront, crossing the Kennedy Bridge and then cutting left beneath a railway overpass, turning north onto Marseiller Strasse. He would then pull over to the right, onto a turnout called Dag-Hammarskjöld-Platz, by the entrance to the Dammtor train station.

The instructions said the *platz* would be blocked off at the far end by traffic bollards and an armed policeman. Mahmoud was supposed to look for a curbside parking space on the left, about fifty feet before the roadblock, which would be marked off by two orange cones. He was then supposed to stop, move the cones, and park the car facing in the opposite direction. He would leave the car unlocked and, without attracting too much attention, place the keys atop the front left tire, out of sight to any passersby.

He was then supposed to board the S-Bahn at the Dammtor station for the short trip back to the main train station, at the foot of Steindamm. From there he would walk back to the mosque. If for any reason he was stopped along the way or prevented from parking, he was supposed to call a number at the bottom of the page and simply say "I am late" to whoever answered. Otherwise he was not to use his phone until returning to the mosque.

He unfolded the map, found his location, and traced the route with his forefinger. It was fairly direct, probably no more than a ten-minute drive. What stopped him was that the route ended at the Hamburg Plaza Hotel, which, as he knew from their discussions, was where the infidel American professor was staying.

Surely Mahmoud's assignment must be part of some action against him. But what sort of part? Logistical support, or something more crucial? He wondered again about the trunk, and what might be inside. There was a handle just below the steering wheel, down to the left, for unlatching the trunk. He touched it, then pulled his hand away. What if it was wired to explode if the lid opened? Nothing he could do about it now anyway, and he didn't want to attract any attention. Stray from the script and he might botch the operation. He was a foot soldier now, a new recruit in a long and costly war. Follow orders or withdraw from the field.

He cleared his throat and sat up straighter, checking the mirrors. Two women with shopping bags were approaching on the sidewalk to his rear. From the opposite direction came an old Turkish man eating a doner kebab from a cylinder of foil, the sauce dribbling onto his chin. Mahmoud reached for the key and started the engine. With some difficulty, he put the car in reverse, turned the wheel, shifted into first, and then eased out of the space. The clutch was stiff and sensitive, and he nearly stalled out. But within a few blocks he had the hang of it.

Was the car riding a little heavily? He didn't think so, but it had been weeks since he'd driven a car and he wasn't familiar with Toyotas, so he couldn't be sure.

A green police van passed him in the opposite direction. He kept his eyes on the road ahead but glanced in the mirror as the van receded. Traffic was heavier once he was rounding the shoreline of the Alster, and he became overly conscious of any car or truck that cut into his lane or swerved around him. It was like driving a carton of eggs, and he accelerated as he realized he was traveling well below the speed limit. That, too, might draw unwanted attention, particularly if the driver looked Middle Eastern in this sea of Nordic whites.

He switched on the radio, caught a blast of American pop music, and immediately switched it off. That told him the car probably didn't belong to anyone in the Al Quds crowd, and he didn't want to dwell on the possible ramifications. Stolen? Borrowed? Just keep moving.

He crossed the Kennedy Bridge, with a pleasant view off to the right of sailboats and sun-dappled water. He considered rolling down his window for some fresh air but decided that the tinted glass was good protection. Straight ahead loomed the Hamburg Plaza Hotel, stabbing the blue sky like a great glass needle. Would his actions leave it in shards upon the ground by day's end? He thought of how open the horizon would look without that monstrous object filling the view, and then he put that thought aside. He supposed that if he'd turned down the job, someone else would have done it.

He was passing the entrance to the Dammtor train station when he saw the roadblock of bollards a hundred yards farther ahead, with a policeman on duty as promised. He began looking for his parking space, the one with the orange cones, and when he spotted it he breathed a little easier, because it was clearly too far back from the hotel—maybe eighty yards—for this to be a strike position for a car bomb. Unless, of course, some other foot soldier came along later to plow through the roadblock, or enter the underground parking garage beneath the hotel, which was over to the right.

He turned the car around, brought it to a stop, and then climbed out to move the cones while the policeman at the roadblock conferred with the driver of another car. Tossing the cones aside, he hastily got back in the car and parallel parked. A getaway car, he thought, or else why would they have instructed him to face it in this direction? Or maybe there was something besides a bomb in the trunk, something as tame and innocent as placards for a demonstration. Why all of the secrecy, then? It was part of his test, he supposed. Just to see if he'd do it without straying from the script, and without asking too many questions. For all he knew, someone had been posted in the nearby park to watch his arrival and make sure he did everything according to plan.

He got out of the car, looked around again, and hurriedly stooped down next to the front left tire. He ran his fingers across the top, pretending to check the tread as he placed the keys on top. Then he stood, wiped his hands—a gesture that felt as symbolic as it was practical—and headed off toward the train station to catch an S-Bahn back toward the mosque. He had carried out his role. He had been a good soldier. The rest, whatever that involved, would be up to others. Maybe he would learn more about everything tonight from Omar and Amir.

Twenty yards down the lane, he turned his head slightly for a final look back at the car. No one was near it, and the policeman at the roadblock wasn't paying it the slightest bit of attention. Silver and still. It reminded him of a crouched animal, lying in wait.

11

Armitage took a while to get warmed up once the interviews began. His first few responses sounded wooden, a trifle rehearsed, but maybe that was Tony's doing. On the plus side, the BBC reporter specialized in covering religion, so she at least seemed to know what questions to ask, and eventually she had Armitage spouting off as if he'd been doing this for years.

The security screen and voice modifier didn't exactly help everyone get comfortable, and the latter gave Armitage's pronouncements an almost sinister air, an Oz-like gravity that made it sound as if he had alighted from on high with his proclamations on the futility of martyrdom. On radio it was going to sound particularly bizarre.

Then again, some of the answers sounded so dry—to Claire's ears, anyway—that maybe they needed an added element of mystery to keep the BBC's listeners from tuning out.

"I began," she heard Armitage say, "from the idea that the language of the Quran must be studied from a historical-linguistic point of view. When it was composed, Arabic did not exist as a written language; thus, it seemed evident to me that it was necessary to take into consideration, above all, Aramaic."

Interesting, she thought, *if a trifle pedantic.* But what about all that controversial business of confusing white grapes for virginal nymphets as the martyr's reward in paradise? That subject finally arose just as the *New York Times* reporter, a disheveled older man in a corduroy jacket, arrived to await his turn.

"We begin from the term 'huri,' for which the Arabic commentators could not find any meaning other than those heavenly virgins," Armitage said. "But if one keeps in mind the derivations from Syro-Aramaic, that expression indicates 'white grapes,' which is one of the symbolic elements of the Christian paradise, recalled in the Last Supper of Jesus. There's another Quranic expression, falsely interpreted as 'the children' or 'the youths' of paradise, which in Aramaic designates the fruit of the vine, which in the Quran is compared to pearls. As for the symbols of paradise, those interpretive errors are probably connected to the male monopoly in Quranic commentary and interpretation."

So there you had it, she supposed. The meat of the issue, and the basis for all of the current security. She had to admit, he certainly sounded convincing, although she was far from an expert on the subject.

"But aren't you worried about a possible fatwa," the reporter asked, "like the one pronounced against Salman Rushdie?"

"I am not a Muslim, so I don't run that risk. Besides, I haven't offended against the Quran."

"Then why employ all of these security measures, or the voice modifier? And why are there no author photos, either in the publicity kit or online?"

"I'm doing that on the advice of Muslim friends who are afraid that some enthusiastic fundamentalist will act on his own initiative, without waiting for a fatwa."

The *Times* reporter, whose name was Scott, took advantage of his moment of eavesdropping to scribble down the gifted quotations. He then leaned toward Claire and, in a lowered voice, said, "So tell me, Mrs. Armitage, what does his voice really sound like?"

"Oh, like a professor's."

"Meaning it would put me to sleep in half an hour?"

"Only if you've had a few cups of coffee."

He laughed and flipped a page in his notebook.

"That's a good one. Mind if I use it?"

"You must not have been a reporter very long if you're actually asking."

He wrote it down.

Claire smiled as she imagined the Agency's director of operations reading her quote in tomorrow's *Times*. Then she considered the rest of the potential audience, and felt a twinge of regret on behalf of the real Brenda, still back there on her motel bed with her soap operas and bonbons.

Claire wondered yet again about the possible effectiveness of this bit of agitprop she was participating in. She was all for harnessing the power of books and the arts to change the hearts and minds of adversaries, and the Agency had a storied history in that department. In the fifties they had circulated copies of *Doctor Zhivago* and other banned books behind the Iron Curtain. In Italy, in the run-up to the crucial elections of 1948, they had promoted showings of the movie *Ninotchka*, a satire on Soviet life with Greta Garbo, to blunt the electoral appeal of the Communists. Garbo had then swamped Joseph Stalin at the polls. But Armitage's book somehow felt more like ridicule, no matter how scholarly or well intentioned. In an angry world, wouldn't this kind of provocation only stir more anger?

After the interviews, Armitage and Tony decamped to the room while Claire set out on a reconnaissance of the stairwells and the areas where the professor would be making further appearances. The route took her through the lobby, where she passed the hotel bar. Her first observation was that these Islamic studies scholars could really put it away, a bit of a surprise since, presumably, some were devout Muslims. It wasn't quite 5 p.m., yet all of the barstools were occupied, as were most of the seats at the dozen tables. Nearly every patron wore plastic ID placards on lanyards that gave them access to the week's events. She made a note to ask the hotel staff for immediate notifications of any reports of lost or stolen IDs.

She eased in among the tables to survey the crowd and quickly realized from snatches of overheard conversation that some of the drinkers were here instead for a convention of German electricians that was also booked for the week. Yet another security headache. Tomorrow a third gathering would arrive: fans of the *Asterix* comic books, a lot of them in costume. Wigs, breastplates, and horned helmets. She could easily imagine an opportunistic bearded jihadi showing up with a scimitar to take a hack at the professor.

The mere thought of it made all those cocktails look pretty inviting.

Maybe this evening she would kick back with a shot from the minibar once Armitage had turned in for the night. Or maybe not, because rules were rules.

She was about to head to her next stop when a face at the end of the bar caught her eye. It was Lute Sherrill, the bodyguard, and he was holding a half-empty glass. He looked up with a sheepish grin as she approached.

"Hello, Lute. Shouldn't you be—?"

"Upstairs?" He nodded. "I figured that while I was down here to get the registration kit I might as well get the lay of the land—plus some caffeine to keep me going."

She picked up his drink and sniffed. Iced coffee. Good boy.

"This jet lag is pretty awful," he said.

"Your first time in Europe?"

"Yeah. My wife was all kinds of jealous. I'm hoping to squeeze in an extra day once the conference is over. Maybe see some sights, get some souvenirs for my boys."

"You have sons?"

"Two. Age three and five."

He reached for his wallet to show her their photos.

Claire usually hated these displays, with all their requisite gushing about offspring she didn't know and would never meet, but Lute's manner was so pridefully bashful, so *homespun*, that she couldn't help but smile.

The boys stood in a gravel driveway in front of a basketball hoop that Lute had probably assembled himself. It was easy to imagine them back home in Iowa, bragging to their friends that their father had gone off to Germany—on a secret mission, no less—and would soon bring them something special. Or maybe that was the outdated thinking of a girl who'd grown up in a small town before the internet existed, when the idea of a transatlantic flight had still been exotic, even glamorous.

"They look sweet." And they really did.

"They're a handful, but that's what makes 'em fun. What about you?"

"Me?"

"Any kids?"

"None, thank you."

"Ah." He seemed momentarily at a loss. His eyes flicked toward his drink, then back up again at Claire. "Mind if I ask a prying question?"

"Depends, but give it a try."

He lowered his voice.

"I'm probably not cleared for this, but are you and Tony, well, maybe some kind of feds or something?"

"You're right, you're not cleared for that. And don't share your theory with the professor, if you please. All the paperwork says we're employed by the foundation, so let's leave it at that."

"Of course."

She noticed now that he was wearing two lanyard IDs—his own and the one for Armitage—and for the moment the professor's tag was more visible. She reached across the table and pulled it closer for a better look.

"Is wearing this a good idea?"

"Sorry. It's just that I'm pretty terrible at keeping track of this kind of stuff—tags, papers, you name it. Figured if I didn't put it around my neck it would end up on a counter somewhere. It's already turned a head or two."

"I'll bet."

"Those guys at the end of the bar wished me luck with the book and offered to buy me a drink."

She suppressed a laugh.

"I suppose a little misdirection never hurt."

"Speaking of which, here comes one of them now."

A thin fellow in a sweater vest approached the table. He had the wide-eyed look of a boy preparing to ask his favorite ballplayer for an autograph.

"Dr. Armitage?"

Two heads turned at the table next to them. Even a passing waiter paused in his orbit for a prolonged glance. So the professor—or his book, at least—really *was* a sensation, here anyway, and probably not for all the right reasons. Claire's fingers clenched into a fist beneath the table.

"Yes?" Lute answered.

"I just wanted to say, well, keep up the good work and, you know, *illegitimi non carborundum* and all that jazz."

"Excuse me?" Lute was out of his depth, and smiling to hide it, so Claire supplied the translation.

"Don't let the bastards get you down."

"Of course."

The fellow nodded nervously and retreated with a wave. The waiter was now talking with some excitement to a server who had just come out of the kitchen.

"See what I mean?" Lute said.

"I wouldn't overdo it."

He nodded and rearranged the tags so that his own was in front.

"Yeah, you're probably right. Kinda fun, though."

Then, for the third time since Claire had sat down, he scanned the room, his eyes on the move. He was alert, watchful, and that would be an asset for them all. Working with a rent-a-cop or any contract hire was always a crapshoot, but this time they seemed to have lucked out. She was betting he was also an attentive father.

Meanwhile, the time was approaching for her first stop on Bridger's auxiliary assignment across the Alster.

"Better get going," she said. "Got a few errands to run."

"I won't ask."

"Good policy. Tell Tony I should be back around eight thirty. Oh, and after you run that upstairs, maybe later you could check the stairwells and the emergency exits. I didn't like the look of the easy access coming up from the basement and the parking deck. Maybe you'll have a few ideas on dealing with that."

"Will do."

"And don't let the professor nap too long or he'll be up all night, which is the last thing we need."

"You especially, I'm guessing."

"You got that right." She smiled and then surprised herself by returning to the subject of Lute's kids. "You know, if you do get a chance to buy something for your boys, there's a chocolate museum in town and I've heard it's got a pretty great gift shop."

His eyes lit up.

"Perfect! They'll love that. Thanks."

She stood.

"See you later, then. If not, then bright and early tomorrow."

Lute nodded. He swallowed the last of his coffee and headed for the elevators. Still alert, eyes moving from side to side as he crossed the lobby. Claire left the hotel feeling a little less burdened than before.

12

Ken Donlan, whose slumped posture was not even close to perfection, glanced at the map on the front seat while he worked the gear shift of his German rental, an Opel Vectra. He was heading for his main target, having come straight from the airport.

Donlan, a special agent with eleven years at the FBI, always tried to hit the ground running on these foreign assignments, if only to distract himself from the funk of jet lag and the inevitable insurrection of his digestive tract.

He was looking for Grillparzerstrasse, every street name here a jumble of consonants. But Hamburg was already a pleasant revelation. Clean sidewalks and orderly pedestrians, everyone moving with assurance, like they knew exactly where they were going. The abundant trees and shaded boulevards were also a surprise, as were the spotless apartment houses, with their big windows and tiled European rooftops. Prosperity across the board, yet the cars and trucks were all downsized, sleek, and nimble, and no one seemed to be driving like an asshole.

Donlan liked it, even if his stomach was already complaining about the early dinner he'd wolfed down an hour ago, and that coffee they'd served on the plane, a connection out of Frankfurt that hadn't landed until midafternoon.

Back home, he could stuff himself with pizza, curry, jalapeños, and a pitcher of beer in a single sitting without the slightest grumble from below. Put him on an overseas flight to another time zone and all systems went into revolt. He gulped Tums like candy and became preoccupied with the whereabouts of the nearest public toilet, preferably at a McDonald's, where you could take a dump for free, and with reliable assurance you wouldn't have to squat over some hole in the floor.

There was his street, just ahead. He turned right and checked the scribbled directions for the next waypoints—Hofweg, then Karlstrasse, which would take him toward the shoreline of the Alster and the home of Mohammed Haydar Zammar, first stop on Donlan's get-acquainted tour with the city's Al Qaeda connections.

Donlan's presence had not been requested by any of Bridger's people. With any luck they wouldn't find out he was here, although you might say he had come in on their coattails after learning what they were up to. He'd been in a position to do so because he, too, worked for the Agency, sort of—as an FBI liaison to Alec station, an outpost of the CIA's Counterterrorism Center.

Alec station, based in one of those generic glass office towers in D.C.'s Virginia suburbs, was the Agency's Osama bin Laden unit, a onetime backwater that had become a hot posting fourteen months earlier, after Al Qaeda operatives bombed U.S. embassies in Nairobi and Dar es Salaam, killing more than two hundred people.

Zammar, a Syrian who'd been living in Germany since he was ten, had turned up on Alec's radar a few months earlier, when various Al Qaeda money trails had converged on Hamburg. That, plus Zammar's earlier travels to Bosnia and Afghanistan, made him an object of curiosity for Donlan. Better still, the fellow never seemed to stop talking, whether he was giving impassioned speeches at his mosque or handing out Al Qaeda pamphlets on a public sidewalk, where, at six foot four and more than three hundred pounds, he was impossible to miss—big and blustery, with a booming voice and a dark, bushy beard.

The Germans had surveilled him for a while but had eventually lost interest, so Donlan, whose specialty was tracking Al Qaeda's financial and logistical routes, had decided to pick up the slack. And the advent of Bridger's op right across town, which seemed guaranteed to kick up a little dust, had seemed like an opportune moment to observe for himself the loudmouth with the massive gut. At best he might witness something actionable. At worst, maybe collect some worthy intelligence to support his latest theory—that Haydar Zammar was now a recruiter and conduit to bin Laden's training camps in Afghanistan.

His CIA boss at Alec hadn't been all that keen on the idea of his visiting while another op was in progress so close by, especially when, technically, Alec wasn't supposed to know about that one. But the blessing and curse of Donlan's hybrid employment status was that he also had a boss in New York, an FBI supervisor who took pleasure in any opportunity to set loose his own people to graze in Agency pastures. And that boss had liked his idea just fine.

So here he was, armed with a camera, a surveillance file, and a list of known associates as he eased the Opel into a curbside space just down the block from Zammar's home.

Donlan switched off the engine and screwed a long lens onto his camera for a closer look. It was a posh four-story apartment house. White plaster walls, ornately molded, with picture windows that looked out at a row of willows to the Alster and beyond. Zammar's apartment, up on the fourth floor, had the biggest windows and best waterfront views. With these digs, and a job record as an unemployed auto mechanic, no wonder everyone had pegged him as a guy who got his income from Al Qaeda.

This was no stakeout, not yet. It was Donlan's way of getting his bearings for the week ahead. He also hoped to stay busy enough to remain awake as long as possible today, so that tonight he would sleep soundly and awaken fresh the next morning. Beating jet lag was as high a priority as beating indigestion.

He snapped a photo and scribbled in his pad, noting the location and the time of day. All was quiet except for the gurgle and whine of his gut.

"Fucking bratwurst." He should've said no to the hot mustard.

He picked up the map and studied his markings. The nearest McDonald's was only five minutes away. With any luck he might hold out for another twenty. He was about to restart the car when a door opened downstairs, and out came Zammar, car keys in hand as he headed for a white Mercedes out front. Huge, just as advertised, and the car sagged as he climbed in. Donlan snapped two more photos. The fat fuck didn't even look around as he pulled away from the curb.

Should Donlan follow? His stomach said no, but his professional instincts countermanded the order. He peeled back the wrapper from a roll of Tums, popped two into his mouth, and put the car in gear, buoyed by this initial run of good fortune. It boded well for the week.

He let Zammar put some distance between them. If he lost the trail, well, he technically wasn't supposed to start snooping around anyway until after he'd checked in with local law enforcement. That was a promise he'd made to his FBI boss, Mike Sheehan, during a stopover in Manhattan on his way to LaGuardia.

Sheehan was the special agent in charge of the Bureau's National Security Division for New York, with a corner office on the twenty-fifth floor of the Javits building. Sheehan had been late for their appointment, but his secretary, Elaine, had ushered Donlan into the office to wait unchaperoned among the mementos displaying Big Mike's connections to presidents and power brokers from all walks of life. That, plus the view—Empire State Building out one window, Brooklyn Bridge out the other—relayed an unmistakable message: *I've got more juice than you, so don't fuck with me.*

Donlan had grown up in Jersey, where he'd met plenty of Mike Sheehans—bluff, fast-talking Irish Catholics who shot their cuffs, gave generously to the local parish, and worked every angle. Yet he had warmed to the man. Sheehan usually got it right, and wasn't afraid to admit it when he didn't. He was deeply loyal to his people, and demanded the same in return, which is why he'd never gotten used to the idea that Donlan was also answerable to the CIA.

Sheehan had rushed into the room with the air of a harried maître d'. As always, there was a white tea rose pinned to his lapel, like he was forever en route to a wedding to give away the bride. Sunlight flashed off a pinkie ring as he moved behind his desk.

"Christ, did Elaine open the goddamn blinds again?"

"It's for your health," she piped up. "You need better air in that tomb."

"Like it makes any goddamn difference with the windows closed."

Elaine smiled and rolled her eyes as she shut the door.

Sheehan got busy shutting blinds until the room had returned to its customary monkish gloom. At work or out on the town, Big Mike was a one-man army of the night.

"So tell me about this overseas boondoggle you're about to throw in on."

"Well, there's this Quranic translation thing with some academic, which I'm happy to steer clear of because it's a little loopy for me."

"Dumbest fucking thing I ever heard of."

"Yeah, well, it's not Alec's doing."

"Your new boss down there—he still working out?"

"Well enough. Says good things about you, by the way, and not just when he knows I'm listening."

"Anything would be an improvement over before."

"I know, I know." Donlan spoke quickly. He had hoped to avoid this topic, which never failed to wind up Sheehan.

"Speaking of whom, any sign of his handiwork in this Quranic road show?"

"From what I've heard, some guy named Bridger is in charge."

"I know the name. Competent—by their standards, anyway. But keep me posted if, you know . . ."

"Of course."

"And you'll be checking in with our German pals in the BND, right?" Another topic he had hoped to duck.

"The guys at Alec want me to lie low. Maybe play the tourist, keep it unofficial."

"No way, Kenny. I won't have any of my people doing business over there without at least giving notice. Besides, it wouldn't be nice to Gunter, and he's a good man to have on our side."

Gunter was Gunter Hauser, a longtime buddy of Sheehan's at the BND. They'd worked together on other cases, and, as with most such people, Sheehan had charmed the rather chilly German with his chummy manner and direct approach.

"You'll make a courtesy call first thing, got it?"

"Yes, sir."

And now here he was, already tailing an Al Qaeda figure who, for all he knew, might still be under surveillance from time to time, which meant Donlan could soon turn up in a BND report before he had even let them know he was here. Big Mike wouldn't like that.

Zammar's Mercedes moved north while Donlan tracked their progress on the map. They were closing in on a big splotch of green called the Stadtpark, and now Zammar was pulling to the curb alongside a fenced lot with dozens of gardens and wooden huts. He'd seen these places before in German cities—private gardens where the locals went to relax among their flower beds and vegetable patches.

Donlan cruised by slowly as Zammar got out of the car, and he watched in the rearview mirror as the big man headed into the gardens. He circled the block and then parked just up the street from the Mercedes. Inside the expanse of greenery he saw a flag being raised on a staff next to one of the huts—the flag of Syria, Zammar's home country. So maybe his family owned one of the plots. Could the flag be some kind of signal?

Donlan checked his watch. He was due at the BND in an hour, probably the last item on their schedule for the day, so it wouldn't do to keep them waiting. Maybe he should ease off. Another rumble from below decided the issue, at least for the moment. He would drive to McDonald's and relieve himself free of charge in an Americanized toilet. But, then, because he was a great believer in fate and happenstance, Donlan resolved to return to see if the Mercedes was still here. If it was, he would then phone the BND to reschedule for tomorrow and would spend the remainder of the evening keeping an eye on Zammar's hut. It was a little dicey in terms of protocol, but with any luck Big Mike would never find out.

With a final glance in the mirror, he pulled away from the curb.

13

Claire's extracurricular marching orders—the ones she'd memorized from the sealed envelope—were both maddening and alluring in their simplicity. Maddening because they included only an address, a daily listing of times when she was supposed to be in place, the names of three targets (accompanied by mug shots and thumbnail bios), and the scantiest of instructions: *Watch, listen, report.* Alluring because, well, that certainly offered leeway to do more than just stay in one place if the targets moved elsewhere, especially since Bridger knew firsthand Claire's tendency to stretch—and sometimes break—the boundaries of assignments. She was assuming he wanted initiative, or whatever initiative was possible within her daily two-to-three-hour window.

The address, over in the St. Georg district, turned out to be for a mosque, so that answered her first question. It wasn't one of those grand and beautiful mosques you sometimes see in Europe—Spain, especially—with minarets, painted tiles, and Moorish arches. This place didn't even have its own building. It was more like an office, up on the second floor of a drab modern building, with an imam slotted between insurance salesmen and real estate brokers.

At least now she understood the sequence of times Bridger had given her—18:51, 18:49, 18:47, 18:44, 18:42—an oddly precise regression that had at first looked like a railway timetable. It must be the schedule for the week's sunset prayers, with punctuality presumably offering the best chance to take note of worshippers as they came and went.

A quick canvas of the surrounding block had produced sightings of several prostitutes already trolling for customers on Brennerstrasse, a quiet cobbled street behind the mosque, where she also passed an Arabic bookstore that had plastered its front window with a copy of the provocative newspaper story that Tony had placed about the professor. It was posted next to a handbill that called for "Death to the Raisin Infidel" in several different languages. Claire winced and marched onward. She supposed that even the placid Germans wouldn't like that sort of language. But by the time their lumbering security bureaucracy reacted, the professor would either be dead or away to his next stop.

The mosque's upstairs location made it impossible to keep an eye on the doorway unless you were willing to camp out in the stairwell, but an easy vantage point for the building's main entrance presented itself right away—a café next door with sidewalk tables. It was a little brisk for dining alfresco, but half the tables were full, and if the hearty Germans could stand it, then so could she. Claire slid into a seat, opened a menu, and peeped over the top.

Upstairs she saw flashes of robed movement behind a smudged window. Listening closely, she thought she could detect the undertone of a muffled drone of voices, like the buzzing of bees within a hive, a lulling sound to soothe the soul. She was reminded of church services she'd had to attend every Sunday as a girl in rural Georgia, when the congregation's rote chanting of the Apostles' Creed had always made her drowsy, especially after lengthy sermons. Claire hadn't stepped inside a church in ages except as a spy, a tourist, or a wedding guest. Plus two funerals she would rather forget.

Her targets, whose names and mug shots she had memorized, were Ramzi bin al-Shibh, nickname Omar; Mohamed Atta, nickname Amir; and Mohammed Haydar Zammar, who went by Haydar. She also needed to stay aware of the time, lest her duties with Armitage be neglected. It was a bit like playing Cinderella. Stay out too late and the professor might turn into a pumpkin, or maybe just get carved up like one. By now Tony and Lute were probably both with him in the room. Secure enough. If not, her phone would be ringing.

A waiter approached. Claire ordered a *milchkaffee*. He nodded and departed. Across the street she noticed a small produce market where women in modest Turkish and Arab garments were coming and going. That could be another vantage point as the week progressed, since she could hardly perch here every evening without being noticed, or if it rained.

Thank goodness Germans were quiet eaters. At an American joint, even out in the open air, she wouldn't have been able to hear herself think, much less eavesdrop on any sidewalk conversations next door. Here it was all discretion and lowered voices. The man at the next table was shielding himself with a book. The waiters bent forward so you wouldn't have to raise your voice.

A few worshippers soon began to emerge from the building. The first four didn't match any of the photos. Three of them continued past her, toward the main train station at the end of Steindamm. The last one lingered, as if waiting for companions. He looked once at his watch and then glanced up at the second-floor window, his face calm, movements unrushed. Mid-twenties, with alert eyes and a beard of recent vintage.

Two more men emerged, and she had her first hit, a sighting of Ramzi bin al-Shibh. The waiting man greeted him warmly in Arabic, which was certainly going to limit her ability to pick up anything of value, although his mention of the name Omar at least confirmed the ID. Omar then helped the cause by replying with the name Mahmoud, so she now had one item of interest. Bridger had told her to file daily written reports, coded, on the back of the hotel laundry form in her room, and then deliver it by hanging it on the doorknob with a bagged item of clothing, which would be picked up at midnight by a daily courier. Cumbersome, but sometimes that's how it went, especially when you were working off-script from the main event.

More worshippers came outside, and three of them joined Omar and Mahmoud. One of them was Mohamed Atta, whom the others greeted as Amir, just like the bio said. An additional name, Jarrah, floated across to her on the evening air. He was worth noting as well, if only because he wore blue jeans and a sweater and had a ready smile. Shave the beard and he could pass for a frat boy on his way to a kegger. Another fellow joined them, although no one spoke his name. There were six of them now, but no sign yet of Haydar Zammar, who was supposedly so huge that he'd be impossible to miss. Still, as the song said, two out of three ain't bad.

As the din of conversation grew, so did the variety of languages. She heard snatches of German, and then of English. It was a measure of their intelligence and their education, she supposed. Also an indication of their potential for mischief in foreign locations, because with those skills they could more easily blend into other cultures. Although for the moment, grouped as they were, they easily stood out as outsiders. A few passing Germans glanced coldly in their direction. One, strolling by just as a loud gust of Arabic came from the group, even waved at the air, as if fanning away a cloud of gnats.

Atta, she knew from the bio, was an engineering student, so they probably had a fair amount of technical skill as well. My, but he was a serious one, stern and nodding, as if passing judgment on every remark. The center of energy gravitated toward Omar, although Amir's nods also drew attention.

And then, like a single organism, they set off away from Claire and up the sidewalk—not toward the train station, as she would've guessed, but in the opposite direction. She supposed she should be relieved, since they would have headed for the *bahnhof* if they were going to the Plaza to stir up any trouble about the professor.

From her study of the map she knew there was an U-Bahn stop only a few blocks in the other direction. So maybe they were on an outing, or headed for a communal dinner. If their destination was a restaurant, she might even be able to eavesdrop from another table, although a quick wardrobe change from the tote bag at her feet might soon be in order.

She glanced at her bill and put a few coins on the table, leaving behind the chump change that passed for a tip over here as she stood to leave. They were quite noisy in their progress, laughing and slapping backs, one big, happy bunch of true believers. Claire was happy, too— all of that gregarious fellowship would make it easier for her to follow without being noticed.

Their laughter swelled as they headed up the block, and she soon saw why. One of the prostitutes had boldly ventured over to Steindamm and was heading toward them. They stopped—not because of her, but because Amir had put up a hand like a traffic cop. He then crossed the street in the middle of the block, and they continued without him, passing the prostitute. Only then did Amir cross back to rejoin them, which triggered further laughter.

So in addition to being stern, he was a prude. Another note for Bridger, she supposed, although she was already wondering how much more time she would have to observe them. She had been away for more than an hour, and it would take at least twenty minutes to get back. But Tony was a good egg who understood that operational demands didn't always run on a schedule, and Lute seemed competent as a backup. And, well, for whatever reason, these extra duties were what Bridger seemed to want from her the most. Maybe her reports would help determine which young men they'd decide to "scoop into their nets," as Bridger had put it, although those words struck her as a little disturbing, given the tame activity she had witnessed so far. Would that sort of action by the Agency pass muster if the Germans found out?

The group of young men was a full block ahead of her now. Unless one of their apartments was nearby, they were almost certainly headed for the U-Bahn, where keeping pace would become trickier.

Claire set off in their wake.

14

The Syrian flag was still flying when Donlan returned, and the Mercedes was still parked at the curb. Donlan phoned his contact at the BND and rescheduled for the following day, citing his delayed flight and an upset stomach—both of which were legit, making the lie easier to deliver.

Within minutes a column of smoke began rising next to the flag, either from a fire pit or a barbecue grill. He was hoping it was the latter, because that could mean Zammar was expecting company.

Donlan rolled down his window, took a sniff, and detected the smell of cooking meat. A barbecue, then. Lamb or beef, certainly not pork. His stomach grumbled, this time in a more agreeable way. The trip to McDonald's had been a success.

He rolled the window back up. The smoked glass allowed for greater privacy, and for the moment the sidewalk was clear in both directions. Nothing to do but wait and see who turned up. He retrieved his briefcase from the back seat and got out the *International Herald Tribune* that he'd picked up at the airport. There was a puny sports page, but the scores were two days old and the main feature was about some soccer player they insisted on calling a footballer. When the Giants played on Sunday, Donlan wouldn't know the outcome until Tuesday unless he checked online, and the hotel's server was bound to be slow and woefully insecure. Well, they'd probably lose anyway. No quarterback worth a damn. Not their year.

He kept an eye on the gardens while he browsed the news, yawning.

Ten minutes later he nodded off, the paper slipping from his grasp, and his forehead thumped the steering wheel. *Stay the fuck awake.* Had he missed anything? The Mercedes was still there, and so was the flag. The smoke was thicker than ever.

A sound got his attention—a gust of male laughter, from just down the block straight ahead. Six young men, all but one in Middle Eastern attire, had just turned onto the street and were strolling his way. One already looked familiar from the surveillance photos in his briefcase.

Donlan got out the photos and thumbed through them. Then he grabbed his camera. He rolled down his window, slid lower in the seat, and zoomed the long lens on the short fellow out front, the one he'd recognized. Those unmistakable high cheekbones, the dead eyes—an Egyptian whom everyone called Amir, although the file said his full name was Mohamed el-Sayed Atta. Toward the back was a skinny, smiling fellow known as Omar. None of the other four was familiar, although Donlan was already curious about the one in the middle, wearing jeans and a crewneck sweater.

He steadied the camera as the group moved closer—forty yards out now—and he snapped three photos just before they turned into an opening in the hedge. As they did so, Omar called out to another guy toward the back. Donlan's Arabic was practically nonexistent, but he picked up a name, Mahmoud, and took note of the young man who replied—earnest, watchful, in the way of a newcomer. Or new to Donlan, at least, since the guy didn't match any of the photos. Neither did the guy in the middle in the jeans and sweater.

The six men made their way deeper into the gardens, heads bobbing above the greenery as they moved toward the column of smoke. Moments later, they vanished from sight. He heard sounds of greeting, some laughter. An Al Qaeda cookout, right here in sunny Hamburg. Too bad nobody had miked the little garden house.

Donlan scribbled "Mahmoud" onto a pad. A small item, as these things went, but a lead was a lead. He looked again at the name and then underlined it twice. Not a bad start to the week.

15

Claire nearly lost track of them at the U-Bahn station. She had to wedge her purse into the closing doors to make it onto the departing train, a move that drew disapproving stares from the orderly riders of Hamburg, who looked doubly scandalized when they realized the malefactor was a woman. She stared back defiantly, and everyone looked away. All that mattered by then was that the six young men were only two cars ahead of her.

At the next stop they switched to another line, and she followed, again two cars back. In the meantime she put on a scarf and sunglasses and pulled her hair back.

The next leg of the journey was longer. The men got out at the fifth stop and walked toward the Stadtpark, still chattering away like the best of friends. Claire was cutting it close on time, but she wanted to at least find out their final destination.

By now she was wondering what the hell could be so important about this role of hers that Bridger was willing to compromise on the professor's safety. It wasn't as if she would be able to find out all that much with only a two-hour window for daily observation, especially given her lack of Arabic. She could take note of names and movements, as she was doing now, plus maybe a few observations on the group's dynamics—its alpha dogs and errand boys, its eager acolytes with stars in their eyes. But all of that would be subjective, and she doubted it would surpass or even equal the information the Germans had already forwarded from their own previous work.

Why bother, then? In fact, when viewed in this light, the assignment had the feel of busywork, a nuisance chore you'd give to someone at the bottom of the food chain. Counterintuitively, this told her there must be something deeply important concealed within, because Bridger was a great believer in the elegance of complexity, a master of applying layer upon layer and then letting his own people peel them back depending on their capabilities. He had once said, long ago, that if you told an operative what to look for in a surveillance, then that's probably what he would observe, to the possible exclusion of more important details. Here she was, then, keeping an open mind even if still at a bit of a loss regarding what she was supposed to be looking for.

The young men strolled into a quiet, tree-lined residential neighborhood, which made following them trickier. They were still making plenty of noise, but hardly anyone else was out and about. She wished she had a bicycle, or a baby stroller, some prop to give her a clearer reason for being there. Instead it was just her with a tote bag, wearing the stupid sunglasses even as dusk closed in. They turned a corner and she slowed down, waiting, and then crept forward to watch their progress from around the trunk of a majestic beech, hands against the smooth bark.

There was a burst of laughter, and she saw them turning into a park—or, no, one of those public plots of mini-gardens, where the locals grew their freesias and chrysanthemums, their cabbages and summer tomatoes, alongside those chockablock brown huts where they liked to putter around on weekends. She spotted a Syrian flag, and that immediately brought to mind the third name on her list, Haydar Zammar, a fellow who, with the right word to the right people, could supposedly set you on the long road to bin Laden's camps in Pakistan and beyond.

Maybe this was what Bridger was after—names and faces for the Al Qaeda pipeline, young prospects to keep an eye on as they were nurtured and grew, like the flowers in this lovely green patch of Germanic kitsch. Gray smoke was rising near the flag. She smelled meat cooking. No wonder they'd all sounded so jolly; they knew a free dinner was waiting at the end of the line.

For a moment she entertained the reckless idea of entering the garden area at the far end and then working her way closer down crosscutting paths, as if progressing through a maze. Then she noticed a car parked farther up the street, an Opel, where a reflected bit of light from an open window on the driver's side caught her eye. Was that a camera lens?

She stepped back, taking better cover behind the beech. If someone from the BND was up there, snapping photos, then this public garden full of Al Qaeda connections was the last place she wanted to be seen. Now, wouldn't that be a fine start to her week: turning up on a glossy that landed on some desk in Berlin? She imagined men in white shirts, sleeves rolled up as they discussed in lowered tones where they'd seen that woman's face before, and why they were seeing it now. She was debating whether to back off and call it quits when her phone buzzed.

A glance at the incoming number showed it was Tony calling. Then she noticed the time—she was appallingly late. She turned to face away from the gardens and kept her voice low.

"Sorry. On my way back now."

"No rush. I was just getting a little worried."

"Did Lute bring up the professor's ID?"

"Yes. He's been keeping us company. Figured we might as well double-team this under the current circumstances, but I'm guessing he'd like to get some dinner fairly soon."

"There's room service."

"Apparently that's off-limits until we've cleared this threat, and, well . . ."

"Message received. On my way now, Tony. See you in twenty."

"Thanks, Claire."

She headed for the nearest likely spot for flagging down a taxi, already feeling guilty about inconveniencing her colleagues. And for what, really? A few first names and a few new faces, plus a snarky anecdote about Amir's aversion to prostitutes. She was still perturbed by that camera lens—if that's what it had been—and wondered how she should characterize it in the report to Bridger, or if she should even mention it at all. Tell him that and he might end the assignment, or send someone else. Not the best of starts. She vowed to be more careful tomorrow.

Claire had a special key card that let her enter through an emergency door at the Plaza so she wouldn't be seen in the lobby or the elevators as she returned. She briskly climbed the back stairs while trying to think of a suitable apology. She hoped Tony had at least let Lute get dinner.

She reached the third floor just as Lute stepped into view from the elevator bay, halfway down the hall. He turned in her direction and, with a sheepish grin, hefted a white plastic bag.

"Sorry, couldn't wait any longer."

"No. Glad you did."

"Got you something, too, just in case."

"Oh, thanks. That was sweet of you."

She was famished.

Lute moved toward her a step or two as she strolled in his direction. There was a ping from another elevator and he turned briefly to acknowledge it before looking back at Claire with another smile.

"Hope Caesar salad is all right. Also got a cheeseburger if you'd rather have that."

"No, the salad sounds—"

Claire gasped as a large man in white lunged into the hallway from the elevator bay, coming up suddenly behind Lute. She broke into a sprint as the man gripped Lute from behind, throwing a forearm across his chest. Lute was trying to twist free when the attacker slashed a huge knife across his throat.

"Lute! No!"

Claire reached them just as the man threw Lute to the floor and backed away, still holding the bloody knife. Lute gargled and gasped and then slumped onto his back while clutching with both hands at a ragged gash across his windpipe. The man in white—hotel staff, by the look of it, either from room service or the kitchen—ran toward the stairwell at the other end of the hall while calling out a breathless and half-hearted "Allahu Akbar" as he fled. Claire fleetingly considered pursuit before dropping to her knees to help Lute. He was thrashing his feet, like a drowning man, in agony. Blood gushed from the wound. Claire pressed her hands against it, but it was too large, too horrible. The blood poured between her fingers, warm and pulsing.

She frantically watched his eyes, which were panicky in one moment, glazing over in the next.

"No, Lute! Stay with me!"

But he was staring now, and still. Even the flow of blood had lost its urgency, oozing in weak surges that came to a halt as his heart stopped.

She sobbed once, but only once, in anger and despair. Then she pulled away her hands and reached into her bag, smearing her phone and everything else with Lute's blood. She could barely work the buttons, they were so slippery, but she somehow managed to punch in the number she'd memorized for the police detail in the lobby.

She shouted down the hallway as it rang.

"Tony! Tony!"

A door opened, but not from the professor's room. It was one of their colleagues from Madrid station. He looked shocked, horrified.

"Call an ambulance! Call Bridger!"

A policeman answered. She told him what had happened and described who to look for.

"I think he was one of the hotel cooks."

"I'm on it."

From his breathing she could tell that the cop was already in motion. His words were clipped and controlled, which made her feel better for about a millisecond until she looked back down at Lute. On the floor just to his left was the white plastic bag, its two foam dinner containers splayed open, spilling lettuce and a hamburger bun onto the carpet. She forced herself to look again at his throat, a deep gash through artery and trachea, and then she searched his eyes. Fixed and staring, no one home.

Claire's phone rang. She stared at it, uncomprehending for a moment as it buzzed on the floor, smeared red. In a daze she snatched it up, nearly letting it slip from her grasp before she could press the button to answer. Bridger spoke in a rush.

"The paramedics will be there in five minutes."

"Cancel them. He's dead."

"Shit. Are you sure?"

"Yes. I'm with him." She sighed, pausing to collect herself. "We're in cleanup mode now, literally and figuratively. The fewer people up here, the better."

"And the attacker?"

"I reached a cop downstairs. They're on it. Someone from the kitchen, I think. He did it with a chef's knife."

"We've got two more people headed your way. Keep Tony and Armitage in the room. You stay with the body until help arrives and I'll handle the rest."

Claire hung up and sagged against a wall. She smeared blood onto everything she touched. The wall, the carpet, her hair. She wanted to stand beneath a hot shower for as long as it took, but she didn't want to abandon Lute. An eerie calm had settled over the hallway, and no other doors were open—a tribute, she supposed, to how well the Agency had controlled the number of guests who were staying on this floor, even if the silence gave her a chill. She tried to think about what she needed to do next. She tried not to look again at Lute, or his throat. If paramedics made it up here, she'd have to head them off. This matter would have to be coordinated carefully with police and the hotel staff to keep it from becoming an even bigger problem. If at all possible, they had to keep it quiet. Difficult, but she'd seen it done.

Look at me, she thought. Plotting contingencies and backup plans when a man was dead, practically in her lap, someone she'd just been speaking to, a friendly man of boyish charm who had bought her dinner, a young father who'd wanted to buy chocolate for his boys. A Corn Belt innocent who'd had no idea what he was up against, partly because, well, they hadn't seen fit to tell him. Too worried about their own security.

A room door opened at the far end of the hallway—Tony, stepping halfway across the threshold, while Armitage peered wide-eyed over his shoulder.

"What the fuck! I just heard from Bridger. We had the TV on and didn't hear a damn thing, and I—"

"Get back inside, both of you. We're handling it."

"But who—?"

"It's Lute. He's dead."

Armitage's face had gone deathly white. Tony nudged him back inside, a nurse with an invalid. The door shut, and once again a cold silence reigned.

Claire forced herself to look one more time at Lute. His eyes stared blankly at the ceiling. She remembered how he'd smiled bashfully when she found him at the bar, with Armitage's ID tag draped around his neck, drawing all that attention—the waiter she'd seen speaking with a cook, the cook probably telling others. God knows how many other people must've pointed him out before he finally left the lobby, the infamous professor, out and about on his own, a marked man before he even knew it.

"A little misdirection never hurt," she'd told him. And then she'd made him wait to get his dinner, so that he'd had to order directly from the kitchen. She had delivered Lute to their doorstep, and his attacker had followed him back up in the elevator.

Nice move, Claire. Brilliant work.

A mere ten hours into the op and they were already a man down.

TUESDAY, OCTOBER 5

16

An exhausted Claire arrived eleven minutes early for her midday meeting with Paul Bridger along the shore of the Alster. As instructed, she sat at the end of a bench beneath a shedding maple and placed a folded newspaper beside her. Then she sipped coffee from a paper cup and tried to take solace from the view—sailboats passing in one direction, rowing crews in the other, lined up like targets in an arcade. Joggers trotted by on a gravel path behind the bench, loping along as if in cadence with the commands of the coxswains. "Eins-zwei-drei-vier!"

Had she slept? Maybe an hour or so, just before dawn. Miraculously, and somewhat unnervingly, Bridger had managed to keep news of the murder from leaking to the news media or to other attendees of the conference, and so far the Hamburg police were complicit in the arrangement.

An unmarked van had arrived at the hotel's rear loading dock to collect Lute's body, which was delivered in a laundry cart, covered by towels and sheets. The hotel manager, who was as eager as Bridger to hush things up, had kept guests and staff away from the crime scene by concocting a story about smoke coming from an ice machine. The attacker, a line cook born in Algiers, had been apprehended by police just as he reached an apparent getaway car parked near the hotel, a silver Toyota that had been reported stolen the day before, with tags from a car that had been abandoned near the waterfront. His knife was found in the stairwell. He had apparently counted on his arrest to make him an instant celebrity, a jihadi hero. Instead, he was now alone in a holding cell while Bridger haggled with police officials over how to handle the case in the quietest possible way.

No word yet on when a replacement for Lute would arrive, but the university had agreed to hire someone recommended by the foundation, meaning it would be an Agency plant. An upgrade, then—a thought that seemed brutally callous, under the circumstances.

Claire had shampooed and scrubbed herself for what felt like hours, yet her fingernails still had deep brown stains beneath them that she hadn't been able to reach. She examined them now and then looked away, off toward the far side of the lake.

She had written a report of the attack at 11 p.m. while seated on the lid of the toilet, after shutting the bathroom door to keep from awakening Armitage, who had needed a few shots from the minibar before collapsing into oblivion. She then wrote a report, for Bridger's eyes only, of her surveillance of the Al Quds crowd, which felt like it had occurred several days ago. She left out any mention of the Opel and the possible camera. After what she'd been through, she felt entitled to be selective. And the last thing she wanted now was to have that side of their mission aborted. If that crowd had played any role in Lute's murder, she wanted to be part of the effort that discovered it.

After placing the report in the laundry bag, along with a pair of the hated polyester slacks, she had hung the bag from the doorknob and listened skittishly for the pickup. Her worry was that the night's events had thrown operations into such chaos that the bag would still be there in the morning, and the wrong person would collect it. But promptly at midnight she heard footsteps approaching, and when she looked through the peephole she recognized the petite young woman in a maid's uniform as a recent hire from London station. Then she went to bed.

Approaching the rendezvous point along the Alster, Claire had noticed two watchers, to the right and left of the bench, each of them about thirty yards off. Neither was familiar to her. Exactly at the appointed hour, a man took a seat on the far end of the bench. She didn't turn to look, but knew it was Bridger from the smell of his soap—sandalwood and moss—which triggered a flashback to a dim morning on the outskirts of Berlin, the two of them sharing a chocolate croissant beneath a wool blanket in a narrow bed, the only warmth coming from their bodies.

He addressed her in German.

"Pardon, madam. Mind if I have a look at your paper?"

"Please do."

He was about to shake it open when his attention was diverted by something out on the water. Claire followed his gaze to a small black bird fussing in the shallows, poking its beak into submerged grasses. It looked like a small, stocky duck with a sawed-off beak, and it was cheeping loudly.

"A coot," Bridger said, switching to English. "They're conspecific brood parasites."

"They're *what*?"

"They like to lay their eggs in other coots' nests. To ease the load of child-rearing."

"Unless some other coot lays eggs in *their* nest."

"Yes. I suppose that happens, too."

"You and your birds. I remember in Berlin, once, you compared a careless asset to a stork building its nest on a smoking chimney."

"Birds fascinate me."

"Watchers fascinate me. Who do those two belong to?"

"They're ours, of course."

"Yes. But reporting to who?"

"It's security, Claire. Don't try to make something out of it that doesn't exist."

"Then why keep your voice down? Why the whole business with the newspaper? Why have someone pick up my reports at the hotel when I could deliver them in person? What is it you're trying to keep them from seeing or hearing?"

"As I said. It's security. How's the professor handling the news?"

"About like you'd expect. The news—is that what we're calling this?"

"What would you suggest?"

Claire glanced at him as he refolded the newspaper. He looked quite pale, although he had spoken calmly from the beginning, a model of composure, and she'd had enough of it. She slid closer, reached for his hand, and squeezed it hard enough to make him flinch, although he didn't try to pull away. If you'd been passing, you might have mistaken them for quarreling lovers on the verge of making up.

He turned to face her.

"I know we're close, Claire, but what are you doing?"

"Checking for a pulse. Or any other sign of humanity."

"That's a bit harsh."

"Paul, we lost a man barely fifteen hours ago. Not one of ours, maybe, but someone working with us, and we let it happen. I saw the life go out of his eyes and was literally up to my elbows in his blood, and all you want to talk about is the job. And I'm fine with that because we're all professionals here, but goddammit, can we also be human beings for maybe just a second and acknowledge that we cost someone his life?"

He inhaled slowly and lowered his head. She relaxed her grip, and he gently squeezed back while the color returned to his face. Or maybe he was blushing.

"How have you managed to keep this under wraps?"

"The usual channels. The police won't be making any charges public for a few days, well after the book has been presented, and they'll probably gloss over a few details."

"Such as motive, location, and the intended target?"

"Oh, I expect the latter will eventually spill out."

"I see."

She squeezed again, her nails digging into flesh.

"Thus giving us a nice sales bump, but well after the professor is back in his research bunker and Lute is in some hole in the ground in the middle of Iowa. Is that your plan, Paul?"

Bridger's voice turned gruff.

"Look, I understand your concern, even your revulsion. Yes, we're going to make the most of this. It's what we're paid for. Maybe you should remind yourself of what we're fighting against, which is why this even happened. And once you've learned more about the rest of this op, I believe you'll acknowledge that my approach is understandable. Necessary, even."

"So that other part of my assignment is still in force?"

"If anything, it's more important than ever."

She nodded and released his hand. At least they agreed on something. They stared at the colorful rowing shells, where the coxswains were still calling out the strokes, the oars sweeping in unison. The coot fluttered its wings in a shimmer of droplets and paddled away.

"Do we think any of those people I'm watching had any role in this?"

"You tell me."

"No, you tell me. You're the one plugged into the cops and whatever they've been able to find out. Somebody said the getaway car had keys left on top of a tire. Sounds to me like the car was delivered."

He gave her a sidelong glance, then nodded.

"Apparently so. They've checked the wheel and the keys for fingerprints, but they haven't come up with a match. No cameras in that area, unfortunately. This cook, with the knife, he wasn't a regular at Al Quds, if that's what you're wondering."

She waited for more, but apparently that was all he had.

"So if I'll still be wandering over to the other side of town every evening, when do we start scooping jihadis into the net?"

Bridger remained silent. Claire had hoped to prod him into revealing more about what she was supposed to be looking for, but if he wanted to stick with his approach, then fine, because she had work to do. The big press conference was coming up in seventy minutes.

"By the way," Bridger said, "in case of some fresh emergency where the phone isn't an option, I'm staying in the Dammtorpalais. You probably passed it on the way here. Six-story apartment building converted into a complex of boutique hotels. Ours is the Wagner, down on the ground floor."

She considered all the possible reasons he might have just told her that.

"Yes, I know the building."

"We've rented five rooms for the week under the name Dewitt, on a dummy corporate account for a Canadian freight handler. So that's who you should ask for."

"Five rooms. That's a lot of support. Who else beyond your usual suspects?"

He put the folded newspaper back on the bench. She picked it up in case he'd enclosed any further instructions.

"I suppose you should get moving. Stay out of harm's way, Claire."

"Seems to me that's exactly where you've put me."

"Yes, well . . ."

She stood and set out for the Plaza.

At the halfway point, Claire doubled back toward Bridger's hotel while keeping an eye out for his minders. She kept to the cover of the trees at the far end of the Moorweide, a pleasant expanse of green where children were playing in the sun. Not long after, the Dammtor-palais loomed into sight, a stately old brick building at the end of a block, with a tiled roof and white mullioned windows. She took up an observation post at the corner across the street and saw Bridger headed toward his hotel, about forty yards from the entrance. The watchers were in his wake, fanned out to either side.

She was about to depart when the front door of the Dammtorpalais opened. In front was a porch shaded by a tarnished copper roof. Out stepped the man she had photographed in Paris, the one with the mole on his cheek, which was visible even from this far away.

The man motioned with his right hand, and the two watchers peeled away in unison to turn back toward the Alster. Then he put his hands in his pockets and smiled at Bridger, who was now only fifteen feet away.

Bridger nodded but did not smile back. They went inside together. Claire opened the newspaper. There was no message hidden there.

17

The turnout for the press conference was everything they'd hoped for. To Claire, that no longer seemed like such a great thing. She was keyed up, scanning the room for any sign of menace in the faces and movements of everyone assembled—nearly a hundred people once you added up all the camera crews, sound techs, scribblers, and photographers. Everyone had been searched at the door, but in Claire's state of mind each long lens still looked like a potential firing point, and every equipment bag seemed primed for an explosion.

Armitage had looked a little pale and rattled as she led him up the steps to his seat on the stage, where he was concealed from the ravening hordes by a security screen. His brow was beaded, his eyes darting.

"Is this screen bulletproof?"

She shook her head, and his Adam's apple bobbed as he swallowed.

"Not to worry, though. Everyone's being searched on entry."

He nodded, but didn't exactly look reassured.

Now she was moving among the crowd, glancing left and right. Tony was across the room doing the same, as was Eduardo, the new bodyguard Bridger had flown in that morning from Berlin station. Two policemen were posted at the door.

She barely paid attention as the questions began, especially once it became apparent that none of the assembled reporters had any idea of what had happened the night before. Most of their queries were similar to the ones she'd already heard in the interviews the previous day. Armitage's answers again sounded surreal coming through the voice modifier. The event's moderator, another Agency plant, stood at a podium to the left of the screen, pointing to the next questioner and keeping everything on schedule. The setup made it feel like a TV quiz show featuring a mystery guest.

A stocky young Australian reporter stood up to Claire's immediate right.

"I'd like to ask the professor if he's worried his book will have the opposite effect of what he has intended, by igniting violence rather than defusing it, especially if his scholarship is interpreted by the Muslim world as further ridicule from the West?"

Not a bad question, but Claire never heard the answer, because she had just spotted trouble toward the back of the room, in the form of the professor's old pal Tom Warden, the bearded fellow she'd been instructed to deflect at all costs.

Somehow he had gotten a press badge—and if he could get in, why couldn't anyone?—and he was moving forward, row by row, like a fan from the upper deck angling for the box seats in hopes the ushers wouldn't notice. She set off to intercept him. He seemed to be charting a course that would allow him to make a move toward the stage after the event, perhaps to shout a friendly hello to Armitage as he exited. Probably harmless, but orders were orders.

She caught up to him just as he'd reached the second row by jostling aside a crouched photographer, who glared up at him. She touched his sleeve. He turned and frowned, but then his eyes lit up as he inspected her ID badge.

"So *you're* Brenda?" he whispered, while Armitage droned on. "His wife?"

"Last I checked."

"*Quiet!*"

One of the scribblers was annoyed. Claire steered Tom toward a couple of empty seats to the side, where he'd be easier to talk to and easier to corral.

"You're not at all what I expected," he whispered.

Oh, dear. Had Armitage shown him a photo of the real Brenda?

"How do you mean?"

"I don't know. He's always joked about how he can never get his wife to even leave the house. Yet here you are in Hamburg, acting like you own the place."

"Well, it's his big break, so I didn't want to miss it, and I'm helping all I can."

"Of course. And I'm glad I bumped into you. All this security is nuts, don't you think?"

"Better safe than sorry. Speaking of which, how'd you get a press pass?"

"Oh, that." He grinned, while yet another journalist shushed them. They lowered their heads and stepped toward the back of the room, mumbling like a couple of conspirators.

"I got these guys to credential me." He held out his badge, which proclaimed that his news organization was the *Journal of Arabic and Islamic Studies*. "They've published some of my papers. Winston's, too. But these goons Wightman hired won't even let my calls through to his room, and his cell number's been disconnected. All I was hoping for was to maybe get him out for some tennis, so maybe you could ask him for me. Tomorrow, if his plate's too full today."

"Tennis?"

"Sure. It's what we always do at these things. Clear our heads, blow off a little steam. God, that one time in Munich we played so long I almost missed a panel I was supposed to moderate."

"By playing tennis?"

The briefing materials hadn't said a thing about hobbies. She probably should have spent more time looking around his house before they left. And now Tom was frowning at her apparent puzzlement, so she had to backtrack.

"Well, yes, of course. But he didn't bring his racket."

Tom looked crestfallen. There was another indignant "Shhh!" and Claire eased them farther toward the back corner.

"The price of fame," Tom said. "Poor Winston. I tried to warn him. And listen to him. God, he sounds like crap."

"His security people said the voice modifier is for his own good."

"Oh, I mean his answers. They're all so rote. And the pity of it is that he has always described this project so beautifully to me, and with such passion. And now? Maybe stardom kills your spontaneity. Listen to him!"

They paused. Armitage's mechanized voice droned on.

"I began from the idea that the language of the Quran must be studied and analyzed from a historical-linguistic point of view."

"That's at least the third time he's used that phrase," Tom said. "Did his publisher write this crap for him?"

Claire didn't know what to say. Maybe this was the inevitable result when you boxed in an active mind with the demands of marketing and safety. She felt a stab of pity for Armitage. A brilliant academic who had reached the pinnacle of his professional life, only to be danced about on a stage in tightly controlled steps behind a screen, like some shadow puppet reading from a script.

A few minutes later, the moderator announced that there was no more time for questions. The room then buzzed in anticipation as hotel staffers wheeled in a long table piled with two hundred review copies of the book.

"Everyone wait your turn!" the moderator said. "There are plenty of copies to go around." But the surge had already begun, with reporters pushing aside chairs and one another to move toward the front. Tom and Claire watched glumly as silhouetted figures behind the screen escorted Armitage toward the rear of the stage before the hordes could close in. Claire exhaled as the door shut behind them. Crisis averted.

Now she could start planning her own escape. Yet some of the things Tom had said were already nagging at the back of her mind.

"Nice to meet you at long last," Tom said, "and do give him my regards. And, well, if he does happen to have a spare moment tomorrow, maybe for a drink or something . . ."

"I'll be sure to let him know, but . . ."

"Yes, I know. Security and all that. Fame, right?"

A disillusioned Tom joined the hordes heading for the door. He seemed friendly enough, and as she watched him depart, she tried without success to imagine him and Armitage playing tennis for hours on end.

18

Ken Donlan couldn't understand what was taking so long with the photos he had snapped of all those guys walking to Haydar Zammar's cookout. It was great work—okay, *lucky* work, but still—and he'd even managed to pick up a new first name, Mahmoud, for his colleagues to work with in providing IDs. Then he'd sent the whole package to Alec station the night before in an encrypted email. Given the time difference, they would've received the message around 2 p.m., leaving plenty of time for them to have answered by now.

Yet here he was at 4 p.m. the next day—10 a.m. back in Northern Virginia—and he still hadn't heard squat.

Fitting, he supposed, because it hadn't been a productive day. He'd slept too late after hitting the snooze bar on the hotel alarm, a jet-lag relapse that had left him feeling groggy when he finally reawakened at 10:30. After breakfast he'd spent an hour getting his digestive tract back in order. European coffee didn't yet seem to agree with him, although by midafternoon he had weathered the storm.

He had then taken care of his overdue courtesy call at the BND, where the Bureau's contact was Gunter Hauser. Hauser was a tall, wiry fellow with Nordic ruddiness and the steady, piercing gaze of someone accustomed to studying surveillance videos for long periods of time. Donlan always figured him for one of those obsessive exercisers who spent his weekends either running ultramarathons or cycling hundreds of miles. He was also a stickler for institutional correctness. Donlan had little doubt that if he ever were to misbehave on German soil, Hauser would be on the phone to Big Mike within seconds.

All of which had made Donlan a bit wary as he tried to gloss over the purpose of his trip, by telling Hauser he was there for "exploratory research, preliminary to a possible extradition request."

Hauser had raised an eyebrow at that bit of sophistry.

"Extradition? Of whom, may I ask?"

"As I said, my work's exploratory. It may amount to nothing."

"Are charges pending?"

"Not at this time."

"Do you anticipate an indictment in the near future?"

"As I said, it's—"

"Exploratory, yes. You Bureau people are not usually so . . . opaque, my friend."

"It's a sensitive assignment."

"So I gather. And what would your colleagues at Alec station, the ones from CIA, have to say if I were to inquire further about your presence?"

"I'd prefer if you didn't rock that particular boat."

"No doubt. But 'that boat,' as you put it, is now sailing in our waters under your FBI flag, so you can see my dilemma, especially if one of my superiors was to raise a concern."

"Well, if it's any comfort, I'm probably here more at Mike Sheehan's bidding than on their behalf."

With that bit of news, Hauser smiled and leaned back in his chair.

"And how *is* my old friend Big Mike?"

"Same as ever."

Donlan always had to suppress a laugh whenever he heard "Big Mike" spoken with a foreign accent, partly because he knew Sheehan would get such a kick out of it.

"He sends his regards, by the way. He was the one who insisted I stop by here first thing."

"The implication being that your Agency colleagues aren't overly concerned with such niceties?"

Donlan shrugged.

"If it makes any difference, I only plan on being here a couple days."

Hauser nodded. Then he paused to scribble a note, which was mildly disturbing, because it suggested follow-up action.

"It's obvious, of course, who you must be interested in. Your colleagues have made it quite clear in the past about who they want us to keep a closer eye on. But you will take pains not to stir them up, I hope."

Then Hauser stood, hand outstretched, a clear signal that it was time for Donlan to do the same. So he did.

"When you leave the country, Mr. Donlan, you'll be so kind as to give notification on your way out, yes?"

"Of course. Big Mike would expect nothing less."

Now, back in his hotel room as he checked his watch for the umpteenth time, Donlan decided that he had been patient long enough, so he got out his secure cell phone for an overseas call. It was an FBI model, one that Sheehan had insisted on. But it was perfectly suitable for this chore as well. He punched in the number for Alec station.

A familiar voice answered, sounding rushed.

"Dave, it's Donlan, in Hamburg. Did I catch you on a coffee break?"

"A break? Shit, man, given what's gone down over there, it'll be all we can do to get out of here by midnight."

"Come again?"

"You haven't heard?"

"Heard what? Something's happened?"

"Jesus, man, don't you guys talk at all? They took a hit on the professor's security detail, some rent-a-cop from the university. Stabbed, right down the hall from the professor's room."

"Today?"

"Last night."

"Fuck. Is he okay?"

"He's fucking dead. They called me in at six thirty this morning, all hands on deck. They think they've got it contained, but shit, who can say for sure? You really had no idea?"

Donlan felt like an idiot. He wondered if Hauser had known anything. No wonder he'd been so leery.

"None. They, uh, didn't want me in their hair, so I've been keeping to myself over in another part of town."

"Well, they sure as hell won't want you around now, either. But what do you need?"

"I sent some photos yesterday afternoon for analysis. I figured somebody might have taken a look by now."

"Oh, right. Wally mentioned those last night. He ran a check. Want me to see what he turned up?"

"That'd be great. Thanks."

He held on while Dave put down the phone, but he was still shocked by the news. He stepped over to the television and switched it on. By now there was probably plenty of coverage, either on CNN International or the local channels. What a monumental fuckup. Those guys did things differently in their shop, but they usually didn't screw up their protection details. How in the hell had someone gotten through to one of their people? Although Dave had said it was a rent-a-cop, so maybe that was part of the problem.

Then his stomach sank. What if one of the six guys from yesterday's photos was involved? For all he knew, they might have been meeting at Zammar's garden house to monitor the action, or even to trigger it with a phone call. Great. And now they'd have photographic evidence that he'd been in position to do something about it. Unfair, sure, but that would be their assessment, their dodge. He'd be the perfect foil—*It was the Bureau's fault, and here's the evidence.* Sheehan would have his ass.

"Kenny?"

"Still here."

"I've got two IDs for you. Wally says the skinny guy who looks like he's laughing is Ramzi bin al-Shibh, nickname Omar. The super-serious one up front is Mohamed el-Sayed Atta, but apparently his buddies call him Amir."

"Yeah, well, those two I recognized. What about the other four? I put in the notes that the guy way in the back was named Mahmoud. I also wanted to know about the guy in jeans."

"Right, I see that."

"Well, what else did they say?"

A long pause, followed by a sigh and a rustle of paper. Maybe someone had interrupted him.

"Dave, you still there?"

"I'm here, Kenny, but I'm not quite sure how to break this to you."

Oh, fuck. One of them was the killer from last night. He was sure of it now.

"This, uh, doesn't have anything to do with the events over at the Plaza, I hope?"

"No, no. They already caught that guy. A line cook from the hotel kitchen. Mustafa something, an Algerian asylum seeker."

"Holy shit." Donlan exhaled in relief. "Well, then, how come—"

"It's above your clearance."

"*What?*"

"These other IDs. They're above your clearance, and that's all I can say on the matter."

"Dave. I'm part of the team there."

"Gotta go, Kenny. More bells going off."

The line clicked.

Above his clearance? How was that even possible? Donlan had access to virtually every file at Alec. It could be true only if this information had come from someone upstairs, or from another station, and even then he should be entitled to at least the names.

Meanwhile, he was also puzzled by what he was seeing—or *not* seeing—on his TV screen. So far, there hadn't been a single mention of a terrorist murder in Hamburg, either on the live reports or the crawler. He flipped open his laptop and scanned the latest news bulletins. Nothing there, either. He refined the search, just in case. Still nothing. Cleanup indeed. If the Agency had managed to keep this under wraps, then at least they'd done *something* right.

Donlan then made a few clicks to call up his photos from the day before. He studied them closely, examining each of the six faces before zeroing in on the guy in jeans and the guy in the back, Mahmoud.

"Above my clearance? Fuck that."

He shook his head in irritation. Who in the hell were these guys?

19

In the bookstore around the corner from the Al Quds mosque, Mahmoud and Omar were still smarting from the lecture that Brother Haydar Zammar had given them the night before at the cookout.

"My hope, dear brothers," Haydar had said, "was that none of you would become involved in the arrangements that have been made for the Godless so-called man of letters who has profaned the Prophet. Yet just this hour I have learned that some of you—brothers who should know better—have allowed one of the newer members of the Al Quds flock to be drawn in."

Mahmoud had reddened in embarrassment. Anyone paying close attention would have also noticed Omar lowering his eyes and looking chastened, although Amir's demeanor didn't change in the slightest. Brother Haydar then softened his rebuke.

"I am sure our brothers' instincts were noble, and I know that we all share their anger against the infidel American. But for now you must all lie low, and that means not taking unnecessary risks. Set your sights upon broader horizons. Your talents have been recognized by important people, and it would be a tragedy to squander them on silencing a single fool."

Omar, as if tacitly confessing to his transgression, had then stepped forward to publicly take the blame on his shoulders alone. The massive Brother Haydar enfolded him in the bulk of his white garments. It was like watching a polar bear embrace a seal, and for a moment Mahmoud wondered if Omar would be crushed. Then the smaller man emerged, smiling in affirmation, and even for a shamed Mahmoud, his joy was contagious.

Saving them for something bigger.

It was a thought to quicken the pulse, to give you strength. Or maybe that was owing to the lamb, grilled the way Mahmoud's father used to do it. The meat slid off the spit in great juicy chunks, encrusted with cumin and coriander yet rosy at the center. He ate as much as he could stand, his best meal in weeks, and by the time all of the earnest talking began, he felt as sated as a pasha.

So yes, then. He would conserve himself for a higher calling, one which they would all work on together, brothers in arms. As he listened to Haydar and watched the others, Mahmoud experienced the deep satisfaction of knowing this was one of those rare moments when he was in exactly the right place among exactly the right people, God willing, positioned perfectly for what he hoped to achieve.

Now, a day later, they were back to their usual topics of discussion as they watched videos and drank tea in the late afternoon. Apart from Mahmoud's minor role, the matter of the professor had been delegated to the able hands of others, Haydar had said, meaning it would soon achieve success. Or so they assumed, until Brother Haydar rumbled through the door, big and burly and loud, an elephant broken loose from a parade. All heads turned his way as he stopped to catch his breath.

"I have news of a great disappointment, my brothers. A would-be martyr has taken action at the hotel, but I have just learned that he took down the wrong target. The infidel professor has survived, and he is distributing his lies to the world as we speak."

"How can this have happened?" Omar cried out. "You said—!"

"I know what I said, Brother Omar. But there was a mix-up, a failure. I don't know how or why, but it has happened. Even worse, I am told that our brother is now in the hands of the police."

Amir erupted.

"He did not martyr himself? He is *alive*?"

Mahmoud swallowed hard. Yes, a getaway car—that must have been what he had provided. Would the police check it for fingerprints? Was he now at risk? Or maybe the attacker never made it that far and the car was still sitting there, undisturbed, with the keys still lying atop the tire. Either way, they had entrusted him with an important job and he had completed it without a hitch. He'd measured up, and they knew it.

"As I said, it was a failure," Brother Haydar said. "He will not speak of any of us, of course. He moved in different circles from all of you at Al Quds, so we have no worries there. But otherwise? I am at a loss. He was positioned in exactly the right place, but it is now clear that he did not have the necessary commitment."

"They should have trusted one of us to do it," Omar said. "You should have insisted."

"No, no. I stand by my judgment. This job was not worthy of you. Something better awaits, and when that time comes I am confident that all of you will be ready."

This lifted their spirits a bit, although Mahmoud continued to worry. He looked over at Omar, who smiled and then shrugged, not exactly a comforting gesture. Someone brewed more tea, and the conversation moved on. Brother Haydar then began entertaining them with an old war story from some forlorn corner of Bosnia where he had once trained with a jihadi unit, tramping through wooded hills beneath the green banner of Islam.

"Here is a jujitsu move that they taught me," he said, stepping back to create room for himself. "I will show you."

He whirled his arms and kicked up his right leg. But in thrusting it outward, he lost his balance and blew the landing. His foot slipped and he sprawled to the floor with a massive thud that shook the building. The ensuing explosion of laughter was probably audible across the street, and even Mahmoud felt a little better.

"That was like something from a silent movie!" Jarrah shouted.

Omar doubled over, laughing until his face was streaked with tears.

Haydar took it all in stride as he pulled himself off the floor, red in the face from the effort.

"Is that the kind of mission you are saving us for?" Omar said. "If we were all to do that in Chechnya, my brothers, we would open a crater in the enemy lines big enough for an entire division to charge through."

Everyone laughed again, except Amir, who had remained silent throughout and still seemed to be brooding over Haydar's news. He sidled up to Mahmoud as the noise subsided and steered him toward the back of the room.

"This failure is no grounds for laughter. I understand why Brother Haydar wants to lift our spirits, but it should remind us of what happens when we do not act with the necessary resolve."

"You're right."

"There are lessons in everything we do, and I am pleased that you, at least, were able to do what you were asked. Later, I of course realized that Brother Haydar was right. This was not an affair worthy of our involvement. We should be saving our resources for a cause of greater magnitude. In case you were wondering, the car you drove was stolen, so the police should not be able to connect it with anyone here."

"Thank you. But I am ready for any sacrifice."

"That is good to know, because tonight Brother Haydar and I will begin discussing our next steps, and I am sure that your name will be mentioned."

"What kind of steps?"

"To other horizons, other callings. I like what you have shown us, Brother Mahmoud, but before I can know you are right for this path, I must see more. So perhaps we will think of a way to see if you are ready for this next step. Would you like that?"

"Of course."

"Good. Then, God willing, it will happen."

"Yes. God willing."

Amir squeezed Mahmoud's shoulder but still did not smile, nor did Mahmoud expect him to. A grave man who made weighty decisions. Someone had to bear that burden, he supposed. And now his own burdens of trust and responsibility would become weightier, exactly as he had hoped.

Mahmoud drew a deep breath, filling his lungs. Pride, apprehension, excitement—all of those emotions were in play. He was ready to move forward.

20

Donlan, still ticked off after getting the brush-off from his colleagues at Alec station, decided to up the ante by moving Mahmoud and the college boy in the crewneck to the top of his target list. Although he supposed that someone else in the photo, as yet unnamed, might have also triggered the reaction. Either way, maybe it was time to pay more attention to the followers than the leaders. To him, at least, they were the unknown quantity.

It was definitely time to ditch the Opel. Having been parked for so long near the garden houses the day before, the car was far more likely to be noticed today. But when he phoned Hertz an hour earlier, they'd said it was too late to deliver another car today, unless he wanted to come all the way out to the airport to do it himself. They promised to send a replacement to his hotel by midday tomorrow.

Fine, he thought. In the States they'd be using vans or vehicles with commercial logos, loaded up with sound equipment. Here he had to be more low-key. So, at around 5 p.m., he drove the Opel over to Haydar Zammar's street, where he parked well down the block from the house. He then followed the white Mercedes from a prudent distance when it pulled away at around 6 p.m.

He had done a little homework on the Mercedes's registration, thanks to some overnight help from the Bureau, and apparently it didn't even belong to Zammar. He was borrowing it from some other guy on their target list, a suspected Al Qaeda moneyman who also lived in Hamburg. So, in addition to being a blowhard and a fat fuck with no apparent job, Zammar was also a mooch.

The Mercedes wound up on Steindamm, just down the street from an address that, according to Donlan's file, was the location of the Al Quds mosque. Zammar had walked around the corner to some other spot for a while, but only moments earlier he had reemerged, trailing six or seven other guys as all of them approached the mosque. Donlan, parked in the Opel, watched the group through his long lens. Mahmoud and the college boy were again part of the jihadi conga line. Above his clearance? Not for long.

Or that was the plan until Zammar and two of the known targets, Amir and Omar, sidetracked him with some behavior too interesting to ignore. The three men emerged from the mosque at dusk and began to argue out on the sidewalk. The skinny one, Omar, seemed the most upset, shouting and pumping his fist while the quiet one, Amir, nodded and folded his arms.

Zammar gestured wildly with his hands, as if in exasperation, and then shook his head, although he said little until Omar went silent. Then he leaned forward and spoke into the little man's ear. Incongruously, Omar laughed. Zammar joined in, Amir did not. Zammar and Omar clasped each other's hands, as though they'd reached some sort of accommodation. They then crossed the street toward Zammar's Mercedes, three abreast and nearly in lockstep.

It had the feel of an important moment in which major decisions were about to be made or discussed. And when several other worshippers began emerging from the mosque—including Mahmoud and the college boy—they sauntered off in the opposite direction toward a kebab shop just down the block, where they disappeared inside. Nothing very important about that, he supposed, so he kept his eyes on the Mercedes as it pulled away from the curb—his three original top targets, he reminded himself, who were now heading somewhere else.

"Shit!" he said. "Shit, shit, and shit."

Mahmoud and the college boy would have to wait for another day. He started the Opel and pulled out into traffic.

21

Claire, watching from behind a table of oranges at the produce market on Steindamm, also wondered what the shouting was all about. At one point she even thought Omar was about to throw a punch, for all the good that would have done against a fleshy, impregnable target like Haydar Zammar. She knew then that she would describe the confrontation in her daily report to Bridger, although she couldn't hear much of what they were saying, beyond a few incomprehensible bursts of Arabic.

If she could have hailed a taxi on short notice—a doubtful proposition in this part of town—she might have set out after the white Mercedes as it cruised away. But the bigger problem was that the damn Opel was again on the scene, and it was already in pursuit. She had noticed it almost from the moment of her arrival, a half hour earlier, when she had ducked into a pharmacy next door to the produce market.

Today she was covered head to toe in the style of a Turkish grandmother from a religiously conservative family. A shopping bag held her purse with her phone and notebook inside. She studied the Opel briefly from inside the pharmacy. Then, convinced that her clothing and sunglasses would make her impossible to recognize, she decided to stroll by the car for a quick reconnaissance.

There was definitely someone inside, apparently alone, although the smoked windows—rolled up today—offered only the murkiest of outlines. More revealing was a bar code sticker on the car's rear window, which told her it was a rental. That almost certainly ruled out the BND, but it opened a wide realm of new possibilities.

She took note of the license tag and began a circuit of the block, working her way back to the produce market just as Omar, Amir, and Zammar began their bit of street theater outside the mosque. And now here she was, still behind a counter full of oranges as she watched the Opel disappear up Steindamm in the wake of the Mercedes. *Happy hunting*, she thought, *whoever you are.*

The car's departure left few remaining targets, although she had noticed some repeat customers from yesterday's cookout crowd entering a kebab shop just down the block from Al Quds. She made her way closer, walked by for a look, and saw that the five young men who'd entered had split into two groups—three at one table, two at another. The twosome interested her more, mostly because she already knew their names—Jarrah, whom she now thought of as a Sigma Nu pledge, and the watchful young Mahmoud.

She drifted slowly down the street, window shopping as she passed a travel agent and a clothing store. There was a bus stop with a bench, so she sat down inside the glassed-in shelter and watched sidelong for movement from the door of the kebab shop.

The good thing about tailing these lesser lights, she supposed, was that they were very unlikely to hop into a Mercedes, or even a cab. They seemed to be the type who'd be careful of their spending, meaning they'd almost certainly travel on foot and via public transportation whenever possible, and that was just about the only kind of surveillance she was equipped for. Had Bridger calculated that into his plan? If so, then maybe she was watching the right people. Let the leaders cook up their plans and keep the Opel preoccupied. She would stick with the rank and file.

Ten minutes later, Jarrah and Mahmoud stepped onto the sidewalk and headed north, away from her. Probably bound once again for the U-Bahn. She checked her watch. By now the professor was probably napping, or maybe he had cracked open something from the minibar, which the hotel had efficiently replenished after his mini-binge the night before. Tony was there, prepping for the next day's events, along with the new hired hand from Berlin station. There were also now two uniformed policemen stationed outside the room, posted at either end of the hall.

Partly because of that, Tony had told her to take as much time as she needed tonight. Had Bridger discreetly passed him the word? Whatever the reason, she planned now to take him up on the offer.

She stood, picked up her shopping bag, and set off after the two young men.

22

Mahmoud was surprised by the prosperous look of Jarrah's ground-floor apartment. It was well appointed and modern, with spotless appliances, generous windows, and freshly painted walls. Plenty of room, too, and the building's six tenants shared a shaded garden in the back.

Jarrah was still something of a puzzle to him. They were roughly the same age, and Mahmoud had been drawn to him right away while watching him in action at Brother Haydar's garden house, where his eyes had gleamed with the hunger of a seeker, a man yearning for certainties. *A bit like me*, Mahmoud thought. Looking for purpose in a life that, until recently, had felt aimless and unmoored.

Jarrah must have sensed this as well, because he had invited Mahmoud over for a visit as soon as they finished their kebabs.

"Omar says you're from Beirut?"

Jarrah laughed.

"Omar thinks that makes me a generous pushover, especially since I come from a prosperous family."

"Well, you do seem to be living better than the rest of us."

Mahmoud said it with a smile so that Jarrah would not take it as a slight.

"True enough. I know I should live more humbly, but I'm spoiled. You should've seen me growing up. Parties every weekend. Smoking weed in a hubble-bubble, and lots of Scotch on the rocks. The good stuff, single malt. Dancing till dawn at the disco."

His face was aglow, as if he could still feel the pleasures of those long-ago nights.

"My sisters wore miniskirts—still do, probably. Our house was always filled with the sound of Western music. I lived that way when I first came to Germany, too, three years ago, to study in Greifswald. It's up on the Baltic." He laughed again. "What a dreary, cloudy place! It's a miracle I didn't drink myself to death that first winter."

"What brought you here? Besides the weather."

"Oh, the weather's not all that great here, either. You'll see. It was my studies. I transferred to the University of Applied Sciences, for engineering. And, well, also because it's a bigger city, and there are more people here to talk to in Arabic. We're thick as thieves at the university. You should come out there for a look. Enroll in some classes—it might even help with your asylum application. Then there's Al Quds, of course, where I can always feel at home and speak my mother tongue. Although my German is now quite good."

"Mine, too."

"That isn't always such a good thing, you know. Even here I probably wasted too much of my time trying to fit in. Parties and all that."

There was again an almost wistful note to his words. He fell silent for a moment, as if to allow the fallout from those misspent days to settle.

"But that way of life never failed to leave me feeling empty. What was the purpose? Where was I going with my life? Nowhere of any importance, as far as I could tell. Al Quds has been the best thing that ever happened to me. I've never had such a clear sense of direction as I do now. I'm healthier, more focused."

"You and me both."

"Of course. Still . . ."

"Still?"

Jarrah sighed. For the first time, Mahmoud noted a flash of uncertainty in his eyes.

"Do you really think you're ready for it, Brother Mahmoud? This higher calling? This level of sacrifice that all of us like to talk about? I *say* that I am, because it fills me with pleasure and brings their approval. Especially when Amir asks. I'd almost be afraid to say no to Amir."

"Amir wouldn't actually, well, hurt anyone, would he?"

"Wait until you see him when he's angry, *really* angry. Once he decides to do something, I wouldn't want to be standing in his way. Still, I'm not always so sure about myself. I have times of doubt even now. The idea of reaching paradise is the only thing that keeps me going."

"I understand. I don't think any of us can know for sure what we'll do when the decisive moment arrives. Except maybe Amir." They both giggled, but not for long—as if worried he would overhear them, even from miles away. "But I'm serious. How can any of us know for sure that we have what it takes?"

"This doubt isn't healthy. My soul won't stand for it. We should just turn ourselves over to God. Let him decide."

Mahmoud was about to answer when another voice—a woman's—called out from the darkened hallway to the bedroom, speaking in German:

"And how will you know that God is deciding, and not one of your new friends making the decision for you?"

She came down the hallway and stepped into the light. Jarrah was scowling, rigid with either anger or embarrassment, but Mahmoud hardly noticed because he was so transfixed by her sudden arrival, like an apparition. He hadn't known anyone else was here, much less a woman. Jarrah hadn't offered the slightest warning. What's more, her head wasn't even covered. Was she his sister? A girlfriend, even?

"She came in yesterday on the train," Jarrah said icily. "I could do nothing to stop her."

"Only a month ago you would have been glad to see me."

She said it solemnly, but without malice, her eyes betraying a sadness that made Mahmoud feel for her.

"Hi," she said, turning his way. "I'm Esma."

"You shouldn't speak to him, nor he to you. It's not proper. There is a train leaving at three. Go and pack your bag."

"I should leave," Mahmoud said abruptly. He stood to go. It was an awkward moment for all of them. Yet he had to wrench his gaze away from Esma, whose dark brown eyes, even in their sadness, were active and alert.

"I'll walk you out," Jarrah said. Then, turning back toward Esma: "Go and pack. I don't want you to miss that train."

The two men headed for the door, although Mahmoud couldn't

help but notice that Esma lingered in their wake. *A woman of spirit*, he thought, then wished he hadn't.

As Jarrah reached for the doorknob, a phone jingled down the hallway.

"That's probably Amir," he said. "I should answer him promptly."

"Of course. Go."

Jarrah called out over his shoulder as he trotted down the hallway toward the bedroom.

"I will see you later, Brother Mahmoud!"

Mahmoud was opening the door to leave when Esma's voice stopped him. She spoke quietly, furtively.

"I'm sorry you had to see that. I should have stayed in the back until you left, but I was hungry. A year ago he would have been happy to introduce me. Can I get you anything? For an Arab, Ziad can be so terrible about hospitality."

"No, thank you," Mahmoud answered stiffly. His hand was still on the doorknob. "Brother Jarrah made us some tea."

It wasn't right or proper for him to linger, now that he was alone with this woman. Yet he found himself unable to leave.

"*Brother* Jarrah. So you are from Al Quds?"

"Yes."

"We're married. Did he tell you he had a wife?"

Mahmoud's mouth fell open, and for a moment Esma looked as if she might laugh. He glanced down the hallway, but Jarrah was out of sight, talking loudly on his phone.

"I didn't know."

"I'm not even sure it is even a lawful ceremony by German standards. But, yes. We had a wedding at Al Quds back in April, the only time I've been invited there. I am still surprised his friends let us have the ceremony there. Maybe they thought it would make me a more proper believer, but they'd never say that now. I don't remember you being there."

"No. I've only been in the city a few weeks."

"Are you sure you don't want some tea biscuits, or maybe some grapes?"

"I couldn't possibly."

"Yes, I thought you'd say that."

Mahmoud again looked down the empty hallway, willing himself to leave even as his feet remained rooted. Footsteps thundered in the bedroom. They again heard Jarrah speaking on his phone. It sounded like he was pacing back and forth.

"Your German is very good," he said, even though it was wrong to be making conversation. Her uncovered hair was quite beautiful— a lustrous black, stylishly cut. It swirled when she turned for a quick glance toward the bedroom.

"I grew up here." She was practically whispering now, which made the exchange feel even sneakier and more forbidden, and only added to its appeal. There was an undeniable warmth in her eyes. "My parents are Turkish. But I also speak your language. A little bit, anyway."

"German is fine. It's good for me to stay in practice."

Besides, speaking to her in Arabic, the language of the Holy Quran, would feel like even more of a transgression. He should go. He again glanced down the hallway, as if gauging the distance of an approaching storm.

"Don't worry. You're one of them, so he won't hold it against you. He'll think you've been trying to save me from myself."

"Do you need saving?"

"I don't think so, but he does. It's him I'm worried for. We are married, yes, but I don't even live here, and I almost never see him anymore. When I arrived yesterday, the first thing he did was leave for the mosque."

"Why are you telling me all this?"

"I'm not sure. Maybe because I'm hoping I can trust you. All of his other friends would have run away."

"That's what I should do."

"But you haven't, which must mean you're different from them. Are you?"

At that moment he certainly wanted to be, if only to please her. If a tremor from deep in the Earth had just shaken the apartment's foundations, he would not have felt as unsettled as he did just then. Yet, alarmed as he was, he still could not bring himself to open the door.

"I might be. Different. I am still trying to prove myself, to them and to me."

"So is he. And now that you're here, I'm sure he'd much rather spend time with you than with me."

"I'm sorry. I—"

"I'm not blaming you. I'm just telling you how he is. I am from his past, and as he has changed, I have remained the same. I have always been someone who takes liberties, as I am doing now with you."

She smiled. He smiled back. It still felt dangerous, but he was growing comfortable with the risk. He enjoyed her company, her presence.

"I have a job," she continued. "I act on my own, I decide things for myself, dress as I please. There was a time when he was attracted to all of that. But now? He says that he needs distance so that he can take himself in another direction."

"You shouldn't be telling me these things, and I shouldn't be listening."

"I know. But I keep saying them because you *are* listening. And because I am worried about him. I think he is determined to do something foolish, in order to give himself a greater sense of purpose. Is that what you'll do as well?"

Mahmoud lowered his eyes, disconcerted. He thought of the job he had carried out only the day before. Driving the car into position, an escape vehicle for a killer. He had been so proud of pulling off the assignment without a hitch, yet now, with her brown eyes upon him, he felt only shame.

A thud resounded from down the hall.

"He is getting my bags down," she said, again in a whisper. "He wants me to leave."

A second thud followed, louder than the first. Jarrah's movements sounded angry.

"Your luggage must be quite large."

They stared at each other for a fraction of a second before bursting into laughter as they held their hands to their mouths. Mahmoud experienced the thrill of a thief who has narrowly avoided being caught in the act. She reached over and touched his arm, and his pleasure doubled. Then her expression turned solemn.

"Go now, before he hears us."

She stepped closer. Mahmoud backpedaled so quickly that he nearly tripped. They flinched at the sound of another thump against the wall. Then she touched his arm a second time.

"Quick. Come outside with me a second. There's something I need to ask of you."

He nodded solemnly and followed her out the door, resisting an urge to take her arm, to hold her hand. These were not the impulses he should be dealing with now, not in this new life. They were part of what he had left behind, separated by time and distance. Yet he could not deny the thrilling nature of this encounter, or the effect that Esma was having on him.

They practically tiptoed to avoid making noise as they made their escape, Mahmoud complicit in her deception. With a final, furtive glance over his shoulder down the empty hallway, he slipped out the door behind her.

23

Mahmoud thought she would stop by the mailboxes in the building's entryway. But she beckoned him onward, and he followed her outside. She didn't stop until they reached the sidewalk, where she turned to face him, her eyes as earnest as before.

"First, I want to thank you for not running away from me."

"I probably should have."

"But you stayed, and that told me that you must not be completely lost, am I right?"

"Lost?"

"To your beliefs."

"I think of it as being found. It's only now that I'm starting to feel a little lost."

She smiled.

"I understand. But maybe I will see you again, yes? You are the only one of those people—from Al Quds, I mean—who has ever talked to me without acting as if they were morally superior."

"Yes, well . . ."

Mahmoud shuffled his feet and glanced toward the doorway of the building. The bedroom was in the back, so at least Jarrah wouldn't see them from the window. He wasn't sure how to answer. Then he realized it probably didn't matter. The issue would soon be resolved for him.

"Of course, if you're leaving on the train this afternoon, then it's not at all likely that I'll see you again."

"I'm not taking the train. That's what I wanted to tell you. I'm going to stay with a friend for a while, because I want to try to speak seriously to Ziad at least one more time. Not to talk him out of his beliefs. I understand that he is devout. But I want to make him see sense when it comes to, well, doing something foolish. Or worse. Do you think you could help me do that?"

Mahmoud knew he should refuse her.

"That will be difficult. I share his beliefs, and his . . . his sense of commitment. So maybe I'm not the right person."

"Maybe so." She lowered her eyes sadly, and it made him feel terrible.

"But I could try."

He felt weak the moment he said it, a backslider unworthy of his new friends. But when Esma looked up at him, her eyes were alive with hope, which made him feel worthy, useful. Humans should help others who were in need. That, too, was an important lesson of the Holy Quran.

"Thank you," she said. "Is there a number where I can reach you?"

Another dangerous idea, but he told her his number, and his heart lifted as he watched her punch it into her phone.

"You'd better go now, before Hurricane Jarrah arrives. And when he brings my bags, I will leave, too. My friend is at Holunderweg 9; that's where I'll be staying."

"For how long?"

"Until I give up, I suppose, but please don't tell him that. Don't tell him any of this."

Holunderweg 9. He told himself it would be wrong to dwell on that address, even as he committed it to memory.

"Keeping your secrets makes me feel disloyal. And, well . . ."

Mahmoud groped for the right words.

"Yes?"

"May I also say that it's nice to have met you?"

"Of course. Glad to have met you as well. This is the first time in days that I have not felt so alone. And don't feel disloyal—this is for his well-being."

"Oh, and my name is Mahmoud."

"I know. I was listening from the bedroom. My last name is Demir. I am Esma Demir."

"Yassin. Mahmoud Yassin."

"Mahmoud, promise me this. That you will look after him, and look after yourself. Don't commit to anything just because someone you respect says so. If you are waiting to hear God's voice, first make sure that you know what it sounds like, yes?"

"Yes."

She smiled.

He smiled back.

Mahmoud left without a further word, his feelings in turmoil.

24

Thirty feet away from them, seated on a bench at a sidewalk bus stop, Claire bowed her head to hide her face as Mahmoud strolled by. She was excited by what she'd just seen and heard. Having watched Jarrah and Mahmoud—Mahmoud Yassin, she told herself, to keep from forgetting—enter the building half an hour earlier, the last thing she'd expected to see was Mahmoud emerging with an attractive young woman.

It was such an unlikely sight—a stoically devout Islamist making nice with an attractive, westernized young woman—that for a moment she'd wondered if the location might be some sort of high-end brothel. But the woman was dressed in jeans and a modest top, and seemed far too earnest. The neighborhood wasn't right for it, either. Clean and well maintained. Lace curtains and window boxes of geraniums. Trim lawns, a tranquil, calm sense of well-being.

So what had she witnessed, then? She had overheard enough of their conversation—in German, no less, another stroke of good fortune—to know that Mahmoud and the woman had just met, yet there was already an element of tension in the dynamics between them. The woman was either Jarrah's sister or his girlfriend, and Claire was betting on the latter, if only because there was no familial resemblance.

And oh, what an impression she'd seemed to make on Mahmoud. His voice had been edgy with excitement, and as he passed on the sidewalk, he even seemed to be walking differently—head held high, his feet almost skipping. Only a few minutes of contact, but the seemingly introspective Mahmoud was momentarily in the clouds. A weakness, then, for this man of rigid beliefs, who otherwise never would have allowed himself to be so familiar with a woman who wasn't family. In surveillance, you were always looking for cracks in a target's armor. Maybe this one would prove to be minor, but she filed it away for later.

Esma Demir was another item for the report. Thanks to her, Claire now knew Jarrah's first name—Ziad—and the young woman was obviously troubled by the intensity of Jarrah's piety and where it might lead him. A smart woman, and quite modern in her outlook and manner of dress. How had she ended up with Jarrah?

All of these observations suggested to Claire that Jarrah and Mahmoud were recent converts to the Al Quds brand of Islam. That would also explain why they were drawn to each other. Fellow pilgrims, new on the scene, feeling their way together on the path to deeper devotion.

Claire waited until Mahmoud had rounded the nearest corner before she stood, already mapping out the quickest way back to the Plaza. She had again overstayed her allotted time, although not as badly as the night before. And tonight there wasn't likely to be a body waiting for her when she returned. Not with all their reinforcements.

She also finally had something interesting to report, because to her mind this encounter represented the existence of a tiny fault line within the group, one that they might even be able to exploit later—but only if she was able to keep track of it, and that was no sure thing, given the limitations of her assignment.

Or maybe Bridger would read her observations and deem them frivolous, a sideshow unworthy of further viewing. But to her, at least, it felt like something significant. For now, that would have to do.

WEDNESDAY, OCTOBER 6

25

Claire was awakened by shouting protesters, their voices chanting Armitage's name three stories below. It was quite a commotion, but the professor was still snoring. Annoyingly, his arm was slung across her chest like a damp tree limb, despite all the room in the king-size bed. She carefully set his arm to one side without waking him and then sat up, listening as the chants and cries grew louder by the second.

She climbed out of bed and pulled back the curtain. There were maybe fifty of them, almost all males, many of them bearded. They were waving signs and shouting in unison, but, thankfully, they didn't seem to pose any immediate threat.

As best she could tell, no vehicles were approaching, and at least a dozen policemen were posted around the perimeter of the protest. They stood calmly, looking a trifle bored, although one of their placards said, in German, "Death to the Infidel who profanes the Holy Quran," so there was that. She wondered if they had any idea what floor he was on, but none of them seemed to be looking up at the windows.

The snoring stopped, and when she glanced back at the bed, the sleeping professor had rolled over onto his stomach. Before going to bed the night before, she had asked him about Tom Warden, the friend she'd spoken to at the news conference.

"Meant to tell you: Tom said hello."

"Who?"

"Tom Warden. From Northwestern?"

"Oh, right. How's my old friend Tom?"

"Hoping to get out for some tennis, apparently. He said he wished you had time for a few sets."

"Right. Of course."

"So you play a lot?"

"Well, not much lately, with all this going on, and, you know . . ."

Then he smiled, as if something pleasant had just occurred to him.

"Tom didn't happen to invite us out for a beer, did he? There's a *hofbräuhaus* near here, right across the park on the ring road. I looked it up in that tourist guide and—"

"*No.*"

"Right. Figured it was worth a try."

Later, after again writing her daily report to Bridger in the bathroom while Armitage slept, she popped open her laptop for a little research. First she opened her copy of the professor's CV for a closer look. She studied it line by line, made a few mental observations, and filed them away. She also did a search for recent news items from his corner of Western Pennsylvania, bookmarking a few curiosities, which then percolated through her dreams.

She had just remembered one of them when the protesters, after a brief pause, suddenly began shouting again. The fresh burst of noise finally roused Armitage, who sat up with a start.

"What's all that racket?"

"It's for you, Doctor Professor Armitage, as our German hosts might say. An angry protest in your honor. Not very many of them, so I wouldn't worry."

He rubbed his eyes and yawned.

"Certainly *sounds* like a lot of them. What do you think they're saying?"

She was about to answer snarkily that her Arabic wasn't all that great when it occurred to her that his was supposedly much better, so instead she just stared at him, which seemed to revive him to a higher state of alertness.

"Oh, I hear it now. Never mind."

"And?"

"The usual stuff about God and infidels. Glory to the former, death to the latter."

"Well, that's a shock."

He climbed out of bed and headed for the bathroom.

She was then distracted by a sharp double knock at the door, followed by a woman's voice, saying briskly, "Your laundry, madam!"

Claire stepped quickly to the door and, looking through the peephole, saw the departing maid, Bridger's courier. This earlier-than-scheduled visit meant that the message must be of some urgency, one that he didn't feel comfortable relaying by phone. She opened the door and grabbed the plastic bag while Armitage was in the bathroom—the shower was running now—and she sat on the end of the bed to read it:

Noon. Same place.

So, then. A crash meeting. Or an unscheduled one, at any rate. She wondered if her report from the night before had unduly upset or excited Bridger. Without knowing the answer, she wasn't sure whether to be upset or excited herself, so instead she settled on hungry and picked up the phone to order room service. With security now beefed up in the hall, and the kitchen staff more firmly vetted, they had finally deemed it safe to order food. She thought about sticking her head in the bathroom to ask Armitage what he wanted but decided he could order for himself. Already acting like a cranky old spouse, she supposed. Fine: It would bolster her cover.

"Yes. This is 309. I'd like to order two fried eggs over easy, with the bowl of berries, a croissant, and a pot of hot coffee, please. Yes, up on the floor with all the policemen. Oh, and also two more eggs, scrambled, with sausage, toast, and a small orange juice."

The latter was what Armitage had ordered the day before, so she figured she might as well save time by ordering for them both. Yes, just like a real spouse, and he'd probably eat it without even saying thanks.

Outside, the chanting and shouting continued at varying volumes throughout breakfast. That plus the unexpected summons to the midday meeting left Claire feeling distracted as they headed downstairs with Tony, accompanied by a policeman, to attend a seminar in a ground-floor conference room where the professor was scheduled to be part of a panel. They had to pass through the lobby on the way, and it was packed with gawkers and policemen, who were all staring out through the plate glass doors at the protest.

Someone had acquired a bullhorn, and the noise was deafening. Heads turned at the sight of the professor and his security escort, and word of his arrival rippled through the crowd. Somehow this news must have reached the mob outside, which reacted with a sudden fury of shoving and shouting.

"Hang him, hang him!" the bullhorn commanded. Several onlookers in the lobby stumbled backward from the force of the surge, and one of the doors shattered.

"Move forward!" she shouted into the professor's ear as she shoved him toward the open door of the conference room.

Several protesters broke through the police cordon and instantly became entangled with three paunchy Germans decked from head to toe in *Asterix* costumes—two with helmets and massive curling red mustaches, and one clad as a Roman legionnaire. The legionnaire took a swipe at one of the protesters with a plastic sword, then gave a huge shove, which sent the man stumbling toward Claire.

Claire grabbed his left arm and twisted it until she had leveraged him onto the floor, where he was quickly handcuffed by a policeman. Another cop turned and inspected Claire, blinking with surprise as he read her name tag: Brenda Armitage.

"It's one of the reasons he married me," she said, snapping him out of his shock in time to do his job and grab a second lunging protester in a headlock. Another member of the *Asterix* crowd, a brawny, bare-armed woman with a wig of waist-length braids who seemed to be particularly enjoying her new role as a crowd control specialist, shoved two of the hapless infiltrators straight through the door of the ladies' room, where they sprawled onto the tiles.

Order was soon restored, and by then the loudest noise from outside was the wailing of sirens as police vans arrived to cart away the offenders.

Claire rejoined Armitage in the conference room, where he was waiting to be escorted to his seat behind a security screen at the front. He looked keyed up, eyes lively, as he experienced the blood rush of the survivor.

"I have a feeling they've already taken their best shot," he said with assurance.

"Yes, and Lute took it for you."

He bowed his head from the scolding. Good. He'd needed that. Claire reflexively checked her fingernails. She had scrubbed them again, but the narrow brown stain was still there.

Once the door was shut and locked, you could barely hear any more of the chaos, and by the time the lights were dimmed for the discussion to begin, the mood was as somber and self-important as every other event they'd attended so far.

Claire sighed in relief and wondered yet again what Bridger had cooked up for her now.

26

Mahmoud rose earlier than usual that morning to attend the sunrise prayer at Al Quds. He needed it to clear away his thoughts of Esma, which had troubled him throughout the night. Desires like those had no place in a mosque, or in polite conversation, or, well, *anywhere*— not if he was going to maintain his footing on this new path he had chosen.

Yet even as Mahmoud kept trying to banish her, Esma continued to reappear—her oval face, her smooth olive skin, the smile that lit up her eyes, the pain in her features every time Jarrah spoke harshly. And Jarrah, who had looked so disapproving in response to her kindness, now seemed so happy and relaxed among the believers, because he, too, had come to the sunrise prayer, his arrival making Mahmoud feel sorry for Esma all over again. She was his wife, yet Jarrah had cast her aside. Was that how faith was supposed to work? As an act of personal abandonment?

One reason for these thoughts was that his brethren had been discussing with some excitement the plans for a wedding that weekend at the mosque. Two lambs would be slaughtered, a feast even grander than the one Brother Haydar had provided, and there would be singing, chanting, and celebration. He would be expected to attend, of course, as would Jarrah. He hoped it would lead to better things than Esma's wedding, and he wondered if she had known even on that day that events would proceed so gloomily from that point forward.

"You look troubled, my brother."

It was Amir, nosing in on Mahmoud's thoughts. He seemed to have a knack for that.

"I am fine. Especially now. I am in the right place here."

"I know that feeling. Sometimes I feel like this is my only refuge."

But Amir was not through with him. He tilted his head as he eyed Mahmoud, like a doctor leaning in to inspect an ailing patient.

"Brother Jarrah tells me that you met his woman."

Mahmoud was taken aback, but tried not to show it.

"Well, yes. At his apartment. Only briefly."

"He calls her his wife, and in the eyes of God I suppose that it is so, because we witnessed their marriage with our own eyes. But she is not a believer in the way that we are. She is not good for him."

"Yes. I can see why you believe this." He paused to gather himself for his next words, which didn't come easily. "You're right, of course."

"We've been trying to help him find a way to leave her behind, but it is not so easy. Jarrah sees in her all the pleasures of his old life, and those can be difficult to part with. When I try to talk with him, it does not always go well, for him or for me. But he likes you, trusts you, so maybe you can help him reach this decision. It will be easier that way."

Mahmoud nodded. Amir seemed to be waiting for a more emphatic answer than that, so he offered one.

"I can certainly try. I want to help."

"Good. Otherwise, there are some of us, me included, who believe that more forceful action will be needed."

"Forceful? You wouldn't hurt her, would you?"

The words came out more heated than Mahmoud would have liked.

"Of course not. She is one of God's creatures, and a Muslim—in name, at least. Still, Jarrah must act soon, and you must help him. You will be helping us, too, by keeping a closer watch on his interests." Amir placed a hand on his shoulder. "Can you do this for us?"

Mahmoud nodded again, but this time he did not speak.

"We must support you better, Brother Mahmoud. You have done whatever we have asked of you, but we have not yet accepted you in all of the most important ways, and that is our failing. I know that you are poor, and Brother Omar says that you are living in quite humble arrangements. Is this true?"

"I'm not troubled by that. I have my own room in a building near here. I share a washroom with nine others. There is no kitchen, but Jarrah is going to lend me a hot plate."

Amir seemed to brighten at the news.

"We can do better for you than that. Brother Saeed—the one who will marry this Saturday?—he is moving out today from his bed at the House of the Followers, into an apartment he will share with his wife. You must take that bed for yourself."

"Are you certain that is possible?"

"Possible, and preferable. For you and for us. I can see now that we must do a better job of holding you closer, Brother Mahmoud. We would be bereft if you strayed."

"I will not stray, Brother Amir. But I thank you for this offer."

"There is also a kitchen there, which you may use as you please, and a common room. We even have a television, although we are careful about what we watch. It is a community of believers, and you will be welcome. And the rent is paid. You need only pitch in with the cooking and cleaning."

Mahmoud was nearly overwhelmed by the generous invitation, if also a little intimidated. Life would take on a new intensity. His piety would have to be evident at all times. He would also feel a bit more controlled and corralled—that certainly seemed to be one of Amir's motives.

But the move would also signal a deeper level of acceptance within the group, the next level of trust. And maybe that, in turn, would offer a quick and painless way for him to stop thinking of Esma. He reminded himself that time and distance were proven remedies for that sort of temptation, as he knew from his own recent past.

Yet a part of him now wanted to warn Esma of what Amir had just said, that she must sever her ties with Jarrah for her own well-being. He could relay the message by phone or, better still, with a brief visit to her friend's house on Holunderweg—a visit he could justify by telling himself he was following Amir's orders, since he would be convincing her to make a clean break and return to Greifswald. That would remove her as a distraction for him as well as for Jarrah.

"It all sounds very generous, Brother Amir. Thank you. But are you certain it will be all right with the others?"

"Of course. Omar has already urged me to do this. Come tonight if you wish. Bring your things. Do not even worry about speaking to your current landlord. Just go. Will you join us?"

Mahmoud took a deep breath and made up his mind.

"I will. Thank you."

"If you'd like, I'll ask Brother Haydar to drive you down in his Mercedes so that you will not have to lug everything on the S-Bahn."

"That would save me all kinds of trouble. Thank you."

Amir nodded in reply, and they embraced as brothers.

Mahmoud left the mosque a few minutes later to begin preparing for the move. It crossed his mind that Amir might have an ulterior motive. From now on, it would be easier for the group to keep an eye on him, just as he was supposed to be keeping an eye on Jarrah. Every coming and going would be seen and noted, and so would his daily behavior. Any lapse in commitment would be common knowledge.

Fine. He was all right with that, because this was what he had sought all along, yes?

Mahmoud's knees were a little wobbly as he exited onto Steindamm. He had reached a point of no return. This new direction seemed almost certain to lead somewhere momentous, God willing.

His phone rang in his pocket. When he saw the number, his heart lifted, and he was so eager to answer that he nearly fumbled his phone onto the sidewalk.

"Esma?"

"Hi. I was worried you wouldn't answer when you saw who was calling. Especially if you were at Al Quds."

"Well. Yes, that might be hard sometimes. But . . ." His voice trailed off, and he looked up at the mosque. No one was watching from any of the windows, but he decided to walk farther down the block.

"Look, all I really wanted to say was how enjoyable it was to meet you the other day."

"I feel the same way." Mahmoud's face flushed with equal parts of joy and shame.

"Good. It's a relief that not all of Ziad's friends think I'm so horrible. But I was wondering . . ."

"Yes?"

"I was wondering if you could see me again at some point. To talk about Ziad."

His first impulse was to say yes right away, but he held his tongue in sudden turmoil. She spoke again before he could answer.

"I'm sorry. I'm being too forward, especially for someone who is married, even though Ziad no longer acts like he's my husband. I think he still cares for me, and I care for him, deeply. But now it is more like we are brother and sister. Quarreling, yes, but brother and sister."

"It's hard for me to know what to say."

"I know. And please don't think I'm belittling your faith. Maybe I just wanted to hear your voice. But if you don't wish to hear mine, then—"

"No, no. That's not what I meant. And maybe you're right. Maybe together we can both help Brother Jarrah. Ziad, I mean."

Mahmoud was more confused than ever. This was the opposite of what Amir would have wanted him to say. But by working with Esma instead of against her, couldn't he still achieve the desired result? Not just for Amir but also for Esma and, ultimately, for Brother Jarrah? Calming her fears would prevent her from disrupting Jarrah's plans and, in turn, keep her out of harm's way.

"Yes, I agree," she said. "Let me think about this some more, and then call you back. Does that sound good?"

He again glanced back toward the entrance of the mosque. No one had come out to join him.

"Yes, that sounds good."

"Thank you, Mahmoud. I'll be in touch."

They hung up. Immediately Mahmoud felt like he'd done something foolish. Amir would have wanted him to refuse her, to discourage her. Instead, he had filled her with hope.

Yet the prospect of seeing her made him happy, so he resolved that if they did meet soon, he would make sure it was for the final time. Or, at least, the final time until Brother Jarrah was free of her influence. A hello, and then a goodbye. Mahmoud would then rededicate himself to what was important.

Despite his turbulent frame of mind, Mahmoud noticed an Opel Vectra parked just down the block as he turned back toward the mosque. It was a new model—dark blue, spotless—and he was certain that he had seen it twice before—yesterday, on Steindamm, and the day before, near Brother Haydar Zammar's garden house, which suddenly felt like one time too many.

Should he mention this to Amir and Omar? Or had they grown accustomed to such things, as targeted believers in a Western city, where almost anyone with strong opinions might attract the attention of law enforcement? Omar had once mentioned the need to keep changing cell phones. Saeed, the fellow who was getting married, cautioned them regularly about careful use of the internet. But Mahmoud hadn't taken their warnings seriously until now.

He passed the mosque and headed farther up Steindamm, toward the U-Bahn stop and away from the Opel. As he approached the first intersection, he allowed himself a quick glance over his shoulder and was surprised to see a man climbing out of the car, heavyset, in Western attire. Half a block later, a second glance revealed that the man was in pursuit—pale-skinned, wearing jeans, a dark polo, and sunglasses. Maybe this was mere coincidence, because Mahmoud had certainly done nothing to warrant such close scrutiny. He went to Al Quds, he prayed, he enjoyed the company of his new friends. But others were the leaders and big talkers, not him.

He bypassed the entrance to the U-Bahn station, and a block later he stooped to tie his shoes. The man was still back there, marginally closer. It made no sense. *I'm a newcomer*, he thought. *I've done nothing. Was this about the Toyota, perhaps?*

He considered breaking into a run, then decided that would only make him look more suspicious, and thus more worthy of pursuit, so he maintained a steady pace until he reached a small grocery on the left, where he ducked inside long enough to buy an apple and then switch directions, heading back toward the U-Bahn. By now the man was watching from a doorway on the opposite side of the street. Mahmoud picked up his pace as he descended the steps to the U-Bahn platform, where, with a few quick maneuvers he had learned as a boy, he was certain he could soon lose his pursuer.

But he could not stop wondering. Of all the people who were regulars at Al Quds, why had *he* become a target?

27

Shortly before noon, Claire approached the park bench by the Alster. Bridger sat in the same spot as before, this time wearing a wool over-coat against the raw wind off the lake. All it took was a glance to see he was upset about something. His jaw was tight and working at something, like he was chewing a piece of gristle. He started talking before she even sat down.

"You and your goddamn camera."

"What?"

But she knew, of course. The motor pool driver in Pennsylvania must have reported her photo, the one she had shot in front of Bridger's apartment.

"You're off the surveillance assignment. Done."

"*What?* Why?"

"A fucking camera, Claire? And then showing the photo all over creation? Have your skills and instincts really eroded that much since I last saw you?"

She was about to protest that he was making far too much out of a minor bit of insubordination when he spoke again.

"Why did you even *bring* one, or did you acquire it after arrival? Either way, you should have told me, because it's the last thing I would have wanted."

And that's when she realized this wasn't about Paris.

"Paul, I didn't bring a camera. And I haven't acquired one, and I haven't taken a single photo since I arrived. I'm a lot of things, but

I'm not a liar. You know that. And I have *not* been shooting photos here."

He turned and stared at her for a few seconds and then shook his head. Then he reached into his folded newspaper and withdrew an item, which he plopped onto the seat between them.

"Then how the hell do you explain this?"

It was a photo of all the young men she'd been following the other day—Omar, Amir, the ones named Jarrah and Mahmoud, and two others. They were relaxed and in motion on a sidewalk in a leafy neighborhood, on their way to the cookout at the garden hut.

"I recognize them, all of them. And I was there—or near there—watching them when that happened. But I didn't take that picture."

She did know who must have taken it, of course—whoever had been in the Opel—a conclusion she couldn't very well mention now, not after she'd withheld that item from her reports.

He stared at her for a while before speaking.

"You're certain?"

"Positive, Paul."

"If that's true, this is even worse than I thought."

"How so?"

"Because this damn thing"—he nodded toward the photo—"has turned the entire operation on its head. And now I'm not even sure who's responsible, or why they would have done it."

"A single photo has done that much damage? How's that even possible?"

"It just is. It's a huge problem."

"For you, or for someone above you?"

No answer, not that she'd expected one.

"So does this mean I'm still on the surveillance?"

"Afraid not." He spoke with an air of resignation. "The damage is done, so we're going to recalibrate. With all of your additional free time, you'll be doubling down on your main mission."

"With the professor, you mean."

"Yes. The thinking now is that you'll extend your stay here by a few days, beginning with some sort of tour day on Friday, right here in Hamburg."

"You're joking."

"I'm not. The idea is to ease him out into the open a bit more, with a few leaks to selected members of the press, in hopes of generating further, edgier coverage. Try to create more of a stir, so to speak."

"So we've truly reached the chum bucket stage. Is the university on board with that?"

"They don't need to be. We're bringing in security reinforcements, and once we finish here we'll be taking the show on the road, depending on what sort of events Tony is able to gin up over the next few days. All we know for sure is that Rome is our next stop. After that, maybe London, Paris."

She sighed at the stupidity of it—the waste of resources, the unnecessary risk of a civilian's life, and a prominent civilian at that. They'd lost one man already. Or was another incident what they were hoping for? Even on his worst day, Paul Bridger had never been this damn cynical. So who was?

"Did you see those protests this morning? Is that what you're after? More of that kind of madness, except maybe multiplied and with heavier ordnance?"

"We'll make it work, Claire."

She shook her head.

"These aren't things you can manage. Keep lighting matches and you'll eventually have a fire you can't put out."

"Look, Claire, maybe we'll tone this down a bit when we've had another day or two to rethink the logistics, but for now all I want you to focus on is the professor and his book. Keep him safe, but keep him in the spotlight. From this moment forward he is our sole raison d'être. Got that?"

The rented Opel. Who had taken this photo, and why? She had the tag number. She had to find out more about it.

"Claire, are you listening?"

Her secure phone buzzed.

"It's Tony, calling from his emergency number. I have to take it."

Bridger sighed but nodded, and then listened as she fielded the call.

"Yes? When? No, don't do that, not yet. I'm on it."

She pressed the button to disconnect and turned toward Bridger.

"Your wish is granted. Looks like we're about to get all the attention we can handle."

"What do you mean? What's happened?"

"Our sole raison d'être has gone missing."

"Missing? He's *disappeared*?"

Claire stood, put her phone in her purse, and began striding back toward the hotel.

Bridger called out after her.

"Where are you going?"

She answered without looking back.

"To clean up your mess and bring him back. Preferably in one piece."

28

Claire was basing the brash confidence of her departure on two things. One was that, according to Tony, the professor had apparently disappeared of his own volition. The other was a strong hunch that she knew exactly where he'd gone—a hunch that took a severe blow five minutes later when Tony called again.

"An update," he said breathlessly. "Not good. Police are reporting a stabbing in the park by the hotel, over in the Japanese garden. I'm headed there now."

"Shit! How the hell did he get away?"

"He had to have planned it. We've already screened some security footage and it looks like he left on his own, so we're still pretty sure it wasn't a kidnapping. But now, well . . ."

"I'll meet you there."

What a fuckup. By all of them, of course, although the Agency would happily lay it at her feet. Worse, Bridger would then close up shop as quickly as possible and hustle them back to their stations, leaving the goal of that other op—whatever it might have been—unknown and unfulfilled.

She then caught herself, realizing that she was thinking just like Bridger. If Armitage was stabbed in the park, *that* would be the worst result. Another casualty, perhaps another life, and this time it was the man she'd been sharing a bed with for the past few nights, a bored and timid academic wholly unprepared for the world they'd shoved him into. A suddenly famous author who was about to become an international tragedy. On her watch, too. She broke into a run and was halfway across the green expanse of the Moorweide when Tony called yet again.

"False alarm. The stabbing victim's a wino. Superficial wounds, probably self-inflicted. Of course, Armitage is still MIA, which could be even worse."

Claire took a deep breath and rethought her route. Her original hunch was back in play.

"I'm betting it isn't. Where are you now?"

"Japanese garden, with the cops. What about you?"

"Eight, nine minutes out, but I'm taking a detour."

"Where?"

"I'll let you know shortly, but stand by. I may need reinforcements fairly soon."

She disconnected before he could ask any questions, and set out on a beeline for her original destination.

Ten minutes later, Claire pushed through the heavy front door of the Hofbräuhaus München, and there was Armitage, seated in the middle of a long table in the main dining room, looking far too satisfied with himself. Claire backed away so he wouldn't spot her, and then punched in Tony's number.

"Found him. Alone and alive, no jihadis in sight. We're at the *hofbräuhaus* on Esplanade 6, just below the park."

"You're fucking kidding me."

"He's about to have lunch, and I'm going to join him."

"We'll send assistance."

"Keep 'em outside. Everyone here seems to be genuine drinkers. Whatever he did to get away, looks like he managed to shake that crowd of protesters outside the hotel. Oh, and please sound the all-clear to Bridger before he drowns himself in the Alster."

"Will do. Thanks, Claire."

She was about to put her phone away, but the mention of Bridger reminded her of another chore that needed attention. She dialed her office in Paris and asked to be connected to Clay, who still owed her dearly for his rescue the week before.

"Didn't expect you'd be back so soon," he said.

"I'm not, but there's something I'd like you to do for me."

"I suppose I'd better get used to you saying things like that."

"That's the spirit."

But he hesitated when she told him what she wanted.

"What's your authorization on this?"

"Do I really need one?"

Even without her phone she might have heard his sigh of resignation all the way from Paris.

"I'm going to be your personal slave for quite a while, aren't I?"

"I certainly hope so."

By now Armitage was poring over a menu. A huge mug of beer sat before him, nearly empty, foam on the sides. Seated at the opposite end of his table, separated by several empty chairs, was a Japanese family of seven, all of them sawing through massive joints of pork. Across an aisle to his right was a smaller table with four actual Germans, perhaps the least represented nationality among the touristy clientele. The beer hall's speakers played an accordion tune that competed with the laughter and the clanking of mugs. It was a place of relentlessly kitschy good cheer.

Still, Claire allowed as how she, too, could use a beer right now, partly in relief, partly in despair, partly in celebration of her newest line of inquiry, despite the stupid plans that Bridger had unloaded on her for a tour day in Hamburg and points beyond. Some food would also be nice. It was nearly 1 p.m., and the Georgia girl in her was already salivating at the idea of one of those pig knuckles.

She plopped down in the opposite seat, and Armitage looked up with a start. He reflexively crouched lower in his, and then smiled sheepishly.

"Hi, wifey. Want a beer?"

"I do, actually."

A waiter came over. He wore colorful suspenders and lederhosen shorts but was so trim and ruddy that he almost managed to not look ridiculous.

"One of those," she said, pointing to the professor's huge mug.

"And I'll have another," Armitage said.

"Make his a *kleine*," meaning a small one. "He has work to do."

The waiter looked to Armitage for confirmation, and the professor nodded grimly. They were almost acting married now, one of those couples where the wife is always tidying at the edges of her husband's sloppier habits.

"Have you ordered lunch yet?"

"No, but I'm hungry. Can we stay?"

She turned back to the waiter.

"Those humongous things they're sawing up over there—is that the *schweinehaxe*?"

"Yes."

"We'll split one."

"Very good." The waiter pivoted away with the precision of a storm trooper.

"What did you just order? A hacksaw what?"

"Haxe. It'll be right down your alley, trust me. Mine, too, for that matter. Big enough to feed a family of four." She glanced to her right. "Unless you're a family of tourists."

He smiled, seeming to like the idea.

"This is exactly what I needed," he said, coming up out of his defensive hunch. "I'll be fine now."

Claire let the remark pass without comment. She eyed him carefully, but he wouldn't meet her gaze.

The waiter returned with their beers. Claire took a long swallow that immediately did her a world of good. She took a closer look at the surroundings. Unfinished floors of blond wood planks, dark timbered ceiling beams that were purely ornamental. The curtains and tablecloths were decorated in the blue-and-white checkerboard pattern of Bavaria. On the walls, cornball adages and slogans were painted in Gothic lettering.

"This place is Bavarian kitsch at its worst, you know. It's about as authentically Hamburg as a hamburger."

Armitage shrugged.

"As long as the beer's cold."

He nodded toward a line of lettering on the nearest wall that read, "Wenn's Arscherl brummt . . . ist's herzel gesund."

"Any idea what that means?"

Claire puzzled it out as best she could, which wasn't hard, because it was the crude sort of thing a schoolboy might carve into his desk.

"Basically, 'When the ass grumbles, the heart is healthy.'"

"The management is suggesting that we fart?"

"Only if the spirit moves you. Or the beer."

He laughed. Maybe he was right. Maybe this was just what he'd needed. And if they were now going to be spending the next week or so together, or even longer . . . She took another swig of beer and tried to think about something else.

The food arrived quickly, probably because they roasted a few hundred of these things every day. The waiter set down a large white platter with a massive hunk of fat-encrusted pork, as big as a child's head, with a steak knife stabbed into the top and a bone poking from the side. It looked like dinner for Fred Flintstone. Next to it were slippery potato dumplings in perfect white spheres and a scoop of fresh, pale sauerkraut, which smelled far better than anything you ever got from a supermarket in the U.S. of A.

She withdrew the knife and, as Armitage watched with something like awe, she carved away a slab of glistening roast pork, plus some crunchy bark of browned fat. She might as well have been standing in line at a pig picking before the Tech–Georgia game. She put some on his plate and some on hers, and then popped a bite into her mouth. Not heaven, but she was at the gates.

Armitage took a bite and his face lit up.

"My God, but this is good. Nice choice, wifey."

"Don't say that word again."

"Sorry."

She rechecked the tables around them, lest she sink too deeply into gastronomic euphoria, but it was still the same collection of tourists and happy Germans. Looking out the windows, she saw that Tony and another of Bridger's hired hands were on the sidewalk, pretending to scroll through messages on their phones. All was safe, so why not enjoy the food and drink? But something was still nagging at her.

"So how did you manage to elude everyone at the hotel and make your way here?"

"Walked, of course."

"No. I mean, without being seen or followed. How'd you give everyone the slip? Our people, the protesters . . ."

He fidgeted, swallowed a chunk of pork, and sought refuge in his small mug of beer.

"I don't know. I just used common sense."

"Elaborate, please."

"You know, the kind of stuff you security guys get paid to do, I guess."

"You mean like that plastic bag next to you on the other chair. Is there a wardrobe change in there?"

She grabbed it before he could stop her, and pulled out a hat, a light sweater, and a pair of sunglasses.

"I left the room while Tony was taking a dump. I wore that stuff out of the hotel. I took the back stairs and then used an emergency exit."

"Very good, Winston. And I'm betting you didn't come here directly."

"First I went into the park. I ducked into a WC along the way and took off the sweater, the hat, and the sunglasses. But I still had this."

He showed her another hat from the chair to his right.

"And after you left the park?"

"I doubled back a few times, caught a cab, that kind of thing."

"Of course. That kind of thing. And where'd you learn all those moves?"

"Oh, you know. Movies. Books."

"I'll bet."

"You don't believe me?"

"I suppose I have to. You're my husband. Trust is everything in a marriage, right?"

"Right. Trust. Agree completely."

"Speaking of which, when I was talking to your friend and colleague Tom the other day—and he is your friend, right?"

"Of course. For quite some time now."

"Including a few years ago during a conference in Munich, he said. And I double-checked your résumé later and saw that you presented a paper there."

"Right. I remember that." He looked down at his plate.

"But of course that made me wonder why you've been so eager since you got here to see an authentic German beer hall. In fact, I remember you saying this might be your one and only chance."

"Well, yeah, because they kept us so busy in Munich that we hardly had a chance to get out of the hotel."

"So busy, Tom said, that the two of you spent almost an entire day playing tennis."

"Too busy to go drinking, I meant."

There was plenty of meat left, but Claire had lost her appetite. She slid the plate toward Armitage, who polished off the remainder while she watched in silence, eyeing him closely.

Later, back at the Plaza, a somewhat woozy Armitage decided he needed a nap to prepare for an afternoon interview, and in short order he was tucked beneath the sheets and snoring softly. Claire set the alarm on the bedside clock for half an hour later, recruited Tony to sit in, and took the elevator to the lobby, where she set out from the hotel.

She had another call to make but preferred a little more security for this one, so she bought a twenty-deutsche-mark phone card at a newsstand and wandered farther afield before entering a yellow Deutsche Telekom phone booth on a quiet street. She slipped her card into the slot and punched in an international number that, somewhat to her surprise, she was able to recall from memory, even though it had been years since she last used it. Maybe nostalgia had preserved it. She checked her watch: nearly 2 p.m., which meant that in the eastern United States it was shortly before eight in the morning.

The call clicked and sorted its way across the Atlantic while she tapped a fingernail against the glass. As the line began to ring, she wondered which room in the house the phone would be answered from at this time of day. A bedroom? A den? The kitchen?

Her guess was a wall phone in the kitchen, although she knew nothing about the house apart from the address, a rural route number in a small town called Poston, on the Maryland Eastern Shore. Home to duck hunters and oystermen, farmers and housewives. Or so she had always imagined, based on Christmas cards that arrived in Paris every December. What she still didn't quite understand was how her friend and former colleague had ever gravitated to such a place? Derailed careers led to odd landings, she supposed.

A familiar voice came onto the line after the third ring.

"Hello?"

"Helen?"

"Yes?" Uncertain, a little wary.

"Got a few minutes for an old friend?"

There was a pause, filled with the crackle of the international line, followed by a gasp of recognition.

"Oh my God. Claire?"

"Hi, sweetie. I'm a little boozed right now. Beer, believe it or not. A Deutsche lager, so you'd feel right at home."

"You're in—?"

"No need to elaborate further."

"Of course."

"We're going to have to speak carefully, if you know what I mean."

"I remember the rules. It's kind of alarming how fast they all come back."

"That's because you were good at it. How long has it been now?" She paused to total it up, but Helen got there first.

"Twenty years. Not counting the last time we did a little business together, and that was, what, six or seven years ago?"

"More like nine."

"Wow. And here I'd just been thinking time moves so slowly."

"Sorry to hear that. As much as I'd love to catch up on things, I'll admit that I'm calling again for some help. Off the books, of course, like last time. Unless that's out of the question now."

"I'm listening."

"This wouldn't be too far from you. A day or two. A little spadework in Western Pennsylvania, if you can manage. But you'd have to start pretty much right away. Nothing dangerous. Not like our first duet."

"That was half the fun, I seem to recall. Although I know I didn't feel that way at the time." She paused. "I don't know. I guess it depends."

In the background, Claire heard a shout—a girl's voice, the rebellious tone of a teenager. Helen covered the receiver and shouted back, the words muffled, before she returned to the line.

"Sorry."

"Is this a bad time?"

"The daily wardrobe debate, with the school bus moments away. Could I call you back?"

"This is international. It would cost you a fortune. Was that your daughter I heard?"

"Yes." Her tone was both proud and exasperated. "She's fifteen. I also have a boy now. He has some, well . . . special needs."

There was sadness in her tone, and weariness, but also love. Claire sensed a whole world of burdens and obligations that she would have liked to know more about, but at the moment there wasn't time.

"Do what you need to do and I'll call you back. Ten minutes?"

"Can we make it fifteen?"

"Absolutely."

"Good. And, well . . ."

Claire waited through another muffled shout, a burst of crackling.

"With a little juggling, I think I can do this. Help you out, I mean. I'm almost ashamed to admit how excited I am by the whole idea, but I guess you'd have to see me here, right now, to really understand."

Then Helen laughed, sounding relieved and excited.

"I'm thrilled you feel that way. Oh, and before I call back, scrounge up something to write with. I'll have names, dates, locations—a full set of marching orders."

"Will do. Talk to you in fifteen."

Claire was smiling when she hung up.

29

Donlan sighed and sipped his cold coffee, more than two hours old, as he stared into the gathering gloom of dusk and walked up the sidewalk. He was far afield from where he was probably supposed to be, having endured a long and fruitless day that was all the more frustrating because it had come on the heels of a long and fruitless night.

The pursuit of Haydar Zammar's Mercedes—the *borrowed* Mercedes, Donlan reminded himself—had ended at Zammar's apartment, where the big man had disappeared inside with Amir and Omar and then none of them had ever come out, or at least not while Donlan was there. He had parked down the block and waited until 2 a.m. before giving up.

Today had offered more of the same, partly because he was still stuck with the damn Opel. Hertz, having promised to deliver another car by midday, had phoned in the morning to tell him it would be closer to 3 p.m. A pleasant young woman had given him the news.

"But if the car you presently have is not functioning properly, you may use taxis and we will deduct the cost from your bill as long as you keep the receipts."

"It's functioning fine. I just want a damn upgrade."

"But, sir, the Volkswagen you've requested is in the same midsize class as the Vectra, so if an upgrade is what you want—"

"Look, just bring the goddamn car, okay? Soon as you can swing it."

He had then driven the Opel yet again to Steindamm, where he was certain that its all-too-familiar presence had spooked Mahmoud.

Or that was what it felt like after Mahmoud, uncharacteristically skittish, had eluded him with a couple of surprisingly nimble moves at the U-Bahn stop.

Donlan had then driven the Opel back to the hotel, and by the time Hertz finally arrived with the VW Passat, he had decided to do the rest of the day's work on foot. He returned to the Al Quds mosque by S-Bahn and, in desperation, or perhaps just to keep himself occupied while he was in such a foul mood, he had settled on a fresh target—a young man who emerged from the mosque with six or seven others in tow.

The only thing that made the fellow interesting was that all the others were intent on slapping his back and congratulating him. A few times they mentioned his name—Saeed—and one gave him a small hand-wrapped box, apparently a gift.

Donlan, in a leap of logic, or maybe simply because he had nothing better to do, thought that this might mean Saeed had been chosen for some special duty or mission, and that the others were wishing him well. More likely it was his birthday, or some special occasion that had nothing to do with either Islam or Al Qaeda.

He followed the man anyway, trudging in his wake down the street to the *bahnhof*, where he boarded an S-Bahn for what turned out to be a long ride south, across the dreary estuarine and industrial wastelands below the city.

At first that excited him. Why would the fellow be journeying to such a far-flung and remote place unless it was for something special? But after a few more stops he began to grow bored. Saeed finally disembarked in the town of Harburg, more than half an hour from the center of Hamburg.

Donlan considered whether to stay on the train or get off to catch a return. But having gone this far, he decided to pursue the man to the bitter end, so he walked through the town and around several corners, trailing him until he reached a narrow, cobbled, sloping street called Marienstrasse, where Saeed entered the door of an apartment house at number 54 and disappeared from sight.

Great, Donlan thought. Soon it would be dusk, and all he had accomplished today was getting a rental Volkswagen that was parked nearly an hour from here in the hotel lot. At the rate he was wasting money for such meager results, either Alec station or Big Mike Sheehan would soon be summoning him home. Maybe he never should have come to begin with. A beer seemed to be in order for tonight. Several of them.

He did a circuit of the neighborhood, partly out of idle curiosity, partly because he couldn't yet allow himself to give up on the day. And that's where he was now as he sipped his cold coffee, preparing to turn back onto Marienstrasse for what he vowed would be the final time.

As he reached the block where number 54 was, a white Mercedes passed him from behind, cruising slowly, as if preparing to stop.

No way. Couldn't be.

The brake lights went red and the car halted right in front of the door of Marienstrasse 54.

Donlan slowed down so he wouldn't get close enough to be recognized, and he tilted the cup of coffee to his face.

A man got out from the passenger side—it was Amir—and then another male got out from the back. Donlan couldn't tell who it was at first, because the fellow was lugging a lumpy green duffel bag.

The two men spoke, and he heard Zammar's voice from the car, followed by a laugh from the guy with the bag.

Son of a bitch. It was Mahmoud, who was now waving goodbye as Amir helped carry a second, smaller bag into the house, where, if Donlan was reading things correctly, Mahmoud seemed to be moving in.

After the door shut, Donlan watched some lights go on upstairs. He crossed the street for a better look.

The blinds were lowered, but you could see enough shadows moving around in a couple of windows to tell that the place was fairly crowded. He remembered from the file that Amir's university was down here, practically right around the corner, so this might be his home as well. The Germans probably already knew this. And now, by all indications, Mahmoud had joined them.

He surveyed the neighborhood again, this time with a more discerning eye, and by the time Donlan was ready to call it a day, he was feeling quite pleased with himself. It was time for those beers. He'd earned them. But not too many, because he was already compiling a checklist for tomorrow, and to get everything done he'd need to be back here bright and early.

THURSDAY, OCTOBER 7

30

One more seminar. Two more interviews. Then, looming tomorrow, the hideous prospect of Tour Day, with its itinerary of museums and harbor walks.

Those were Claire's waking thoughts now that the most interesting part of her assignment had been declared null and void. And after Tour Day there would be another week—maybe more—of further travels with the professor. Tony had already booked their flights for Rome, a destination that would normally be glorious at this time of year, offering strolls along the Tiber, maybe some shopping on the Via Veneto, and then a leisurely dinner under the stars, without shivering as she had the other evening at the café next to Al Quds. But with the professor and a phalanx of security minions in tow, none of that would be practical.

In the clarity of morning, as she sipped her first cup of coffee while Armitage slumbered, she felt foolish for having set her old friend Helen off on some vague hunting expedition in the hinterlands of Pennsylvania.

Based on what? On the professor's intense desire to visit a beer hall, even though he'd already been to Germany? His failure to look or move like a tennis pro? His surprisingly clever escape from the hotel? His wooden answers and generally uninspired public appearances? She had seen enough of his colleagues by now to know that wooden answers and uninspired rhetoric were the order of the day for this crowd. They mumbled, they repeated themselves, they bored her to tears; and, as she had gleaned by skimming some of their books on offer at the tables set up by the academic publishing houses, most of them didn't write particularly well, either.

The atmosphere here was that of a gathering of moles who had come up out of the ground for a few delirious hours of sunlight, needful and blinking, but also with a wary eye out for any hawks that might snatch them away during their few hours of enjoyment before it was time to scurry back down into their archival tunnels. And so, *of course* Armitage had sought to break loose, and, being of sound intelligence and an analytical frame of mind, he had found a way to do so. Big deal.

Oh, well. Too late to recall Helen now. As long as she didn't get herself arrested by some small-town cop, maybe the trip would give her some escape from her dull life. Or was Claire the one with the dull life? No children, no spouse, no life-or-death decisions about animals and crop cycles while living hard up against the daily whims of nature. She instead stayed busy pretending that her work was more important than it really was. Even Bridger's other assignment had probably been empty at the core, once you peeled away all the layers. Why else would he have canceled it on such seemingly shaky grounds?

Here she was, then, the fake wife of a bland academic, readying herself for a week of package-tour boredom in some of the world's most wonderful cities.

The professor sat up in bed and stretched.

"Last day of the conference," he said, sounding quite chipper about it.

"So you're glad, too?"

"Oh, I'm not cut out for this. All this press stuff, the constant attention. And the protests, although God knows I've been threatened before. Occupational hazard."

"Yes," she said, still searching for possible double meanings, although her heart was no longer in it.

"Tony says I'll be getting out more once we're on the road." He sighed with contentment. "That will make it much better. And is it true what they were saying last night?"

"Is what true?"

"That they've added Spain to the schedule?"

"I'd be the last to know at this point. And whatever you say this morning, please don't say anything with the word 'wifey' in it."

He laughed and shuffled off to take a shower. At least someone in the room was a happy camper.

On one level, she supposed the trip had been a success. When she checked online the night before, she'd seen that Armitage's book was up to number 6 in the Amazon sales rankings, and when it came to book sales, Amazon was supposedly the next big thing.

Would that make any sort of dent on opinions in the Islamic world? Perhaps among scholars and deep thinkers, she supposed. Among jihadis like Amir and Omar and their younger recruits? Doubtful. In her long career of watching human beings of supposedly high intelligence shamble and stumble and make fools of themselves across half of Europe, she knew that the deluded weren't easily swayed, even when you offered them the alternative of a far sturdier delusion. Impressionable young men would keep lining up for martyrdom whether the reward was virgins or a box of raisins. Anger and hopelessness stirred them to action, not the idea of some sexual paradise.

But more power to Armitage, she supposed, who would at least get to cash in. No box of raisins for him. He'd be able to visit all the kitschy beer halls he liked. She hoped the real Brenda was out buying a better grade of chocolates this morning if she, too, was tracking the sales results.

"You okay?" Armitage asked.

He was buttoning his shirt now, his expression one of genuine concern, the very model of spousal empathy.

"I'm fine. I suppose we should call room service for breakfast."

She did so for both of them and, while waiting, wondered idly if, orders or no orders, she might have one last chance this afternoon to sneak a peek at Al Quds just before sunset prayers. Unofficially, of course, or even more unofficially than before. Then she dismissed the idea as pointless. From here on out, all of Claire's roads led to Rome.

Twenty minutes later, as she bit into a strawberry with the firmness and flavor of a rubber ball, her phone rang. It was Clay, calling from Paris.

"About that car," he said.

"Ah, yes." Yesterday that had all seemed so important. "Any luck?"

"None. Lots of skill, though. And you were right: It was a rental. Straight from the Hertz counter at Hamburg airport."

"No surprise there. What else?"

"Plenty, and I think you'll like it. Maybe even enough to say we're all even."

"Doubtful."

But when she heard what Clay had to say, she had to admit that he was very nearly correct.

31

They were watching television at the House of the Followers on Marienstrasse when Mahmoud saw Amir laugh for the first time. The show was a documentary on the Intifada, the Palestinian uprising against Israeli occupation forces back in the late eighties. There was a vignette about an Arab suicide bomber who detonated prematurely, injuring only himself. An ambulance rushed him, unconscious, to an Israeli hospital, where he awoke on an operating table. Gazing up at the doctors and nurses clad in white, he asked groggily, "Is this heaven?"

"Do you think there will be Jews in heaven?" a doctor replied.

"No."

"Then I guess you're not there yet."

Everyone burst out laughing, and even Amir was swept along. Omar, seated beside him, slapped him on the back as if to reward this hopeful sign of mirth.

"That's the spirit, my man!"

Amir smiled back. For a change, he didn't seem to mind being an object of fun. Then someone opened a bag of pastries while someone else went off to the kitchen to brew tea, and the mood was downright festive.

It was a relief to kick back. Mahmoud had already gathered that television wasn't an every-night event. Group discussions were more the norm, and he had already been craving some release from the household's rituals and routines. He was also still getting used to the cramped living conditions. With his arrival, the apartment now housed seven young men from North Africa and the Middle East.

He had moved in the night before, slinging down his duffel in a room shared by two others before sacking out on a twin bed with a hard, thin mattress. Theirs was a three-bedroom upstairs flat in a drab four-story building with a stucco facade. It was in Harburg, near Amir's university, on a treeless street with cars parked on both sides. The surrounding buildings were similarly drab. Their only notable features were ceramic historic plaques that noted the years when some of the buildings had been destroyed by Allied bombers during the Second World War and then rebuilt. *Zerstoert 1944, Aufgebaut 1955*. Most of the neighbors seemed to be Germans, and Mahmoud wondered what they must make of this crowded and often noisy little household.

Omar brought in a tray from the kitchen and helped pour glasses of hot, sweet tea. There were ten young men here tonight, and the air was a bit stuffy, so someone opened a window. The night air rushed in, fresh but raw. Mahmoud went to fetch a sweater.

Once he reached his room, he was tempted to stay. The voices out in the living room were muffled as he stood alone in the dark, and he felt his chest muscles relax. He finally had space to think. Not that his bedroom was particularly cheerful or welcoming. In the dimness, he surveyed the bare vinyl floor with clothes tossed here and there. Two of the beds were unmade. A plate of uneaten grapes sat in a corner next to cracker crumbs on a paper towel. Grapes like the ones Esma had offered. He thought of her face, the deep sense of empathy in her eyes.

He sighed and stepped over to the window to pull back the blinds. Same parked cars as earlier. No Opel Vectra, so he supposed that was an improvement. Maybe he would retire early tonight, although it would be antisocial to do so now, especially on only his second night of residence.

A voice from down the hall rose in anger. Amir's. So much for his lighter mood, or the prospect of a fun evening. Mahmoud's chest tightened. Dawn to dusk—that had to be his level of commitment now.

Earlier that day, on his first morning, they had awakened him for prayers before sunrise. He had washed himself in silence and unrolled his rug alongside the others on the living room floor. Everyone bowing and chanting, a calming morning rhythm with words to soothe your soul. *Prayer is better than sleep.* Unless you were Omar, missing in action. As the group's top fixer and motivator, he often worked late into the night, making calls on his little cell phone, which he changed every few days. The work was so valuable that Amir had apparently granted him a dispensation to sleep in.

Mahmoud drew a deep breath and counted slowly to ten. Better. He supposed he would settle into the domestic routines soon enough. He strolled down the hallway, cleared his throat as if to announce his return, and then rejoined the others just as Ziad Jarrah arrived at the front door. The young Beiruti held two boxes and was out of breath from having carried them up the stairs.

"Brother Jarrah, what have you brought us?" Omar asked.

"Books! From my apartment. Is there somewhere I could store them?"

Mahmoud seized the opportunity. He wanted a moment alone with Jarrah.

"Put them in my room. They'll fit under my bed. Here, let me help you."

He took a box and headed down the hallway. He'd been meaning to probe Jarrah a bit more, in keeping with Amir's request. He admitted to himself that he also hoped to learn more news of Esma. After all, didn't Amir want him to keep track of her?

"Slide them under here," he said, showing Jarrah.

"Are you sure? Your room looks a little cramped."

"It is. You're lucky to have your own place."

"Not for long. That's why I'm getting rid of some things, like these books."

"You're not moving back in with Esma, are you?"

"Oh, no. Quite the opposite." He frowned and lowered his voice. "But she's still in Hamburg. She lied to me about taking the train and went to a friend's house instead. She called and asked me to meet her tomorrow for lunch, but I won't because I've already told her."

"Told her what?"

"That I'm moving out and moving on, leaving this place behind. I'll be traveling in the next few days, so now she will *have* to leave the city, and soon. It's the only way I'll have the peace of mind to prepare properly for my departure."

"You're traveling?"

"Brother Haydar has arranged my passage. I have been chosen."

"For what? For where?"

He smiled and shook his head. There was a faraway look in his eyes—part wonder, part wistful.

"I am not supposed to say, not yet, but everyone will know soon enough. Others will join me. It will be the first big step of many, for all of us."

"Well, congratulations."

"What about you, Mahmoud? Have you put your affairs in order for when you're called?"

"I don't have much in the way of possessions."

"That's not what I meant. A last will and testament. A power of attorney agreement. Things to leave behind for your family. You must be prepared for anything. I'm sure that Brother Haydar will soon ask you to do these things."

"He might not want me for that kind of work."

"Oh, but he will. He has his eye on you. You speak English, yes?"

"Yes. My mother was American."

"He knows that. And he has heard your German, which is also quite good. All of these things are of value, to him and to the people above him. Do you have any technical skills, maybe in science or engineering?"

"No."

"Not to worry. The language skills are what he values most. You'll see. Come, let's join the others."

By now, as if summoned by Jarrah's words, Haydar Zammar had also arrived, and the big man was loudly regaling the room with a tale of an ornery pack mule in a supply caravan crossing the deserts of Baluchistan.

"And then the bastard, he tries to bite my *ear*, and instead takes a chunk out of my shalwar!" A roar of laughter. "So I dispatched him with a shot to the head. And for dinner we roasted his haunches on the campfire."

"You're making that part of it up!" Omar said.

Brother Haydar laughed as if to confirm it. Then he nodded toward Amir, who was watching, stone-faced, from a doorway.

"Have you told our new recruit what we need from him?" Haydar asked.

Amir shook his head.

"Brother Mahmoud, can you spare us a moment in the kitchen?"

"You see?" Jarrah whispered. "It's all beginning for you."

They clasped hands. Then Mahmoud headed for the kitchen.

Amir shut the door behind them. The kitchen was lit only by a light above the stove, and Haydar stood by the refrigerator with his arms folded. Amir spoke first, in a burst of English, the words taking Mahmoud by surprise.

"Tell me how you are liking it here, Brother Mahmoud. Are your accommodations satisfactory?"

If not for Jarrah's tipoff—that Haydar was interested in his language skills—he might have wondered if Amir's question was some sort of trick, designed to trip him up. Instead, he collected himself and answered calmly in English.

"I am liking it here a great deal. Everyone has made me feel comfortable and welcome. I only hope I can become an asset to the house."

Amir looked to Haydar, who unfolded his arms and nodded toward a table in the corner. Everyone sat, Haydar's chair groaning beneath his bulk. Then the big man spoke.

"If you are so inclined, Brother Mahmoud, I believe that you can become an asset to something much larger than this house. Tell me, would you be willing to give me your passport so that I can make a few travel arrangements on your behalf?"

"Where will I be going?"

Haydar answered with silence. Mahmoud looked to Amir, who also said nothing. The message was clear. *You must trust us before we can trust you.*

"Yes. Of course I'll give you my passport."

"Very good. I'll get to work on it tomorrow. You won't be disappointed, and you won't be alone. Others will soon begin leaving—one at a time, to avoid attracting notice. Different destinations, at first. A beginning only. But, well, if you remain vigilant, your name might someday be immortal."

Mahmoud had no trouble mustering an awestruck expression. He answered in a whisper.

"Thank you."

Haydar gripped his shoulder and stood. Mahmoud was about to follow suit when Amir took his arm, as if to take possession from Haydar.

"I will leave you in the care of Brother Amir," Haydar said. He went off to join the others, and an awkward silence followed.

"It is good that you inspire such great confidence in Brother Haydar," Amir said, "but I'll admit that I am not yet fully convinced. I was pleased with your action the other day, and your willingness to do what we asked. But I still sense a certain weakness in you."

"Weakness?"

"Maybe 'softness' is the better word."

"I can be as tough as you need me to be."

"I'll let you show me. But first I want to know what you've learned from observing Brother Jarrah. I saw you take him aside a little while ago. Where do things stand with that woman of his?"

"I wouldn't worry about her. She'll be leaving Hamburg soon."

Amir raised his eyebrows.

"She is still *here*? Jarrah had told me otherwise. This is not good. This must be remedied."

Mahmoud belatedly realized his mistake. He had just put Esma in Amir's crosshairs.

"I could be wrong. She may have already left."

"No, no. There was something troubling in Brother Jarrah's eyes when he walked in the door. When I called out to him, he wouldn't look me in the eye, and this has to be the reason why. I must deal with the problem."

"It won't be a problem much longer. Jarrah said he has already seen her for the last time."

"*Jarrah* is not the problem, Brother Mahmoud. *She* is the problem. He is at a critical moment, and we must free him from any further worries about her. If she stays, she will continue to try to meddle in his life. I will deal with her."

"How so?"

"It is not your worry, Brother Mahmoud. I will act quickly, decisively."

Mahmoud was alarmed. His slip of the tongue had caused this, and only he could make it right.

"Let me," he said. "I'll deal with it."

"No, no. There isn't time. Your next test will come later. If I need help, I'll get it from Brother Omar."

Perhaps they would only put her on a train, or threaten her, but Mahmoud couldn't live with the uncertainty.

"You and Omar don't know where to find her," he said, gambling that they didn't have Esma's friend's address. "I'm not even sure Brother Jarrah knows. He may deny to you that she's still here. And if that happens, we'll only risk pushing him away from us, maybe even back to her."

Now it was Amir who looked alarmed. He furrowed his brow in thought, then nodded.

"You may be right. But how would *you* find her?"

"I . . . I obtained her phone number. From looking at Jarrah's phone. I was doing as you'd asked, trying to learn more, and, well . . ."

"It's all right. You were correct in your actions. I am even a little impressed. But do you think she will speak to you, much less tell you where to find her?"

"If I am careful, I think that she will. I can tell her that Jarrah wants to arrange a reconciliation with her. She will be too curious to say no."

Amir considered this for a few seconds. Then he nodded.

"Do it, then, as soon as you can. Brother Jarrah will be leaving Sunday, the morning after Saeed's wedding, and we cannot afford any last-minute disruptions to his life. Everything must stay on schedule."

Mahmoud nodded. Amir moved closer and put a hand on his shoulder.

"This will be your final test, to show us your toughness. Force may be in order, and you must be willing to use it."

"How much force?"

"That is for you to decide. But the break must be clean and complete. Brother Jarrah must have no possible path back to her. Do you understand what I am saying? It must be an act of permanence."

Mahmoud was unable to come up with suitable words for an answer, so he again nodded. Amir squeezed his shoulder and nodded back, sealing the bargain.

32

Ken Donlan stood in the dark and rubbed his hands against the chill of the empty apartment. A light came on in a window across the street, at Marienstrasse 54. He'd been watching the place for a few hours, and his knees were aching, but at least he had already seen a few things worth noting. A little earlier, the college boy had turned up on the doorstep, followed by the fat fuck Haydar Zammar. Now someone was looking out one of the windows, and he was pretty sure it was the guy called Mahmoud.

Donlan sipped cold coffee, which had become his default beverage in Hamburg. A second guy was also in the room now, but standing too far from the window for Donlan to make an ID. College boy, maybe? Their movements looked free and easy, like they were buddies.

Donlan groaned and flexed his legs. For a few D-marks he could buy a folding chair. He should also stock the refrigerator with a few snacks, some bottled water. Get a coffeemaker, maybe even a cot with a blanket so he could sleep here when necessary. Sheehan would blow a fuse when the bill arrived for his share of all this, but, hey, in for a penny and all that. And if Alec station complained? Well, fuck them for freezing him out.

So far Donlan had counted ten different young men of probable African or Middle Eastern origin coming and going from number 54, and he had snapped a photo of each of them through his long lens. This was the perfect vantage point, far better than having to hang around out in the open, outside the mosque.

Finding the vacant apartment had been a stroke of luck. After watching Mahmoud enter Marienstrasse 54, he had spotted a "Zu Vermieten" sign—"For Rent"—in the window of an apartment across the street during his subsequent reconnaissance of the neighborhood.

He'd gone back to the address first thing this morning and had seen someone inside, tidying up. The sign was still in place. He pressed the buzzer for entry, and an older gentleman in baggy pants buzzed him in.

"Speak any English?" Donlan had asked.

"Yes," the man said, eyeing him warily.

Donlan told him that his wife was German, and that their son would soon be arriving to study engineering at the technical university. He said he was scouting out possible apartments for their son, who needed a place big enough to also accommodate his parents when they came over for visits. Could he have a look?

The guy showed him around, and in stilted English he described the terms of the lease and the rules of the building. Donlan offered to pay a month's rent to hold the place until his son could see it, maybe in a week or two. The landlord frowned and asked for two months, saying it would all be credited going forward as long as his son took the place. Donlan knew that once he spent the money, the Bureau—or Alec, or whoever ended up footing this extravagant bill—would never get it back, and that it would go into the books as a strike against him. So he hemmed and hawed for a while, trying to negotiate, but the guy in baggy pants wouldn't budge. Donlan, still motivated by his anger, swallowed hard and said okay.

They went to the landlord's office to sign some papers, and Donlan had wound up back here with a key and a fresh cup of coffee just in time to see Mahmoud and the wiry Omar returning from a neighborhood errand, carrying a couple of bags of groceries. And now he was standing in the dark, watching as Mahmoud lowered the blinds on the window.

He checked his watch. Just after 11 p.m. Probably a good time to head back to the hotel. Tomorrow he would start even earlier, and maybe follow a few of them as they left the house. Start assembling a profile of who lived there, what their habits were, who came to visit them, and so on. With Mahmoud and the college boy coming in for extra attention, of course, because the whole issue of his photo still stuck in his craw.

The long ride on the S-Bahn crossed a lot of desolate ground—salt marshes, the fringes of Hamburg's port, an industrialized heath. Gantry cranes and container ships loomed up in the darkness, lit like rides in an amusement park. Donlan felt the chill of the glittering water below as they crossed rivers and tidal streams. He sank his hands into his pockets and hugged himself for warmth.

Heat began blowing from a floor vent, and he finally began to relax. It was a relief to let his guard down after so many hours of watchfulness, and he soon grew drowsy. He nodded off, nearly missed his stop, and then flagged down a cab for the final leg to his hotel just before midnight. Maybe tomorrow he'd drive the rental VW to Harburg and park it a few blocks away.

He overtipped the driver, feeling expansive now that he'd decided to blow open his budget. Plus, he was worn out, and an earlier takeout dinner of currywurst and fries had left him feeling bloated and gassy. All of which helped explain why his guard was down as he unlocked the door of his darkened room. Otherwise he might have noticed the crouching figure lurking behind the half-open bathroom door.

Instead he turned on the overhead light, headed farther into the room, and sprawled heedlessly onto the bed. With a groan of satisfaction he rolled onto his back, kicked off his shoes, and stared up at the ceiling with his hands behind his head. He slipped his feet under a folded duvet for extra warmth. Maybe he'd sleep for a while without bothering to get undressed. He was that damn tired. There was a switch for the light by the bed, so he reached over and flipped it off. Sweet darkness. He immediately began to drift off, lulled by the muffled drone of traffic from the streets below.

An odd noise caught his attention, like that of a door moving on its hinges, followed by the scuff of a shoe on the carpet. He jolted to attention, although he remained flat on his back.

"Who's there?"

There was a rush of movement in the shadows at the foot of the bed. The worst part was that he couldn't have been more vulnerable, and there was no weapon within reach—not even a pencil or the TV remote—and with his feet under the banket, even kicking wasn't an option.

Then the light came on, and in a blinding flash he saw that it was hopeless: game over.

33

Mahmoud's phone buzzed him awake shortly after midnight. He extricated himself from a tangle of sheets to shut it off before it disturbed his roommates, and then he checked the incoming number. Esma. At this hour, it had to be important, maybe even an emergency, but it was too risky to answer here, so he shut it down and considered his options.

Jarrah had stayed over at the House of the Followers, so she wasn't in danger from him. Had Amir changed his mind and decided to handle things himself? He put his feet on the floor, trying not to wake the others. Then he dressed quietly and stepped into the hall. The common room was dark and empty. Even Omar had gone to bed by now, but a light was showing in the crack beneath Amir's door, and for a moment he considered heading back to bed.

Contact with Esma meant trouble, maybe for both of them, especially after Amir had made his wishes known—"an act of permanence," he'd said. Mahmoud wouldn't let himself dwell on what that might mean.

But Amir had also wanted him and Esma to be in touch. It was the only way he'd be able to handle this "problem," as he had promised to do. He steadied himself and crept down the hallway, a burglar wondering how he'd explain himself if Amir's door were to fly open. A cough issued from inside as he passed, and it froze him for a few seconds. Then he exhaled and continued. The dead-bolt lock on the main door clicked as he slid it open. He double-checked his pocket for his key and then he eased into the stairwell, where he began to breathe easier

as he put on his shoes. Nine other pairs were on the landing—quite a
sight for the building's other tenants, no doubt.

It was chilly out on the street, and he wished he'd thought to grab a
sweater. He stepped onto the cobbles and looked back up at the house.
The only light came from Amir's room, but the blinds were drawn.
He walked uphill, quickening the pace to keep warm, and turned at
the first corner to take himself out of sight before heading toward the
park. Once he reached it, he punched in Esma's number. Her voice
was breathless with relief.

"I'm so glad you called back. There's something I have to show you,
before it's too late."

"Tonight?"

"If you can."

He didn't have his wallet or his transit pass, and he'd be taking a
huge risk by reentering the house to retrieve them. And given how
long it would take to reach Esma on the north side of Hamburg, the
S-Bahn wouldn't be running by the time he needed to return, meaning
he wouldn't make it back in time for predawn ablutions and prayers,
where his absence would be noted.

"I can't. But I can get there tomorrow, if that's okay."

"All right. It's just that I'm so upset. These things that I've found.
Ziad's things."

"I thought he moved everything out?"

"He left a few items, in a box he set aside for his family. You'll see.
But don't wait any longer than you have to. I think he's leaving town
soon."

"He is. This Sunday morning."

She gasped. Maybe he shouldn't have told her.

"Then tomorrow, for sure. There's so little time. You have to help
me. He will no longer listen to me, but maybe he'll listen to you."

"I'll come in the evening. Holunderweg, right?"

"Yes, number 9. But can't you come sooner?"

"I can't. Too many obligations."

"At the mosque?"

He paused.

"Yes."

"Maybe you're not the right person, then. Maybe no one is."

"I'll come. I'll try to help."

Help how? Without knowing what she had discovered, how could he know what she would want him to do? But he needed to see her, partly so he could tell Amir that he had taken care of matters, partly for his own reasons, his own needs—an admission that made him blush.

"You promise?"

"Yes, I promise."

Meaning that he had now pledged to help both of them, Amir and Esma, goals that were inherently incompatible. God must be laughing at him.

"Tomorrow evening, then. As early as you can." Her voice again breathless, which sent a thrill through him. His hands and feet were frigid, but he was warm at his core.

He walked back to Marienstrasse. If he were caught now, he'd simply say he hadn't been able to sleep. Surely Amir would understand that, given the gravity of his marching orders.

But by the time he reached the house, all of the lights were out, so he relaxed. A glance up and down the block showed no sign of anyone. He unlocked the downstairs door, climbed to their floor, left his shoes on the landing, and crept back into bed, where he dreamed troubled dreams of Esma.

34

Claire knew better than to gloat as she stood at the foot of the bed, towering over a prone and obviously startled Ken Donlan. Professional pride was at stake, and she needed to get him on her side. It helped that they'd met before, although it had been a while. So the first thing she did was confess to having cheated in order to get the drop on him.

"Your own people told me where to find you. A hotel maid did the rest."

Donlan exhaled loudly and blinked into the light.

"Shit, Claire. Did you have to scare the bejeezus out of me like that?"

"Sorry. I was betting you'd come into the bathroom first, so that's where I was waiting."

"With the lights out."

"Well, I couldn't very well just wait for you downstairs, where someone might see us. I guess I was hoping to make an impression."

"Mission accomplished."

He raised himself into a sitting position and shook his head like a wet dog, as if to convince himself he was still among the living.

"And if by 'my own people' you mean the guys at Alec, we haven't exactly been pals lately. Tell me, does this have anything to do with that goddamn photo I took the other day?"

"Good guess."

"Meaning Alec sent you?"

"No one sent me. This is way off the books, for my sake as much as yours."

He frowned, more confused than ever.

"Do me a favor, will ya? Reach into that mini-fridge and grab me a brew. Get something for yourself while you're at it."

They had met a little more than three years ago, at an interagency cookout at the FBI training center in Quantico. The get-together had been Mike Sheehan's idea. Big Mike had invited counterterrorism employees from both agencies in hopes of promoting a spirit of cooperation and goodwill. Claire was included because she'd just completed a surveillance op on a suspected terror cell in a suburb of Paris. It was a pleasant afternoon of burgers and beer. They even got to use the FBI shooting range, a bonus for Claire, who was qualified as a markswoman with both a Smith & Wesson .38 revolver and a Colt .45 automatic but almost never got to practice.

Donlan had been trying to meet as many Agency people as possible, because he had just been assigned to Alec station, and he had come across as a pudgy, good-natured digger, eager to please. Claire had been chatting with him when everyone's beepers went off with news of the terrorist bombing of Khobar Towers, a U.S. military housing complex in Saudi Arabia. Everyone had headed straight to work—Bureau people in one direction, Agency people in the other.

She hadn't seen him since, but when Clay gave her Donlan's name as the renter of the Opel, plus his whereabouts and probable mission, thanks to a source at Alec, she had realized right away that they might be able to do business.

She popped the caps off a couple of beers and handed him one. Donlan swung his legs over the side of the bed to the floor, and she sat down beside him as he took a long, recuperative swig. Claire did likewise in solidarity. Less than a week out of Paris and she was drinking like a German.

"You owe me some answers," he said.

"Fair enough. Ask away."

"Are you part of that wacko op of Paul Bridger's, babysitting that egghead who's supposed to end martyrdom for all time?"

She nodded and checked her watch. She had managed to slip away from the Plaza only by telling Tony that she had to do some last-minute location scouting for Tour Day. At this hour, that excuse wouldn't work indefinitely.

"That's us. I'm undercover for security, posing as his wife."

"You guys managed to get anybody else killed yet?"

She lowered her beer and glared at him.

"And here I was feeling sorry for you," she said.

Donlan looked down at his socks.

"Apologies. That was out of line."

"He wasn't one of ours, not that it makes it any better. And this gig with the professor wasn't the only thing Bridger had me working on."

She described her surveillance duties and the locations she'd been covering, plus her repeated sightings of the Opel.

"Yeah, I got sloppy with that. Goddamn Hertz didn't help, either. But here's what I really want to know. What's the big deal with these Al Quds guys?"

"I was hoping you'd be able to tell me. About all of them."

"Well, somebody must fucking know, the way Alec slammed the door in my face."

He told her about the reaction his photo had gotten.

"Above your clearance? They really said that?"

"And I've been there three years now, since we first met at Quantico."

She told him how the photo had derailed her assignment as well, although not before she'd at least heard Mahmoud's last name, Yassin. She also gave him the ID for the college boy, Ziad Jarrah, and told him about the young woman, Esma Demir. But that was about all she had for him, and they ended up shaking their heads at what it all might mean.

It only confirmed her suspicion that something bigger was at work, at a depth she hadn't yet plumbed before Bridger had angrily yanked her to the surface—to his own disadvantage, she suspected, which was one reason she was taking this risk. Or that was her justification anyway—that this kind of insubordination was okay because it was for the good of the aborted op. Which reminded her of one of the reasons she'd come here.

"Now I've got a question for you," she said.

She stood and got her bag, pulled out her laptop, and plopped back down. Donlan watched over her shoulder as the screen came to life. She clicked on the photo she had taken in Paris of the man with the mole on his cheek, the fellow she had already seen calling the shots here with Bridger's minders, and then turned the screen in Donlan's direction.

"Any idea who this is?"

"Ho-lee shit. Did you shoot this?"

"Yes."

"When and where?"

"Last week in Paris, but he's here now. The power behind the throne on this entire boondoggle, far as I can tell. I take it you know him."

"Mark fucking Wharton."

It took a second for the name to click.

"The guy who used to run Alec?"

"Yeah. My boss until a year ago, after that shit show of the bombings in Nairobi and Dar es Salaam got him canned. None of that was his fault, but he was the man in charge, so . . ."

"How come I didn't meet him that day at Quantico?"

"Because he didn't come. An intentional snub, and my Bureau boss, Mike Sheehan, didn't mind a bit."

"They're not exactly friends?"

"Let's just say that bin Laden is probably the one guy they both hate more than each other. And even that might be a stretch."

"Ego?"

"That's part of it. The rest? Well, you know the deal."

She did indeed. An interagency rivalry had existed since the CIA's birth, in 1947, when a petulant J. Edgar Hoover ordered FBI agents in Latin America to destroy their files rather than turn them over to the nation's newest practitioner of foreign intelligence. Now each side had its own boilerplate excuse for not sharing intelligence. The Agency: *It will jeopardize our sources and methods.* The Bureau: *It will jeopardize any prosecution.*

"Big Mike *still* bitches and moans about the time Wharton wanted to get bin Laden by calling in a missile strike on a bird-hunting party in Kandahar, which would've wiped out half the royal family from the Emirates."

"Didn't you guys come up with something equally stupid?"

"Damn right, and I wasted two weeks training for it. We rigged up a C-130 with a dentist chair in the cargo hold, figuring we'd swoop into the Afghan hills, snatch up bin Laden, and strap him down so I could interrogate him all the way back to some secret landing strip near El Paso. But Wharton's *here*? And fully employed? Last I heard, he'd been exiled to some reading room in Langley. Everyone had written him off as a burnout."

"Maybe this is his comeback tour."

"No wonder my photo set off such a shit storm. He's still got lots of friends at Alec. Somebody must have shown it to him."

"And then he took it to Bridger. But why? There's nothing in it. Or nothing but a bunch of guys we already knew about."

"Except the Mahmoud guy, and the frat boy in the sweater. Ziad Jarrah, you said?"

"Yeah, and he does sort of stick out like a sore thumb."

"Yet another reason I don't like the smug fuck. I don't get any of this, unless Wharton just got pissed off by the whole idea of someone poking around with the jihadis while his little op was in progress across the Alster."

"That would certainly explain why Bridger dropped the hammer on me," Claire said. "Self-defense, or maybe just cutting his losses to keep the boss happy. But is Wharton really that petty?"

"Didn't used to be, except when Big Mike was involved. Speaking of whom . . ."

"You're not going to tell him, I hope?"

Donlan sighed.

"Not if I can help it. But his last request before he took me to LaGuardia was to let him know the second I got wind of any involvement by his old friend Mark fucking Wharton. Like that was even a remote possibility at the time. How the fuck he even knew to ask is, well, kinda creepy. But there you are."

"Yes, but—"

"I know. Rough seas already, so why stir 'em up more? But I just dropped a bundle setting up a surveillance down in Harburg, and if he gets wind of that before I come up with any results, well . . . a little name-dropping might be the only way I can stay in the game. Unless you've got some ideas on picking up the slack."

"I came here hoping *you* could pick up the slack. Unless Bridger—or Wharton—changes his mind, they're sending me out of here on Saturday for more of this dog and pony show. But it's this surveillance op, slim as it is, that feels like something bigger. I'm convinced there's something hidden down at the next level that we're not seeing yet, and we need to find out what it is."

"Even if Alec already knows?"

"I guess that's possible. But I'm doubting it, or Bridger wouldn't have had me poking around. And for now, you're our only eyes and ears."

He shook his head.

"I doubt I'm good for more than another week, unless I can come up with something big. Less, if someone from accounting blows the whistle. I'm spending money out the wazoo."

Donlan told her about the apartment he'd just rented on Marienstrasse, down in Harburg. Claire was encouraged and impressed. But she also saw the danger.

"No wonder you're sweating the bean counters."

"Yeah. Two months' rent, paid in advance. But it's the perfect setup, a picture window on every coming and going from their happy little home."

"Stay in touch, then, and I'll do the same."

They exchanged phone numbers and a few other details. Claire packed away her laptop.

"Oh, and next time? Try not to scare me halfway to Berlin and back. Just wait in a chair with the lights on."

She smiled, tossed her empty beer bottle into the trash, and set out for the Plaza.

FRIDAY, OCTOBER 8

35

Helen Abell was literally up with the chickens, mostly because they were the first item that needed attention this morning—sixty thousand of them, clucking and fretting and pecking in two long houses.

One of the ventilation fans was sounding creaky, and the level of grain in the feed silo was a little too low for comfort. The water lines weren't leaking, but that was always subject to change.

Helen hated the damn chickens—their smell, their shuffling stupidity, the idiotic way they'd been bioengineered to be as top-heavy as strippers, and the whole idea that every few months you sent them all away to be killed, only to replace them with yet another batch of victims. But her husband was tending to the fields this morning, where the soybeans had been harvested and the winter wheat was just beginning to sprout, so if she didn't do this, then no one would. Plus, she was feeling more than a little guilty after having spent the previous two days away from the farm, on a jaunt to Western Pennsylvania, where she had enjoyed herself far more than she'd ever be able to admit.

Her family believed she had been in Georgia to see an ailing aunt. She had given them a number for a cell phone with a Valdosta area code, a phone that Claire had provided via FedEx delivery to an office supply store in Uniontown, Pennsylvania, along with a packet of all sorts of other helpful items sent via someone named Clay in Paris. She had used the aunt's name years ago for cover on a similar errand, and it had worked smoothly on both occasions. Her husband was trusting and incurious, partly because, apart from these visits to her "aunt," Helen had never given him any reason to be otherwise. She had never told her family about her brief long-ago career with the Agency, and she never planned to. This was partly because she never wanted to have to explain what had happened then, and partly because some of the secrets she had acquired back then remained potent, even dangerous. Being a spy was a little bit like exposing yourself to radiation, and she didn't want to poison her family with any of her forbidden knowledge.

Was she ashamed of this deception? Not really. No infidelity was involved, and she was now making up for her absence with a penance of additional chores. Besides, she was giddy with satisfaction, because she was pretty certain she had gained what her long-ago bosses at the Agency would have called "a result," and that knowledge kept her going as she made her morning rounds, with one eye on the clock.

It was 6:30 a.m., meaning that Claire would already be deep into her workday in Europe. Helen would have phoned her when she'd finished up in Pennsylvania, but by then it had been 8 p.m.—2 a.m. in Europe.

She had also needed to drive back down to Maryland in order to return the rental car to the Baltimore airport and retrieve her own car from the long-term parking lot for the ride across the Bay Bridge back to the Eastern Shore, and she hadn't gotten home until around midnight. Her plan this morning was to wait until her husband was out in the fields and her daughter, Anna, had caught the bus to school. Her son, Willard, would still be in the house, but anything she said in his presence would go in one ear and out the other, poor boy, so she had no need to seek privacy on his account.

Upon rising this morning, she had peeked hurriedly at her notes while the coffee brewed. They were folded deep within her purse, along with the secret phone. After reporting in, she would use the old ways to get rid of the papers, burning them and then flushing the ashes down the toilet. Maybe the manure pile would be a good final resting place for the phone, once she had removed and destroyed the SIM card.

Thinking of the notes made her giddy again, even though her work had involved a close brush with a campus cop at Wightman U., where she had gotten out of town in the nick of time. She'd then had another near miss with the feds up in that remote part of the state, where, posing as a newspaper reporter, she had talked to a pleasant old fellow in a sheriff's office. He'd obviously opened up to her largely out of boredom. Most of the time he probably had nothing better to do than run down leads on missing hikers and runaway livestock. Thanks to her farm experience, she had known exactly what to say to get him talking, to the point that he had eventually felt compelled to check in about her with "one of those fellas down in Washington who came up here about all this."

"Those fellas" had apparently not been pleased to hear about her, so she had promised to wait for their arrival at a little café around the corner. And now she was here instead, with the car returned and her day-old fake ID melted in a trash can at a rest stop on the Pennsylvania Turnpike.

Helen checked the kitchen clock as she came back into the house. The stench of the chickens clung to her like steam from a long shower. Everyone would want breakfast soon, but because the shopping had gone untended these past few days, she would have to make do with four eggs for the three of them, with only cold cereal for herself. Just as well for her waistline. Farm life, with its high-carb diet and all those hours on your feet, eventually turned every woman into a Russian peasant, with sturdy calves and the shapeliness of a matryoshka doll.

She again checked the clock. Fifty more minutes. She hadn't been this excited about, well, pretty much anything in quite a while. In many ways she envied her old friend Claire—Hamburg this week, who knows where the next, with Paris always waiting at the end of the rainbow. But Helen also knew there was never anyone to greet her when she got home. Reading between the lines of their annual exchange of holiday cards always made her suspect that Claire had left behind something along the way, something valuable that she wished she had held on to.

Helen opened the fridge and got out the eggs and bacon, but the smell of the chickens was still so strong that she decided to dash down the hall for a quick change of clothes. Yes, a brioche and an espresso would definitely taste much better right now than anything here.

She threw open her closet and glanced at the digital clock on the bedside table.

Forty-six minutes and counting.

36

The first major finding of Tour Day was that Claire and Armitage were not compatible as fellow tourists. So far they'd been going to all of the kitschy stops that he loved and she hated.

The second was that not a single member of the media had shown up to cover it, although Tony had helpfully distributed their itinerary to TV, newspapers, and a couple of free weeklies. Even the demonstrators were no-shows. Apparently they hadn't been resourceful enough to ferret out the information. Or maybe now, with the conference over, they simply no longer cared.

There were plenty of police and plainclothes security people in evidence, however, moving among the crowds to scout out entrances and exits and to check possible vantage points for snipers or car bombers. Claire easily spotted these reinforcements by looking for anyone who appeared to be talking into their sleeves or their ties. Had there been any actual press attention, it would have felt like being part of a presidential visit.

"So glad we were ordered to arrange this," Claire muttered to Tony.

"Things should pick up in Rome."

"Oh, absolutely. Maybe the professor can wear a centurion's uniform and peddle his book by the Colosseum. *Veni, vidi, vici.*"

On the touristy part of the waterfront, where centuries of industry were inevitably giving way to retail, restaurants, and high-end housing, the joints of the long docks had whined and groaned like an orchestra tuning up. Moored among the many pleasure boats was a barge tricked out to look like a Mississippi steamboat. Dozens of ticket holders were eagerly lining up to go aboard, which Claire thought was about as stupid as paying to see an oompah band in New Orleans.

A nearby guide, noting her interest, perked up and said, "Mark Twain, ja?"

"Ja. The innocents abroad, that's us."

"Can we ride it?" Armitage asked.

"No."

For once, she was glad they were on a strict schedule, and for the umpteenth time that morning she wondered how many more days of this she would have to endure.

They then paid to take an elevator to the top of the bell tower of St. Michael's Church, for a panoramic view of the city through a cloak of mist that tasted vaguely like the sea. They stood at the rear of a knot of visitors to wait for the elevator back down, everyone anxious with the knowledge that there would be room for only about half of them. The elbowing began even before the door opened. When Armitage hesitated, Claire took his arm and steered him into the heart of the throng, and they squeezed aboard.

"You're good at this," he said, sounding a little appalled.

"I'm impatient," she said. "And, yes, I'm very good at that."

Now they were in the gift shop of the chocolate museum, and as Armitage piled some goodies into a shining bag, she couldn't help but think of Lute and that photo of his smiling boys, who would never get their treats from Germany. She considered having a box shipped to them but decided against it. It would probably only make them sad.

"How 'bout these?" Armitage asked. "What kind of flavor is *haselnuss*?"

"Hazelnut."

"Oh." He frowned and put them back. "The next tour's in ten minutes. Think they'll mind if I take some merchandise along?"

"As long as you pay before you start eating it."

"Ha! Good one."

Poor Lute.

Her phone buzzed in her purse. She walked toward a corner to answer.

It was Helen. She heard a sudden blast of noise in the background, a television blaring brassy music.

"Oh, God. Sorry, Claire. My son just put in a tape for his thousandth viewing of *Star Wars*. I'll have to go out to the barn. Hold on a second."

The noise of the trumpets receded, followed by the shutting of a door and then the creak and rumble of what must have been a big gate.

"There. Much better."

"You have a barn?"

"Of course we have a barn. It's a farm."

"Well, okay."

"And don't sound so damn smug about it."

Claire laughed, realizing that she needed it. The two of them really should find a way to see each other again. Soon enough they would all be dead and in the grave, with their secrets and their stories, and she doubtless had some catching up to do. Even if Helen had come up empty, this call would tide her over for the next several days. Eat well, live well, and roll with another punch. Maybe she would write a long letter to Helen from Rome and try to really get caught up on things. Or as much as the rules of security allowed.

"Tell me what you've got, then. Even if it's nothing."

"I think it might actually be something. Maybe a lot of something. That photo you sent? The guy from the university?"

"Yes?"

"I discreetly showed it around, like you wanted. His neighbors, people on campus. Nobody recognized him. Not a soul. Even the secretaries in his department. When I dropped the name, Armitage, well, then everything changed almost immediately. They all started chattering about his book, and what a star he'd become, and how nice and humble he was, and some of them wondered if he'd ever be coming back, now that he was so famous. But it was quite obvious that this fellow in the photo had nothing to do with any of that."

"And you say the neighbors didn't recognize it, either?"

"No. And one of them had her *own* photo. From a cookout a few years ago. Kind of fuzzy, and hair sort of like the fellow in yours. But this guy was in tennis shorts, and really in shape, and they said he liked to get up into the hills, to hike and camp."

Claire looked across the room at Armitage—or at the man calling himself Armitage—while she listened. He was still poking around among the boxes of chocolate, as pale and puffy as an uncooked merengue. Outdoorsy? Not a chance.

"Did you make it to the Laurel Highlands?"

"Right at the end of the day. Apparently I got out of Wightman just before the campus police descended on the department, after one of the secretaries must have called. Their car was parked out front when I drove by on the way out of town. Fortunately, they only seemed to have one car."

Helen had presented press credentials when she got to the Highlands, telling them she was a reporter up from Baltimore on a story that was very hush-hush.

"I asked about that news account you sent me, and said everything would of course be off the record. And this one bored little sheriff finally gave me what I needed. He told me about the body—he said another hiker had found him—and he said his people never did get an ID, or not before a bunch of feds in black cars swarmed in, even before the county medical examiner could have a look. That's why your little newspaper story was so short and so vague. All the sheriff ever heard for sure was that the victim was a white male, middle fifties. Plus the cause of death."

"Which was?"

"Hit in the chest by an arrow, probably a bolt from a crossbow. A hunting accident, or that's what the feds told them."

"Sure, because the feds always get involved on those."

"Exactly, but he still didn't want to say much more. It was like someone had put the fear of God in him. And when I kept asking questions, he mumbled something about a nondisclosure agreement and said he didn't want to lose his pension. As I was driving away, I passed two incoming Suburbans doing over seventy, about five miles out of town. Fortunately, I'd parked a few blocks from his office, so no one had gotten a look at my car."

Across the room, the fake Professor Armitage held high a jumbo bag of chocolates, motioned toward the register, and then pointed to his watch. Claire nodded back and gave him a wide, genuine smile, which seemed to please him.

"Helen, this is wonderful. I mean, not wonderful, obviously, but it's exactly what I needed."

"Well, good, because there's one more thing."

"Yes?"

Claire heard a shuffle of papers as Helen moved the phone to her other ear.

"Don't worry, I'll burn all these notes as soon as I hang up. Ah. Here it is. Look, I know this wasn't part of my assignment, and I may have, well, overstepped things a little. But once I realized this guy in the photo wasn't a match with the name, I took the liberty of, well, getting in touch with an old colleague of ours. Our friend in archives?"

"Oh, my. Okay."

Claire wasn't sure that was wise, but she probably would've done the same. They had always been alike in that way, pushing the boundaries of every assignment. And the archivist had been one of their illicit allies, even though she was a good bit older than them.

"I thought she'd be retired by now."

"Not for a few years yet, she said. She was a little frosty at first, but she agreed to take a look when I told her it was for you. Hope that was okay."

It wasn't, but it was too late to object now, and Helen had done such fine work otherwise that Claire wouldn't have had the heart to say so.

"Just this time."

"Hmm. You don't sound so sure. Sorry, I'm very rusty. Anyway, she ran the image through a few scans and almost immediately came up with a match. From human resources."

"*Our* human resources?"

"Well, yours, anyway. An analyst, based in Langley. Want his name and all the rest?"

Of course she did, even more than Armitage wanted his chocolate. So Helen told her, and Claire filed it away. The ammunition she had now was more than sufficient for what she needed to do next.

"You did ask her to keep this quiet, yes?"

"Of course, and she seemed oddly happy to do so."

"Thank you. Thank you so much. You've succeeded beyond my wildest hopes, but I suppose I should have expected nothing less."

"A stroke of luck, really."

"Luck is the residue of design. Some baseball guy said that once. And you just made my day. My whole week, in fact."

"And you made mine by saying so. Now I'll have the strength to face all those smelly chickens for the rest of the week."

"Love and kisses to your children."

"If they don't kill me first. Put this to good use in your glamorous life."

"In which I'm about to tour a kitschy museum with a dumpy analyst who's been duping me for days. I'll let you guess his name."

Helen was still laughing when they hung up.

Claire crossed the room toward the register, where the fake professor had just completed his transaction.

"Well, you certainly look happy, wifey. Oops. Didn't mean to use that word."

"No problem at all, as long as you don't mind if I call you Mr. Weeks. Do you go by Warren, or is there some nickname I'm unaware of?"

His smile disappeared and he set down his bag of chocolates on the counter, as if they'd suddenly become too heavy for him to carry. His eyes went very wide, and in the space of a few seconds he transformed back into the timid man who had fearfully gazed out the hotel window while asking why she and Tony had just said something about snipers.

Then he sighed.

"Does this mean we're not going to Rome?"

"You'll probably still be going. I can't imagine Mark Wharton will want to let this operation come to an end just because I've discovered it's a fraud and a con job. But I won't be accompanying you, so you're half right."

She shouted across the room.

"Tony?"

Tony scurried over.

"I hate to do this to you, but I've got work to do."

"Work?"

"Elsewhere. Because I'm done here."

"Done? What do you mean, done?"

"With this whole business. Him. The tour. Because I'm betting that you knew, too. About Warren, I mean. Warren Weeks, analyst for Central American affairs."

Tony and Warren exchanged looks, two guilty parties if ever she'd seen them.

"Yes, I thought so."

"You know how it goes sometimes," Tony said, lowering his voice. "With 'need to know' and all that.'"

"I do. Except this time I was apparently the only one not to know. So I'm done."

"Claire, really. You can't be *that* angry, can you? It's the business we're in."

He had a good point, of course, even if cutting her out of the loop had been, at the very least, an insult to her ability to play along with the illusion. You could also question the ethics of fooling the entire world of Islamic scholarship, although that wasn't part of her job description.

But in order to justify what Claire was about to do, she needed to at least *appear* to be as angrily indignant as possible, and Helen's findings had given her the necessary pretext. Wharton would no doubt call it an overreaction by an overly emotional female, but if that helped sell her act, then she might as well use it to her advantage.

So she handed Tony the folder of promotional materials with their schedule for the rest of the week.

"Please give this to whomever they choose to replace me."

"But you can't be replaced," Warren said. "You're my *wife*."

"Then I guess this is our divorce."

And with that she left.

37

By late afternoon, Mahmoud had worked himself into a state of high agitation. By most measures, he was exactly where he wanted to be— on the threshold of life-changing adventure, a foreign journey, an unknown mission of high importance. Yet the very sorts of secular worries that had derailed his previous life were now threatening to interfere. How could he possibly fulfill Esma's wishes while also doing Amir's bidding? Sever her ties to Jarrah, yet reassure her about Jarrah's future. It didn't seem possible, and to even try might put her in danger and threaten his own prospects, his own mission.

In the meantime, there were still errands to run in preparation for Saeed's wedding. The man who was roasting the lambs had to be paid and assured of transportation on Saturday. Other contributors—of rice dishes, vegetables, pastries, and beverages—had to be tended to as well. Several of them had earlier swept and cleaned the room where the celebrants would gather—separated by gender, of course, divided by a screen running down the middle.

Mahmoud helped arrange for transportation of the groom's family, which proved to be a little tricky, partly because Saeed's mother, a German, was not all that keen on the direction her son's life had taken in recent years. They would attend, but it seemed unlikely they would fit in very well with the Al Quds regulars.

Mahmoud then accompanied several others in a rented truck to haul gifts of food and furniture to the couple's new apartment, where the bride would be moving in on Saturday night. He was assembling a set of Ikea bookshelves in the dining room with a screwdriver and an Allen wrench when Amir filled the doorway and eyed him with a questioning gaze.

"It is good to see you so busy on Saeed's behalf, Brother Mahmoud, but don't you have other, more important duties to attend to?"

Two other young men who were setting up a dining room table stopped what they were doing to watch the exchange, with obvious curiosity about what other task Amir could be referring to. Mahmoud put down the screwdriver and stood, brushing himself off.

"Yes. I suppose I do."

"Have you decided upon a course of action?"

"I have. It will depend upon the circumstances that I find when I arrive."

"You will do nothing in a way that will arouse the interest of the authorities, I hope."

"Of course."

Did this mean Amir had backed down from his initial demand, or was he only exhorting Mahmoud to act with great care? Or maybe by "an act of permanence" he was only hoping that Esma would be gone from Hamburg by day's end—even if only by plane or train. Mahmoud decided to interpret the comment that way, and it immediately eased his mind.

"Very well." Amir then gestured toward the bookshelves. "Please, leave the rest of that job to someone else. You must act soon, for the good of us all."

Mahmoud nodded, and Amir departed. The two other men looked up at Mahmoud with an unmistakable air of newfound respect, even envy. To them it seemed apparent that he had been entrusted with important work, and Mahmoud supposed that was true, even if he still wasn't yet certain if he would succeed. On his way out, he stopped in the bathroom, where he hastily washed up and tried to comb his hair with his fingers.

The mirror showed a flushed face, creased with worry, so he blinked and tried to relax. God willing, he would handle this in a way that would allow both parties to come away with some satisfaction. His phone buzzed in his pocket, and when he took it out he saw a text from Esma.

Are you still coming?

He pecked in a reply on the awkward keypad. In the excitement of anticipation, he moved his fingers so clumsily that he had to halt several times to clean up mistakes.

On my way now.

38

Ken Donlan headed for his hotel as darkness closed in, feeling gloomily as though he'd already let down the team—meaning him and Claire. Their meeting the night before had energized him, and her news of the Agency's recent machinations in Hamburg had convinced him that, as she believed, something was afoot at some deeper level.

But for all his good intentions and heightened energy, a day that had begun with promising results had pretty much turned into a disaster.

He had set up shop on Marienstrasse at 6 a.m. This time he'd put his coffee in a thermos so it wouldn't go cold, and he'd bought a bag of sugared pastries from a *bäckerei* around the corner. The weather had turned chilly and gray, but the furnace seemed to be working fine. Another expense, he supposed. He screwed in the long lens of his camera, got out his notebook, wrote down the time, and began watching.

Almost immediately, young men in Middle Eastern attire began to come and go from the apartment building across the street. He scribbled notes and took photo after photo. At 9:31 a.m., Mahmoud and the college boy, Jarrah, left the house together, and he set off after them. Their destination was a butcher shop, where he watched them speak to a man in a bloody apron who gesticulated as he talked. They strolled into the back of the shop and disappeared into a meat locker. When they emerged a few minutes later, Mahmoud paid with some money from his wallet, and then they left.

On their way back to Marienstrasse, the duo made two more stops. The first was at a caterer, where they handed over another payment.

That plus the payment to the butcher seemed to indicate that some sort of big event was in the works, maybe a party, even though these Al Quds guys didn't exactly strike him as party animals. The other stop was at the home of a family that, as best he could determine, seemed to be your typical upper-middle-class German burghers. He got a glance at the lady of the house as she bade them farewell at the front door, and he noted with interest her stiff body language. To say that she seemed distant toward the two young men would have been an understatement, although she did not appear to be rude or angry.

Donlan snapped more photos and wrote it all down, complete with addresses for each stop. Not much to get excited about, he supposed, but you never knew when some seemingly random thread might turn out to be important later, so he kept at it.

Then, at around 3 p.m.—or 9 a.m. Manhattan time—Big Mike Sheehan called on his cell phone as Donlan was eating a late lunch of bratwurst and fries.

"Hi, Kenny. I'm guessing you know exactly why I'm calling."

"Does this have anything to do with money?"

"You're goddamn right it does. I just got off the phone with accounting. They've flagged a cash advance for something you describe as *rent*?"

"That's right."

"Mother of God, Kenny, are you keeping a mistress over there?"

"It's for surveillance."

"Of what? Bin Laden's love nest? Anything less and you're way over budget."

Donlan spelled it out for him, step by step, beginning with how he'd first tailed the guys to an outdoor cookout at Haydar Zammar's garden house. Sheehan didn't interrupt until Donlan described how the guys at Alec had frozen him out on providing IDs for the lesser figures in his photo.

"*Above your clearance?* They actually said that?"

"Exact words."

"Jesus. Is one of these guys bin Laden's nephew or something?"

"No idea. My first instinct was that these guys were probably no big deal. But now I'm more curious than ever, because why else would Alec hold out on me?"

"Hell, Kenny, I don't really have to tell you that, do I? They're stiffing you because they can. And if you press them—even if *I* press them—they'll give us the same stupid song and dance they always do. 'Sources and methods.' So I can see why you're pissed. Hell, *I'm* pissed just hearing about it."

Big Mike paused then, as if to digest it all from a few thousand miles away, and for a moment Donlan felt like he was on the verge of carrying the point.

"Even so, Kenny." Or maybe not. "As bad as that is—and it's fucking inexcusable—it's no grounds for spending money like a drunken sailor, not unless you've got something more solid than a hunch."

"I think I'll have a better idea of that in a day or two."

"No, no. You need to see about getting out of that lease, and right away. 'Cause I'm sure as hell not having it in our books, and I'm betting Alec won't want it in theirs."

So, in desperation, Donlan fired the one missile he had hoped he wouldn't have to deploy, the one missile that Claire had explicitly asked him to keep in the silo.

"Yeah, but Mike, there's more."

"Then let's have it."

"The Agency guy behind all this—and he's here in Hamburg, running the show—it's, well . . ."

"Mark Wharton?"

Donlan took a deep breath.

"Yes, sir. And that's not just me blowing smoke. I have it firsthand from one of their own people. She's seen him."

"I fucking knew it. From the first second I heard about this screwball op of theirs, it just had that feel to it, right from the beginning. So Wharton has finally rehabbed and come up for air, then. Didn't I tell you?"

"Well, you asked about him, yeah."

"And now he's fucking around with you—one of my people. Because that's got to be why your buddies at Alec won't play ball, don't you think?"

"It could be, I guess, but—"

"No. Has to be. And we can't have that."

"No, sir."

"You stay put, then. I'm still not sure we can leave this in the books, but we'll find some other way. Stay on top of it. Oh, and Kenny?"

"Yes, sir?"

"Send me that photo. Before you do another goddamn thing, I want a copy."

Donlan got a sick feeling, deep in his stomach, and it wasn't from the bratwurst.

"I don't know if that's a good idea, sir, especially if—"

"Who's paying your bills, Kenny?"

"Got it. But, sir?"

"Yeah?"

"It would help if we could keep this quiet, not make any waves. For one thing, I don't want to burn my source on this Wharton thing."

"Of course, Kenny. Anything I do, I'll be discreet about it."

"Or maybe for a day or two you could do nothing."

"Discretion, Kenny. That's the key. You won't notice a thing."

That's what he was afraid of. That no one would notice a thing until the walls started collapsing, due to mysterious tremors from on high. But it was too late now to stop Big Mike.

Telling Claire about it was another matter, especially since he now had a second item of bad news, one involving Mahmoud from just a few minutes ago.

Donlan had resumed surveillance as soon as he got off the phone with Big Mike, and in the late afternoon things had started to get interesting. A rental truck pulled up in front of the Marienstrasse apartment and Mahmoud got in, along with another guy. Images of truck bombings immediately came to mind.

But neither guy who had climbed aboard had looked armed, and they were both acting pretty casual, even a little bored. He decided not to worry unless it looked like the truck was heading for the Plaza Hotel.

Instead, it rolled off toward a drab apartment complex on the city's outskirts, where the driver, Mahmoud, and the other guy got out and began unloading furniture, boxes, and other items. The fellow named Saeed, the one he'd clocked the other day outside the mosque accepting a gift from his pals, came out to meet them, and thanked them profusely. And that's when Donlan figured it out. Shit, they were helping the guy move. They were unloading women's items too, so maybe

Saeed was getting married, a conclusion that also fit with the idea they were preparing for a big party. Had to be. And any wedding among these guys would almost certainly be held at the mosque.

Mahmoud had been in the apartment for at least an hour when Amir came strolling up from the direction of the nearest bus stop to join the others, who were still inside. Ten minutes later, Mahmoud emerged alone, moving quickly and stuffing his phone in his pocket. He looked in both directions, seemingly on full alert, and headed briskly up a sidewalk.

Donlan set off after him, only to lose him half an hour later at a bus transfer terminal. There one minute, gone the next. And, just like before in the U-Bahn station, it felt like Mahmoud had intentionally been trying to lose him.

So here he was now in a taxi, feeling gloomily incompetent and deeply guilty just as his hotel was looming into view. Then his phone rang with a call from Claire.

"Good news," she said. "I'm back on the beat, and if I play this right I should be here for at least a few more days. Only don't say so if anyone else happens to ask."

"Sounds sketchy."

"Very." She laughed, and seemed to be enjoying herself. It was almost enough to make him feel better about his lousy day. "How 'bout things at your end?"

He swallowed his pride and told her—part of it, anyway, including his growing certainty that some sort of big event was in the works, probably a wedding. She reacted in silence to his news about what he'd revealed to Big Mike about Wharton's involvement. Finally she answered with a long sigh, which convinced him—for the moment, at least—to withhold the news about sending the photo to Sheehan.

But she perked up as soon as he told her that Mahmoud had eluded him less than half an hour earlier, which was kind of odd, because he'd expected a scolding.

"Interesting. And you think he lost you intentionally?"

"Oh, yeah. He was being extra careful. He had that look about him. Of all those guys at Al Quds, he's one of the few with any kind of radar. He might be more experienced than we've been thinking."

"Or maybe the others are just used to the attention by now. What was his general heading at the time?"

"Into the city."

"Toward the airport?"

"Maybe. You think he left town?"

"No, but there's an address up that way he might be interested in, and if I'm right, we could be onto something we can use."

"Yeah? How so?"

"I'll let you know. But keep an eye on that house in Harburg, and if he comes back to Marienstrasse I want to know right away."

"Will do."

They hung up as the taxi pulled in front of Donlan's hotel. Instead of getting out, he asked the driver to keep going, this time all the way to Harburg. Then he looked inside his wallet: not nearly enough cash to take him all the way to Harburg.

"Check that," he told the driver. "Just drop me off at the nearest S-Bahn."

His long day was about to get longer.

39

Mahmoud sagged into his seat on the bus, finally underway on the final leg to Holunderweg. Esma had texted him three times in the past half hour to ask what was taking him so long. He had kept his answer to himself: fear and suspicion.

He had been running scared for the past half hour, alarmed by the sudden reappearance of the guy with the Opel—except this time without the car—on the street outside Saeed's apartment.

He still couldn't understand why he was attracting this sort of attention. Of all the people he prayed and ate and lived with, Mahmoud figured he had given the least cause for alarm among the local authorities. Unless, of course, someone had found out he had driven the getaway car to the Plaza Hotel. But if that were the case, why hadn't he simply been arrested and charged, or detained for questioning? Maybe they had grown bored with keeping an eye on his better-known, established friends, and were interested in him precisely because he was a newcomer.

Whatever the case, it freaked him out, so he took his time reaching Esma. He rode the first bus to a nearby transfer terminal and then, as he had the previous time he spotted this big fellow following him, he employed a few of his boyhood ruses from the streets of Morocco. That seemed to do the trick, and he lost the guy among all his comings and goings.

By now he was so skittish that he was wondering whether Amir might also have sent someone after him, to make sure he got the job done with Esma. But the bus was practically empty. All six of the other passengers looked German, and all were dressed for office jobs. They slouched in their seats, wearily headed home at the end of the work-week. One by one they got off before he did, and the new riders who boarded looked every bit as worn out as their predecessors.

A four-block walk from the bus stop took him to the house on Ho-lunderweg, where Esma greeted him at the door.

"There you are!" she said, flushing as she spoke. "I was so worried that something had happened to you."

She touched his arm as she took him inside, just as she had done at Jarrah's apartment, a forbidden thrill that sent a charge of energy straight to his chest.

"Is your friend at home?"

"She's away for the weekend with her family, so I can show you what I found in privacy. It's here, in this box." She gestured toward the couch. "He left it for me to mail to his parents."

"In Beirut?"

"Yes."

He went over for a look. It was a small cardboard box, of the size for packing books. Having already torn off a strip of tape from the top, Esma opened the flaps and pulled out a small booklet with a faux leather cover.

"It's his journal. Don't you think it's significant that he didn't take it with him?"

"Maybe he feels like he has put that part of his life behind him."

"Or maybe he's preparing himself for an ending. But that's not the scary part. You have to see what he's been writing."

She sat on the couch and made room for him to her left. Settling in beside her, Mahmoud smelled the soap on her skin from her shower, the shampoo on her hair. She was about to open the journal when she sighed in apparent exasperation. Thinking it was a reaction to him, he was about to slide farther down the couch when he realized she was upset with herself.

"Look at me. I'm so horrible. I'm like some salesman, getting straight down to business. This won't do."

She put the book aside and stood.

"I'll make tea. Or would you rather have coffee? I can do that, too."

"Tea is fine, but it's not necessary."

"Oh, but it is. You came all this way and I'm acting terribly. My mother would disown me, if she hasn't already. Come on. We can talk in the kitchen."

He was glad for the invitation, not wanting to be apart from her for even a few minutes, now that he had finally reached her. The idea that they were alone in the darkening house was thrilling but a little dangerous. He wondered where Jarrah was, and what he would think of the two of them talking about him behind his back. It made him feel disloyal. Then he remembered what Amir had wanted him to do, which confused him even more.

"What's troubling you?" She took two mugs from a cabinet and switched on an electric kettle.

"I shouldn't be here. Or not for this."

"What do you mean?"

"Don't you think it would be best for everyone if you left Hamburg, at least until Ziad has made up his mind?"

"By then it will be too late. You'll see. That's what I want to show you."

"But . . ."

He faltered. He was weak, a failure.

"What?"

"I am supposed to make you leave. It is one reason I came. I don't think it is safe for you to still be here."

"Did Ziad ask you to do this?"

"No. Brother Amir."

"Amir. The one who never smiles."

"Yes. They tease him about that."

"I'm glad someone is doing some teasing over there." She smiled and got out the sugar and a pair of tea bags. "And how were you supposed to make me leave?"

"He didn't say. That was up to me. Otherwise he was going to send Omar."

Her smile disappeared.

"Omar, the one who laughs so much. Don't be fooled by his smiles. He came right up into my face one day and held a pencil under my chin like it was knife. He was smiling then, too, but his words were not at all nice."

This was the point where Mahmoud knew he should act. He should take her arm, be forceful, even threaten her if necessary. She watched him as he steeled himself, as if his turmoil was something visible. Then, before he could decide what to do next, she reached over and touched his arm. All of his resolve slipped away.

"I know that you would never do me harm. Maybe that's why you're telling me all of this."

"Maybe."

He looked down, ashamed yet relieved. He touched her hand in return, but he felt shaky, because he could easily imagine all sorts of horrible things he might have done if he hadn't been so susceptible to Esma's warmth, or that someone else might have done at Amir's bidding. Each possibility involved blood and screams and, in the end, a terrible silence. He raised his hands to his face and covered his eyes.

"I only want to help, but I am also trying to not betray my friends."

He felt her breath on his cheek.

"It's all right," she said softly. "I understand."

He opened his eyes to see hers, inches away. He wanted to hold her, to feel her skin against his, but every instinct told him that would be wrong for both of them.

"It's good that you feel this way," she said. "It will help you better understand what Ziad must be going through, and why you need to save him. Not for me, but for himself. Together we can do that."

She returned to the counter, where she poured hot water into the mugs and handed him one. They took their tea into the living room and sat, marginally closer than before. Esma switched on a lamp, and for a few minutes they sipped in silence, letting the steam drift up into their faces. Mahmoud felt himself growing calmer. Yes, he was weak, but he also felt righteous, and he supposed that should count for something.

Esma set down her mug and picked up the journal.

She thumbed through the pages with the assurance of someone who knew exactly what she was looking for. Jarrah's tiny, neat handwriting flashed at him in blue and black ink as the pages flipped by. Mahmoud wondered how much of it she had read, and he felt a twinge of guilt at this violation of his friend's privacy.

"Should we really be doing this?"

"Please. First you have to listen. Here. He wrote this only a few days ago."

Esma drew a breath and spoke in a quavering voice.

"It's from last week, the day before I got here. He writes that he has been chosen, and that he will travel soon. Then he says, 'The morning will come. The victors will come, will come. We swear to beat you. The earth will shake beneath your feet.'"

She shook her head in apparent disbelief and flipped to the next page.

"'Amir has entrusted me with much that is important. He took me into his room and showed me names, dates, and photos of all the places we will go, and my part in their plans. His trust empowers me, even though I know he still thinks of me as weak. This is why he will send me first, to strengthen my resolve. I welcome it.'"

Esma flipped through a few more pages and then took a deep breath.

"Here is the part that scared me the most. He wrote this only yesterday, just before he ended his writings and put the journal away: 'I came to you with men who love death just as you love life.' And then, a few lines later: 'The mujahideen give their money for the weapons, food, and journeys to win and die for Allah's cause, but the unhappy ones will be killed. Oh, the smell of paradise is rising.'"

She let the words hang in the stillness of the house. Then she closed the cover of the journal with the solemn air of a sacred ritual and placed the book at her side.

Mahmoud believed the words were important, and deeply personal, but he found them to be more interesting than alarming.

"He is speaking of his commitment to a cause greater than himself. It sounds like the words we use in some of our discussions."

"He is speaking of *death*, for himself and for others, perhaps many others."

"We often speak of that kind of sacrifice when we are with each other, as an expression of our devotion."

"Yes, but he wrote these words when he was alone, and facing only himself. There was no one else in the room he needed to impress."

"Except God. Perhaps he was only speaking to God."

"Then why is he going to Afghanistan? To see God?"

Mahmoud was unable to keep the look of surprise off his face. "Afghanistan?"

"Did you not know this?"

"I knew only that he was traveling soon, on Sunday. Are you sure?"

"I saw his air tickets, to Karachi via Dubai, and some notes about a rendezvous in Quetta, out in the desert, with directions to a guesthouse across the border from Pakistan. So, yes, I am sure. Then there was this. I found it under the desk in his room. I think he must have dropped it when he was packing."

It was a yellow sheet of paper torn from a legal pad, scribbled with a couple of American-sounding names—Arnold Wallace and Ned Stewart—next to phone numbers with U.S. area codes and, below each, a dollar amount, as if someone had quoted a price.

"I found that page after he spent about an hour searching online. He was very excited about whatever he found, but this was all he wrote down."

"Do you know anything about these people? This . . . Arnold and Ned?"

"No. But I'm sure they're important. He seemed to think so, anyway."

"Maybe. But it could have something to do with his schoolwork. It may have nothing to do with Al Quds."

"*All* his actions now have something to do with Al Quds. You should know that as well as anyone."

That was probably true, and the travel plans were exciting in their own right. Would he, too, soon be headed for the same destination? Haydar Zammar had certainly implied as much, and if anyone could follow through on those sorts of travel plans, it was Brother Haydar.

Mahmoud had to restrain himself from smiling pridefully at the mere thought of the possibility. He pictured all of them together in some training camp, the ultimate access granted to him, the ultimate trust. Exactly what he was hoping for. Then he remembered why he had come here: to calm Esma and to convince her to leave the city, because it was in her own best interest.

"You are right, it all sounds very serious."

"Do you think you can stop him from traveling?"

Mahmoud wanted badly to please her, but he felt like he needed to be honest.

"I could no sooner stop him than I could stop the sun from rising tomorrow."

"Then you're as lost as him."

"You may be right. I will let God answer that question. But what I know for sure is that you must protect yourself. You must leave Hamburg as soon as you can, because they still see you as a danger who might stand in his way, even though we both know that nothing will stop him."

"You are only saying that because of Amir. I won't let that grouchy Egyptian make my decisions for me."

"I am saying it because if you stay, he will send someone other than me next time, someone who might do you harm."

"Let him. There are laws here. He has to live by them just as I do."

Mahmoud frowned. This was going badly wrong.

"Amir doesn't feel bound by those kinds of laws. But you're not going to be able to see Jarrah again anyway, not before he leaves, because he'll be too busy. All of us will. We've spent the whole day helping Saeed get ready for his wedding, and tomorrow there won't be a minute to spare. But I'll talk to him, I promise. I'll make sure that he looks out for himself, and not just for what Amir wants. I'll do that, okay? For both of us."

"There's a wedding tomorrow?"

"Yes. Brother Saeed's."

"In the meeting hall at Al Quds?"

"Of course."

"So Ziad will be happy, then, and relaxed."

Mahmoud didn't like where this was headed.

"What are you thinking?"

"You won't need to speak to him at all. I'll do it myself."

"No! You can't risk that. There won't be time, and if the others see you—"

"They won't know it's me. I'll be covered head to toe like every other woman there. And I'm sure they'll put all the women on the other side of the room, yes? They'll hang something down the middle so the men can't even see them, because they're so silly about those things. Then afterward, when everyone's leaving, I'll wait for my chance and take him aside. It will only take a minute or two, and no one will notice."

"No, Esma, it isn't right."

"Listen to you. You sound like them, telling me what's right and what's wrong. I'll decide that for myself."

"It's not that. I'm worried for you. After what Amir said to me, well . . . Promise you won't do anything to put yourself at risk."

Her expression softened.

"Thank you for coming, Mahmoud. I'm glad I was able to show you these things. I think that someone besides me needed to see them. But I really can take care of myself, even around Amir."

He shook his head.

"You don't know him the way I do. He's capable of more than you think."

"So am I."

She stood. He put down his mug, and she showed him to the door. They lingered for a moment on the threshold, as if uncertain what to say, now that it was time for him to go.

"I will speak with Ziad, and then I will report back to you." He hoped this would be enough to keep her away from the wedding. She nodded, but he wasn't convinced.

"I want you to do something else for me as well," she said.

"Yes. Of course."

"After you've spoken with Ziad, I want you to have a long talk with yourself, to ask if these are really the people you want to be following into the next part of your life. And if you need me to join that conversation, I will."

"Thank you. But they have been good to me. And they're loyal."

"In their own way, I'm sure that's true. But if they would do me harm, then they would do the same to you."

He frowned. He could have rebutted her point, but not in a way that would come easily, or quickly. So instead he made a final plea.

"There is no good reason for you to come to the wedding tomorrow. It's too much of a risk, not just for you but also for Ziad." *And also for me,* he could have added. "He has made up his mind to leave the country."

"I'm sure he thinks that he has. But Amir is right: There is still a softness in Ziad, and I mean that in a good way because I also see it in you—a softness that could save you, or else you would not have come here to warn me. And I thank you for that."

She raised a forefinger to her lips, kissed it, and then placed it on his forehead, a gesture that left him speechless. Then, ever so briefly, she leaned against him, as if otherwise she might fall. He nearly lost balance, and had to steady himself by putting his hands on her hips. A thrilling moment, but dangerous, and Esma almost immediately pulled away from him, as if she, too, had sensed where this might lead.

"Goodbye, Mahmoud. I hope that I'll next see you under better circumstances."

But not tomorrow, he hoped. Anytime but tomorrow.

"Goodbye, Esma."

He wanted to touch her again, a deeper embrace, but didn't yet dare. Later, he hoped, after Jarrah was gone. Then he stepped away into the night, more troubled than when he had arrived.

40

Claire had turned off her phone by the time she reached Holunderweg. Five calls from Paul Bridger did the trick, buzzing like a fly beneath a lampshade until she could no longer stand it. She was in no mood to speak to him. Besides, he deserved to fret and stew and worry about what she might be up to in this, her fifth hour of walkabout since leaving the chocolate museum.

She considered removing the SIM card from her phone but didn't believe that Bridger would go so far as to track her, or not yet, not after what Tony must have told him. He would see this as her way of blowing off steam and would wait for her to calm down, when in fact she was already turning the moment into much more—an opportunity to bolster her own case for what she hoped to do next.

First she needed time to figure out how to best employ the leverage she'd earned with her discovery that the professor was a fake, a stand-in, a PR prop for a dead man in Western Pennsylvania. Had the real Brenda Armitage endorsed this charade? She doubted it. The university? Probably, as long as the price was right. Or maybe they, too, were among the duped, because hadn't the real Armitage supposedly been on sabbatical?

The more important question was whether Bridger's debt to her was great enough to overcome whatever obligation he had to Mark Wharton. But Ken Donlan's phone call had refocused her attention on the more pressing issue of Mahmoud and what he might really be up to with his friends at Al Quds. So now she was strolling toward the house where Esma was supposedly staying with a friend.

There had been no opportunity along the way for a wardrobe change. Fortunately, Holunderweg's tidy and prosperous look was a perfect match for her Tour Day clothes, a polyester dress-for-success business suit that made her look like a workingwoman on her way home from the office.

The address was just ahead on her left, a two-story stucco home with big windows, a steeply pitched roof, and a tiny, well-groomed lawn with a pot of red geraniums on the front porch.

As if to signal her arrival, a light came on in a big window downstairs as she approached, and she slowed down for a closer look. Behind lace curtains, two heads appeared in silhouette, as if projected onto a movie screen. One was male, the other female. They were close, but not close enough to call the scene intimate, and she would have bet a lot of D-marks that the heads belonged to Mahmoud and Esma.

Farther down the block, an older man was out walking his dog, doddering in fits and starts as the animal stopped to sniff at fence posts and shrubs. Otherwise she had the street to herself. Neither of those heads in the window had turned to look outside, and she doubted they would. There was no bus stop in sight, nor any other vantage point that would give her a plausible excuse to linger for an extended time. She decided to take a risk by just standing there, watching, waiting, until circumstances dictated otherwise. This might be her only chance for a breakthrough before she confronted Bridger, which made boldness feel excusable.

She watched for several minutes, but the two heads barely moved. Down the block, the old man with the dog had barely moved. Had Wharton put someone on her tail without her noticing? She strolled toward him. The dog was doing its business on the edge of a lawn. He stooped to pick it up with a plastic bag. Then he looked up, nodded, and continued. She waited until he was out of sight. False alarm, she supposed.

By the time she made it back to the house, both silhouetted figures were standing. The male head bobbed up and down, as if in affirmation of something, and then both of them faded from view.

The front door opened, and Claire eased behind a beech tree in front of the house next door. She heard their voices as they stepped onto the threshold. Yes, it was Mahmoud and Esma, and they were facing each other as if saying goodbye. Even from here, it looked to Claire like every muscle in Mahmoud's body was tense.

They were speaking in German. Down the street, a dog barked, and Claire cursed beneath her breath. Then the neighborhood went quiet enough for her to make out at least some of Mahmoud's parting remarks:

"There is no good reason for you to come to the wedding tomorrow," he said. "It's too much of a risk, not just for you but also for Ziad."

Esma's answer was too soft to make out, but her eyes shone with care and concern. Then the dog began barking again, and she couldn't hear the rest of their conversation. She did, however, see Esma touch a finger to her lips and then to Mahmoud's forehead, a chaste moment of tenderness followed by a brief and awkward embrace. All of it seemed quite daring, considering Mahmoud's beliefs. They broke apart. He then hesitated, as if on the verge of taking her in his arms. Then he turned and departed. Fortunately for Claire, he headed in the opposite direction. Esma stood in the open doorway, backlit, waiting until he was out of sight before she went back inside. The door clicked shut. Mahmoud's footsteps were the only noise as Claire watched him recede into a patch of darkness between two streetlamps.

So then. Donlan's hunch about an upcoming wedding had apparently been a good one. And it was tomorrow. A great opportunity, perhaps, to observe many of these characters at once, and also to snap photos and collect names of everyone else who showed up. Find out who all of their benefactors were.

But what could all of these conversations between Mahmoud and Esma mean, and why was he warning her off from the wedding? Claire's hope—and this was what she planned to report to Bridger—was that she was witnessing the beginning of a rare fault line of discord within the Al Quds crowd. Perhaps Mahmoud's relationship with Esma offered a potential wedge that they could exploit. In her wildest dreams, it might even lead to recruiting one of them as an informant, although she knew the possibility was remote, given the cultural and spiritual barriers. Still, a woman could dream. She set off after Mahmoud, curious to see where he might go next.

She followed him for several blocks. Fortunately, he soon reached a busier street with shops and restaurants, and enough cars and pedestrians to let her ease closer. He walked like a man in a trance, face slightly upturned, glancing at nothing to either side, and proceeding at a leisurely pace.

Then he stopped outside a Turkish sandwich shop and sniffed at the air, almost like a dog, as if it had suddenly occurred to him that he was hungry. Claire kept on going as he went inside, and she found a spot by a Telekom phone box where she could observe him at the counter, placing his order with a large man in a stained white T-shirt, who then turned and began slicing shards of charred meat from a glistening column of fatty lamb rotating on an upright spit—a doner kebab, Germany's favorite imported sandwich, with shaved meat stuffed in a pocket of Turkish bread with lettuce, tomatoes, and yogurt sauce.

The counterman wrapped the doner and dropped it into a yellow plastic bag. Mahmoud paid him and took it to a small table, where he unwrapped the sandwich and began to eat. After a few dripping mouthfuls, he set aside the doner, wiped his hands with a napkin, and reached into his trouser pockets for a stubby pencil and a folded sheet of paper. Smoothing the paper onto the table, he began to write, the pencil moving quickly in the glare of the fluorescent lighting.

A love note, Claire guessed. Still trying to explain himself to the sweet and becoming Esma. Afterward, he would probably go back to Holunderweg to post it on the door or stuff it into the mailbox. Maybe what they had here was a love triangle. Mahmoud, Esma, and Jarrah. A fraught arrangement in any culture, but especially explosive in theirs. Yes, this could be ripe for exploitation, which made her more eager than ever to pass along her findings.

But Mahmoud did not return to Holunderweg. Instead he refolded the paper, placed it into the yellow plastic bag, and finished his dinner. He cleaned his face and hands, picked up the bag, and headed for the exit.

Claire stepped into the phone box and shut the door, turning her face away as the light came on. She heard Mahmoud's footsteps pass behind her on the sidewalk, and when he was twenty yards along, she again set off in pursuit.

A few blocks later he caught an U-Bahn at a crowded station that made it easy for her to slip onto the same train, two cars back. He got off at a junction with an S-Bahn line that ran all the way south to Harburg. But, to her surprise, he exited the station and returned to the streets.

Following him here was trickier, because it was mostly houses and apartment buildings, so Claire dropped back. He then caught her short by stopping suddenly in front of an empty three-story stone house that appeared to be under renovation. The windows were boarded up, and a small cement mixer was parked on a muddy spit of land out front.

Mahmoud sat on the front stoop as Claire eased back into the shadows near the end of the block. He reached into the plastic bag and got out the paper, which he unfolded and began to read. He made further marks with his pencil, as if editing whatever he'd written, and then refolded the paper and put it back into the bag. Was he having second thoughts?

He checked his watch and looked down the street in the opposite direction, as if expecting someone. Claire checked her own watch: It was two minutes before the hour. A minute later, he stood and looped the plastic bag around the end of the railing by the front steps. Then he walked away, continuing in the direction he had been going. Seconds later, he disappeared around a corner.

How odd. Did he know the owner of the house? Or had he decided, perhaps, that whatever he'd written was in vain, and discarded it? Claire wanted to rush over and grab the note, but she worried that Mahmoud might reconsider and return, catching her in the act. She supposed he might even have seen her, and had done this to trap her.

As she waited, frozen in place, she heard a rhythmic clicking sound—*tap, tap, tap*—a sound of metal against metal that grew in volume as it approached from down the darkened sidewalk. It was a bicycle, an old one, with the pedal striking a glancing blow against the frame on every revolution. *Tap, tap, tap.* The rider was small, either a child or a young woman.

The tapping stopped abruptly as the bicycle braked to a halt next to the steps where Mahmoud had been sitting. The rider stopped only long enough to reach over to the railing and snatch up the yellow plastic bag. Then the bike resumed its progress. *Tap, tap, tap.* It made a U-turn beneath a streetlight to head back in the direction from which it had come, and in a faint flash Claire saw that the rider was a petite young woman, the same one who had been collecting her laundry-bag dispatches every midnight at the Plaza. A courier, in other words, one of Bridger's own.

The shock of it took a few seconds to sink in. But then, with a thrilling but coldly logical shift of thought deep within her, Claire realized that Mahmoud's message was not an act of love, or of abandonment, but one of tradecraft, careful and calculated. He was no potential fault line; he was an insider, a source. He was, in fact, that one very valuable item that the Agency had never managed to create within an organization as seemingly impenetrable as Al Qaeda.

Mahmoud was an asset, Bridger's own.

It was so extraordinary—indeed, so outlandish—that she couldn't fully accept it until she'd taken a few moments to review everything she had observed and overheard during the past several days, while weighing it all on the scales of Bridger's own strange behavior. And when she was done, it still added up, clearer than ever: Mahmoud was a mole.

She had to sit down to absorb the revelatory power of it all, although she was already plotting in her head what she needed to do next. One thing she knew for sure: She would not be leaving Hamburg for a while yet.

41

Paul Bridger stared out at the night gloom of the Alster. Claire was gone for good, he supposed—operationally speaking, anyway. Perhaps she had even left Hamburg. A ferry would've been his favored means of escape, so maybe it was hers. By now she could be out on the North Sea, standing at the rail as salt breezes whipped at her hair and white-caps bloomed in the darkness.

A footstep crunched the gravel to his rear, but Bridger didn't turn. One of Wharton's minders, no doubt, inching closer. Precious little left for them to discover since the photo had turned up. The best-laid plans, so easily disrupted. And now the support network he had hoped to build was losing its key players before most of them had even found out the true nature of their mission.

For the first time in ages, failure loomed—his biggest since, well, Berlin—so he had walked here an hour ago in hopes of clearing his head, regrouping. Instead, the waterfront view kept taking him back to The Aftermath, as he still thought of it—those weeks after Berlin when he had sought refuge in the wild, a retreat into solitude.

His first stop had been a beach house on the Outer Banks of North Carolina, where, much as he was doing now, he spent the first three days staring out across the Pamlico Sound as the sun transited the sky. Speechless, motionless. Dozing off every night in a rope hammock on the screened porch, from torpor and too much gin.

On the third sunset, his gaze was drawn to an old yellow kayak up on blocks behind the house, with grass growing up around the hull.

He launched it the following morning and paddled into the sound without a hat, lifejacket, sunscreen, or water bottle. An audience of egrets, herons, and pelicans watched as he entered an estuarial maze of saw grass and tidal creeks, eddying pools of blackness. He glided up a narrowing channel as land crabs scuttled away across the mud. An otter slid from the water and disappeared into the reeds. Beneath the boat, the wingbeat of a startled ray stirred a rolling cloud of silt.

The channel ended at a hammock of scrubby pines, and the kayak skidded to rest on a shoal. The only way out was to turn around. He sat very still while flies bit his neck and his face burned red. Perhaps this would be a fitting end. The tide was falling, and he wouldn't have to wait long before heat and dehydration took him out. Then nightfall would come, with clouds of mosquitoes to drain him of blood, sip by sip. By dawn his body would be an invitation to the turkey vultures, and in a spot this remote he might not be found for months, a slumped skeleton in the cockpit.

The image made him laugh, a croak that startled a heron. He braced his paddle against the mud, heaved the boat into deeper water, and paddled out. Later, after rehydrating with a shower and a pitcher of gimlets, he realized that he had acquired a taste for hardening himself by ordeal, so he decided to up the ante.

A week later he arrived in the Boundary Waters of Minnesota, where he set out alone in an aluminum canoe. On day two he decided to skip a grueling mile-long portage by shooting a dangerous run of rapids, even though he had no previous experience of whitewater.

At the first steep plunge, he instantly found himself in trouble. The rushing water turned the canoe like the needle of a compass and pinned it broadside against a boulder. When he leaned to push off, the hull tipped and water poured in, dumping him into the current as the hull swung again, which trapped him against another rock and pushed him deeper. It was all he could do to keep his nostrils above the surface, breathing with difficulty as his chest constricted in the icy water.

In desperation, he grabbed a fallen limb as it swept by, and he managed to lever away the boat just enough for the current to do the rest, washing him and the canoe downstream. He banged his way through the rapids until the stream emptied him into the next lake, where he stood shakily, bruised and coughing in the tea-colored shallows.

He recovered the dented boat and the scarred paddle and soggily paddled to the nearest campsite, where, blowing like a bellows, he kindled a warming fire from birch bark and twigs. That night he decided it was time to begin rebuilding himself.

The rental company charged him for the damages and he kept the cracked paddle, which he shipped to Paris and then mounted in a frame as a daily reminder of the need for vigilance against all odds. Once a year he headed back into the wilderness for a refresher course. It was all designed to toughen him by degrees for the next existential challenge.

Now that crisis had arrived, and, just as in Berlin, Claire was part of it. Was he ready? Time to find out. He squinted into the darkness. The ideas would come, even if Claire didn't.

But he probably wouldn't come up with anything on an empty stomach, so he decided to get dinner before all the restaurants closed. He stood from the bench. The watchers stirred at their posts.

Ten minutes later he reached a quaint cobbled lane with old, timbered buildings, lovingly restored so that wealthy people could shop and eat in tasteful surroundings. The minders were keeping pace, no longer even trying to disguise their intentions from anyone who might be watching. It made Bridger feel like a prisoner out for a stroll on the yard. Bolt for the shadows and he'd half expect the beam of a spotlight to fall on him from a guard tower, with Wharton barking orders through a megaphone.

There was a decent Chinese restaurant just ahead, on the second floor of a charming stucco building, and the lighted windows looked warm and inviting. As he reached the door, he raised a hand as if to signal his minders that he had arrived at his destination, and he heard them peel away, footsteps receding. As he climbed the stairs he wondered what sort of fast food they would choose for themselves tonight. It was a relief to be truly alone.

He asked for a corner table out of habit. The hostess handed him a menu and informed him that the kitchen would be closing in fifteen minutes. The only other customers were an older man and woman on the far side, with cleared plates and a depleted wine bottle. He gazed out the window, down into the empty cobbled lane.

He studied the menu, with its stylized red peppers in the margins, the dishes described in both German and English. Footsteps approached—

the waitress, no doubt, already pressing him for a decision—so he decided to buy time by ordering a Hefeweizen, even though the weather had turned a little cool for that treat, partly because he knew it would be delivered in one of those tall, sculpted glasses with a tiny waistline, like a model on a runway, or maybe like Claire.

When he looked up to make his request, there she was—Claire herself, still as shapely as that glass of his dreams. To his surprise, she was smiling, although not very nicely.

"I saw the goons letting you off the leash for dinner and decided to join you. How long will they be gone?"

He shrugged. The thought crossed his mind that she might be about to make a scene, but deeper down he knew that wasn't her style. Besides, she'd earned the right to deliver a scolding, even a lecture, so he gestured toward the opposite chair.

"They won't come up here. As long as I'm the first one to leave, you shouldn't have a problem with them."

"Good, because we have plenty to talk about."

He handed her the menu, and the waitress approached as Claire slid gracefully into the seat, a movement that reminded him of that otter in the marsh all those years ago.

Bridger ordered his beer and the crispy duck. Claire asked for mineral water and a spring roll. They waited in silence until the food arrived, in near-record time. Amazing what you could accomplish with a wok when everyone in the kitchen wanted to get the hell home.

With the waitress gone and the other couple now departed, he tore open the paper sleeve around his chopsticks and nodded, as if to signal that the floor was now Claire's.

Then she began.

42

During the hour it had taken Claire to find Bridger, she still hadn't come down from her high about what she had learned about Mahmoud. In all of the Agency's work in all of the world's most dangerous corners, Al Qaeda was their single greatest blind spot—the shadowy room into which they could never shine a light.

Yet if what she had just witnessed was as it seemed, then Bridger's op had at least managed to light a candle, and the possibilities were exhilarating.

She wondered how many other people knew. It wasn't the sort of knowledge you tended to set loose in the corridors of Langley, even in the highest echelons. And if Bridger had been going it alone up to now, that would certainly explain his anger over the surveillance photo. Maybe he had been forced to clue in Wharton, who had reacted badly. But why? Professional jealousy? Surely any wounded feelings over being kept in the dark would be overcome by the benefits.

Or maybe Wharton had also been in on this from the beginning, and was equally upset by the photo. No one wanted their most valuable asset to start showing up in images circulating within the intelligence community.

Claire's hour on the move had also given her time to reassess the Mahmoud-Esma-Jarrah dynamic. It was not, as she'd first thought, an opportunity to be exploited, but instead a dangerous vulnerability, an unnecessary risk. Mahmoud falling for Esma could jeopardize his entire standing with the Al Quds crowd, and she doubted Bridger knew just how precarious the young man's position had become.

But before addressing that, she had some grievances to air, a few debts to collect, some leverage to exert. She had plans, too, regarding her own role and how it might evolve going forward. And that was the discussion she would open with, here and now, before Bridger even had time to dig his chopsticks into those chunks of crispy duck.

"So were you ever going to tell me that the real professor was dead?"

To his credit, Bridger did not look away.

"Not if I could help it."

"It's one thing to play the lead in a sideshow, Paul. But a charade?"

"We're in the business of charades."

"Not when it means duping your own people."

"The reasoning was that you'd be a more convincing wife if you thought he was the real thing. That said, it wasn't my call."

"Meaning it was Mark Wharton's?"

Bridger's chopsticks halted in midair. A glistening piece of duck fell back onto the plate.

"Impressive. How long have you known about Wharton?"

"Not long enough to protect myself against his stupidest decisions. But I'm getting there."

"Yes, I believe you are."

"And you can't keep putting this all on him."

"You're right, I should've told you. I owed you at least that much."

"Owed me? Why, because of Berlin? I'm not paid by the hour for weekends like that. But now you owe me big-time."

"What is it you want, then? Within reason, of course."

"We'll get to that. First I want to know who killed the real professor and why you hushed it up?"

"Who told you all this?"

"It's true, isn't it?"

"Well . . . yes. But it's a closely guarded secret. Even the university doesn't know."

"How I found out isn't relevant, or not until you've told me what happened."

"I did mention he'd already had a few death threats."

"Yes."

"Well, one of those turned out to be quite serious. We were already planning this whole thing last May, with the professor's cooperation. We hadn't yet firmed up the publishing contract, but Hamburg was looking like the right time and place to release the book. Then we got wind that a couple of bad actors from Baluchistan had flown into the country and set off in his general direction. One was a fellow known for his skills with a crossbow. We warned him, of course—the real professor, I mean—but before we could calm him down, he took off into the woods with a backpack and his own crazy idea of riding out the storm. His wife said he often did that sort of thing."

"Hiking and tennis. Not exactly the hobbies of Warren Weeks."

"Yes, well, if the real Armitage had been a couch potato like Weeks, he'd still be alive. We took off after him, of course, but we reached him about fifteen minutes after the fellow with the crossbow."

"Which at least gave you the opportunity to grab the killers and hush it all up."

"And to erase the photos of the dead Armitage off the killer's camera memory card before he had a chance to send them anywhere. The irony is that the professor's killing was what convinced the director of just how powerful a weapon his book might be, as a means of getting attention in the Islamic world."

"So why not just publish it posthumously? And you still could have unveiled it here, to all his former colleagues. Our very own martyr author, with his own heavenly box of white raisins."

"That was my argument—minus the raisins, of course. Then Wharton got involved. He'd been licking his wounds up in the Agency library for a few months and saw this as his way back into the game. And, well, he wanted the whole dog and pony show, complete with a fake professor and his duped wife."

"I'm guessing he used the word 'synergy' at least once."

Bridger smiled ruefully.

"Early and often. And the director went for it."

"And the real Mrs. Armitage? Brenda? What did she think of Wharton's marketing plan?"

"Apparently she's been too busy spending the advance to object. She's been relocated under a new identity."

"The cover wife is about to do the same. That's my first demand.

Give Warren Weeks all the security you want, but I'm off the tour bus for good, with your full and official blessing."

"I think even Wharton will see the wisdom in that. We can have you on a flight to Dulles tomorrow afternoon. From there you can ease out of cover and head back to Paris."

"Good. Tell Wharton that's what I'm doing. You can even buy the damn ticket. Wave it in his face and have a courier bring it to me at the Plaza while Tony watches. But what I really want is the same thing you do."

"And what might that be, Claire?"

He said it flippantly, so she paused for her big reveal.

"I want to help keep your asset Mahmoud up and running, and out of harm's way. So my plan is to remain in place for as long as you need me."

Bridger's chopsticks clattered into the rice bowl. One bounced to the floor. His mouth slowly opened and shut, like a landed trout gasping for air. He seemed impressed, but also alarmed. And why not, because if Claire had figured out his greatest secret, well . . .

He leaned forward and lowered his voice.

"How in the *hell* did you—?"

"I saw him making a mail drop, just this evening. And then your little girl Friday out of London pedaled by to snatch it up. It's brilliant, what you've done, but I have to say I'm a little worried that it may be about to come apart at the seams."

His brow creased. Then he cleared his throat as he stooped to pick up the fallen chopstick before sitting up straighter in his chair. Whatever you thought of Bridger's strengths and weaknesses, he adjusted quickly to thunderbolts and changing circumstances.

"Coming apart? How so?"

"No, no. First let's back up. If I'm going to be of any value here, then I have to be fully in the picture. So I want to know everything about this op of Mahmoud's, including whatever you're still hiding from Wharton."

"Claire, you know how these things work."

"I do. I also know that I'm now in a very strong position of leverage. So, while it's certainly still your call . . ."

He took a bite of food and chewed slowly. Then he sighed, nodded, and again lowered his voice.

"His real name is Malachy Yassin."

"*Malachy?* You're joking, right?"

"Please, not so loud. His mother was Irish American. Practically breast-fed him on Guinness, to hear him tell it. His father's Moroccan, from Rabat. They met in Germany, when Mom was working as a mechanic for the U.S. Air Force, Ramstein Air Base. It's where Malachy was born."

"Him and Lois Lane."

Bridger raised his eyebrows.

"Really?"

"You'd know that if you'd taken your nose out of those bird books long enough to read some comics. Did he always live abroad?"

"Moved to the States when he was ten, but Dad took them to Morocco a few times every year. He went to mosque on Fridays and to mass on Sundays. Perfect training for what he's doing now. We knew to start with the Al Quds bunch from the surveillance materials the Germans had shared with us."

"And the gang just smiled and said, 'Come on in?'"

"They were leery at first, as you'd expect. But they're big on outreach, especially that fat fuck Haydar Zammar. And Omar, the one with all the personality. You've seen them."

"I have. And what were you hoping to accomplish, exactly, by sending me over every evening to look at them?"

"First I wanted to know if Malachy passed the look test. If you came back thinking he seemed out of place, well . . ."

"Oh, he fits right in. It's the frat boy, Jarrah, who stands out, but they seem to trust him as well."

"Yes. So Malachy says in his reports. Eventually I was going to clue you in. This whole media show for the professor was mostly to provide cover to build a support network for Malachy as he eased deeper into the mix. I was also counting on the professor's arrival to be a test for his circle of friends. If they were recruited to take part in some local action—like the stabbing—then we would've given the Germans what we had so they could round up the guilty parties for prosecution, to take them off the board. But if the group's leadership ducked it and started grooming their people for something bigger, well, then we'd be onto something bigger, too."

"Sounds too clever by half."

"It nearly was. Apparently Mahmoud helped supply the getaway car for the guy who stabbed Lute. Fortunately, the police don't have any leads that would implicate him, and that seems to be the extent of their involvement. So we were still on track, and probably could have kept it that way if Wharton hadn't come aboard. That made everything a little too complicated."

"Meaning you haven't even told the *director* what you're up to with Malachy?"

Bridger shrugged dismissively.

"Sometimes 'need to know' means keeping your superiors in the dark."

"Good advice. Someday I'll quote it back to you."

"In this case it was necessary. I was the only one with any clout who still had faith in him."

"In Malachy?"

"His last assignment didn't end well. He was in Nairobi, spring of last year. We'd placed him in a job with a shady NGO that was employing known jihadis, funneling money and support to all the wrong people. He made nice with a few big talkers and started sniffing around. A month later the embassy was bombed. Turned out it was the quiet ones he should have been paying attention to."

"And they blamed *him*? You can't always back the right horse."

"His case officer decided it was either a deliberate oversight or some variation on the Stockholm syndrome. Although by then the case officer was going through some problems of his own. Burnout was the official explanation, but by the time that judgment was rendered he'd badmouthed Malachy to anybody who'd listen, the director included."

And that's when Claire figured it out.

"Malachy's case officer was Mark Wharton."

"Yes. He was running the whole show out of Alec station. In the aftermath they both got the sack, which in Wharton's case meant he was temporarily banished to the reading room in Langley, licking his wounds until something better came long."

"And in Malachy's case?"

"Exiled without pay to his rat trap of an apartment in Queens, from which he was never supposed to return."

"Shit. No wonder the photo was a problem."

"When Wharton saw Malachy was here in Hamburg, it was all I could do to keep him from pulling the plug on the whole op. Instead he did the next worst thing, by sending you off on that Tour Day boondoggle, right when I was ready to start using you more for support."

"But why pull the plug now? Malachy's *in*, he's made it. Maybe he failed before, but this time he's exactly where we want him to be, where we *need* him to be."

"Wharton doesn't trust him, not after the embassy bombings. He thinks Malachy, at heart, is one of them, and that he might even be intentionally misleading us."

"Seriously? Is he one of those idiots who freak out whenever he sees someone unrolling a prayer rug?"

"He was always a little inclined that way. Malachy said the first time they met he had to down a double whiskey just to put the man at ease. But I think the bigger problem is that Wharton sat in on a lot of the suspect interrogations in the wake of the bombings. I think he saw a light in their eyes that he also saw in Malachy's, and it scared him because he couldn't tell them apart. The only reason he hasn't blown this whole op to the director and, well, everyone else, is that he doesn't want to admit to any higher-ups that he'd let me dupe him for this long. So instead he's basically shutting me down. Two days ago he canceled the lease on Malachy's safe house, and by now the landlord will have changed all the locks. Not that Malachy's ever had to use it yet, but still. And this morning Wharton found out about my courier, Janis."

"The bicyclist from London station?"

Bridger nodded.

"By this time tomorrow she, too, will be on her way home. And that will close my last line of communication with Malachy, unless I can find a way to check the mailbox myself."

"While your handlers watch from half a block away."

"Exactly."

"Did Wharton tell you who took the photo?"

"No. Once I'd ruled you out, I figured it was the BND. Had to have been."

"It wasn't."

She told him about Donlan, and what he was up to, and how even he had been stonewalled by his colleagues—and Wharton's former team—at Alec station.

"How do you know all this?"

She explained that as well.

"I last spoke to him a few hours ago."

"Interesting. And what else have you and Kenny Donlan been cooking up?"

"Sometimes 'need to know' means keeping your superiors in the dark."

"That was a fast turnaround."

"Isn't your dinner getting cold?"

This finally got a smile out of him, but it didn't last.

"You said something earlier about things falling apart at the seams. What did you mean?"

She told him about the complicated triangle developing between Jarrah, Mahmoud, and Esma, whom she described as Jarrah's probable girlfriend.

"Yikes," Bridger said. "She's not just Jarrah's girlfriend. She's his fucking wife."

Claire took a moment to absorb this.

"That makes Malachy's position even more tenuous. Has he mentioned her in his reports?"

"Only as possible collateral damage. A few days ago he was asking if we might provide a little protection for her if things got dicey. I told him that was out of the question."

"From what I've seen, he's taken on that role for himself. And from what they were saying to each other, she may be intent on making a scene at some wedding tomorrow."

"That would be unfortunate in the extreme. This wedding's going to be quite the big event. Malachy thinks it may be a sort of jumping-off point for some of them. The start of their next phase in planning for, well, whatever it is they're building toward. Disrupting that wouldn't sit well. And if he gets caught in the middle of *that* . . ."

Bridger's voice trailed off. He sighed and shoved away his plate. The waitress, watching from a far corner, bustled over to ask if he wanted it boxed.

"You can do the same with the spring roll," Claire said, even though it was soggy and cold.

They waited for her to depart.

"I guess I should've anticipated something like this," Bridger said. "When I recruited him to the job, his girlfriend had just left him. At the time I was thinking that was a plus."

"No attachments, meaning he was prime material for a long-term infiltration."

"Yes."

"I'd have reached the same conclusion."

"But he's still a human being."

"And by all appearances, a lonely man. Esma has obviously made a connection, and in his current state of mind she's important to him."

"Right when they seemed to be grooming him for something big."

"How so?"

He told her about Malachy's recent reports, which rekindled her excitement. The op was clearly on the cusp of achieving something momentous, if only they could keep the lines of communication open. If Malachy headed off to training camps in Pakistan, Afghanistan, and points beyond, they might be able to uncover just about anything Al Qaeda was planning, perhaps for years to come—provided Malachy lasted that long.

Bridger continued.

"This wedding tomorrow, it's for one of his new friends, Saeed Bahaji. Apparently it's also going to be a sort of farewell to Jarrah, and he's only the first in line for departure. The others will soon begin heading east as well, one by one. Jarrah, Amir, Omar—and even our Malachy. As long as he doesn't blow it first."

"Or Wharton doesn't blow it for him."

"Yes, there's that as well."

"Have you told Malachy that Wharton knows?"

Bridger sighed and lowered his head.

"Haven't had the heart. Nor the intestinal fortitude. It's tough enough doing what he's doing without finding out that your greatest detractor has learned what you're up to. He also doesn't know he's about to lose the better part of his support network. Christ, he doesn't even know he no longer has a safe house."

"That's it, then. I'm staying. I'll help provide backup and communications until he gets away safely. Whatever you need."

"Hard to imagine how you'll manage that if we're putting you on a plane tomorrow."

"Oh, I've got that part figured out, but I'll need your help, and you'll have to move fast."

Then she told him exactly how everything was going to work.

SATURDAY, OCTOBER 9

43

Mahmoud awoke to the sound of footsteps, muffled voices, the clatter of a teapot. It was barely dawn and the house was astir, everyone else up and getting ready for the day's big events—Saeed Bahaji's wedding and Jarrah's farewell. He realized with a start that he had slept through the first prayer, but after the events of the night before he supposed it was understandable.

His thoughts turned to Esma, and he swallowed hard. If she showed up at the wedding, they would both be in trouble, but she most of all. He was still angry with Bridger for ignoring his earlier appeal for help on this front. With a little protection, she never would have become this vulnerable. It was the least they could do, especially considering all of the vital information she had helped Mahmoud uncover.

So now, of course, he felt obligated to look after her, even if it meant jeopardizing his own security. Or so he told himself, while wondering whether he was letting his heart overrule his head.

Mahmoud sat up beneath the sheets. He had an erection, which annoyed him. Fortunately, both of his roommates were already gone. Their discarded clothes were strewn across the floor, their beds unmade, and he could smell the remnants of a carton of yogurt one of them had left on the windowsill.

The mess reminded him of how his apartment in Queens had looked six months ago when Paul Bridger came calling without warning. Mahmoud—or Malachy, an identity that now felt remote to him—

had been living like a pauper at the time. Counting out his change in the grocery line. Holes in his socks and underwear. His books and newspapers came from the library, and he had sworn off visits to the doctor unless he was at death's door. Most of his dinners were from the falafel cart down the block.

But the worst of it was that he was still emotionally bruised from the three-week debriefing that had followed his failure in Nairobi. The same numbing questions, over and over, many of which he was sure had been fed to his interrogators by Mark Wharton:

Tell us how you managed to misread them, Malachy. How did it happen? How did they control you? Did you succumb to their charms, their delusions? Did they wear you down, or were you under duress? Was it repetition, or was it doctrine? Tell us again about each of your friendships at the NGO. Did you willfully ignore the danger signs? Did you, just maybe, let things slide when you should have been at your sharpest? Willingly or unwillingly, Malachy? Write down a log of your daily movements and contacts as best you can remember them. Yes, we know you've already done that, but do it again. For the whole month, please. How did you manage to misread them, Malachy? How did it happen?

Afterward the Agency had cut him loose—a probationary period only, they said, an indefinite suspension without pay. They reserved the right to rehire him later but suggested it might only be on a contract basis, if at all. The timing was still under discussion, they said. In the meantime, they promised to supply him with a few job references. *Maybe you should find something in the private sector, Malachy, but not in the security realm, if you please. Don't call us, we'll call you.*

And that was how he had thought matters would end, with a distance that would widen over time as their voices faded—the less said about it, the better—until Bridger knocked on his door.

He had come bearing gifts—a six-pack of Guinness and a carton of Marlboros, as if to show right off the bat that *he*, at least, harbored no illusions about Malachy's loyalty to the secular West. And Bridger had neither flinched nor even wrinkled his nose at the ungodly, odiferous mess in his kitchen, a hoarder's paradise of unwashed dishes and empty cans, the crumbs indistinguishable from the mouse droppings.

They made small talk for a minute or two and went for a walk, strolling around the corner to a Brazilian diner with steamy windows and scalding coffee, sliding as comfortably as old pals into opposite sides of a corner booth.

"You look a little down in the mouth, Malachy. Can't say that I blame you, given the way they handled everything."

The statement seemed to cover a wide range of Agency transgressions, and Malachy had felt more grateful than he wanted to admit.

"I've been better."

"Top of your class at the Farm, and one of our few Arabic speakers in the field. One hiccup and they toss you aside like the warranty's expired."

"Not so sure I'd call Nairobi a hiccup."

"Oh, it was a full-blown convulsion. But your part in it wasn't. You fell in with the wrong people. The talkers, not the doers. An unfortunate choice, but it happens. Or that's how I see it."

"It's not how Langley sees it. Wharton especially."

"His problem, not ours. I understand your girlfriend's gone, too."

Malachy looked up as if Bridger had slapped him. Bridger held up a hand to forestall any protest.

"That happens, too," Bridger said. "Not just the breakup, but my interest in it. Occupational hazard. Believe me, I wouldn't have gone to the trouble to poke around if I didn't think you were still worth it."

Malachy nodded but was back on his guard, mostly because Bridger's intel was accurate. Cara had walked out on him only two weeks earlier. Quiet and compassionate Cara, who had waited patiently while he was overseas, but lost hope when he returned damaged and unable—or unwilling, anyway—to talk about what had happened. For security reasons, he'd said, which was true but also convenient, and she had sensed that.

Even here in Hamburg, the ache of her departure had lingered for a while. During his first days in the city, Malachy had heard her name from time to time, hiding in the rhythms of certain noises—the ticking of a radiator, the clacking of the rails beneath the S-Bahn, the drip of a faucet—*Cara, Cara, Cara*. And then, after months of loneliness, he had met Esma, with that same gleam in her eyes, her barely concealed sense of play, that luster in her hair. Yet another woman with a doomed loyalty to an untethered man who was straying beyond her reach, so of course he had felt protective.

"There's no cure for it, that's my experience," Bridger had said at the diner. "So you might as well be working instead of moping, don't you think?"

"I am working. Part-time."

"So I heard. Valet parking at a two-star hotel. Teaching a little English to new arrivals. But I was referring to real work, the kind you were born to do."

"Is this official?"

"*I'm* official, Malachy, that's all that matters for now. And I've come here about a job. One that will properly use your greatest talents at a time when they're more necessary than ever. Provided you're willing to start out by working a little bit under the radar, as far as the Company is concerned."

"Under contract, you mean?"

"Something like that. More of a one-on-one arrangement. No paperwork, at least for a while. But you'll be paid, of course."

"Unsupported?"

"Not completely. There's me, for starters. As for the longer term, I've come up with a way to budget a network that will go into action once you're more firmly established. Initially, yes, you may be a bit on your own. But not to worry, the cavalry will arrive."

But apparently no one from the cavalry could be spared to help Jarrah's wife Esma, and his housemates were already on full alert with regard to her. That had been made clear to Mahmoud the previous night, not long after he returned to the house.

The place had been dark and quiet by then, everyone seemingly snug in their beds. Mahmoud had hoped to creep up to his bedroom without notice. Then Amir ambushed him at the top of the stairs, emerging from his room as if he'd been waiting eagerly for a progress report.

"So you have taken care of things, Brother Mahmoud?"

Fortunately, Mahmoud had used his return trip to concoct a cover story, in which he had forcefully put Esma aboard an outbound train. He was halfway through this tale, whispering in the darkened hallway, when Amir suddenly grabbed his shirt, leaned closer, and sniffed, like a dog on the hunt.

"What's wrong, Brother Amir?"

"You, my brother. You smell of woman. You smell of *her*. You had better tell me why."

Mahmoud had answered with further dissembling, although more haltingly, a story in which a weeping Esma had pleadingly clung to him, nearly collapsing, shedding tears on his shoulder. It had been wrong to let her touch him, of course, quite impermissible, but it was the only way to keep her moving and get her aboard the train.

Amir let go of his shirt and eyed him closely.

"And you are sure that's all it was, and that she is gone from us now?"

"Absolutely." Thus upping the stakes if she were to turn up this afternoon.

"And she does not know his plans?"

"Brother Jarrah's?"

"Of course."

"No, I don't think so. She only knows that he's going away."

The lies, piling up like boxcars now. Another pause. Another long and probing stare.

"I hope that you are correct."

Mahmoud got out of bed and picked up his clothes from the night before. He raised his shirt to his face. Amir was right, it *did* smell of Esma, which only troubled him more and resurrected his fading erection. Her eyes. Her expression of desperate hope. Then he recalled Jarrah's journal, with its alarming words of resolve as he steeled himself for God knew what sort of deed.

A burst of laughter from downstairs jolted Mahmoud back to the present. He dropped the shirt to the floor. Now he smelled coffee, toast, and brewing tea. It was time to join his housemates in their joyous and industrious preparations. Time to get on with the important work of this important day.

44

Gunter Hauser stared yet again at the photo that had ruined his week-end. The damn Americans, meddling in forbidden places. And in his own backyard, no less, which was why he now sat in an otherwise empty office of the BND on a glorious Saturday morning.

His old pal Mike Sheehan had sent the photo at about four thirty on Friday afternoon. Hauser wasn't yet certain he should be thankful for the favor, and he definitely didn't approve of its timing. Half an hour later and Hauser would have been out the door until Monday, and right now he'd be pedaling his ultralight Bianchi road bike across the tidewater plains along the North Sea, a trip he'd been planning for weeks with his two best cycling buddies. Obviously, Big Mike had no concept of how sacrosanct the idleness of a Friday afternoon was to the German civil servant, no matter how vital his duties.

It wasn't as if the photo itself was all that interesting—a shot of a few fellows from that noisy crowd over at the Al Quds mosque as they strolled down a sidewalk near a bunch of garden houses. The BND already knew about them—or most of them, anyway. A year or so ear-lier, Hauser and his colleagues had even tried to secure an indictment of one of their financial backers, but the prosecutor had blown them off. And with no prospect of any further legal action, the BND's inter-est had faded. Hauser still sent out a surveillance van from time to time for an update, and tapped into a phone line or two. But their efforts weren't as thorough as before, which hadn't pleased the Americans.

That's why Hauser had easily guessed who Ken Donlan's targets would be when the FBI man paid his courtesy call earlier that week. The visit had made him a little uneasy, but he hadn't expected any major disruptions.

Then the photo had arrived, with two faces circled, and, with it, Sheehan's note:

FYI, a few new targets for your people, perhaps? The guy toward the back is named Mahmoud, but there's no further info because mutual friends at the Agency have told our man that it's "above his clearance." If you have anything more, we'd certainly love to be in the know before matters progress further.

The obvious intimation, even if phrased in Sheehan's collegially roundabout way, was that the Agency had made an end run around the BND with regard to at least two figures in the Al Quds universe. It was embarrassing, because Hauser also had no idea who either this Mahmoud fellow or the guy in blue jeans was.

For all that, he probably would have waited until Monday to look into the matter further if he hadn't decided to make a single exploratory phone call to Richard Karner, his best contact with the Hamburg police, just in case they'd compiled a dossier or arrest record on the young man.

Their conversation had immediately veered off in an unexpected direction.

"Gunter, I've been wondering when you'd call. My only surprise is that it's taken this long. This is about the Americans, right?"

"Ah, so you've seen this photo as well?"

"Photo?"

"The one with this young fellow Mahmoud at Al Quds, plus another young man with no ID?"

"No, no. I meant this whole business over at the Plaza. Surely by now you're up to speed on all *that*, yes?"

Hauser sighed. Obviously he was out of the loop on something, and Karner was enjoying letting him know. As badly as he hated to admit to his ignorance, he was already captive to his curiosity. And late on a Friday, no less. He never should have called.

"I'm not up to speed at all, actually."

"Well, then, I was probably wrong to have opened my mouth."

"Too late to go silent on me now, Richard."

"Yes, well, you should have probably been told anyway, considering the source. He calls himself Williams."

"This is an American you're speaking of?"

"Says he's the acting cultural officer at the consulate. But when I checked with my friend there—and you know how those Americans love to talk—he says they don't currently have any TDYers on posting. That's their acronym for a temporary employer."

"Yes, Richard, I know what the fuck a TDY is. And there's no one on staff named Williams?"

"Correct. But he did say he overheard someone talking about a colleague who was in town, by the name of Bridger, and that the fellow saying this had then entered one of their locked hallways."

"Locked hallways" was Richard's coy way of referring to the Agency. And "Bridger" was almost certainly Paul Bridger, whom Hauser had heard of but had never met. His inner radar began to beep.

"Go on."

"I take it you know this name?"

"We'll discuss that in a moment."

"We'll discuss it now if you want the rest of my story."

"If he's calling himself an acting cultural officer, I don't think you need me to tell you what that means. I know there's a Bridger based in Paris who handles things on the covert side. And he's here, you say, at the Plaza?"

"Not staying there, no. But he got involved in a little cleanup on something that happened there last Monday."

Hauser, who by now had fully emerged from his late-Friday lethargy, quickly figured out at least part of the connection.

"The only relevant thing I'm aware of at the Plaza this week is the press conference by that American professor with the new book, the one that all the Islamists hate."

"Yes. We've had our hands full all week with demos and crackpots, but thank God the fellow is leaving tomorrow."

"You think the Agency is fronting for him?"

"Not sure I'd go that far, but they're certainly part of his security detail, maybe partly as a means of IDing new targets."

"But without telling me, of course."

It was inexcusable. Bridger should have personally contacted him, even if all they were doing was providing extra muscle. But if the professor and his CIA escort were indeed leaving town on Saturday, then maybe Hauser's weekend plans could remain intact. With his attention already beginning to wander, he clicked on his desktop to a Saturday weather forecast for the region where he'd be cycling, just as Karner spoke again.

"Yes, and while working with my boss to hush up a murder, no less."

Hauser let go of the mouse and refocused.

"Did you say murder?"

"At the Plaza, yes."

Karner then told him the rest of the story. Hauser took meticulous notes, and by the time he hung up he was convinced that the Agency's deflection of the Donlan photo must somehow be related to Bridger's attempt to bury the news of the murder of the American security man. Related how? He had no idea, not yet. But now that a murder was involved, Hauser could no longer afford to wait until Monday to get up to speed. Or not without risking an embarrassing lapse, especially if further and possibly bloodier events were to unfold this weekend while he was out cycling.

So the first thing he did was send a copy of the Donlan photo to Karner, who cross-checked it against a few of their own images and records, came up empty, and then promised to ask around a bit on Monday.

Hauser had then scrounged up enough spare personnel to put together a couple of surveillance teams for weekend duty. He decided to post one near the Al Quds mosque and the other near the house in Harburg where several of those characters lived.

Admittedly, the pickings had been slim when it came to available employees, especially in the case of Heinz Wiedemann, who would be running the Al Quds surveillance. Wiedemann was reasonably competent but had worn out his welcome with that crowd a year ago, when he dogged them so often that they had learned to recognize him and his van. Once he had supposedly even taunted them as he stood by the curb during a cigarette break, although Wiedemann had denied it.

The other problem was that neither team would be moving into place until noon, so Hauser would be blind to anything important that happened in the morning.

Still, on weekends you took what was available and made the best of it, so here he was on a sunny Saturday, dressed in jeans and a polo instead of his cycling clothes as he picked up his phone and punched in the number for the leader of the team that would be posted in Harburg.

"Yes?"

"Just making sure you're still on schedule for today."

"We're assembling in a few hours. You're lucky to have us at all, you know. We were supposed to be on for something up in Kiel, but they called it off."

"I'll take what I can get."

"Now there's gratitude for you. And this is overtime, right? For all of us?"

"Except Vogel. He was on standby shift already."

"I'll break the happy news to him. Maybe we'll also let him buy lunch."

Hauser heard him laughing as he hung up.

So, then, everything was set, meaning that his ass would be covered as long as Wiedemann didn't do something stupidly provocative, like flip them the bird out the window of his van. He hoped they'd come up with something noteworthy enough to justify the extra expense.

He sighed again. At this rate he'd also be working Sunday. And then of course it would be just his luck that by next Wednesday or so the first cold fingers of another gray and clammy winter would close around the city like a fist, and that would be the end of any hopes for a pleasant weekend of cycling until mid-April at the earliest.

Hauser stared intently at his notes and picked up the phone. He was going to find out all that he could about these two fellows, and he would start with the one named Mahmoud.

45

One of Bridger's minders followed Claire to the airport. She'd expected nothing less, although she was a little surprised he was making it so obvious. Wharton's way of sending a message, she supposed: *Good riddance and bon voyage.*

His taxi stopped right behind hers. He hopped out when she did and followed her through the big revolving doors into the cavernous main lobby, where he stood off to the side, sipping coffee through a plastic lid while she waited in line to check her bags and collect her boarding pass. It was noon, far later than Claire had hoped to get started on such a potentially eventful day, but flight schedules hadn't allowed for anything earlier.

From the check-in counter the minder tailed her to the security checkpoint, and when Claire's carry-on bag cleared the conveyer belt she turned to wave goodbye. He at least had the good grace to nod. Was that a smile, or a grimace from the bitter taste of his coffee? He turned to head for his next observation post, probably downstairs. Bridger had told her his name was Chris, although that probably was fake. She supposed she'd be seeing him later. The key question was whether he'd see her.

Her airport contact, recruited overnight by Bridger from his vast array of assets, was supposed to be seated in the waiting area for Gate 33, after having arrived earlier on a LOT nonstop out of Warsaw. Black skirt, cream blouse, red scarf, red pumps, black sunglasses, blond wig—

that was the working description from an overnight text. She would be reading a copy of *Der Spiegel*, with a blue carry-on bag at her feet.

Claire had been on virtual lockdown since the night before, when Bridger, in a calculated display of solidarity with Wharton, had handed her over to his minders outside the Chinese restaurant. Claire had done her best to act shocked and betrayed. One of the minders—Chris, in fact—had then escorted her to the Plaza, where he checked her into a new room and arranged for delivery of her things from the one she'd been sharing with the fake professor.

"Mr. Armitage said to tell you goodbye, and that he was sorry," Chris said.

She let the remark pass without comment but was surprised to realize she'd developed a soft spot for the pudgy little analyst, who, like the real professor Armitage, had gotten into something way over his head. She hoped no one would take a potshot at Weeks as he and Tony continued their folly of a media tour. Most of her anger now had to do with poor Lute, who had been killed protecting an impostor. She doubted that Wharton or even Bridger would give it a second thought, and that also ticked her off.

Now it was Mahmoud, or Malachy, whose safety and security were in doubt. He, at least, was fully aware of the dangers of his assignment. She marveled at what he had already been able to accomplish and was somewhat in awe of his willingness to commit to such a long-term immersion. She doubted she'd ever be able to manage that. It wasn't her lack of skills; it was her unwillingness to walk away from her own life for months at a time, maybe longer.

She knew there were often hidden motivators in accepting such assignments. Personal upheaval, or great loss. Deep undercover work sometimes functioned as the spy's equivalent of retreating to an ashram to rethink your life. That might well be the case with Mahmoud, given his fall from grace. And now Wharton had dismantled the young man's support network, just when he might need it the most.

Until she got free, the only person watching over him would be Donlan, who by now was probably at his surveillance post in Harburg. Claire had phoned him late the night before to tell him everything she had learned. He had sounded as excited as you'd expect, and had readily agreed to help. But she had also detected a note of worry, which made her wonder if Donlan's boss, Sheehan, had already become a problem. And that prospect was making her impatient, antsy. Time to get her little disappearing act done and dusted, as the Brits liked to say.

But when she reached Gate 33, the only person in the waiting area was a cleaning woman, emptying a trash bag. She strolled to the big board where the arrival and departure times were posted. The flight from Warsaw, which should have landed eighty minutes ago, was delayed. It wouldn't be here for at least another two hours.

She strolled to her own gate, where passengers for the flight to Dulles were already fidgeting with anticipation. The status board at the counter said boarding would begin in forty minutes. This wasn't going to work.

Claire phoned Bridger.

"Yes?"

"Are you able to talk?"

"I've got a ten-minute window. And some bad news."

"I've already seen it. Her flight's delayed. Another two hours, it says."

"I'm told it may actually be worse. Par for the course on this LOT route, I'm afraid, but working this close to a deadline didn't give me enough time for a plan B."

"I'd have arranged my own if you hadn't put me under lock and key."

"Wharton had to believe I'd fully taken charge of you, Claire."

"But now we're fucked, unless you can do something at your end in the next forty minutes."

"Not even the full power of the U.S. government can make an airline be on time."

"But you can certainly do something about delaying *my* flight, yes?"

"Excellent point. I'm on it."

Claire settled in. She was still dressed in her Mrs. Armitage wardrobe, and the baggy polyester clothing was more irritating than ever.

Fifteen minutes later, a collective groan issued from the people around her. The status board now said her flight was delayed for an hour. Not enough, but if Bridger could arrange this on short notice, perhaps he could arrange for more.

A woman's voice crackled over the PA system.

"For all United passengers on Flight 1320 to Washington Dulles, scheduled for departure at 1:42 p.m., that flight has now been delayed at least an hour due to an apparent documentation error. An airline official is now en route to clear up the problem, but we are not yet able to offer a firm departure time. We will keep you informed of any updates as they occur. In the meantime, for your convenience and comfort, a snack cart will soon arrive at the gate with complimentary items for all our passengers."

There was another chorus of groans. To her left, a prosperous-looking American in a pinstripe suit glanced impatiently at his massive watch and said, "Only in fucking Germany would you have a paper-work delay."

To her right, a German of comparable age and attire volleyed back, "And only an American company would think it could buy you off with a bag of potato chips."

"You're both right," Claire said as she stood to take a walk. Maybe burning off some energy would calm her nerves. Already she could sense that time was growing short for Mahmoud.

46

Ken Donlan, watching from the empty apartment in Harburg, couldn't decide if excitement or caffeine was more responsible for keeping him going. All he knew for sure was that he needed both, given the lousy night's sleep he had endured.

He had gotten out of bed at least five times, restless, his mind flitting from thought to thought like a cat chasing bugs in the dark. A few times he sat at the end of the bed and scribbled ideas onto a notepad. He then scratched them out, tore them into pieces, and burned them over the toilet while trying not to set off the smoke alarm. He poured himself a drink, only to leave it untouched, and then killed an hour watching a godawful German TV talk show hosted by a flabby woman who sat naked on a rotating couch. Or had he dreamed that? No, he'd seen it, weirdest thing ever.

Twice he picked up the phone to call Sheehan, then thought better of it. By dawn he was too exhausted to do anything but page room service for a pot of coffee. He then drove down to Harburg, with the windows open for the bracing air, as the sun came up across the marshes to his left.

Claire's news the night before had keyed him up as much as anything since the Giants won the Super Bowl in '91, a game that still made him anxious whenever he thought about the last-second field goal attempt that had nearly defeated them, the ball tumbling end over end toward the goalposts like a blade aimed straight at his heart until . . .

Wide right! And now his worry was that, partly in response to his own actions, Big Mike Sheehan might tee up some kind of meddlesome play that would scuttle this apparent victory over Al Qaeda. Mahmoud was a mole. Donlan could hardly believe it.

But that damn photo. He never should have sent it to the boss. And he definitely should've told Claire that Sheehan now had a copy, just to give her a heads-up. Maybe he'd tell her when they were a little more in control of the situation. Better still, maybe Sheehan would show some restraint. Even if that happened, too many secrets had now been shared among too many people for him to feel comfortable about Mahmoud's security.

At least now he didn't feel so bad about having twice lost track of the guy in surveillance. A trained spy, Langley's own: That was Mahmoud. And to hear Claire tell it, he was now on the verge of easing himself even deeper into the Al Quds crowd, with the looming prospect of foreign travel and a special mission.

Unless they blew it, of course, right here at crunch time. Already today he had seen some interesting activity at the house on Marien-strasse. Several comings and goings, both involving young men loading items into a car. Supplies for the big wedding, Donlan supposed. He'd been pleased when Claire confirmed his speculation on that count.

No sign yet of Mahmoud, not even a twitch of his window blinds, and that was beginning to bother him. It was now early afternoon—shouldn't he have shown his face by now? Was everything all right inside the house? Was Mahmoud even there?

Donlan then spotted something troubling off to the left—a brown van, creeping up the hill as if searching for a parking spot. It eased into a space about twenty feet to the left of his vantage point and shut off the engine. The windshield was smoked glass, totally opaque. Donlan waited for someone to get out, but no one did. Maybe it was a repair-man, gathering his tools or double-checking the address.

Five minutes passed, and still no one emerged or even rolled down a window. Not a repairman, then. Donlan's fallback hope was that the van had come to pick up someone, and that the driver was waiting for that someone to come out of a house. But five more minutes passed and no one appeared. The likeliest explanation now was the one he dreaded most: This was a surveillance van, and he doubted that Claire had ordered it up. Another set of eyes on Mahmoud, then, but who were they working for? Wharton? The BND? And why now?

From the other direction, a white Mercedes turned the nearest corner and headed for the house, where it stopped out front. Haydar Zammar was back, honking his horn. And there, finally, was a sign of life from Mahmoud's room as someone briefly moved the blinds aside to glance down at the street.

Shortly afterward, the door opened downstairs. Four young men piled down the steps, each of them familiar to Donlan: Amir, Omar, Mahmoud, and Jarrah. All were neatly dressed, although hardly up to the standard of what Donlan would expect for a wedding. No coats and ties for these radical Muslims, he thought. Perhaps only the groom bothered with all that. Having never been to a Muslim wedding, he had no idea.

They walked single-file toward the Mercedes. If Donlan hadn't been pretty certain about where they were going, he would have been grabbing his car keys and preparing to bolt out the door in pursuit. Instead he remained calm, knowing he could hang back for a few minutes. His rental Passat was parked around the corner, and he'd easily reach Al Quds before the wedding began.

The first of the four young men was opening the back door of the Mercedes when Mahmoud, last in line, stopped and held up a hand. He said something unintelligible and pivoted back toward the house, jogging now as he ascended the steps and disappeared back into the building. Had he forgotten something?

To the left, the brown van remained as watchful as a crouching predator. Donlan didn't like it one bit. Claire needed to know. Maybe she'd even have an explanation, but at this hour he didn't want to risk disrupting her with a phone call at an awkward moment. He checked his watch. Shouldn't she have been in touch by now?

Several minutes passed, and Mahmoud's waiting friends seemed to be growing restless. Omar called out loudly, something in Arabic that was probably the equivalent of "Move your ass!" Zammar beeped his horn, a short toot followed by a three-second blast that caused curtains to open up and down the block.

Then Amir took action. Scowling and businesslike, he mounted the steps, threw open the door, and disappeared back into the building.

This, too, disturbed Donlan. Maybe he was overreacting, now that he knew Mahmoud's true role, but he didn't believe he was wrong in thinking that something about this dynamic felt off, even a little dangerous. It was then that he realized he had no idea what the rules of engagement were if it became clear that Mahmoud was in trouble. Was he supposed to merely observe? Intervene? Call the cops? Call Claire? Go outside and bang on the side of that fucking van?

He began pacing the dusty floor of the empty apartment. He and Claire needed reinforcements, and they needed a clearer idea of what to do in case of an emergency. He stared at the upstairs windows in the house across the street, wondering what was happening behind the blinds. Then he voiced his emotions, in the same way that he always shouted at his TV during the tensest moments of a Giants game.

"C'mon, Mahmoud. Get your ass back out here where I can see you!"

But the door to the house remained closed. Zammar again honked the horn. Donlan checked his watch and began counting the seconds.

47

As his housemates departed for Saeed's wedding, it occurred to Mahmoud that a rare opportunity was at hand. Only four of them remained—him, Jarrah, Omar, and Amir—and when Brother Haydar came to pick them up in his Mercedes, it would mean the house was empty.

With some nimble footwork, he could double back for a quick reconnaissance of Amir's room, a possibility that had enticed him since the night before, when Esma had read the passage from Jarrah's journal that said, "Amir has entrusted me with much that is important. He took me into his room and showed me names, dates, and photos of all the places we will go. It is a plan, and I am part of it."

Mahmoud wanted to see all of that, especially if he would soon be traveling to a part of the world where it would be difficult, if not impossible, to relay a message to Bridger. He might be able to glean at least a sketchy preview of whatever they were planning. Worth a try, anyway, because once you disappeared into a place like Afghanistan, you might never return. Was he ready for that possibility? Probably not, but he supposed that was what he had signed on for.

Frankly, he was also worried that if Esma showed up, today could be his last opportunity to gather vital information. An angry Amir might react by kicking Mahmoud out of the group. It would be an especially stupid way for the op to fall apart, and he'd have only himself to blame. All the more reason, then, to try to find out everything he could before it was too late.

So, fifteen minutes later, as everyone traipsed down the sidewalk to pile into Brother Haydar's car, Mahmoud raised a hand and exclaimed, "Forgot something. Be right back!"

He turned and ran into the building before anyone could object. On the stairwell he quickened his pace, taking the steps two at a time as he listened for anyone who might have followed. They were an impatient bunch, so he didn't have much time.

His first stop was his own room, where he grabbed a comb off the top of the dresser and stuffed it in his pocket. That would be his excuse for returning.

He stepped across the hall to Amir's doorway. The house was silent. He turned the handle, not at all surprised that the door was unlocked, since, by their rules of communal living, it would have been selfish and even ungodly for Amir to keep his possessions under lock and key.

The room was clean and spartan, with bare plaster walls, no carpeting. The window blind was closed, fortunately. He could hear his housemates chattering on the walkway below. No one was yet calling out for him to hurry.

Along the wall to the left was a single bed with an iron frame, like something in a college dorm. It was covered by an army surplus wool blanket, tucked neatly. To the right was a chest of drawers, scratched and battered, and beside it a narrow closet with the door shut. At the foot of the bed was a rolled prayer rug and a pair of blue plastic shower sandals. Straight ahead, level with the windowsill, was a small wooden desk with a single lamp, two side drawers, and a metal folding chair.

Mahmoud got to work. On top of the desk were two copies of the Holy Quran—one quite old, with a dog-eared leather cover and a cracked binding, and one much newer, bound in white vinyl. He flipped the pages quickly, finding nothing concealed in either copy. Stacked to the right were bills and repair invoices for the house. To the left was another pile of papers, with neat handwriting in German. Judging by the wording and a few diagrams, they were Amir's notes toward his dissertation for a doctorate in urban planning. Next to them were three weighty volumes—textbooks—with titles in German. Nothing inside them, either.

There was a shallow middle drawer, unlocked, which was stuffed with bank stubs, erasers, a pocket calculator, two Ritter Sport chocolate bars, a box of paper clips, and a logjam of pens and pencils.

A shout from below broke the silence—Omar's voice, loud and shrill: "What's taking so long? Let's get going!"

Then Brother Haydar laid on the horn, a toot followed by a long blast.

He listened for footsteps. None were coming, as far as he could tell. He was sweating from haste and nerves. He pulled open the top drawer with such force that it nearly flew off its runners, and that certainly wouldn't have been easy to explain.

Inside were more notes from Amir's college work, some of them marked up in red by a professor, with handwritten notes in Arabic in the margins. The second drawer held a user's guide for spreadsheet software, a DIY manual on car repair, a textbook on electrical engineering.

Didn't he even keep a laptop here? Apparently not, which seemed odd.

Mahmoud was running out of time, but he couldn't stop now, with so little to show for his efforts. There was a thud from downstairs, probably from the main doorway, followed by footsteps in the stairwell. Time was short.

Mahmoud threw open the closet door but quickly surmised that there was nothing in there but clothes and shoes, and precious few of those. Amir lived like a fucking monk. But where did he keep all of those records that Jarrah had seen? Had he moved them? Destroyed them, even?

He stooped to look beneath the bed and saw a cardboard box, flaps loose. Finally.

He dropped to his knees and slid the box out, but when he pulled back the flaps, all he found was more textbooks with German titles. He pushed the box back beneath the bed just as he heard the door of the apartment rattle open.

Mahmoud stood so fast that he nearly lost his balance. He left the room and shut the door behind him as gently as possible, and no sooner had he turned toward his own door than he heard footsteps rounding the corner at the end of the hall. He pulled his own door shut, took a second to compose himself, and turned to face whoever it was.

"Brother Amir."

Mahmoud's face was perspiring. He should have wiped it dry. Amir stood there, stern and unsmiling, arms akimbo. His brown eyes were as cold as stones in a stream.

"We were beginning to wonder where you had gone," Amir said.

"Forgot my comb."

Mahmoud pulled it awkwardly from his pocket, flashing it like an entry pass back to freedom.

Amir, expression unchanged, slowly shook his head.

"Vanity."

"Yes, I suppose it is. But it's also out of respect for Saeed and his bride. We should all look our best for them."

Amir's face registered no reaction. Instead he stepped closer, coming up the hallway until he reached his own door and turned the handle. He looked inside, and something he noticed made him freeze. He walked in and shut the door behind him while Mahmoud remained in the hallway, trying to control his breathing.

Another blast of the horn sounded from the street. Then Omar shouted again, as impatient as ever. Mahmoud didn't know whether he should make his escape or wait. Surely Amir must have figured out what he'd been up to, because Mahmoud could now hear drawers opening and closing. But why? There was nothing in there to protect, unless he had missed something in his search.

Mahmoud was on the verge of heading down the hallway when the door opened again. Amir looked surprised to see Mahmoud waiting, and it seemed to bring him up short. Then Amir reached into his pocket and, almost sheepishly, he, too, raised a comb for inspection.

"You are right, Brother Mahmoud. We should look our best for Saeed. And also for God. Maybe that is vanity as well."

"Maybe."

Mahmoud exhaled a bit too loudly, and followed Amir downstairs to the street, where the others had already piled into the waiting car.

Preparations were already in full swing by the time they arrived at the mosque. Mahmoud and the others joined right in, setting up chairs and tables and making sure that the food deliveries were handled properly.

Saeed arrived, wearing a suit and tie. He stood at the back of the room, pacing, looking as nervous as, well, a groom on his wedding day.

"Your family is still coming, yes?" Omar shouted from across the room.

"Of course. Why wouldn't they?"

"Well, it's just that your mother . . ."

"Oh, she wishes me well. She's over all that other business."

Mahmoud wasn't so sure about that. When they visited her the day before, he had sensed her disapproval of Saeed's friends at Al Quds, and she obviously hadn't given up on her efforts to change him back into the young man he had once been.

"That beard still has to go," she'd told him, joking but not joking.

"Sorry, Mom. The beard stays."

Mahmoud wondered how she'd react when they started singing songs of jihad—as they were bound to do at some point—during the reception. He was guessing that, if anything, Saeed's father—a Moroccan, just like Mahmoud's dad—would be even more appalled. Their fathers probably would have gotten along quite well—they were the same sort of Muslim, observant and devout, but not all that strict about the rules.

He imagined his own parents attending an event like this. He pictured them keeping to themselves over in a corner, bewildered, sipping nonalcoholic punch, both of them craving wine and a cigarette. Dad with his worry beads, Mom with her rosary.

"Mahmoud," someone shouted, "can you help me move this table?"

"Sure."

He got back to work. They finished setting up the room and began hanging a big privacy curtain down the middle of the room to separate the men from the women. You wouldn't need that for a less traditional wedding, but for this one it would remain in place even during the celebratory feast.

As the barrier went up, he wondered if his worries about Esma were overblown. Even if she dared to drop by, she was too smart to make herself easily known. She would dress conservatively, and plan any intervention with care. She would probably try to cull Jarrah from the herd as he left for the bathroom, or maybe when he departed for home.

Mahmoud doubted Jarrah would do her any physical harm, even in anger, although he might sound the alarm to the others. If so, perhaps Mahmoud could cover for her just long enough for Esma to get away. But then he, too, would be in trouble, for having failed at his assignment. It was all such a mess, and largely on account of his own weakness. Mahmoud needed to stay alert for any possibility.

They finished hanging the curtain. Mahmoud dusted off his hands and watched the others. Omar, eyes gleaming, bustled from place to place like the maître d' of a fine restaurant on opening night. He seemed supercharged by the prospect of a big social gathering where he could turn on the charm to its highest wattage.

"Amir!" he called out.

"Yes, Brother Omar."

"Where are those song lyrics you wrote down for me?"

"I put them away down the hall."

"In your study?"

"Yes, on top of the desk. The imam has a key."

"Why not just give me yours?"

"Use the imam's."

Of course. A study. Amir must have kept his most secretive papers right here at the mosque, and no doubt the imam was happy to let him do so. Mahmoud was thrilled by the whole idea of it. It had to be where Jarrah had seen all of those items, and today offered the perfect opportunity for a look.

He supposed that, like Omar, he could find some excuse for asking the imam for the key. But if word got back to Amir—and why wouldn't it?—it would raise too many uncomfortable questions. Besides, he doubted that any lock on an interior door at the mosque was very sturdy, and he kept a small, slender steel tool in a hidden sleeve of his wallet for just such a purpose.

But for now, the guests were beginning to arrive—women heading to one side, men to the other. Esma was not among them, and, with his hopes for a productive day now burgeoning, Mahmoud was beginning to believe she would not come at all.

Later, then, when everyone was eating and celebrating. That's when he would make his move.

48

The flight from Warsaw finally landed.

By now Claire had checked in by phone with Donlan, who had just moved from his perch in Harburg to a spot on Steindamm near the Al Quds mosque, watching from his Passat.

She was ticked off that she had already missed so much of the day, and she was worried by his report of possible surveillance vans, one at each location. She supposed that might be Bridger's doing. If he could rustle up an asset from Warsaw on such short notice, maybe he'd also conjured up a pair of surveillance teams.

But she doubted it, and he probably would have told her about it during their last phone call, if only to reassure her that Mahmoud was already under close observation.

"You think it's the BND?" she asked Donlan.

"Who else would it be?"

"But why? And why now?"

Donlan sighed, then confessed that he had sent a copy of the photo to Sheehan.

"Fuck."

"I know. My bad, but it was a direct order. I told him to play it cool, but, well . . ."

"Fuck, Kenny. Half the known world is going to have a photo of him by the time we're done."

"I know, I know. And I should've told you yesterday. But, well, yeah, I just should've."

"As long as it's true confessions time, I'm not exactly thrilled with the idea of the BND spotting me, either."

"How come?"

"Long story, very old, and the last thing I should be worried about, considering everything else that's happening. And you've seen no sign of Esma?"

She had described Esma to him the night before.

"None, and pretty much everybody has arrived. The wedding must've started by now."

"Well, if she's coming it'll probably be toward the end, when she's less likely to attract attention. Maybe by then I'll be in place."

"Let's hope. Good luck at your end."

"Same."

Now she was watching the Warsaw arrivals emerge from the jetway. Like Claire, the contact was supposed to be slender, and about five and a half feet tall. Unlike her, she was not yet forty, an age difference that Claire decided to take as a compliment after Bridger told her he'd deployed the closest possible match.

There she was, strolling past the gate attendant, dressed just as promised, and now it was clear that she had spotted Claire—not exactly a tough chore, since Claire was wearing an orange blouse and the despised baggy brown polyester pantsuit.

Claire followed from about twenty yards back as the woman continued down the concourse toward the nearest restroom, where a cleaning woman had blocked the doorway with one of those folding "Closed for Cleaning" signs, a ruse ensuring that Claire and her contact would have their choice of all eight stalls.

As the contact entered, the cleaning woman exited. Claire went inside and walked to the last stall on the right, where she entered and shut the door. She heard someone unzipping a skirt in the next stall.

Claire began to undress. Off came the hideous fabrics with their Halloween colors. She thrust them beneath the partition, where unseen hands took possession. She similarly jettisoned her sensible shoes, chunky black monstrosities built for asylum wardens and prison guards.

Shortly after that, a neatly folded cream-colored silk blouse appeared at the opening below. Claire took it and hung it on the hook on the back of the door. A black skirt followed, and then the red scarf, the sunglasses, the blue-carry-on. Next came the red pumps. Surprisingly, they were a perfect fit, and looked better than she could have hoped for. The last contributions were the blond wig and a big brown Louis Vuitton handbag with leather handles.

Inside the handbag was a wallet with a fresh supply of D-marks, a credit card, a New Jersey driver's license, and a U.S. passport with Claire's photo and the name of Rebecca Joan Thompson, age forty-one—another dose of flattery—of Nutley, New Jersey. She inspected it closely, flipping the pages with their visa stamps and slightly worn feel. Very nice for a rush job. Bridger had outdone himself, and the miracle of it was that he had probably managed most of it from his room at the Dammtorpalais, almost literally under Wharton's nose. She smiled and removed her phone from her old handbag and then slid the bag beneath the partition, along with her boarding pass and all of the documentation for Mrs. Brenda Armitage.

She flushed the toilet, smoothed her skirt, and emerged for a look in the mirror, already blooming with pleasure at how good it felt to no longer be draped in all of that billowing excess, with the reptilian feel of polyester. Yes, it was silly to draw this much pleasure out of a silk blouse and a crepe de chine pencil skirt, but after nearly a week dressed so horribly, it felt as if she had reentered her own skin, her own personality. Even the head-to-toe coverings of her guise as an older Turkish woman had been preferable to the Brenda Armitage collection.

The door of the other stall opened behind her. Glancing in the mirror, Claire saw her counterpart emerge in the hated costume.

"Good God!" the woman muttered under her breath. They were still the only two customers in the restroom, so Claire felt free to check her out. Attractive, with lively and intelligent eyes, which made her wonder if there had ever been more to her relationship with Bridger than just work. She knew firsthand the sort of loyalty he inspired among his Janes and Joes—the kind that, under certain stresses, could easily become a tad too personal.

They exchanged glances in the mirror. A glint in the other woman's eyes made Claire wonder if she was engaging in the same speculation.

"Hope you at least get a few extra days in the States to unwind," Claire said.

"Of course. Plus, for now, the usual cheap thrill of pulling this off."

"Yes, there's always that."

They exchanged smiles of professional approval, and at that moment Claire wouldn't have traded her job for any other.

"Good luck," the woman said, "whatever it is you're doing."

"Thanks."

Then two other women came through the door, ending the conversation. Claire gathered up her carry-on and the handbag and departed. A few minutes later, having cleared passport control, she was riding the escalator down to the exits near baggage claim. Chris the minder was there, just as she'd expected, scanning the departing passengers. He'd presumably remain in place until he received confirmation from airline personnel at the departure gate that the flight to Dulles had left with Mrs. Armitage on board.

She found his diligence oddly reassuring. Sloppy tradecraft irritated Claire, even among adversaries, and technically this fellow was working for her side.

Nonetheless, she whisked right past him, no more than fifteen feet to his left. Then she cleared customs, crossed the lower level of the terminal and rode another escalator down to the underground station for the S-Bahn, where she boarded a waiting train and, five minutes later, departed for the city center.

No cell phone reception down there, so she would be out of touch for a while if there were any further updates from Donlan. But at least now she was free and clear to worry about more important things. Namely, Mahmoud, the Agency's most important asset since, well, since she had first come aboard, nearly twenty-five years ago. And now she was in the thick of the operation that was running him. Late to the party, but invited nonetheless.

Fifteen minutes later, the S-Bahn reached her stop. Bridger was supposed to be waiting in a rental car just around the corner, provided he'd slipped the leash of his own minder. She came up the stairs and turned the corner. A dark blue Ford Mondeo flashed its blinkers from just up the block. Bridger was ready to roll. And just in time, because if Mahmoud needed help today, it was likely to be soon.

"You certainly look sharp," he said, doing a double take as she slid onto the seat.

"Let's hope the BND thinks so as well." He frowned as she told him about the surveillance vans.

"I was hoping maybe they were your handiwork," she said.

"Not a chance. We won't even get Janis back in action until this evening at the earliest."

"So you've recalled her, too."

"Your disobedience inspired me. I'm now officially in full revolt."

"And Wharton hasn't called?"

"I'm guessing my minder is still looking for me, and hasn't yet had the guts to report he lost me. Plus, I turned off my phone the second I saw you come up from the S-Bahn."

"So we really are on our own."

"Which is good in one way, bad in another. From everything you've told me, this feels like the worst possible time to be shorthanded."

She nodded and settled back into the seat as Bridger accelerated toward the Al Quds mosque, their sense of urgency palpable.

Finally, her real work had begun.

49

Donlan was still antsy about the goddamn vans. He no longer had any doubts about their purpose.

Even under the best of circumstances, it was hard to commence a security intervention without either spooking your targets or endangering your asset. On foreign soil the odds got longer. And with the resident intelligence agency watching, ready to film the whole thing, the dangers multiplied for everyone. Even if you pulled it off, you risked losing your job, or, at the very least, your employer's good standing with the locals. Donlan could wind up being persona non grata for life with the Germans. Sheehan would have his ass.

Meanwhile, the wedding celebration was apparently in full swing. Someone upstairs had opened a window, and Donlan could hear singing in Arabic from his perch across the street. Male voices in full cry, loud and jolly, with a driving beat. And all of it without a single drop of alcohol; he wondered how that was even possible. He had attended only one dry wedding, a reception in the basement of a Baptist church in rural North Carolina. He and his friends had escaped as fast as they could from the petrified church ladies, with their punch bowls and congealed salads, decamping to the bride and groom's home, where the real party had finally begun. But it was good to be hearing music, he supposed. Even if they were singing about holy war, it meant they must be happy, which could only be good news for Mahmoud.

A few moments later, a trim young woman approached on the sidewalk on his side of the street, and he knew almost instantly that it must be the mysterious Esma.

She was quite attractive: dark-haired and serious looking, with an assured stride. And now she was stopped at the curb, gazing directly across Steindamm at the entrance to the mosque. No doubt she heard the music, but she seemed to be deep in thought, as if considering her next move.

Maybe he should call Claire. He had figured she'd be here by now. He picked up his phone to do so, then put it down to watch Esma. Her posture was rigid, her eyes wide. Scared, maybe, a brave young woman mustering the nerve for a potentially dangerous confrontation. The male voices from across the way reached a crescendo and then went quiet, subsiding in a backwash of laughter and applause. But Esma remained in place while Donlan watched, transfixed.

Five minutes passed, then ten, and still she did nothing but watch, her face angled up toward the open window across the street. If anything, her expression was more determined than before. Donlan decided it was like watching a long fuse burn slowly but inevitably— their very own stick of dynamite, that was Esma, and she looked set to explode any second.

Donlan again reached for his phone, then hesitated. He had no way of knowing if Claire had yet escaped her minder. But if things started to go wrong here, he'd have no choice, and he had a bad feeling Mahmoud would need reinforcements fairly soon.

He set his phone on the car seat, and kept his eyes on Esma.

50

Mahmoud seized his chance not long after Omar began belting out songs of jihad. By now the feast was nearly over. Two whole lambs, splayed and seasoned and roasted, had been stripped to the bone. Platters of bread, tomatoes, salad, and baked plums were wiped clean. The big containers of tea and lemonade were down to a trickle, and the caterers had begun brewing coffee and carrying in trays of Moroccan sweets.

He felt a little sorry for Saeed's family. Not just his mom and dad, who seemed bewildered by the boisterous passions of the Al Quds regulars, but Saeed's brother, Markus. They had met after Mahmoud took his loaded dinner plate to a folding chair in the corner, well away from the others, a vantage point that had allowed him to furtively keep an eye on the women's side of the room through a narrow opening in the curtain, in case Esma showed up.

Markus had introduced himself. Then he'd nodded toward Omar and some of the others, a knot of seven or eight young men, with Saeed in the middle.

"Do you think they're always like this?" he'd asked, obviously unaware that Mahmoud was one of the elect.

"Like what?"

"So intense. So cut off from everyone else. It's like the rest of us don't exist. My brother's not even normal anymore. I pity his poor wife."

"I suppose they are a bit zealous. But friendly when you get to know them. Welcoming, too."

Markus paused to reassess him.

"Sorry. I hadn't realized that . . ."

"It's okay. I understand. We can take a little getting used to."

As if to drive home the point, Omar had then begun a speech, gesturing emphatically and raising his voice as his flock gathered closer in support. Others who were standing nearby, not among the faithful, drifted toward the corners but kept watching Omar with expressions of appalled fascination. An Al Quds regular switched on a video camera and began filming.

"For so many of us, it feels like now we are back in school, taking our lessons in Arabic," Omar said. "And we know that at the end of all this, there will be a big test. Some of us will pass, some will not. But I hope that all of us will be ready. Like our brother Saeed. And like our Brother Jarrah, who is saying farewell to us today!"

Jarrah and Saeed linked arms with Omar, and everyone broke into song. The lyrics, in Arabic, weren't exactly standard wedding fare:

We follow the voice of your call, we are aglow with readiness for action, we will crush the throne of the oppressor!

Markus, who, like Saeed, must have learned Arabic from his dad, shook his head.

"Well, that's all very cheery and appropriate to the occasion, isn't it?"

Mahmoud suppressed a smile and stood.

"We'll calm down in a while. But I'm afraid that first we'll have to sing it out of our system. Excuse me, I'd better take part or they'll think I've become a timid old stick in the mud."

Mahmoud, familiar with all their usual anthems, joined in, linking arms with Jarrah. Haydar Zammar appeared on his left, and at the end of the song he pulled Mahmoud aside, a task made more cumbersome by a large plate balanced in Brother Haydar's left hand, filled with sweets. A droplet of honey glazed a corner of his mouth.

"This almond briouat must have come straight from the heavens. So tasty. You brothers outdid yourselves with the catering."

"That was Omar's doing. The master of logistics."

"Speaking of good deeds, Brother Amir tells me you have finally freed Brother Jarrah from his deadly anchor, that woman of his."

"Well, I hope so."

"You are not sure?"

"People who leave on trains can also return on trains. Who can ever say for sure with women, yes?"

Haydar, smiling, seemed to take it as a joke, but Mahmoud felt better that he had hedged his bets in case Esma turned up later.

"By the way, Brother Mahmoud, I have chosen a course for you."

"A course?"

"A route. For your next journey in life."

"Oh. That's gratifying to know. And exciting. Thank you."

"You are welcome, Brother Mahmoud. Soon I will have a visa for you, and a date of departure. From here you will travel to faraway places. But first you must purify your heart. Cleanse it of all earthly matters. The time of fun and waste in your life has gone."

"Of course."

"The time of judgment has arrived."

"Absolutely. Yes, I agree."

Brother Haydar nodded and then drifted back toward the sweets table as Omar launched into another song. A cake had just arrived. It felt like an opportune moment to slip away. If anyone asked, Mahmoud would say he was going to the men's room.

He stepped into the hallway and made his way toward Amir's study. As he passed the stairwell, he nearly collided with a smocked employee of the caterer, rushing up with yet another load of goodies.

"There are more trays to be brought up from our truck," he said. "Can some of you help us?"

"Ask in there."

Mahmoud gestured over his shoulder, then headed to the end of the hall. He turned the corner, walked the length of the hallway, and then turned another corner to make his way back toward the front of the building. It was dark here, and much quieter. There was a row of three doors, all of them shut. The first opened onto a storage closet with cleaning equipment and office supplies. The second, also unlocked, was the imam's office. Mahmoud had been there before and knew that it didn't lead anywhere else.

The third door was locked. There was a keyhole in the middle of the handle. Mahmoud took out his wallet, removed his steel tool, and inserted it into the hole. It took him only a few seconds to spring the push-button lock. He entered and shut the door behind him.

It was a narrow office with a single window facing the street, and a desk and office chair to the side. The blinds were open. He considered shutting them, but for the moment there was just enough daylight left for him to poke around without having to turn on a light, so he left them open.

He knew right away that this must be the place, because a familiar tote bag of Amir's sat atop the desk, next to a Dell laptop. But it was the view out the window that next caught his attention, because there was Esma, one floor below, standing directly across the street in a watchful pose.

His first impulse was to run downstairs so that he could persuade her to leave. He then realized she probably wasn't moving anytime soon. In fact, she appeared to be rooted to her vantage point. Was it possible that she had already come upstairs and then retreated, after deeming her mission to be futile? Or maybe she had decided to wait for however long it took Jarrah to emerge from the building. He decided to start searching the room while trying to keep an eye on her.

He switched on the laptop and it began to boot up. Then he opened the top drawer of the desk. An airline ticket was there, with a departure date of ten days from now. Next to that was Amir's Egyptian passport, and inside that was a visa for Pakistan, issued only a week earlier. Amir's eventual destination was almost certainly Quetta, out in the desert reaches of Baluchistan and close to the border of Afghanistan. Also in the drawer, folded neatly, was a printout of an email from Haydar Zammar with a list of names and dates. All the key players from their inner circle were listed. The dates for Jarrah and Amir coincided with their air tickets, so apparently this was the master travel plan for the whole group. Five of them were scheduled to leave for Pakistan over the next two weeks, with the departure dates staggered at intervals of two to four days.

At the bottom of the list, scribbled in pencil, was his own name, next to a question mark. And now, based on what Brother Haydar had told him only moments ago, that question would soon be answered. Mahmoud would be the last one in line, the final piece in whatever operational puzzle they were assembling. He assumed they'd all be reuniting overseas. For training and, presumably, to receive marching orders from some higher figure in the Al Qaeda hierarchy. He supposed that meeting bin Laden himself was even a possibility, given the location. Mahmoud's heartbeat quickened. He took a deep breath, steadied himself, and wiped his palms on his trousers.

In living with these fellows from day to day, all of their recurring bluster had at times taken on the feel of empty boasts—rote displays with more bark than bite. Now that he had seen this schedule with everyone's names, the songs he had just been hearing felt portentous and prophetic. Ditto for Jarrah's journal entries. Clearly, their planning was fairly advanced. Clearly, those songs of jihad were not just hot air. Saeed's brother Markus was right to be appalled. This was leading to something bigger, and soon.

He realized he hadn't checked on Esma for several minutes. A glance out the window confirmed that she was still frozen in place—either by reluctance or indecision. *Good. Stay that way.* He just needed five more minutes and then he would attend to her.

He opened the lower drawer. It was stuffed with file folders. But by this time the laptop was ready to roll. It was password protected, of course, so he couldn't open any emails or documents. Maybe later in the week he could return with a memory stick, to try to download the contents. For now he contented himself with scanning the icons on the screen. They were about what you'd expect, with one exception—a link to Flight Simulator software. He noted that with interest, then turned toward the file drawer.

Another glance out the window told him that Esma was still standing at the curb.

The folders in the file drawer covered a range of Al Quds business. A few were for keeping track of Amir's Islamic study groups—one at his university, one at the mosque. Another was labeled "Maps." Mahmoud removed it and opened it on the desk. Inside were folded city maps for Hamburg, London, New York, and Islamabad. But the oddest item was an air navigation map for the Eastern Seaboard of the United States. He stared at it for a few seconds, baffled by its concentric circles and coded waypoint markings. Then he refolded it carefully and put the folder back into the drawer.

Another glance outside. Esma remained in place.

He looked for anything to do with aircraft or flying, and he quickly found two more items. The first was a pilot's manual for a Boeing 737, dog-eared and worn. He set it aside on the seat of the office chair and took out another folder, marked "Flight Schools," which he opened on the desk. It was stuffed with colorful brochures for at least a dozen places. At least six were in the United States, and two of those—Huffman Aviation, in Venice, Florida, and FlightSafety Academy, in Vero Beach, Florida—had phone numbers that matched the ones that he had memorized from the yellow sheet of paper that Jarrah had folded into his journal.

Mahmoud, his excitement growing, also spotted both of the names Jarrah had written down. Arnold Wallace was the contact at Huffman Aviation. Ned Stewart was the contact at FlightSafety Academy. Would Florida be the next stop after Pakistan?

So there you go, he thought. Some sort of plot involving airplanes—perhaps commercial jets, judging by the Boeing manual. Hijackings were the obvious conclusion. By why take pilot lessons when you already had a pilot on board to do your bidding? Whatever the plans involved, he was apparently about to become part of them, as soon as Brother Haydar had completed his travel arrangements. He again paused to wipe his palms.

He checked out the window and saw with alarm that Esma was in motion, wrapping herself with a headscarf.

Don't do it, he thought. *Stay there, or at least wait until I've had a chance to talk to you.* Esma stepped from the curb into the street, paused, then continued. He needed to get downstairs. Now.

He switched off the laptop and folded it shut. Glancing quickly around the room, he piled all the flight school brochures back into the folder and dropped it into its place before shutting the drawer and shoving the office chair back beneath the desk. He locked the door behind himself and took off down the hallway, where he again nearly collided with a caterer as he rounded the last corner into the stairwell.

He had to prevent Esma from making it upstairs. With what he now knew, that seemed more important than ever.

51

On their way to Al Quds they got stuck in a horrible traffic jam, the result of an accident near the Stadtpark. Claire got out her phone to check in with Donlan, but it rang before she could punch in his number.

"Kenny?"

"How close are you?"

"Only a few miles, but we've hit a wall of traffic. We're scouting for a way around it."

"Things are coming to a head. Our girl has arrived."

"Shit."

"And he just came out of the building, right as she was about to go inside. But that little fucker Omar is out here, too, and now there's a bunch of yelling going on and it's likely to get worse before it gets better."

"And our German friends?"

"Sitting tight in the van, probably laughing their asses off."

"Do you think they've made you?"

"No idea, but I've been here a while now, so at the very least they've taken down my tags. Oh, and now Amir has come outside. And the fat fuck Zammar is right behind him."

"We're taking a detour now, Kenny. Still slow going, but at least we're moving again."

"Got an ETA?"

"Ten minutes? Fifteen? Let's keep the line open."

"They just turned her loose."

"Esma?"

"Yeah, she's running. Couldn't see exactly what happened right beforehand, but she's out of there like a shot."

"Is he with her?"

"Negative. He's still with his pals. Don't know if that's good or bad. And now they're having some kind of confab—looks fairly intense."

"Crisis averted?"

"Too early to say. None of them looks very happy. Amir's got his hand on Mahmoud's shoulder now."

"That doesn't sound good."

"I dunno. It looks kind of brotherly from here. And . . . oh, shit."

"What?"

"He's staring at the van now, at our German friends."

"Who is?"

"Amir. And, Jesus . . . unbelievable . . ."

"What is it, Kenny? What's happening?"

"One of the guys in the van just got out from the back and is staring right back at him. And he's *smiling*, for Chrissakes. Almost like he's taunting him."

"Taunting Amir?"

"Yeah, the dumb fuck. And Amir, well, he looks pissed. But now he's heading back inside. They all are."

"So they know they've been rumbled, that they're back under surveillance."

"I'd say so, yeah."

"Just great. Let's hope they don't take it out on our guy."

"Fuck . . . Look, my battery's getting low. I'll call with anything new. Just get here when you can."

"Doing our best, Kenny. Stay on it."

Claire hung up. She looked over at Bridger, who shook his head.

"This route's not getting it done," he said. "There's a map in the glove compartment. Get us the hell out of here."

Claire got to work, unfolding the map on her lap as she began seeking any possible clearer path to Al Quds. But all she could keep thinking of was Mahmoud, somewhere inside that building.

52

Mahmoud got to Esma just as she was about to enter the main door downstairs. He was out of breath but managed to push her back with a forceful shove of the door that threw her off balance. He saw the flash of surprise in her eyes, the only part of her face that was visible, and he reached out to keep her from stumbling backward across the sidewalk. By the time he'd steadied her, they were nearly at the curb.

"Sorry," he said. "But it's not a good time now. Not for you, and not for me."

"I'll decide that."

She tried to twist her arm free, but he held on tightly. For a moment he thought she might spit in his face, but her anger emerged in words instead.

"You're as horrible as the rest of them if you think you have a right to stop me. He's my husband. Let me go!"

"No. I'm doing this because you're right, Esma. You're *right*. They're planning something—Jarrah, all of them. I don't know what, exactly, but I think it's big, and I think they're further along than either of us knows."

She stopped trying to pull away as his words sank in. He had her full attention.

"If you get in their way now, they'll hurt you, maybe even kill you. I'm sure of that."

He let go of her arm, and she did not try to rush past him. Her scarf had fallen away from her face, and much of her hair was now visible as well—Esma, in all her glory, face flushed by anger and frustration. But her eyes were pleading, so he began trying to talk her down. He needed to get her back across the street before someone from the group saw her.

And that's how things might have ended, with a few words of counsel and perhaps a promise to stay in touch, if Omar hadn't then appeared, coming up the sidewalk as he carried a tray of sweets from the caterer's nearby van.

Mahmoud heard his voice before he saw him.

"It is her!"

Omar shouted the words, which were nearly drowned out by a clatter of metal as he dropped the tray he was carrying, scattering pastries all over the sidewalk. Oblivious to the mess, Omar stepped forward, rage in his eyes.

"Why is she here?" he asked. Then he screamed it: *"Why is she here!"*

Esma backed away. Mahmoud turned to protect her, holding his hands out to fend off Omar. People around them on the sidewalk stopped to stare. A caterer holding another tray stood rooted, his mouth open. Worse, they were now drawing attention from upstairs. Mahmoud heard exclamations of surprise filtering through the open window, and a quick glance showed a line of curious faces, everyone watching.

"Go," he said over his shoulder. "Go and don't come back. Now!"

She broke into a run, barely missing being hit by a car that swerved and honked its horn. Mahmoud turned back toward Omar, bracing himself to stop any pursuit, only to see that Omar's fury was now focused on him. Omar stepped forward, fists clenched, until a commanding voice halted him. The voice of Amir, who had just emerged from the building.

"No, Brother Omar. It is not his doing."

Amir, too, looked angry, but his gaze was not directed at either Mahmoud or Esma, who by this time was well on her way to safety. He instead watched a white van parked across the street, where a disheveled German man with a widow's peak and hooded eyes stood by the open rear door, grinning from ear to ear as he smoked and watched the commotion. More than just an idle spectator, of course—Mahmoud knew that right away, even if Omar didn't. And Amir, no doubt a veteran of previous surveillance, also seemed to know. It was a precarious moment at so many different levels that Mahmoud wasn't certain what he should say or do.

"But he lied to us!" Omar shouted as he took a defiant step forward. "He said he had handled things. He said this was done."

Amir closed in, and clamped a restraining hand on Omar's bony shoulder.

"I understand why you think that is so, Brother Omar. But let us not judge too quickly."

Mahmoud began to relax. For all that had gone wrong, this unlikely role reversal might yet salvage his position within the group.

"But you saw her. She came here, when he had told us she was gone."

"Yes, I saw her. But, as Brother Mahmoud said to Brother Haydar, just because you put someone on a train does not mean they can't take another train back. She is a willful woman. That is the very reason she is so dangerous for Brother Jarrah. So why blame ourselves, especially when there are better reasons to be angry."

Amir's eyes turned back toward the German, who tossed his cigarette to the pavement, crushed it beneath his shoe, and then boldly nodded in acknowledgment before climbing into the van and shutting the door.

"Who is that?" Omar asked.

"We will discuss these matters upstairs, away from their prying eyes and their microphones. Come, all of us."

He placed a hand on Mahmoud's back, firmly but in apparent warmth—or as much warmth as Amir ever seemed to muster—and they headed back inside. Mahmoud was still on edge, but he felt like he had weathered the storm. His earlier offhand remark to Haydar Zammar about Esma and the train had paid an unexpected dividend. Such were the small turns of fortune on which a sensitive operation could rise or fall.

"Omar is right," he said to Amir. "I was not harsh enough. I should have done more."

"You were weak, it is true," Amir answered. "But your intentions were good. Come; not here."

They climbed the stairs. Haydar Zammar was waiting for them on the next floor. Amir nodded to him and said, "Let's go to my study."

Mahmoud's stomach fluttered at the mention of the room where he had just been poking around. Then he calmed himself. The door was again locked, the laptop closed, the drawers shut. He had covered all of his tracks.

"Who was that man you were watching?" Omar asked.

"Didn't you recognize him?" Brother Haydar asked. "Brother Amir and I noticed their van earlier, and then when he showed his face, well . . ."

"The same ones who were watching us last summer?" Omar asked.

"The same," Amir said. "And at the worst possible time, would you not agree?"

"But why?"

"The woman, don't you think? Surely she must be the one who contacted them. It's why we shouldn't judge Brother Mahmoud so harshly. She would have taken this action no matter what, because she knows they are watching us, and watching her. And if we had harmed her? Well, they would have acted with force. We will have to deal with this problem simply by leaving it behind."

They had rounded the final corner. Zammar switched on a hallway light and Amir reached for his key. Mahmoud eyed the door handle carefully, hoping he hadn't scratched it, hoping the lock would open as easily for Amir as it had before.

The key slipped in and turned. The lock clicked and the door opened. He exhaled. Amir switched on the light and they entered. Mahmoud, to his relief, saw that everything looked exactly as before.

"We must go back over all our planning of the past few days, brothers, to make sure we have not done anything within their sight that made us vulnerable."

Omar shook his head, agitated.

"I still blame him," Omar said, pointing at Mahmoud.

Amir took him by the elbow.

"You must calm down, my brother, so that we can think clearly. Here, sit down."

Amir pulled out the office chair from beneath the desk. Then he frowned, and he froze. Mahmoud immediately saw why, and it kept him from swallowing. In his haste to tidy up before racing downstairs, he had forgotten the Boeing pilot's manual, which had remained out of sight on the chair.

Amir stared at it like it was a toxic object, then leaned forward to pick it up. He flipped its pages, examining it carefully. Then he opened the file drawer. The others, unaware of what had prompted his concern, watched in silence.

Even from across the room, the folder with the flight school brochures looked noticeably sloppier than the others. Amir, always a neat freak, zeroed in on it right away.

"Brother Haydar," Amir asked, "were you in this office earlier?"

"No. There was no reason."

"I was here, remember?" Omar said, "When you asked me to get the words for that song. They were right on top of your desk, just like you said."

"And was this manual here, on this chair?"

Omar stepped closer.

"I'm not sure. I don't think so."

"But you did not put it there?"

"No. I touched nothing but the sheet of songs. And the imam locked up when I left. I saw him do it."

Amir again opened the file drawer while the rest of them watched in hushed silence. He pawed some of the contents and bent lower, almost as if he were sniffing, a dog on the hunt, reminding Mahmoud of the eerie way he had detected Esma's scent on his clothes the night before.

"Could the German have come up here?" Omar asked. "While we were all singing, maybe?"

"No, no. Brother Haydar has had someone watching them since I first noticed the van."

Amir's face was blank, the way it always got whenever he was working over some problem in his head. Then, blinking, he appeared to emerge from his mini-trance, as if he had finally added up all the pieces to his satisfaction.

"I was wrong," he said. "In fact, I have been wrong all along. It was not the girl who brought them to our door. Because I remember now someone who was absent earlier from much of our singing. He also kept us waiting while he went back upstairs to our rooms at the House of the Followers."

Amir turned toward Mahmoud, whose stomach slid as if he were on the deck of a pitching ship at sea.

"So, Brother Mahmoud. Were you in here looking for your comb again? Or was this some other type of vanity?"

Omar went slack-jawed.

"What are you saying, Brother Amir? You think Brother Mahmoud was in here?"

Amir didn't respond. He only had eyes for Mahmoud, and he crossed the floor toward him like a prosecuting attorney closing in on a weakened witness.

"How did you get in? You must have a key. Did you take the imam's?"

"I wasn't in here. And I don't have a key."

"Check his pockets."

Omar looked back and forth between Amir and Mahmoud, as if uncertain what to do next.

"But, Brother Amir, what if—?"

"You heard me. Check his pockets!"

Omar, who moments earlier had been so angry, now shrugged apologetically as he stepped forward. He reached into Mahmoud's right pocket, and then his left. All he found were a few pfennig coins and a key for the House of the Followers. His face brightened as he held them aloft for inspection.

"Only some loose change and the key to our house, Brother Amir."

"Take his wallet."

Omar sighed and plucked it out. Amir held out his hand. All the while, he and Mahmoud stared at each other, a battle of wills. Mahmoud tried to convey a sense of betrayal and aggrievement, but it didn't feel convincing.

"Bring it to me."

The wallet was thin, with only a few D-marks, a photo ID card, a library card, and Mahmoud's Anmeldebestätigung, the stamped form that showed he had registered his presence with the local police. All of them had one.

Amir examined and replaced each item with meticulous care. He was about to hand it back when something about the feel or weight of the wallet made him frown. He bent it back and forth, as if checking its flexibility, and his eyes narrowed. He reopened it and, looking closer, discovered the hidden slit in the leather interior, from which he pulled out Mahmoud's sliver of polished steel.

Haydar Zammar's sudden intake of breath was the only sound in the room as Amir examined the items. Mahmoud maintained a game face, but knew his odds for success had just plummeted.

"Is this not a key in its own right, Brother Mahmoud? I have not seen a tool like this since I was a boy, at my uncle's jewelry stall in the Khan El Khalili bazaar. A young thief tried to open a display case with one of these."

Mahmoud lowered his head, partly in shame, partly to give himself a moment to come up with an answer. He spoke haltingly.

"I am . . . sometimes a thief. I confess to that freely, Brother Amir. I have stolen things in this city. Food mostly. Because, as you have seen, I am not a man of generous means. I am ashamed of this, but I took nothing from this room. Check all you like, and you can search me from head to toe."

"Then why did you come in here?"

He sagged, playing his role. He had come up with a story—a weak one, but weak options seemed to be the only ones left, and this one stood a chance of working only if he sold it with conviction and with seeming candor. He looked Amir in the eye and continued.

"I wanted to see what your plans for me were, to find out whether I was going to be part of the great series of journeys that Brother Jarrah had hinted were about to begin. Earlier this afternoon, Brother Haydar told me my time was coming, and I became so excited that I could no longer wait to find out more in the proper manner, so . . ." He gestured toward the desk where the folder lay open.

Amir turned toward Haydar.

"Is this true, Brother Haydar?"

"It is. But I did not instruct him to go poking about in your things."

"That was my error, my sin," Mahmoud said. "I was overeager, and it was wrong to come here."

"Why didn't you just ask me?"

He sighed, fidgeted, playing it for all it was worth.

"Because sometimes you scare me, Brother Amir."

Omar hid a smile, which could only be a positive sign.

Amir continued to stare. Then he rendered his verdict.

"I do not believe you, Brother Mahmoud." He held aloft the lock pick. "Nor do I believe that you came by this tool on your own. It is too finely made for a mere street thief. I believe those people in the van supplied it, and that you are working for them."

"That's not true!" For once he was able to argue with genuine conviction.

Amir held up a hand to silence him. Omar and Brother Haydar were dumbstruck, and listening closely.

"Maybe you agreed to do so only to help Jarrah's woman, because you are weak and she has tempted you. Or maybe it is because they are paying you. As you said, you are desperate for money. But we are going to find out more about all of this, and we are going to do it now."

Omar nodded. His expression was grave. There was no longer any doubt about who he believed. The case was also closed for Haydar Zammar, who scowled in anger.

"This is not the proper place for continuing this meeting. There are too many other people nearby, right down the hall. Brother Saeed's celebration must continue. We must also leave Brother Jarrah here. The rest of us will go elsewhere. Brother Haydar, do you have the keys to your hideaway with you?"

"The one in Jarrestadt?"

"Yes."

"I do. But there is no heat or light there, and the windows are boarded."

"All the better for our needs. Brother Omar has a flashlight in the supply cabinet, plus some other things we will need."

Omar nodded. Brother Haydar got out his keys. Mahmoud said nothing. His prospects for escape, even survival, were dimming by the second. Worse, he was almost certainly alone, with no help nearby unless you counted the Germans in the van, who he felt quite sure wouldn't give a shit about one more tawdry little Moroccan asylum seeker, no matter how brutally he might soon be handled.

"I'll drive us," Brother Haydar said.

"I have bungee cords. Should we tie his hands first?" Omar asked.

"No. If they see that from the van, they might try to help him. But bring the cords with you. Do not try to run from us, Mahmoud."

"I won't, because I am innocent of what you say."

"We will see. Let us go."

53

Claire had worked out a better route to Al Quds, but they were still moving slowly when Donlan called again.

"Our boy just left with the others, and it didn't look good," he said, loud enough for both of them to hear. "I don't know for sure, but I'm guessing he's being forced. None of them looked happy, and they all piled into Zammar's car."

"What makes you think he's being forced?"

"Just their posture, and his. Plus the look on their faces. I know it's subjective, but it had that vibe. And after the whole scene with Esma, well . . . Ten minutes ago they were all brotherhood and unity. Now it's like he's public enemy number one. I'm tailing 'em."

"What's their heading?"

"Straight up Steindamm, but now they're turning. Left on Mühlendamm, which means they're moving due north."

"So they're headed our way."

"That's the good news. The bad news is I've gotta turn off this phone 'cause the battery's about to die. I'll call back as soon as I get a fix on a destination."

The call ended. The silence in the car was ghastly.

"Turn left up here," Claire said, eyeing the map. "Then three blocks and another right. We're angling in their general direction."

A pause, then she unloaded.

"You should've brought me in sooner, Paul. Me, or *anyone*."

"I know."

"You've become too much of a loner to be keeping someone out on the edge like this. I understand why you couldn't tell Wharton, given the history, but—"

"I *know*."

She held her tongue. The damage was done, so why prod him further? But he needed to hear it. He sighed and shook his head.

"It's because of the way I've taught myself to see the world—self-reliance or nothing—ever since, well . . ."

"Berlin?"

"Yes."

"Look, I know you've spent every year since then looking for a way back to your younger, bolder self, but—"

"For someone who hasn't seen me in almost a decade, you're making an awful lot of assumptions."

"Am I? Maybe everyone else is fooled by your summer disappearing acts into the wild, but not me. Fine, if that's what it takes. But did it ever occur to you there were also consequences in the aftermath for me? Not so much from the operational fallout as from what the two of us resorted to in that one weekend of solace?"

"Oh, Claire. Were you . . . ? Did you . . . ?"

"What I did then is not your business. It might have been if I'd ever heard from you."

"I'm sorry. I . . ."

"I don't want an apology. We both chose those actions. Partly out of fear, partly out of passion. It was your silence I can't forgive, your long retreat into yourself, with no regard for anyone else. And now it feels like you've done the same thing to Malachy—deemed your own skin more valuable than his."

He was stunned. "Maybe so. With you, I was too ashamed to get in touch."

"And I was too proud to ask, so there's that. But now there's another life at risk, a man in trouble, so take this next left and stay on that heading until we hear from Kenny."

Bridger started to reply just as Claire's phone rang.

"Yes?"

"They just pulled over on Lorenzengasse, off Barmbeker Strasse."

"I see it on the map. We're close."

"They took him into number 7."

"Took him? Or was it voluntary?"

"They had him surrounded, like he might bolt. He didn't look any worse for wear, so I guess nothing happened in the car. But this place—Jesus. It's the end section of a big apartment building, five stories. The part they went into looks like it's being renovated, and I'm guessing it's empty. Classic dumping ground is what I'm thinking."

"Let's not get ahead of ourselves. Did the Germans come along for the ride?"

"No. A couple guys from the mosque stood in front of the van, to block it in until Zammar's car was out of sight. It's just me now. Should I go in?"

"Sit tight. We're two blocks away. We'll be turning the nearest corner to the west of you any second."

"Yeah, I see you."

"It's that long building on the left?"

"Down at the end, yeah. What do we do?"

"Not enough information to know yet, so I'm going inside to find out."

Bridger turned sharply toward her but didn't speak as he eased the car into a spot across the street.

"You sure that's wise?" Donlan said. "I mean, he's your guy and all, but . . ."

"I'm open to any better ideas. Got any?"

"No."

"I'll have to play it by ear once I'm inside. Check your watch. If I'm not out within ten minutes, Bridger will come in after me. You'll be his backup."

"Okay."

"For now, hang up and save your battery in case you need to call the cops. If I need help sooner I'll call Paul. If you see him go in, follow."

"Got it. Good luck."

They were right across from Zammar's Mercedes, and just down the block from Donlan's Jetta. They could see him behind the wheel. The apartment block in question was in good shape, for the most part. The neighborhood, as with most of Hamburg, looked solid, well kept. The exception, as Donlan had noted, was the unit at the far end, where most of the windows across the front had no curtains, and the ones on the third floor were covered with plywood. It was dusk, but no lights were on.

"You sure about this?" Bridger said. "Maybe the van rattled them and they're just meeting to regroup."

"Possibly. We could be risking everything. But I'm guessing Malachy's ass is on the line, and if we do nothing he could be dead by the time the rest of them come back out the door. So are we agreed?"

He nodded. She reached for the door latch, then paused.

"Better turn your phone back on."

"Just did."

"I'm turning off the ringer on mine, in case you need to warn me. Otherwise, ten minutes, no later."

He nodded and set his watch. "Ten minutes, starting now."

She got out of the car. Donlan was right: The setup looked like a dumping ground, or a crash pad. The downstairs door wasn't locked, and it creaked open on damaged hinges.

Claire eased inside. The stairwell was cold. It looked dark all the way to the top, and some of the steps were rotted. Already she could hear the mutter and rumble of voices. The words were in Arabic, and there was some heat behind them. Third floor, that was her guess, the one with boarded-up windows.

She checked her watch. Bridger and Donlan could no longer see her. For the next nine minutes she'd be on her own. Taking a deep breath to calm herself, she held the banister for support and began creeping up the stairs.

54

Omar bound Mahmoud's hands and tied him to the back of a folding chair with the bungee cord, stretching it tightly enough to cut off circulation. It was painful within seconds.

The air was so cold and musty that he felt like sneezing. Other than the chair, and another one folded in a corner, the room had only a bare mattress and a floor lamp with no shade. Omar switched it on and pocketed the flashlight he'd used to guide them up the stairs. The windows were boarded.

Amir had called this place Brother Haydar's hideaway. Presumably Haydar used it to stow contraband or shelter people in transit. An Al Qaeda safe house, then, which also made it a perfect place for aggressive interrogation. This end of the building was clearly empty. Even if he screamed for help, no one would hear.

The ride over had been quiet, which gave Mahmoud time to think about what he might say or do to get himself out of this mess. He hadn't yet come up with an answer, and now the questions were about to begin.

Amir crouched until his face was level with Mahmoud's, a foot away.

"Who do you report to, my fallen Mahmoud?"

"I don't report to anyone. I'm not working for the Germans."

"Did they promise you asylum for your cooperation? Is that the arrangement?"

"There is no arrangement. I am not reporting to them."

"Or did Jarrah's woman set this up, after the two of you were touching each other the other night?"

Omar shifted his stance and angrily spoke up.

"Is that true, Brother Mahmoud? You were touching her?"

"Quiet, Omar. I will handle this. And he is no longer our brother. What have you told them, Mahmoud?"

"I have told nothing to anyone, because I am not reporting to anyone. And I did not touch Esma, not like you're thinking. I told her to stay away, but she came anyway. I put her on a train, but she came back."

"You did nothing of the sort. You are working with her, and with them, and if we do not stop you, then you will destroy us all."

Amir stood and backed away. His next question was for Haydar Zammar.

"You must have had problems like this in wartime, Brother Haydar. How did you handle them?"

Haydar bent his knees, but he couldn't crouch as low as Amir. He did, however, maintain his balance well enough to deliver a sweeping punch, which landed with a solid smack against Mahmoud's jaw, like a board against a bony side of beef. Mahmoud saw a burst of bright lights, and his neck wrenched sideways. His jaw felt like it might be broken, and as the seconds passed the agony intensified.

"Like that, Brother Amir. How much more should I do?"

"As much as you believe is necessary."

Haydar nodded and again bent his knees. Mahmoud's vision was still blurry from the first blow, but he could focus well enough to detect a lively malice in Zammar's eyes. It told him that all of the man's tales of combat and war zones were not completely embroidered. This was someone inured to casual and sudden violence.

The second blow was so sharp and powerful that he cried out. Omar turned away, but Amir kept staring, steadfast. Mahmoud must have blacked out for a second, because the next thing he knew someone was lightly slapping his cheek. It was Amir, crouching by his side.

"That's it. Come back to us, Mahmoud. And tell us now, who do you report to?"

Mahmoud tried to answer, but his mouth would not form the words. He hazily realized that one of the biggest dangers facing him now was their utter lack of professionalism. A pro could make this type of abuse last for hours and still leave you conscious and mostly unmarked—

a rendering of strategically inflicted pain, calculated to gradually break you down while leaving you lucid enough to spill your secrets. This was blunt-force brutality. Even if he wanted to tell them everything, he'd find it hard to do so now. One more punch might make it impossible.

That meant he had to come up with something—anything—to make them stop and think, or at least redirect their line of questioning. Blood was filling his mouth. If he were to gasp for breath, he might choke.

"I . . ."

"Yes, Mahmoud?"

"I . . ."

He gurgled, slobbering blood, but was unable to form any words. At the edge of his field of vision, the massive Haydar Zammar reared back for another heaving blow.

55

Claire was horrified by what she was hearing—the thuds and groans, the angry words—even though she couldn't understand a single one. She recognized Malachy's voice and could tell he was already laboring to speak. They were beating him badly. This was no longer a mission to save the operation. Malachy's life was in danger. She had to act.

The numbers weren't good—one of her, three of them, including the huge Haydar Zammar—but in two more minutes she would have a reinforcement, maybe two. Even in a standoff, they'd at least be able to stop any further damage to Malachy. She thought of calling Bridger but worried they'd hear her, and since they were outnumbered, she at least wanted to maintain the advantage of surprise.

She heard the next blow, a sickening sound. They clearly didn't know what they were doing, unless they were trying to just beat him to death. It was time to take a gamble. Claire stepped quickly down to the landing between the second and third floors. She then called out loudly, in the most authoritative tone she could muster:

"Polizei! Kommen Sie raus!"

The effect was almost instantaneous.

A drumbeat of footsteps told her that she had at least stopped the beating. A door flew open. The footsteps paused. She shouted again from below.

"Polizei! Halt! Wir kommen!"

A quick burst of Arabic, followed by the sound of at least two of them climbing toward the higher floors. She checked her watch. Only a minute until the cavalry arrived, meaning she didn't need to waste time making a call. She ran up to the third floor, threw open the door, and saw immediately that Malachy was not the only one remaining. The wiry Omar stood with his legs set widely apart, as if braced for an attack. There was rage in his eyes, and he towered over Malachy, who was slumped in a folding chair, his mouth dripping blood, hands bound behind him.

She ran forward. Omar tensed to deliver a blow. Only then did she realize he was holding a knife.

56

A few seconds before go time, Bridger's phone rang. He was already unlatching the car door when he answered, only to hear Wharton's voice instead of Claire's.

"Goddammit, Paul, you disappeared on me, and I'm guessing it was premeditated."

"Not a good time for this, Mark."

"You're not out there still trying to manage *him*, are you? Not after what we agreed on?"

He stepped out of his car.

"Look, Mark, things are fluid out here, and—"

"No, *you* look—and I'll bring the director in on this if I have to, because I've just spoken to Gunter Hauser, who's convinced we're running something under his nose, and if that's how this unfolds, then you're as good as finished, do you understand?"

Every instinct told Bridger to drop the phone and bolt. Donlan was out of his Jetta and was signaling frantically with his arms, as if to ask, "Stay or go?"

Bridger had spent ten years steeling himself for this moment, and now Wharton had hit him with a sucker punch, threatening not his life but his career, and Bridger, with no counterpunch, was reeling. He waved Donlan toward the building, trying to signal him to advance as he took a tentative step forward while still holding the phone. But Donlan, having been instructed to follow, was hesitating, and precious seconds were elapsing.

"Mark! We have someone in trouble here. I have to go!"

"Malachy is practically one of them, Paul. Let the Germans deal with him!"

"It's Claire, goddammit!"

And with that he finally broke into a run, pocketing his phone as Wharton's voice continued to yammer. Donlan took off behind him, panting and grunting as he pumped his arms in Bridger's wake toward the entrance. They were already a minute behind schedule.

57

Omar lunged at her, slashing with the knife. She grabbed his wrist and, in the same fluid motion, twisted it violently so that his fingers opened as he cried out in pain. The knife fell with a thunk. Claire tried to kick it away, but the point of the blade had lodged in the floor. She stepped toward Omar as he backed away. With a lunge of her own, she grabbed his shoulders and kneed him in the groin while he flailed back at her face.

He grunted in pain, spun free, and ran for the door, disappearing toward the stairs.

Fine. She was more concerned about Malachy, who was motionless in the chair, his head slumped forward and dripping blood onto his lap. And where the fuck was Paul? The only footsteps on the stairs were Omar's, headed upstairs, where the others had gone. They had either taken refuge up there or climbed out a window onto the fire escape.

She dropped to her knees on the floor next to Malachy, nearly slipping on a pool of blood that had spilled from his lap. She took his head in her hands, lifting it gently. He had a weak pulse and was barely breathing. They had to call for help. His eyelids fluttered, and then opened halfway.

"You're safe now, Malachy. It's going to be all right."

He mumbled something in reply, but she couldn't make out the words.

"What? 'Fly?' Is that what you said?"

"Fly soo'." The words spluttered out in a bloody whisper.

"Fly soon?"

He shook his head slightly, either to say no or to try to clear the cob-webs. She held his chin and gently raised his face so he could see her better, and for a moment his eyes came fully open. She could see their urgency. This was not an incoherent moment of free association. He was trying to tell her something important, she was certain of that now.

"Fly soo'," he gasped again, his lips moving clumsily. "Stop 'em."

Then his eyes shut, and she felt his neck muscles go limp. She low-ered his head so that his chin rested against his chest. Checking again for a pulse, she felt his heartbeat judder and stumble before steadying itself, but faintly and at a slower pace. They were losing him. Where was her help?

As if in answer, footsteps now pounded on the stairs. She stood and turned in relief but saw to her dismay that it was the hulking Haydar Zammar, moving with surprising agility and speed, straight at her.

He unloaded a sweeping punch, which she might have avoided if she hadn't backed into the chair holding Malachy. The stumble left her open to the worst of the blow, and she staggered sideways, just managing to keep her footing so she could defend herself from the next punch.

Instead she saw that Zammar had turned back toward Malachy, and she realized that he had come back not to attack her but to finish him off. She lunged at him just as he threw a punch, which softened the blow but did not stop it from making contact with Malachy's battered face.

Then Zammar unloaded on her, his fist crashing into her jaw just as she heard more footsteps clattering closer.

The room spun.

Claire felt herself falling but did not feel herself land.

FRIDAY,
OCTOBER 15

58

The nurse tiptoed past Claire to check the beeping monitor.

"It's okay, I'm awake. Any change?"

"None," the nurse answered. "Doctor says there probably won't be anytime soon. He took quite a blow to the head."

"Several, in fact. But, yes, that last one in particular certainly didn't help. At least his face is looking better."

"The swelling's down. The discoloration will take a while longer. You're looking better, too. That bruise, I mean."

"A little makeup works wonders. But thank you."

The nurse fussed with the pillows and the intravenous tubes. She swapped out an empty drip bottle for a full one, then replaced a full plastic pouch with a new one to collect the yellow outflow. Garbage in, garbage out, six days running, and Malachy had remained motionless throughout.

Everyone else had left Hamburg, leaving Claire as the Agency's sole representative for this vigil. It was a sort of punishment detail, she supposed, a way of letting her contemplate her many misdeeds before they recalled her to Paris or, worse, all the way to Langley for some sort of after-action atonement.

Five days ago she had awakened in a bed just down the hall, after spending a woozy night in which she had been vaguely aware of the hovering presence of a penitent Paul Bridger. The clarity of morning, however, had shown that the only bedside presence was Kenny Donlan, who handed her pills for her crashing headache as he filled her in on the latest.

"Malachy's still touch and go, but the doc thinks he'll pull through."

"All of him, or part of him?"

"Too early to say."

She nodded, then stopped, because her head throbbed every time she moved it.

"Did I hear Paul in here last night, or did I dream that?"

"Yeah, he was here. Said to give you his best."

"He left?"

"Summoned home. So he said." Donlan looked away, seemingly embarrassed. He crossed and uncrossed his legs, then cleared his throat and got up to look out the window. Claire decided to do him a favor by breaking the awkward silence.

"He's never been very good at farewells. Besides, the bigger issue is the matter of his late arrival up there on the third floor. Care to enlighten me on that?"

Donlan settled back into his chair with a heaving sigh.

"He got a call from Wharton right as he was getting out of his car. I saw him talking on his phone and figured it was you. So I waited, too. Not long, but still." A pause, followed by a defeated shrug. "We fucked up."

"I hope you're including me in that assessment."

"I wasn't."

"Doesn't matter. Each of us let Malachy down in our own way."

"He'd be dead if you hadn't gone in."

"He may die yet, but I appreciate the sentiment. I don't suppose anyone's keeping track of our friends at Al Quds, are they?"

Donlan frowned and again looked out the window. He reminded Claire of a marooned man on a life raft, searching the skies for any sign of rescue.

"Nobody on our side is. I saw the report you sent to my guys at the bin Laden unit. Good stuff."

"I couldn't really say anything about Malachy, of course. But I included everything he'd reported to us about their plans. Sketchy, but who knows?"

"I'll make sure it gets as wide a circulation as possible, but . . ."

"What?"

He shrugged and again looked away.

"They think they've already got a pretty good handle on those guys."

"That's what they said?"

"Pretty much."

"Maybe they do. As long as they stay on top of it."

"Yeah, that's the key. If the Germans are still watching those guys, they're not saying. Or not to me, anyway. Understandable, I guess."

"Some fences to mend?"

"Oh, yeah. They did tell me that Jarrah took off as scheduled."

"So by now he's probably in Afghanistan."

"Wonder if he's still wearing those Sigma Nu crewnecks."

They had shared a laugh over that image, although Claire had to cut hers short because of the pain. She then noticed a packed suitcase at Donlan's feet, and he told her he was booked on a flight leaving in a few hours. Big Mike Sheehan's doing. The chain of command was reeling in the evidence of its mistakes, link by link.

Except for her, of course.

Claire dozed in her chair after the nurse left. The sky was clear, the blinds were open, and the autumn sunlight was warm and comforting on her face. She had just slipped into a dream of an empty beach in the South of France when a shadow fell, causing her to open her eyes.

Standing before her in a camel cashmere overcoat, hands in pockets, was Mark Wharton.

"Hello, Claire. I'm—"

"I know who you are. I thought you left with everyone else."

"I did. Now I'm back."

"To check on your victim?"

He smiled in what he probably believed was a tolerant manner and took a seat, facing her from a few feet away.

"Malachy is his own worst enemy. Always has been. Too easily seduced by whomever he's keeping company with."

"Do you really believe that, or do you just use it to make you feel better about your own screwups?"

"The results speak for themselves. Malachy let a woman turn his head, then his friends kicked his ass."

"The results, as you call them, won't be known for months, maybe years. But by then I guess you'll have come up with all kinds of other rationalizations. Yes, Malachy let a woman turn his head. But he was succeeding, and he was trying to warn us about something. When I found him up there, bleeding, his first words were—"

"'Fly soon.' Paul told me. Not so hard to figure that one out."

"'Fly *soo*', actually. Maybe that second word was 'soon,' maybe it was something else. He wasn't all that easy to understand."

"It was definitely 'soon,' judging from his last report. His new friends were about to put him on a plane. He'd been accepted into whatever pie-in-the-sky training fantasy they'd come up with on one of their wacky Fridays at the mosque. He was bragging, Claire. Bragging that he'd become one of the elect. And what a feather in our cap that would've been—a CIA-trained Al Qaeda foot soldier, someone to warn them about every possible trap or tripwire we might set for them down the road."

"Then why were his next words 'Stop them'?"

Wharton looked troubled by the question, but only for a second or two. He waved away his worries as if they were a cloud of gnats.

"Stop them from beating him, obviously. Which you did. For the most part."

"And now the word is they've all left town—Amir, Omar, even Haydar Zammar."

"Of course they're gone. Our man Malachy scared them away."

"Or maybe it's by design. They could all be in some bin Laden training camp by now."

"In which case all of them will probably be dead and smoldering on some jihadi battlefront before long. Chechnya, that's where most of them seem to be expiring lately. If anything, we saved Malachy from that fate."

Claire clenched her fists, took a deep breath, and unclenched them. She glanced over at Malachy, and hoped he wasn't hearing all of this bullshit.

"So why are you here? To give me the ax?"

"Oh, no. You shouldn't have to pay for someone else's mistake. I take some blame, too. Should have checked your background a little better before I let Paul bring you aboard. Then I would have known for sure that you two were likely to try something foolish. Berlin, wasn't it?"

She looked away, and was angry with herself for doing so. When she looked back, Wharton was smiling.

"No surprise you'd still be a little ashamed of that. Holed up together on the run, sharing all sorts of secrets you weren't supposed to be sharing. You know, that weekend is still not completely accounted for in any of the reports. Paul said it was a matter of seeking refuge. Licking your wounds, I guess. Or was it something more than that?"

"You're drawing a lot of conclusions no one else ever has."

"Maybe I'm better at reading between the lines. Whatever the case, it made you two the perfect partners in crime for an unauthorized venture. And I should have figured that out. So now we'll do what the Agency always does when a potential embarrassment arises. No punishment, just a few well-placed doses of ecclesiastical silence."

Wharton reached into the pocket of his overcoat and handed her a folded sheet of paper. He uncapped a fountain pen that probably cost more than her best pair of earrings, and handed it over as well.

"What's this?"

"A nondisclosure agreement. But only if you wish to remain employed."

Claire looked it over. Boilerplate, mostly, except for a section referring to Operation Sidewinder, although even that part made no mention of Bridger's placement of an Al Qaeda mole.

"Sidewinder. Is that what Paul was calling it?"

"It's what I'm calling it. You know Langley. Eventually everything needs a name, and Sidewinder seems appropriate enough for this misadventure, although the full after-action report will be made available only to the director."

Claire took note of everything the form said and, more to the point, everything it didn't say. And that was when she figured out what was really going on.

"I don't believe you."

Wharton frowned. He looked genuinely hurt. In Claire's experience, well-practiced liars always took it personally when you didn't fall for their fictions.

"Which part?"

"All of it. I don't believe you've told *anyone* what really happened here, not even the director. And this is to make sure no one else ever does. Silence me and the only loose ends are Donlan and Sheehan. But once Kenny tells Big Mike the cost of his meddling, that problem will be taken care of. I'm guessing you've come up with some sort of tame-as-possible cover story to explain how a couple of field people ended up in a hospital. That's what these last few days have been about. The Mark Wharton cover-up."

"You're not going to sign it?"

"And you're not going to fire me."

"Just try me."

"Oh, I will."

"If you take this upstairs, it won't do any good."

"I'm aware of that. I'm also aware that if they punished anyone, it would probably be Bridger. Or, worse, Malachy, for being here at all. Either way, you win. But I won't sign your bogus document with its bogus operational name. And I'll never believe Malachy wasn't onto something real, maybe even something important. And if I sign this, that's exactly what I'll be saying, and I'll be bound to that version for life. So no. I won't do it. But you can have your pen back."

She handed it to him.

"The document, too, please."

He held out his hand. She folded it and put it in her purse. He stood and reached for it, then hesitated. Then she stood and backed away, holding her purse to her chest.

"Go ahead. I'm not afraid to defend myself, and I'm not afraid to hit an assistant to the director, or whatever the hell you're calling yourself now. Afterward they'll get you a bed right down the hall. Then you'll have even more explaining to do."

He pursed his lips as if he were about to reply. Then he walked out of the room without a further word.

Claire felt no sense of victory from the moment, but she did take solace in having managed to unsettle his abiding smugness. Then she looked again at Malachy and was overcome by a nagging sense of shame and the beginning of another headache.

She went over to the bed, where she listened to the beeping monitor for a few seconds before reaching out to touch his face. Even if he awakened, would he feel like this had been worth it?

Fly soo'.

The words again came to mind. Still a puzzle, one that she would not solve for nearly two years.

TUESDAY, SEPTEMBER 11, 2001

59

By afternoon the rising sun was napping behind an overcast sky. It was a warm and lazy day, conducive to long lunches and early exits. Or so it seemed to Claire until a little after 3 p.m., when their phones began ringing and the Paris chief of station, Marston, switched on the television in the conference room.

Claire headed over for a look just in time to see replay footage of a commercial jetliner stabbing the South Tower of New York's World Trade Center. She then saw that both towers were on fire, pouring black smoke into the bright blue of a Manhattan morning.

"Bin Laden. Has to be," a colleague near the TV said.

Claire felt a chill, but she couldn't look away. The station switched to an image of a fire burning at the Pentagon, where yet another jet-liner had turned itself into a missile. Minutes passed, and no one said a word. It felt like all of them should be working, even though it also felt like there was not a damn thing any of them could do.

"They're saying four planes in all now," Marston said. "The FAA has shut down U.S. airspace."

The TV was again showing a view of the burning towers when a guy sitting near the screen put a hand to his mouth and cried out in distress.

"Oh, my God. Is it *falling*?"

It was. The South Tower, all 110 stories of it, was collapsing like a column of ash, and the only thing Claire could think of was the hundreds, maybe thousands, of people who were still inside, a cold horror unlike anything she'd ever experienced. Several people who were standing had to sit down.

Half an hour later, the North Tower followed, and by then there was news that the fourth plane had crashed into a field in Western Pennsylvania.

Marston snapped out of his funk to do his job. He clapped three times to bring everyone to attention, and ordered all hands to return to work.

"I'm sure leads are going to start rolling in from all over, but until they do I want everyone with any experience in dealing with terror networks to start culling your sources, your files, your memories— anything you might think is relevant. Especially those of you who've brushed up against bin Laden's networks. Because, as Barry said earlier, this sure looks like his handiwork."

So they all got to work, even though for a while it felt frenetically aimless.

For Claire, as for everyone, it was hard to focus. She kept thinking of the crumbling towers, the rolling billow of smoke and ruin as it spread through the city. A few hours later, Marston appeared at her desk.

"There's something you need to see," he said.

She followed him back to his office, where three others were poring over a long printout on his desk.

"FBI Dallas has come up with the passenger lists for all four of the planes, and they've already flagged a few names. Have a look."

Her colleagues silently made room for her as she began to scan the list. Three of the names might as well have been written in neon, and she was nearly sickened by the sight of them.

Mohamed Atta, whom she remembered as Amir, had been in Seat 8D on Flight 11, which had struck the North Tower at 8:46 a.m. New York time.

Ziad Jarrah, the damn frat boy in a crewneck, was a passenger on Flight 93, which had crashed in Pennsylvania.

Marwan al-Shehhi, hardly a leader but still one of the Al Quds regulars, had been on Flight 175, the plane that she'd watched slam into the South Tower.

She checked the list again, slower this time, partly because she kept expecting to see Ramzi Bin al-Shibh, the one they called Omar. He wasn't there. It would be a few days more before she would find out he'd been unable to get a visa to enter the United States. Haydar Zammar also wasn't on the list, although that wasn't so surprising, given his role as an Al Qaeda logistics man and travel agent.

She was about to tell her colleagues all about it when someone appeared at the door of the office, out of breath and holding another printout.

"FBI says some of those guys were enrolled in a flight school down in Florida in the past few months," he said.

"Flight schools?" Marston said. "Jesus. How the hell did that get under the radar? These were guys on the terror watch list, and they were enrolled in fucking *flight schools*?"

His repetition of the words made Claire's mouth go dry. It was hard to say which of her emotions was more powerful—shock, horror, or anger—although anger was now overtaking the others. For a second she felt like she might vomit.

"Are you okay?" Marston asked.

"I will be."

She walked out of his office, barely noticing what was going on around her.

"Claire, what did you see, where are you going? There's a war on now, in case you haven't noticed."

"And I'll be back in ten to help fight it," she called out over her shoulder.

Because first, before she could face another moment of this, she needed one for herself, and for Malachy, and even for Paul Bridger—a moment to contemplate what might have been for all three of them, and to consider where she could possibly go from here.

Flight schools. Not fly soo'. That was what a woozy Malachy had been trying to warn them about as he slurred his words through blood and stupor. He had seen something, or heard something—the first stirrings of preparation for this horrendous plot—and he had spoken the words right into her ear, only she hadn't been able to make them out.

All she knew of Malachy in the time since then was that he had finally emerged into consciousness two weeks after Wharton's visit, with a walloping headache and no memory of anything that had happened since his arrival in Hamburg. Only one name came to the surface—Esma—although Malachy wasn't able to say who she was or why she was significant.

He was now back in Queens, reportedly living in squalor and teaching English to Arabic-speaking new arrivals. There had been some debate about granting him a pension, and the Agency had deemed him permanently unfit for further operational use. Bridger was still in Paris and still working on his own, running ops across Europe. Wharton had lodged himself into some high office without a name—or no name she knew, anyway. He was in Langley, reporting directly to the top.

For months after the op in Hamburg, Claire had emailed and phoned to Alec station at least once every week, either to ask for updates or to prod for more information on all of Malachy's former pals at Al Quds. And when they dropped off the map, so to speak, she had encouraged her colleagues to redouble their efforts. She had done so with such annoying persistence that Langley had ordered Marston to shut her down. "Let Alec do its job," he'd told her. "This isn't yours anymore. It probably never was." She had no illusions about where that decree must have come from.

Now, feeling sick and dejected, Claire went to a window and looked out at the street. Parisians were gathering in the park across from the embassy to lay bouquets of flowers. They were milling around as if stunned. The sight of it nearly made her cry out, a noise that lodged in her throat. She wiped her eyes, took a deep breath, and spent a few more seconds collecting herself. Being here was like working inside a burial shrine, but at least now she knew what had to be done next.

She returned to Marston's office and announced her conclusions to him and the others.

"I know three of those names. I'm guessing all of them were pilots. They were living in Hamburg when I was there two years ago, and they were all going to the same mosque. The Germans had them under surveillance, and for a while so did we."

Marston was speechless for a moment. Then he cleared his throat.

"You need to report all of this to Langley," he said. "Everything you know about them."

"Everything?"

"Well, sure."

"Good. Just wanted to get that on the record."

The others looked a little puzzled by the statement, but Claire didn't mind. She retreated to her desk, where a search of a file drawer turned up Wharton's nondisclosure form, the one with "Operation Sidewinder" appearing near the top of the page.

She set it off to one side, fired up her desktop terminal, and began to write. Even as she typed, she knew that the bulk of the most crucial information would never see the light of day. That's the way these things always worked. But there would still be a few rewards—a little payback, perhaps a letter of resignation from someone in a high place, and, quite possibly, a small measure of redemption for a few people who still mattered to her.

"Fly soo'," she whispered, shaking her head, dismayed, then angry. They were so close.

Acknowledgments

Any reader familiar with the terrorist plot that led to 9/11 will easily recognize several of this book's characters. Mohamed Atta ("Amir"), Ramzi bin al-Shibh ("Omar"), Ziad Jarrah, Marwan al-Shehhi and Haydar Zammar are the most notable. The existence of this so-called Hamburg Cell has been well documented, and its members were indeed regulars at locales depicted on these pages, such as the Al Quds Mosque on Steindamm, the "House of the Followers" residence at Marienstrasse 54 in Harburg, and Zammar's garden house near the Stadtpark.

A research trip to Hamburg in early February 2020, just before the COVID-19 pandemic shut down the world, was invaluable in helping me map out the orbits of their lives during that period of ferment and preparation before, one by one, they headed off to al-Qaeda training camps in Afghanistan in late 1999. And, yes, German intelligence and the CIA were quite aware of their existence at the time.

Much has been written and broadcast about their Hamburg years, but the two most helpful references were the books, *Perfect Soldiers*, by Terry McDermott, and *The Looming Tower*, by Lawrence Wright. The journal entries of 9/11 hijacker Ziad Jarrah that appear in this novel are in some cases drawn from his actual writings. Others are my own doing.

Professor Armitage is my own creation, but his controversial translation of the Holy Quran—particularly with regard to his assertion that 72 white raisins, not virgins, await martyrs in paradise—has a real-life counterpart in the work of "Christoph Luxenberg," pseudonym of a mysterious figure most often believed to be a German scholar of Semitic languages. Lux-

ACKNOWLEDGMENTS

enberg published his findings in the year 2000, in a book titled, *The Syro-Aramaic Reading of the Koran: A Contribution to the Decoding of the Language of the Qur'an.* By 2002 it had generated a fair amount of publicity, and later it was translated into English.

In navigating the waters of Islamic scholarship, and of Islamic customs and traditions in events such as the wedding depicted in the book, I am indebted to the help of Lema Chehimi and Julnar Doueik, who helped steer me around several shoals. In any cases where I have nonetheless run aground, the fault is entirely my own.

I would like to warmly thank my agent, Ann Rittenberg, for helping me persevere through a difficult year. I also owe deep gratitude to my Knopf editor, Edward Kastenmeier, whose work was invaluable in shaping and strengthening the characters and plot lines in these pages. His help—and that of everyone at Knopf—has been all the more remarkable for how they managed it while laboring not only in the shadow of the pandemic, but also in the shadow of grief and loss following the death of Knopf publisher Sonny Mehta on the penultimate day of 2019. Sonny edited all but one of my previous books, and I have often wondered what he would have made of the strange and trying year we've just endured. He was generous with his wisdom, support, and encouragement for all of us, and I can probably best honor his memory by thanking a few of the fine people at Knopf who have been so kind and helpful to me through the years: Marty Asher, Gabrielle Brooks, Abigail Endler, Pam Kaufman, Ruth Liebmann, Diana Miller, Leslie Levine, Sherry Virtz, Lori Zook and many others, too numerous to list.

Dan Fesperman,
February 2021

A Note About the Author

Dan Fesperman's travels as a journalist and novelist have taken him to thirty countries and three war zones. *Lie in the Dark* won the Crime Writers' Association of Britain's John Creasey Memorial Dagger Award for best first crime novel, *The Small Boat of Great Sorrows* won their Ian Fleming Steel Dagger Award for best thriller, and *The Prisoner of Guantánamo* won the Dashiell Hammett Award from the International Association of Crime Writers. He lives in Baltimore.

A Note on the Type

This book was set in Janson, a typeface named for the Dutchman Anton Janson, but is actually the work of Nicholas Kis (1650–1702). The type is an excellent example of the influential and sturdy Dutch types that prevailed in England up to the time William Caslon (1692–1766) developed his own incomparable designs from them.

Typeset by Scribe,
Philadelphia, Pennsylvania

Printed and bound by Berryville Graphics,
Berryville, Virginia